THE MINNESOTA STORIES
OF SINCLAIR LEWIS

THE MINNESOTA STORIES

OF

SINCLAIR LEWIS

Edited and with an
introduction by

SALLY E. PARRY

BOREALIS
BOOKS

Borealis Books is an imprint of the Minnesota Historical Society Press.

www.borealisbooks.org

www.mhspress.org

The Minnesota Historical Society Press is a member of the
Association of American University Presses.

Manufactured in the United States of America

10 9 8 7 6 5 4 3 2 1

∞ The paper used in this publication meets the minimum requirements of the
American National Standard for Information Sciences—Permanence for Printed
Library Materials, ANSI Z39.48-1984.

International Standard Book Number 0-87351-515-3

Library of Congress Cataloging-in-Publication Data

Lewis, Sinclair, 1885–1951.
    The Minnesota stories of Sinclair Lewis / edited and with an introduction by
Sally E. Parry.
        p. cm.
    Includes bibliographical references.
    ISBN 0-87351-515-3 (pbk. : alk. paper)
    1. Minnesota—Social life and customs—Fiction.
    I. Parry, Sally E.
    II. Title.

PS3523.E94A6 2005b
813'.52—dc22   2005001155

Frontispiece:
Sinclair Lewis, ca. 1922 (photo by Charles Figaro; Minnesota Historical Society)

THE MINNESOTA STORIES OF SINCLAIR LEWIS

INTRODUCTION

SALLY E. PARRY

THE FICTIONAL TOWN OF GOPHER PRAIRIE, MINNESOTA, was a dreary place at the turn of the twentieth century. "The huddled low wooden houses broke the plains scarcely more than would a hazel thicket. The fields swept up to it, past it. It was unprotected and unprotecting; there was no dignity in it nor any hope of greatness. Only the tall red grain-elevator and a few tinny church-steeples rose from the mass. It was a frontier camp. It was not a place to live in, not possibly, not conceivably."

In 1902, at about the same time, the very real seventeen-year-old boy who would write those words set off for prep school from his home town of Sauk Centre, Minnesota. Marked forever by his Minnesota boyhood, Harry Sinclair Lewis — Red, to his friends — used Sauk Centre as the inspiration for Gopher Prairie in his spectacularly successful novel *Main Street* (1920); his other novels also bore his home state's stamp. The short stories in this volume, all set in Minnesota, are striking examples of his ambivalent feelings: they portray flawed and often narrow-minded midwestern Americans who nonetheless demonstrate fundamental human values.

Even in his early years, Sinclair Lewis wanted nothing more than to leave home. At the age of thirteen, he walked out of town with the intention of volunteering as a drummer boy for the Spanish-American War, and his father had to fetch him back. He was a dreamer in a practical land, set apart from his schoolfellows. He left as soon as he was able, traveling to the East Coast for college, to the West Coast for adventure, and to Europe for romance.

Wherever went, he wrote. He even sold plots for stories to

other writers with less imagination, including Jack London. Between 1912 and 1951, he produced twenty-three novels and about 126 short stories. Most of his stories focus on modern life, often setting up a contrast between the values of the city and the small town. Although his stories still contain the satire for which his novels are known, they tend to be somewhat less caustic, partly because magazine editors did not want him to risk offending their popular audience by being too critical of contemporary society, and partly because he did have a lot of empathy for the average American citizen. As Sheldon Grebstein notes, "Like Whitman, he contained multitudes." Mark Schorer finds his short stories "contrived," but does not seem to appreciate that the stories provide only a snapshot of a place or character, while the novels have the room to develop the dynamics of an entire community. Lewis's writing was best when he could provide details on everything from what his characters wore and read to where they lived and what they drove.

Lewis's short stories were very popular and appeared in many of the leading publications of the day: the *Saturday Evening Post, McClure's, Harper's, The Cosmopolitan,* and *Good Housekeeping.* Like F. Scott Fitzgerald, Lewis was well paid for them, and because of their success he was able to give up his job with a publishing firm and turn his full attention to writing.

His writing made it clear that he sometimes despaired of the provincial nature of the state and the town in which he was born. As a writer, though, Lewis came to feel that his roots in the American heartland gave him particular insight into the American psyche, and he always identified himself as a Minnesotan. He referred with pride to his native state in 1930, when he became the first American to win the Nobel Prize for Literature.

About two dozen of his stories are set in Minnesota or focus on characters from the state. The best of these, selected for this collection, illustrate Lewis's interest in the people and landscape of his native state, and they show how, in his opinion, Minnesota served as a microcosm for America. Many have not been reprinted since they were originally published and one, "Main Street Goes to War," has never been published.

The first piece in this collection is not a short story, but an essay that Lewis wrote during the height of his literary success, in 1923, for *The Nation.* Lewis returned to the state off and on over the years — to visit his family, to find inspiration for his novels, to reconnect with the landscape that shaped him. In "Minnesota, the Norse State," he reflected on the way the state had changed in the previous seventy-five years, from a wilderness to a place that encompassed farming, manufacturing, and culture. An almost romantic sense of history vies with the rapid change he observes. He refers to the Indian tribes that preceded the white settlers and mentions the various races and ethnicities that make up Minnesota's population. He notes, "To understand America, it is merely necessary to understand Minnesota. But to understand Minnesota you must be an historian, an ethnologist, a poet, a cynic, and graduate prophet all in one." He had a vast knowledge of Minnesota history and boasted of it, sometimes insulting fellow Minnesotans who were not as well versed in this history. In his 1945 novel *Cass Timberlane,* the title character, a judge, also has an interest in Minnesota history; when he is bored during trials, he keeps awake by naming to himself the counties of Minnesota and their county seats.

When the tall, red-headed Lewis left Sauk Centre in 1902, it was to attend Oberlin College as a preparation for attending Yale University. At Yale Lewis wrote for school magazines, especially romantic verse and stories, often set overseas in places he had never seen, like Japan, Germany, and Italy. Most of these stories, like the ones he would later write for popular magazines, were formulaic. Occasionally, though, he would write of what he knew. His earliest published story set in Minnesota is "A Theory of Values," written for *Yale Monthly Magazine* in 1906 when he was twenty-one. The Minnesota country boy Karl Nelson who longs to be educated but never leaves home can be seen as the Lewis who might have been. In a letter to a friend, Karl writes, "I want to do something in and for the world; not rot away in this dull, little town, and die unheard of."

The ever ambitious Lewis sought out a variety of experiences to write about. He worked as a janitor at Helicon Hall, Upton Sinclair's utopian society in New Jersey; he traveled to California to serve as secretary for two writers; and he worked as a reporter in Iowa. He wrote essays for magazines, translated articles, and even wrote children's verse, before going to work for a publishing company in New York. The heroes of several of his early novels share his wanderlust. *Hike and the Aeroplane* (1912) and *The Trail of the Hawk* (1915) feature young men who find romance in flying, while William Wrenn, of *Our Mr. Wrenn* (1914), escapes from his mundane life as an office clerk by taking a cattle boat to England, just as Lewis did while a student at Yale.

Although much of Lewis's early writing depicted the lives of romantic would-be world travelers, it was when he focused on the Midwest that he found his voice. As he wrote in an autobiographical statement for the Nobel Foundation, his foreign travel was really "a flight from reality. My real traveling has been sitting in Pullman smoking cars, in a Minnesota village, on a Vermont farm, in a hotel in Kansas City or Savannah listening to the normal daily drone of what are to me the most fascinating and exotic people in the world—the Average Citizens of the United States." In his speech accepting the Nobel Prize, he noted that Hamlin Garland's *Main-Travelled Roads* transformed his writing, for he "discovered that there was one man who believed that Midwestern peasants were sometimes bewildered and hungry and vile—and heroic. And, given this vision, I was released; I could write of life as living life."

Two of his early stories, "He Loved His Country" (1916) and "The Tamarack Lover" (1918), present nineteenth-century Minnesota pioneers who persevere under harsh conditions. Lewis shows the tensions that crop up between immigrants with rough and "foreign" ways and those people whose families have been in Minnesota for more than a generation. "He Loved His Country," one of Lewis's best short stories, focuses on a German Civil War veteran who feels torn between his love for his native land and the country in which he has spent most of his life, a love that is called into question when World War I breaks out. Lewis showed empathy with the disempowered throughout his life, partly because he often felt like an outsider himself. He refused to fire a nursemaid of German heritage during the war; a crucial scene in *Main Street* criticizes Gopher Prairie inhabitants who approve of a mob beating up a boy for having a German name. "The Tamarack Lover" also deals with Minnesota's early settlers, this time a tough widow who runs a combination bar, hotel, and general store. Like his novel *The Job* (1917), the story focuses on a woman who must support herself and becomes successful in the business world. Strong women appear throughout Lewis's writing. He was also an early supporter of woman suffrage.

Although Lewis had written half a dozen novels before 1920, *Main Street* brought him to national prominence. He also wrote several short stories set in Gopher Prairie, a town truly in the middle of the plains. "The broad, straight, unenticing gashes of the streets let in the grasping prairie on every side. She realized the vastness and emptiness of the land." "She" is Carol Kennicott, a librarian from St. Paul who marries a doctor and comes to Gopher Prairie, her new husband's home. The town challenges her, expecting her to fit in and disregarding her hopes. Lewis shows the insularity of such small towns as she learns to cope with the unfriendly landscape. He even drew on his first wife Grace's visits to Sauk Centre and the somewhat chilly reception she received because of her cosmopolitan ways. Lewis's feminist sympathies show women's frustrations at their limited choices.

When *Main Street* was published, Lewis attained lasting literary and critical fame. Ludwig Lewisohn wrote, "Perhaps no novel since 'Uncle Tom's Cabin' had struck so deep over so wide a surface of the national life." Mark Schorer, Lewis's first biographer, noted that it "was the most sensational event in twentieth-century American publishing history."

Of the four short pieces set in Gopher Prairie, two were written before *Main Street* and provide a somewhat nostalgic look at the prairie village. The romantic "A Woman by Candlelight" (1917) focuses on a salesman who is caught in a snowstorm in Gopher Prairie and falls in love with a milliner several years his senior. The story re-creates the days before department stores, when drummers came to town selling everything from corsets to anvils to band instruments.

"A Rose for Little Eva" (1918) brings the exotic to Gopher Prairie when a theatrical troupe, specializing in performing *Uncle Tom's Cabin,* comes to the realization that their heyday is past. Uncle Tom shows, based on the novel by Harriet Beecher Stowe, were popular across the United States in the late nineteenth and early twentieth centuries. The story is both an affectionate salute to a dying theatrical tradition and a satire of racist attitudes, featuring heavily exaggerated southern dialects, the audience's mocking of the production, and the sly comments of the author, who would later contribute to the NAACP and the Urban League.

The variety of dialects used by the performers as well as the language of the townspeople demonstrate Lewis's facility with dialogue. He was a natural mimic. To prepare for writing, he often acted as his own characters in a public setting—a bar or a party—one day sounding like a real estate salesman and the next like a defrocked minister.

In 1924 Lewis returned to his Gopher Prairie, situating himself as a character arriving in town on assignment from the *Nation* to see what people thought of the presidential election. The *Nation* supported Robert M. La Follette, running on the Progressive Party line, but in "Main Street's Been Paved!" Lewis finds out that almost everyone in town will vote for Calvin Coolidge. Lewis the character takes a ride through town with Carol's husband Will, viewing the many improvements and catching up on all the news. It is interesting to see how he thinks that his characters have aged in the past four years. As William Faulkner felt about the inhabitants of Yoknapatowpha County, Lewis believed that his characters had a life to them that existed beyond the bounds of his books. This is illustrated even more strongly in the unproduced radio drama, "Main Street Goes to War," written in 1942. Here we see Gopher Prairie contributing to the war effort: Will and Carol's son Hugh is in the army; their daughter Betty is in the Service Club; Carol collects scrap rubber and sells war bonds. Starting in 1942, Lewis returned with increasing frequency to Minnesota, and in a diary entry dated the same year as his radio play, he wrote about how prairie villages have changed over time, wondering, "Did the complaining Carol Kennicott help?"

In the same 1924 series for the *Nation,* Lewis also visits Zenith, a town in the Minnesota-like fictional state of Winnemac and the home of George F. Babbitt, for "Be Brisk with Babbitt." Lewis's novel *Babbitt,* published in 1922, was a study of a middle-aged, middle-class businessman in the Midwest. Like *Main Street,* this novel contained much detail—on the description of houses, the placement of streets and businesses in the town, and the life stories of many characters, including Babbitt's friends, neighbors, and business rivals. The portrayal of the everyday life of a businessman capitalized on the excessive consumerism of the 1920s when the business of America was business. Lewis is again both character and commentator, asking Babbitt and his friends their opinion of the presidential election. It's hard to say how effective Lewis's essays were as a means of promoting La Follette, since Lewis was much more caught up in his characters and their activities.

The 1920s was the decade of Lewis's biggest literary successes, with the publication of five best-selling novels, *Main Street, Babbitt, Arrowsmith* (1925), *Elmer Gantry* (1927), and *Dodsworth* (1929), capped by his winning the 1930 Nobel Prize.

In the first part of the 1920s, as Lewis was becoming a well-known author, he continued to write short stories, setting several in small and medium-sized towns in Minnesota. Vernon, the setting of "Things" and "A Matter of Business," is not as big as Zenith but suffers from growing pains, as the divide between classes becomes more pronounced. "They are transitional metropolises," Lewis writes, "but that transition will take a few hundred years, if the custom persists of making it a heresy punishable by hanging or even by ostracism to venture to say that Cleveland or Minneapolis or Baltimore or Buffalo is not the wisest, gayest, kindliest, usefullest city in all the world." "Things" (1919) focuses on a family, newly rich from iron mines, who find themselves cut off from their old friends and old values. "A Matter of Business" (1921) features a Babbitt-like businessman in Vernon, Mr. Jimmy Candee, who sells novelties and stationery and faces a moral problem of whether to sell handmade dolls or mass-produced cheaply made ones that offer a larger profit. "The Kidnaped Memorial" (1919), set in the nearby towns of Joralemon and Wakimin, like the earlier "He Loved His Country," considers notions of patriotism. A lawyer from Alabama who once fought for the Confederacy helps organize a parade in a Minnesota town that has become too busy to celebrate Decoration Day. Finally, "The Hack Driver" (1923), set in a small town like Gopher Prairie, is an amusing critique of city slickers who think they are smarter than small-town inhabitants.

By 1930 Lewis had become one of the most famous authors in America. Both honored and humbled by receiving the Nobel Prize, he felt stress from public expectations about his writing and this contributed to a growing dependence on alcohol. Some felt that he did not deserve the Nobel because of his criticisms of America, but he felt that was part of his duty as both a writer and a citizen. In a 1927 self-portrait he wrote, "He hates, equally, politicians who lie and bully and steal under cover of windy and banal eloquence, and doctors who unnecessarily and most lucratively convince their patients that they are ill; merchants who misrepresent their wares, and manufacturers who pose as philanthropists while underpaying their workmen; professors who in wartime try to prove that the enemy are all fiends, and novelists who are afraid to say what seems to them the truth." The results of such practices for a country are seen clearly in his 1935 novel *It Can't Happen Here,* about an alternative future where fascists take over from a complacent populace.

Lewis, with his height and red hair, had created quite an impression on others when he first came onto the literary scene. As he grew older, he became gaunt and cadaverous, redeemed, however, by his electric way of speaking. John Hersey, who served as Lewis's secretary in the late 1930s, described him this way: "The first impression . . . was of a thin man put together with connections unlike those of most human beings. . . . Next, piercing pale blue eyes, the bluer for being lashed into the pink face of a redhead. Thinning light-red hair, ill-brushed and tufted, over a wide dome of a forehead. Then, in better focus, terrible cheeks, riddled, ravaged, and pitted where many precancerous keratoses had been burned away by dermatologists' electric needles. Narrow, dry lips, and a slender chin. I would have sworn that he was hideously ugly until he started to talk, when his face suddenly turned on, like a delicate, brilliant lamp."

With the exception of *It Can't Happen Here,* Lewis's writing in the 1930s was of variable quality. He developed a serious interest in theater, which led to dramatizing *It Can't Happen Here* for the Federal Theater Project in 1936; acting in several plays, including one that he co-wrote with Fay Wray; and writing the 1940 novel about theater life, *Bethel Merriday.* In the 1940s he wrote several novels: *Gideon Planish* (1943) about charity scams; *Cass Timberlane* (1945), an examination of the state of marriage; *Kingsblood Royal* (1947), a scathing expose of contemporary race relations; and *The God-Seeker* (1949), his only historical novel, about a missionary in nineteenth-century Minnesota. *Cass Timberlane* and *Kingsblood Royal,* both set in Grand Republic, Minnesota, a city similar to Duluth, show the problems of large industrial cities that appear progressive, but beneath the surface harbor social and economic repression. In 1943, Lewis created a similar city, Cornucopia, for four short stories which, like *Cass Timberlane,* focus on marital problems of the upper class and feature vigorous women without jobs who exercise their energy in destructive ways.

Lewis had experience to draw on, as by the beginning of 1942 he had married and divorced two strong-minded women. His first wife, Grace Hegger, had been a writer for *Cosmopolitan* before their marriage, and his second, Dorothy Thompson, was a prominent foreign correspondent and journalist. Thompson was an inspiration for his *Ann Vickers* (1933), the story of a woman who rises from suffragette to social worker to prison reformer during the course of a tumultuous life. When his second marriage soured, he satirized Thompson as "The Talking Woman" in *Gideon Planish.* Her domineering character informs the depiction of the women in these stories.

The two Cornucopia stories presented here display both Lewis's tense feelings toward marriage and the ennui he identified in the upper-middle class housewife. "All Wives Are Angels" features an irascible woman who is dissatisfied with being a dutiful wife. Like "Main Street Goes to War," the story seems to air Lewis's romantic desires for a successful marriage, something that would always escape him. (Alpha Orchard, the heroine of "Green Eyes," another 1943 story not reprinted here, also expresses this desire to be useful. She tells her husband, "I've always had too much energy, too much imagination. . . . I can't go on living the way women did in 1910, or even 1930. Seems like I'm not the enviable sort of girl that can stay home and be contented, so I can either go on being old-fashioned and jealous, or old-fashioned and dissipated, or new-fashioned and have a job.") A creative writing course that Lewis taught at the University of Wisconsin inspired "Nobody to Write About." A young married woman believes she has the potential to be a great author but does not understand the main maxims of authorship: "apply the seat of the pants to the seat of the chair" and realize that everyone has a story. Lewis had been approached for advice by many would-be writers since he had become famous, and he despaired of the wild expectations of most of them. "For this is the law of instruction in writing, as it is in all other education—to him that hath shall be given, and he shall refuse it, because he needs it not; and to no one can you teach anything save to him who already knows it of himself and is bored by your instruction."

After the Cornucopia quartet, Lewis wrote four more short stories before his death in Italy in 1951 at the age of 65. His last novel, *World So Wide,* was published posthumously. He was cremated and his ashes were buried at the Greenwood Cemetery in Sauk Centre.

Although fewer than ten percent of Lewis's short stories are specifically set in Minnesota, the state was the greatest source of inspiration for much of his best fiction. And the themes of these short stories mirror in many ways the themes of his greatest novels. As Lewis wrote in a piece for the fiftieth anniversary issue of *O-Sa-Ge,* his high school annual, "It is extraordinary how deep the impression made by the place of one's birth and rearing, and how lasting are its memories."

THE MINNESOTA STORIES
OF SINCLAIR LEWIS

A MINNESOTA PRIMER

MINNESOTA, THE NORSE STATE

ON MAY 9, 1922, Mr. Henry Lorenz of Pleasantdale, Saskatchewan, milked the cows and fed the horses and received the calls
of his next farm neighbors. Obviously he was still young and
lively, though it did happen that on May 9 he was one hundred
and seventeen years old. When St. Paul, Mendota, and Marine, the
first towns in Minnesota, were established, Henry was a man in his
mid-thirties—yes, and President Eliot was seven and Uncle Joe
Cannon was five. As for Minneapolis, now a city of four hundred
thousand people, seventy-five years ago it consisted of one cabin.
Before 1837, there were less than three hundred whites and mixed
breeds in all this Minnesotan domain of eighty thousand square
miles—the size of England and Scotland put together.

It is so incredibly new; it has grown so dizzyingly. Here is a village which during the Civil War was merely a stockade with two
or three log stores and a company of infantry, a refuge for the settlers when the Sioux came raiding. During a raid in 1863, a settler was scalped within sight of the stockade.

Now, on the spot where the settler was scalped, is a bungalow
farmhouse, with leaded casement windows, with radio and phonograph, and electric lights in house and garage and barns. A hundred blooded cows are milked there by machinery. The farmer
goes into town for Kiwanis Club meetings, and last year he drove
his Buick to Los Angeles. He is, or was, too prosperous to belong
to the Nonpartisan League or to vote the Farmer-Labor ticket.

Minnesota is unknown to the Average Easterner, say to a Hart-
ford insurance man or to a New York garment-worker, not so
much because it is new as because it is neither Western and violent, nor Eastern and crystallized. Factories and shore hotels are
inevitably associated with New Jersey, cowpunchers and buttes

The Nation, May 30, 1923
Collected in *The Man from Main Street* (1953)

with Montana; California is apparent, and Florida and Maine. But Minnesota is unplaced. I have heard a Yale junior speculate: "Now you take those Minnesota cities—say take Milwaukee, for instance. Why, it must have a couple of hundred thousand population, hasn't it?" (Nor is this fiction. He really said it.)

This would be a composite Eastern impression of Minnesota: a vastness of wind-beaten prairie, flat as a parade ground, wholly given up to wheat-growing save for a fringe of pines at the north and a few market-towns at the south; these steppes inhabited by a few splendid Yankees—one's own sort of people—and by Swedes who always begin sentences with "Vell, Aye tank," who are farmhands, kitchen-maids, and icemen, and who are invariably humorous.

This popular outline bears examination as well as most popular beliefs; quite as well as the concept that Negroes born in Chicago are less courteous than those born in Alabama. Minnesota is not flat. It is far less flat than the province of Quebec. Most of it is prairie, but the prairie rolls and dips and curves; it lures the motorist like the English roads of Broad Highway fiction. Along the skyline the cumulus clouds forever belly and, with our dry air, nothing is more spectacular than the crimson chaos of our sunsets. But our most obvious beauty is the lakes. There are thousands of them—nine or ten thousand—brilliant among suave grain fields or masked by cool birch and maples. On the dozen mile-wide lakes of the north are summer cottages of the prosperous from Missouri, Illinois, even Texas.

Leagues of the prairie are utterly treeless, except for artificial windbreaks of willows and cottonwoods encircling the farmhouses. Here the German Catholic spire can be seen a dozen miles off, and the smoke of the Soo Line freight two stations away. But from this plains country you come into a northern pine wilderness, "the Big Woods," a land of lumber camps and reservation Indians and lonely tote-roads, kingdom of Paul Bunyan, the mythical hero of the lumberjacks.

The second error is to suppose that Minnesota is entirely a wheat State. It was, at one time, and the Minneapolis flour mills are still the largest in the world. Not even Castoria is hymned by more billboards than is Minneapolis flour. But today it is Montana and Saskatchewan and the Dakotas which produce most of the wheat for our mills, while the Minnesota farmers, building tall red silos which adorn their barns like the turrets of Picardy, turn increasingly to dairying. We ship beef to London, butter to Philadelphia. The iron from our Mesaba mines is in Alaskan rails and South African bridges, and as to manufacturing, our refrigerators and heat-regulators comfort Park Avenue apartment houses, while our chief underwear factory would satisfy a Massachusetts Brahmin or even a Chicago advertising man.

Greatest error of all is to believe that Minnesota is entirely Yankee and Scandinavian, and that the Swedes are helots and somehow ludicrous.

A school principal in New Duluth analyzed his three hundred and thirty children as Slovene, 49; Italian, 47; Serbian, 39; American, 37; Polish, 30; Austrian and Swedish, 22 each; Croatian, 20; colored, 9 (it is instructive to note that he did not include them among the "Americans"); Finnish, 7; Scotch, 6; Slav unspecified, 5; German, French, Bohemian, and Jewish, 4 each; Rumanian, Norwegian, and Canadian, 3 each; Scandinavian, unspecified, 8; Lithuanian, Irish, Ukrainian, and Greek, 2 each; Russian and English, 1 each — 60 per cent of them from Southern and Eastern Europe!

Such a Slavification would, of course, be true only of an industrial or mining community, but it does indicate that the whole Mid-Western population may alter as much as has the East. In most of the State there is a predomination of Yankees, Germans, Irish, and all branches of Scandinavians, Icelanders and Danes as well as Swedes and Norwegians. And among all racial misconceptions none is more vigorously absurd than the belief that the Minnesota Scandinavians are, no matter how long they remain here, like the characters of that estimable old stock-company play "Yon Yonson"—a tribe humorous, inferior, and unassimilable. To generalize, any popular generalization about Scandinavians in America is completely and ingeniously and always wrong.

In Minnesota itself one does not hear (from the superior Yankees whom one questions about that sort of thing) that the Scandinavians are a comic people, but rather that they are surly, that they are Socialistic, that they "won't Americanize." Manufacturers and employing lumbermen speak of their Swedish employees precisely as wealthy Seattleites speak of the Japs, Bostonians of the Irish, Southwesterners of the Mexicans, New Yorkers of the Jews, marine officers of the Haitians, and Mr. Rudyard Kipling of nationalist Hindus—or nationalist Americans. Unconsciously, all of them give away the Inferior Race Theory, which is this: An inferior race is one whose members work for me. They are treacherous, ungrateful, ignorant, lazy, and agitator-ridden, because they ask for higher wages and thus seek to rob me of the dollars which I desire for my wife's frocks and for the charities which glorify me. This inferiority is inherent. Never can they become Good Americans (or English Gentlemen, or High-wellborn Prussians). I know that this is so, because all my university classmates and bridge-partners agree with me.

The truth is that the Scandinavians Americanize only too quickly. They Americanize much more quickly than Americans. For generation after generation there is a remnant of stubborn American abolitionist stock which either supports forlorn causes and in jail sings low ballads in a Harvard accent, or else upholds, like Lodge, an Adams tradition which is as poisonous as Communism to a joy in brotherly boosting. So thorough are the Scandinavians about it that in 1963 we shall be hearing Norwegian Trygavasons and Icelandic Gislasons saying of the Montenegrins and Letts: "They're reg'lar hogs about wages, but the worst is, they simply won't Americanize. They won't vote either the Rotary or the Ku Klux ticket. They keep hollering about wanting some kind of a doggone Third Party."

Scandinavians take to American commerce and schooling and journalism as do Scotsmen or Cockneys. Particularly they take to American politics, the good old politics of Harrison and McKinley and Charley Murphy. Usually, they bring nothing new from their own experimental countries. They permit their traditions to be snatched away. True, many of them have labored for the Nonpartisan League, for woman suffrage, for co-operative societies. The late Governor John Johnson of Minnesota seems to have been a man of destiny; had he lived he would probably have been President, and possibly a President of power and originality. But again—there was Senator Knute Nelson, who made McCumber look like a left-wing syndicalist and Judge Gary like François Villon. There is Congressman Steenerson of Minnesota, chairman of the House postal committee. Mr. Steenerson once produced, out of a rich talent matured by a quarter of a century in the House, an immortal sentence. He had been complaining at lunch that the Nonpartisan League had introduced the obscene writings of "this Russian woman, Ellen Key," into the innocent public schools. Someone hinted to the Scandinavian Mr. Steenerson, "But I thought she was a Swede."

He answered: *"No, the Key woman comes from Finland and the rest of Red Russia, where they nationalize the women."*

Naturally it is the two new Senators, Hendrik Shipstead and Magnus Johnson, who now represent to the world the Scandinavian element in Minnesota. How much they may bring to the cautious respectability of the Senate cannot be predicted but certainly, like John Johnson, they vigorously represent everything that is pioneer, democratic, realistic, *American* in our history.

Good and bad, the Scandinavians monopolize Minnesota politics. Of the last nine governors of the State including Senatorial-Candidate Preus, six have been Scandinavians. So is Harold Knutson, Republican whip of the House. Scandinavians make up a

9

large proportion of the Minnesota State Legislature, and while in Santa Fé the Mexican legislators speak Spanish, while in Quebec the representatives still debate in French, though for generations they have been citizens of a British dominion, in Minnesota the politicians who were born abroad are zealous to speak nothing but Americanese. Thus it is in business and the home. Though a man may not have left Scandinavia till he was twenty, his sons will use the same English, good and bad, as the sons of settlers from Maine, and his daughters will go into music clubs or into cocktail sets, into college or into factories, with the same prejudices and ideals and intonations as girls named Smith and Brewster.

The curious newness of Minnesota has been suggested, but the really astonishing thing is not the newness—it is the oldness, the solid, traditionalized, cotton-wrapped oldness. A study of it would be damaging to the Free and Fluid Young America theory. While parts of the State are still so raw that the villages among the furrows or the dusty pines are but frontier camps, in the cities and in a few of the towns there is as firm a financial oligarchy and almost as definite a social system as London, and this power is behind all Sound Politics, in direct or indirect control of all business. It has its Old Families, who tend to marry only within their set. Anywhere in the world, an Old Family is one which has had wealth for at least thirty years longer than average families of the same neighborhood. In England, it takes (at most) five generations to absorb "parvenus" and "profiteers" into the gentry, whether they were steel profiteers in the Great War or yet untitled land profiteers under William the Conqueror. In New York it takes three generations— often. In the Middle West it takes one and a half.

No fable is more bracing, or more absurd, than that all the sons and grandsons of the pioneers, in Minnesota or in California, in Arizona or Nebraska, are racy and breezy, unmannerly but intoxicatingly free. The grandchildren of men who in 1862 fought the Minnesota Indians, who dogtrotted a hundred miles over swamp-blurred trails to bear the alarm to the nearest troops—some of them are still clearing the land, but some of them are complaining of the un-English quality of the Orange Pekoe in dainty painty city tea-rooms which stand where three generations ago the Red River fur-carts rested; their chauffeurs await them in Pierce-Arrow limousines (special bodies by Kimball, silver fittings from Tiffany); they present Schnitzler and St. John Ervine at their Little Theaters; between rehearsals they chatter of meeting James Joyce in Paris; and always in high-pitched Mayfair laughter they ridicule the Scandinavians and Finns who are trying to shoulder into their sacred, ancient Yankee caste. A good many of their names are German.

Naturally, beneath this Junker class there is a useful, sophisticated, and growing company of doctors, teachers, newspapermen, liberal lawyers, musicians who have given up Munich and Milan for the interest of developing orchestras in the new land. There is a scientific body of farmers. The agricultural school of the huge University of Minnesota is sound and creative. And still more naturally, between Labor and Aristocracy there is an army of the peppy, poker-playing, sales hustling He-men who are our most characteristic Americans. But even the He-men are not so obvious as they seem. What their future is, no man knows—and no woman dares believe. It is conceivable that, instead of being a menace in their naïve boosting and their fear of the unusual, they may pass only too soon; it is possible that their standardized bathrooms and Overlands will change to an equally standardized and formula-bound culture—yearning Culture, arty Art. We have been hurled from tobacco-chewing to tea-drinking with gasping speed; we may as quickly dash from boosting to a beautiful and languorous death. If it is necessary to be Fabian in politics, to keep the reformers (left wing or rigid right) from making us perfect too rapidly, it is yet more necessary to be a little doubtful about the ardent souls who would sell Culture; and if the Tired Business Man is unlovely and a little dull, at least he is real, and we shall build only on reality.

Small is the ducal set which controls these other classes. It need be but small. In our rapid accumulation of wealth we have been able to create an oligarchy with ease and efficiency, with none of the vulgar risks which sword-girt Norfolks and Percys encountered. This is one of the jests which we have perpetrated. The nimbler among our pioneering grandfathers appropriated to their private uses some thousands of square miles in northern Minnesota, and cut off—or cheerfully lost by forest fire—certain billions of feet of such lumber as will never be seen again. When the lumber was gone, the land seemed worthless. It was good for nothing but agriculture, which is an unromantic occupation, incapable of making millionaires in one generation. The owners had few of them acquired more than a million dollars, and now they could scarcely give their holdings away. Suddenly, on parts of this scraggly land, iron was discovered, iron in preposterous quantities, to be mined in the open pit, as easily as hauling out gravel. Here is the chief supply of the Gary and South Chicago mills. The owners of the land do not mine the ore. They have gracefully leased it—though we are but Westerners, we have our subsidiary of the United States Steel Company. The landowner himself has only to go abroad and sit in beauty like a flower, and every time a steam shovel dips into the ore, a quarter drops into his pocket.

So at last our iron-lumber-flour railroad aristocracy has begun to rival the beef barons of Chicago, the coal lords of Pennsylvania, and the bond princes of New York.

This article is intended to be a secret but flagrant boost. It is meant to increase civic pride and the value of Minnesota real estate. Yet the writer wonders if he will completely satisfy his chambers of commerce. There is a chance that they would prefer a statement of the value of our dairy products, the number of our admirable new school buildings, the number of motor tourists visiting our lakes, and an account of James J. Hill's encouraging progress from poverty to magnificence. But a skilled press agent knows that this would not be a boost; it would be an admission of commerce-ruled barrenness. The interesting thing in Minnesota is the swift evolution of a complex social system, and, since in two generations we have changed from wilderness to country clubs, the question is what the next two generations will produce. It defies certain answer; it demands a scrupulous speculation free equally from the bland certitudes of chambers of commerce and the sardonic impatience of professional radicals. To a realistic philosopher, the existence of an aristocracy is not (since it does exist) a thing to be bewailed, but to be examined as a fact.

There is one merit not of Minnesota alone but of all the Middle West which must be considered. The rulers of our new land may to the eye seem altogether like the rulers of the East — of New England, New York, Pennsylvania. Both groups are chiefly reverent toward banking, sound Republicanism, the playing of golf and bridge, and the possession of large motors. But whereas the Easterner is content with these symbols and smugly desires nothing else, the Westerner, however golfocentric he may be, is not altogether satisfied; and raucously though he may snortle at his wife's "fool suffrage ideas" and "all this highbrow junk the lecture-hounds spring on you," yet secretly, wistfully he desires a beauty that he does not understand.

As a pendant, to hint that our society has become somewhat involved in the few years since Mr. Henry Lorenz of Saskatchewan was seventy, let me illogically lump a few personal observations of Minnesota:

Here is an ex-professor of history in the State University, an excellent scholar who, retiring after many years of service, cheerfully grows potatoes in a backwoods farm among the northern Minnesota pines, and builds up co-operative selling for all the farmers of his district.

Here is the head of a Minneapolis school for kindergartners, a woman who is summoned all over the country to address teachers' associations. She will not admit candidates for matriculation until she is sure that they have a gift for teaching. She does something of the work of a Montessori, with none of the trumpeting and anguish of the dottoressa.

Here is the greatest, or certainly the largest, medical clinic in the world—the Mayo Clinic, with over a hundred medical specialists besides the clerks and nurses. It is the supreme court of diagnosis. Though it is situated in a small town, off the through rail routes, it is besieged by patients from Utah and Ontario and New York as much as by Minnesotans. When the famous European doctors come to America, they may look at the Rockefeller Institute, they may stop at Harvard and Rush and Johns Hopkins and the headquarters of the American Medical Association, but certainly they will go on to Rochester. The names of "Charley" and "Will" have something of the familiarity of "R.L.S." and "T.R."

Here is a Chippewa as silent and swart as his grandfather, an active person whom the cavalry used to hunt every open season. The grandson conducts a garage, and he actually understands ignition. His farm among the lowering Norway pines he plows with a tractor.

Here is a new bookshop which is publishing the first English translation of the letters of Abélard. The translator, Henry Bellows, is a Ph.D., an editor, and a colonel of militia.

Here are really glorious buildings: the Minneapolis Art Institute, the State Capitol, the St. Paul Public Library, and Ralph Adams Cram's loveliest church. Here, on the shore of Lake of the Isles, is an Italian palace built by a wheat speculator. Here where five years ago were muddy ruts are perfect cement roads.

Here is a small town, a "typical prairie town," which has just constructed a competent golf course. From this town came a minister to Siam and a professor of history in Columbia.

And here are certain Minnesota authors. You know what Mid-Western authors are—rough fellows but vigorous, ignorant of the classics and of Burgundy, yet close to the heart of humanity. They write about farmyards and wear flannel shirts. Let us confirm this portrait by a sketch of eleven Minnesota authors, most of them born in the State:

Charles Flandrau, author of *Harvard Episodes* and *Viva Mexico,* one-time Harvard instructor, now wandering in Spain (Agnes Repplier has called him the swiftest blade among American essayists); Scott Fitzgerald, very much a Minnesotan, yet the father of the Long Island flapper, the prophet of the Ritz, the idol of every Junior League; Alice Ames Winter, recently president of the General Federation of Women's Clubs; Claude Washburn, author of *The Lonely Warrior* and several other novels which, though they are laid in America, imply a European background (he has lived for years now in France and Italy); Margaret Banning, author of *Spellbinders;* Thomas Boyd, author of that valiant impression of youth in battle, *Through the Wheat;* Grace Flandrau, of *Being Respectable* and other authentically sophisticated novels; Woodward Boyd, whose first novel, *The Love Legend,* is a raid on the domestic sentimentalists; Carlton Miles, a dramatic critic who gives his Minnesota readers the latest news of the continental stage (he is just back from a European year spent with such men as Shaw, Drinkwater, and the director of La Scala); Brenda Ueland, who lives in Greenwich Village and writes for the *Atlantic Monthly;* Sinclair Lewis, known publicly as a scolding corn-belt realist, but actually (as betrayed by the samite-yclad, Tennyson-and-water verse which he wrote when he was in college) a yearner over what in private life he probably calls "quaint ivied cottages."

Seventy-five years ago—a Chippewa-haunted wilderness. To-day—a complex civilization with a future which, stirring or dismaying or both, is altogether unknowable. To understand America, it is merely necessary to understand Minnesota. But to understand Minnesota you must be an historian, an ethnologist, a poet, a cynic, and a graduate prophet all in one.

THE EARLY MINNESOTA STORIES

A THEORY OF VALUES

(Karl Nelson to James Bradford, University of Minn.)

"Linton, Minn., Nov 10.

DEAR JIM: — It isn't easy to write on a rough kitchen table, beside a hand-kerosene lamp; but I must thank you for showing me about Minneapolis.

The poplars, the bristling stubble-fields, Hjolme's general store, — these have been the world to me, as seen from our white district school.

Learning has seemed an unreachable, useless thing. That's why I have to keep looking into a pocket Webster's as I write this.

But hustling Minneapolis, and your chat of courses at the U. of Minn., of books and of occupations possible for the college man, have given me something beside the weather to think about.

I want to do something in and for the world; not rot away in this dull, little town, and die unheard of. Here there is nothing to do; and I want to be doing — doing — doing — .

That telephone job which my brother Ole got for me ought to support me nicely until the "Minneapolis Night School" gets me ready for the U. I think I should die, if I couldn't go there.

My new clothes must have helped to show how much the city waked me up. Did I tell you that the telephone manager said to me, "Born here in the city?" And a man on Nicollet Avenue asked me a direction.

Coming home wasn't pleasant. At Mooreville, Orin Svenson, a Linton fellow, got on the train. He smoked a two-for-a-nickel cigar, and talked like this: "Hey dar, Karl! Aye hayrd you been down to the city. You have pretty gude tam with the girls, hein?"

And I once admired him! Of course he aint had a year in the High School, like me, — but why is he so shiftless?

The smell of cabbage cooking, and a feeling of the farm loneliness, greeted me at home, where———."

Old Anton Nelson painfully removed his shoeless feet from a chair beside the stove, and glanced at the kitchen alarm clock. He winked at his knitting wife to express a secret fondness for son Karl, whose letter writing he interrupted by growling, "Aint it time you go to the Ole Bull Association?"

"Gee, guess it is, dad." And Karl started for the district schoolhouse.

Presiding was Chris Peterson, the schoolmaster, whose chef d'oeuvre was the title of the "The Ole Bull Musical and Literary Association for the Cultivation of the Mind," an organization more social than intellectual; where oratorical lions roared to impress the lionesses whom they gigglingly "saw home."

Chris Peterson crossed his legs, clad in the shiny black trousers of his prized black cut-away, and demanded, "The meetin' come to order. Pete Yensen and Karl Nelson, they will debate on the affirmative and negative of, 'Resolved, That fashionable saloons are worse than rum holes.'"

With slow forging of mixed metaphores, Pete enlarged on an article about gin palaces, found in the plate matter of the "Mooreville Avalanche."

Heavy applause, plow shoes stamping; in the midst of which Karl, nervously stroking his light curls, began to dazzle the Association by the description of a gaudy Rathskeller, seen at its best at ten-thirty. He added an unconscious plagiarism from a Minneapolis temperance lecturer, describing the effects of the "rum holes" upon honest working men. His reference to the dignity of their labor brought him the decision of the judge.

An eager listener was Hjolme, keeper of the general store; a fabulous plutocrat, said to clear quite two thousand a year; so wealthy that he played poker in the bar-room of the Mooreville

Hotel, and had run for legislature. Karl's description recalled Minneapolis, dear, wicked Minneapolis; where he had an annual spree, during the excitement of State Fair Week.

"Aye tank Karl, he been kind a' waked up, in the city," he reflected. "Aye might give him the place in mine store what I fired Llarid from."

When Hjolme made his offer to Anton Nelson, promising that Karl should be able to do the chores at home, and help his father at harvest time, old Nelson was filled with dreams such as came to Mrs. Nickleby when Kate entered Mantellini's. Hastening over the mile between the store and his farm, as fast as rheumatism let him, Anton announced the news to Karl, who was husking corn. As he hobbled about the yard, mending the broken boards of a "lumber wagon," the old man, for the first time in years, sang, in a cracked voice, snapping his fingers at old Grouse, the dog.

Although he had not intended to relate his plans for some time, Karl entered the kitchen, and broke his usual reserve in a flood of complaints to his mother. Like many of the prisoners of the farm cook-stove, she had toiled till she was as shapeless as a bag of potatoes. She had never learned a dozen words of English. Karl longed to take her with him to Minneapolis at once.

If he left them, she said, the weight of Anton's rheumatism and of the interest on the mortgage would become too hard to bear. Living at home, his wages could go toward the common purse; clothing would be his only expense. Doing the chores and helping at harvest would be great aids. In the city his expenses would eat up his income, as in the case of his brother who had become a night-miller in one of the mills, towering like castles beside the Mississippi.

As she began to speak querulously of the mortgage, Karl returned to the shed and bowed his head on his patched arm for a minute. Then setting his teeth, he began to husk corn like a machine.

At the store, in the morning, the dirty six-paned show window, displaying sticky-candy, and gaudy Mackinaws, had never seemed less splendid to Karl. As he entered, above the shelves of fly-specked canned goods, rose a vision of the Minneapolis he had seen from the court-house tower; beyond the great river, the halls of the University; like a star on the horizon the dome of the state Capitol, in St. Paul.

Out of the cellar, where he had been drawing bottles of "Hjolme's Kidney and Liver Cure" from a hogshead, came the merchant, saying kindly, "Aye tank you better sweep the back room, Karl. Wait till you get to making money, and there won't be nothing like da old store."

The vision faded; the reality of the rows of cans and boxes remained.

When spring had brought the grass-like sprouting wheat Karl was well established. He interested the farmers; as on an April day when two of them lounged on a dry-goods box, talking of the Russo-Japanese War, then in progress.

"I tell you," interrupted Karl, "the Russians are going to win."

"Them Japs, dey spend next April in Sain' Pe'ersburg," grinned Madlund. "The Revolution knock out da Russians."

"That's just why they'll win. As soon as they get a republic they'll get up a decent army and knock the stuffin' out o' the Japs, just like we would."

"You're right," said Barney Petersen. "You been a purty good arguer, Karl. You goin' to run for Legislature, some day, like Hjolme?"

"Sure!"

"Who's that feller comin' in liv'ry rig?"

"By golly, it's Jack Burton. Travels for the St. Paul Hide Company. Hello, Jack!"

"Mornin', Karl. Whoa! Where's Hjolme?"

"Eatin' dinner."

"Well, how are you anyway? They tell me you are just runnin' the store. How'j' like it?"

"All right. Keeps me busy."

"Goin' to go down to the city and get ready for the University this fall?"

"No," hesitatingly. "But prob'ly I'm goin' next year, when I've got enough money saved up to pay the interest on dad's mortgage for a while."

"How about you'n' 'Mandy Hjolme?"

"'Manda?" blushing, "She's all right."

"Still readin' Dickins?"

"Yuh."

"How'j' like it?"

"Great, but I don't have a whole lot of time to read. Keep up on politics, in the papers, though."

Burton, remarking on Karl's attention to business, and warning him to keep up his reading, told the latest "tales of the road" which made Karl blush slightly, but roll with laughter, like the rest of the drummer's audience.

With many such gatherings, passed the seasons, Karl ever busier and more versed in local politics. In the fall of the next year, when the fields were covered with bristling wheat-stubble, where sportsmen hunted prairie chickens, Karl had been made the agent for a cream separator company.

Witness him installing a separator at Barney Petersen's farm. As he finished his eloquence on the subject of the improved steel bowl, his blond Norse face flushed with interest, Barney said, "It's yust lak I told you, Karl; you talk lak a William Yennings Bryan. Do you go by the University pretty quick?"

"Sure, Barney, in a year or so. I'm going to take a couple of years in the law school, and go into politics."

"You goin' to stick to business, too, hein?"

"You bet! I'm makin' a good thing out o' the store, and this separator business. Put in two last month. Fields aren't so good for wheat now, are they?"

"They get purty much played out."

"Keeps me hustling, but I like it."

The hustle increased, and Karl enjoyed keenly a vacation at the

Sac County Agriculture Fair, at Mooreville, when another year had passed.

In the evening of the first day of the fair, the bar-room of the "First-class, two dollar a day House" was crowded. Farmers, owners of race-horses, petty merchants, shouted bets on the morrow's races. Some were clamoring out plans to beat the saloon's nickel-in-the-slot gambling machine, the winners on which were sure to restore their earnings directly. At which with a feeble grin, they would quaver, "Come on you, ——, —— old ——'s. I guess the drinks are on me."

And invariably the retort, "I told you, you ought to play the red all the time." Whereupon the adviser would lose a quarter to show his good faith in the plan.

At the bar, a red-faced man in shirt sleeves, his derby on the back of his head, was "Settin' 'em up" to a crowd, roaring out at intervals, "What drink's most called for in America?" to which his clients replied, an eye on their empty glasses, "The same"; jeering at the newcomers, who answered "Beer."

At the temporary roulette wheel, a man of large paunch and impassive face was raking in the savings of farmer and clerk.

Karl, who had brought Amanda Hjolme to the fair, had left her at the house of a friend, after dancing in a booth of pine floor roofed with boughs. Orin Svenson, in a red and green sweater, had been the star, winking impartially at all the girls who lined the sides, and "jollying" the players on the fiddle and parlor organ, who quavered out, "In the Good Old Summer Time," or "Mandy." At the latter Karl had nudged Amanda liberally, thumping bravely through the square dances.

At the hotel "sample room" he found Jack Burton, who greeted him with, "Hello Karl; didn't know you drank."

"Oh, a business man's got to be a sport, you know."

"What'll you have? All right. Two ginger ale high-balls, Tom."

"This tastes good to me. The Scandahoofians up my way don't drink much but alcohol!"

"Been out to the fair grounds?"

"Sure, went with 'Manda. Did you see the stuff in the Exhibition Hall?"

"No."

"Gee, there was everything from quilts to paintings on glass. Bet I get the prize for my Baldwin apples. First grown 'round Linton. I been takin' awful good care of 'em."

"Good bunch of horses, wasn't there?"

"Yuh; I made fifteen dollars on the races. Hank Smith is so popular everybody was givin' odds on him, and I took 'em."

"Were you in the grandstand?"

"No; what's the use of blowin' in money uselessly?"

"Speakin' of money, how goes the store?"

"Great. I'll have to get back before the fair is over, for a deal Hjolme is makin' on some cattle he's goin' to ship."

"What about the University?"

"Oh—I don't know. I guess I'll go down sometime and take a couple of years in the Law School. I want to be somethin' bigger than a one-horse clerk."

"Are you keepin' up your readin'?"

"N-no. I don't have time. What'll you have? Two more, Tom."

"Hey, you, Burton. Bring your friend, and get into the game," came a voice from the tiny booth where a young lawyer and a tailor were shuffling cards. From an adjoining booth, of closed door, came the click of poker chips.

"Goin' to get in, Jack?" queried Karl.

"Sure,—but you'd better not. You're too young."

"Maybe; but I don't want to be scared out. A business man's got to learn to take his chances. I'll risk what I won on the races."

By four in the morning, Karl had lost the fifteen and ten more. "To keep it from feelin' lonely," as he said weakly. His occasional winnings had gone to treat the crowd to high-balls and beer, and he had but a confused notion of his surroundings.

Burton took Karl up to his own room, and returned to play calmly till breakfast time. Without undressing, the boy threw himself on the bed, muttering, "Be darned sorry 'bout this, mornin', but got to learn to play the game. Know how to handle them fellers yet."

For another year Karl went on in his learning to handle men as he found them. He became an expert in buying cattle for Hjolme to ship. He was proud of Linton's second grain elevator, of the new church, and the saloon, which he rarely entered save when treating an important customer.

One October evening, he brought home beside the *Weekly Avalanche* a letter from his brother Ole, which said, with certain eccentricities of spelling, —

"A member of our mill firm is in your separator firm. He say you are making big sales. I told him about your wanting to come to the University, and he say if you come down for night school, they give you a place in the headquarters.

"From what you wrote, you must have enough saved up to pay the interest on the mortgage for four or five years."

As Karl sat in thought, his feet, sans shoes, cocked up by the kitchen stove, his day-dreams began drifting into sleep when his mother's voice aroused him.

"Oh, hang the U.!" he sighed. "I'm goin' to have a big place here before long."

"Shall I read the paper to you, mother?"

The last news which he translated to her was an account of the shaving of the Sophomore class president's head by University Freshman.

"What chumps they are," laughed Karl. "They are fooling around, instead of saving money, like me. Well, I must get to the store early in the morning. Let's be good and go to bed like dad has. Yes, I'll make the fire when I get up. Goo' night." And as he drowsily clumped up the narrow stairs, thinking of the morrow's work, he hummed "Mandy."

HE LOVED HIS COUNTRY

I
. . . . .

HUGO BROMENSHENKEL had almost forgotten that he was born in Germany. Fifty years, now, he had lived at Curlew, where the woods ring the Minnesota lakes. His wife was Yankee, and his four sons were American business men of Minneapolis and Duluth and Chicago. Seventy-five years old was Hugo, wizened and fringe-bearded and elf-locked with gray, a fiery and affectionate little man, who could still plow all day and afterward whistle boyishly as he fed his cattle. On winter days when the thermometer was forty below and the trees shivered with the incredible cold, Hugo would still put on his coonskin coat and shoepacks, caper about the kitchen crying, "I am the dancing bear!" then take his tip-ups and axe and go down the appallingly snow-bright alleys of the woods to the lake and fish for pickerel.

A very simple man, common as earth and fruitful as earth, trusting much, enduring much, laboring unceasingly, and rejoicing in love for his wife, with her luminous eyes and clear cheeks and comforting hands, and hair that was black as woodland loam to his eyes, though to others it may have seemed ragged with gray. In awe Hugo watched the processional of the seasons and mutely praised the goodness of God, Who brought him the first stirring softness of spring and the shimmering old-gold of the July wheat-fields.

"I worship God with an axe and a plow — and with love for my *Liebling*," he told his wife, and she, who had never lost her bridehood's passion for the little man, answered: "You worship Him with everything you do, Hugo, and I worship Him because He gave me you, my soldier!"

Hugo Bromenshenkel loved his country, his America, because

Everybody's Magazine, October 1916
Collected in *I'm a Stranger Here Myself and Other Stories* (1962)

he was one of the men who had made it. Fresh from the Old Country he had fought through the Civil War, a chirping, dancing, daring private—and "Grant" was the name he later gave to his oldest boy. After the war he had hiked from St. Paul to Curlew by ox-team, and his wife, daughter of Sergeant Whipple of Maine, he had met among the settlers huddled in a stockade during a Sioux uprising. He had found his farm a chaos of woods; he had made it a paradise; he had whitewashed the outbuildings, and helped his wife in the planting of honeysuckle and geraniums. A grim home for wolves he had made into a gardenland, therefore he loved it—and loved America.

He had no German neighbors near by; the Germans of his section of Minnesota were mostly clustered on the prairies, while Hugo was, like the Scandinavians, a man of the woods, of stump-jagged clearings and hills and small hardy lakes. Norwegian and Yankee were his neighbors in Curlew, with half-a-dozen Irishmen and French Canucks, and the Englishman of mystery, Laxton the saloon-keeper, who read Greek and scowled. Good people, good Americans, all of them, and Hugo loved them, and forgot that he was German as well as American, except once a month or so, when he had a letter from his sister in Prussia. Then Hugo proudly and wistfully remembered that he also was of the good German blood.

In annual photographs he had watched his nephews in the Old Country grow to manhood. It was hard to believe that his tender, slender little sister was the mother of bearded sons; but there they were, ardent men of power: Franz, the chemist, who was none other than Herr Docent Franz Fritz Stegner of Bonn; Hermann, who had stuck to the soil; and even the youngest, plump, laughing Ludwig, who was to be sent to South America, and was feverishly studying for his career. They were as real to Hugo as his own eldest son Grant, the curt and successful business man of Chicago. As he read of them on his ragged farm, more than four thousand miles away, old Hugo became a German again, and with pride remembered the house of his fathers. If America was his Brideland,

Germany was, in no mere sentimental phrasing but in very fact, his Fatherland.

Sometimes on a summer Sunday evening, when the lake bore the flat notes of a church bell from Curlew and made them musical, and when a letter from his sister was still warm from her hands, Hugo would stand on the lake shore and in a dream that was like prayer remember the Old Country: land of rosy children, of Christmas cakes and carols and kindly greetings, of ancient towns where bells sounded down cobbled streets, of whispering woods and somber-haunted castles; land of his fathers, the warriors of old, grave, bearded men brandishing swords whose hilts were ponderous iron crosses. His fathers and his Fatherland Hugo loved no less because they were colored by memory and myth—far-off, venerable, not lightly to be forsaken.

II
. . . . .

To a certain American farmer, Hugo Bromenshenkel, the exploding of the great European war meant very little—at first. It couldn't last. Three months and it would be over. Germany would take Paris and punish the impudent frog-eaters. Germany's firm ally, America, would be glad—secretly however, for of course we had to be strictly neutral. All of this the American farmer demonstrated to his fellow-farmers and they uneasily accepted his explanations, for he was a Grand Army man and esteemed as an authority on war.

Hugo said nothing when the two French Canucks or Laxton, the Englishman, were about, since they were his neighbors, his friends, his fellow-Americans, and he wished not to hurt their feelings. Hadn't he held Laxton in his arms all night, when the Englishman had struggled and foamed with delirium tremens? And hadn't Laxton in turn come grimly skiing over nine-foot drifts of snow to bring coffee and flour and bacon and a Sunday newspaper to the Bromenshenkels, the winter of the big snow? How could a neighbor, who loved them despite their alien blood, who knew every pathetic weakness in their games of cribbage and casino and life, be other than silent regarding the triumphant march of the Germans to cleanse with blood and iron those streets of Paris which, of course, puritan America and puritan Germany equally detested?

Then—

While the battles of the Aisne and the Marne incredibly began the war to destroy civilization, Laxton and the Canucks—and Sweep Monohan, the storekeeper, who in one week had changed from a Fenian into a British Imperialist—in their turn kept silence when Hugo Bromenshenkel rode anxiously in for the news. . . . Mrs. Bromenshenkel had suckled Mrs. Monohan's child when mother and child were edging toward the ease of death; and once Ladour, the Canuck, being crippled with rheumatism, had heard a clanking at the door, and found Hugo beginning to saw his wood.

Then—

The war became a world-habit instead of an illness, and the bright young cartoonists of the American press, in their ardent desire for honor and truth, pictured the Kaiser and his men as hogs, as Huns, as baby-killers, while Hugo and his friends began to argue about the war—just a little, not belligerently. It was a matter of history and geography: "Look here now; if the French come round here on the right—" All that these American neutrals said, some fifty or sixty millions of other American neutrals from Bangor to Calexico were also saying, over and over.

Laxton suddenly sold his saloon to a Dane from Dakota, and started for Canada, to see, as he said, "if I'm valuable to the Empire as anything but a specimen genus Oxonian well preserved in alcohol." Hugo didn't understand that—and he didn't quite realize that Laxton was going off to fight Hugo's own nephews. He pounded Laxton's shoulders at parting, and brought a little present down to the train for him.

Then—

The report of the Belgian atrocities, and the sinking of the *Lusitania,* and a letter from Hugo's sister wailing that her baby, her ambitious Ludwig, who was to have made wealth for her in South America, had been killed, and Hermann wounded, while Franz, the chemist, the zealot who had spent fourteen hours at a time in the laboratory, was glad to be out in the trenches, because he believed the life of Germany was threatened. Hugo wrote awkwardly to Grant, his eldest son, that the little cousin was dead. . . . Grant did not answer him, but then Grant was always very busy.

The Danish saloon-keeper, Laxton's successor, proved to be a man of wrath. He hated Germany, and he shouted "hog" and "Hun" and "baby-killer" to prove all sorts of things, and Hugo answered him savagely as, in bewildered reveries over the dead Ludwig, he began to believe that this really was a life-struggle for his own kinsmen. At first Hugo had lamented the sinking of the *Lusitania,* as a murderous error. Now, with stumbling unhappy phrases, he began to defend it, and to blame the Britishers for using passengers as a screen for munitions-carrying. Gradually his neighbors, his friends, began to join the Dane in arguments— and the American farmer Hugo Bromenshenkel began to change into a German-American.

He had read the *Twin City Morning Sun* for years, but, because its cartoons and editorials represented the dead Ludwig's comrades as fiends, he stopped it and took the *Volks-Zeitung* instead— though he scarce could read it, so deteutonized was he! But he labored over it daily, and daily he became more German-American.

Now for the first time in their years of perfect understanding, he was trying to befool his wife. He pretended that he was not worried. He finally resubscribed to the *Twin City Sun,* lest she think he was disturbed by its attacks. Whenever she rode into Curlew with him he avoided the Dane, and all mention of the war. He lauded the spirit of the Canadians who, from the country just a few score miles to the north, were going to join Kitchener, and he anecdotally recalled the Canadians in his own company in the Civil War.

He could not deceive her. She saw decay in the blue-brown crescents under his eyes, agony in his trembling prayer when they knelt together by their bed, his arm tight about her, as they had knelt every night for forty-eight years, ever since their wild bridal-night during a Minnesota blizzard. The clash between his love of the Fatherland and his love of the Brideland brought them to-gether, as sorrows had always done.

It did not occur to Hugo that he must not be just what he now was, a German-American: but that he must be either an Ameri-can or a German. It was the phrase "hyphenated citizen" which brought to him the doctrine of the red-blooded — that only trai-tors and weaklings can continue to love both sides in a disagree-ment. It must, he felt, be evident to his friends that he was not a hog or a Hun or a baby-killer, and therefore that the other Ger-mans were not. But the question of "hyphenation" could not be so settled.

At first he did not understand the phrase in all its force. The emphatic Dane saw to that, however. He was tremendous about Turn-Vereins. In fact the Dane became as fond of denouncing the sin of being hyphenated as he was of expatiating on the wicked-ness of not teaching the Danish tongue and history to all Danish-American children. But even when the Dane had made Hugo feel like a false husband to the Brideland, even when the *Twin City Sun* began to talk of defense, even when Hugo remembered that he himself had fought in an American War of Brothers, still it never seemed to his fixed old brain conceivable that Germany and America could have any contention which could not be settled by frank explanations. Why, they were both honest, manly; they were not trying to steal anything from each other. So he said, being very simple and not understanding about honor.

The great blow was dealt him suddenly, at a sacred hour.

There was no G.A.R. post at Curlew, and once or twice a year

Hugo went down to the nearest post, at Joralemon, for a camp-fire. In November, 1915, the Joralemon G.A.R. was to have an anniversary meeting, with a special motion-picture show donated by the manager of the Joralemon Theatre, and an address by the young but Honorable Mr. Vickery, the state legislator who was slated to run for Congress. Hugo had constantly become more retiring, and his very seclusion brought signs of old age to his uneasy lips, to his more slowly bending joints. Strong he was, and healthy as a plowed field, but hesitant, doubtful. In a panic his wife urged him to go to the G.A.R. camp-fire: she pressed his blue coat and cleaned the black slouch hat with the gold cord, and drove with him to the station, and kissed him sideways in the hollow between chin and lower lip, a silly trick that these incurable lovers had never given up.

Hugo had not gone five miles on the train before he began to miss her, querulously, as the old do. But in Joralemon the sight of dozens of comrades from towns about made him as expectant as a small boy who is going to a party. The Women's Relief Corps had a supper for them in the basement of the Baptist Church—chicken fricassee, sweet potatoes, beans, coffee, ice-cream, sweet pickles, banana layer cake, and one of Mrs. Williams's famous chocolate cakes, with the chocolate on top as shiny as patent leather. Like most primitive people Hugo liked to eat, and he sampled everything and pretended to quarrel with old Mrs. Williams and cackled with her over memories of stockade days, while he kept glancing with affectionate satisfaction at his comrades, the lively white-pated men who were heroes—tonight—and could eat all they wanted to, and tell the ancient stories and the ancient jokes. Jigtime was in Hugo's step as they marched to G.A.R. Hall together, frail old men—leaves before the winter wind.

All the stories of the Joralemon comrades he had heard, but there was a new comrade present tonight, Dr. James of Iowa, who told of following the trail of Mosby. Hugo had for weeks wondered if he ought ever to have fought in any war, and he was a little self-conscious in the big city of Joralemon with its three thousand people and its cement walks and three-story brick hotel. But he forgot his diffidence; he sprang up and narrated his adventures in patrol duty on the Rappahannock. He laughed; he felt safe, with a place of his own, an American among Americans.

He had stood too close to the hot stove, and when he sat down he felt faint. He heard the benediction through a sick blur, and when the others formed to march to the Joralemon Theatre, for the motion-picture in their honor, he quavered: "I'll join you in a few minutes. No, it's all right, doc—I just talk too much yet!"

He staggered behind them to the drugstore. The November air restored him, but he sat for a few minutes in the cool space behind the prescription-counter. Half-drowsing, he was very happy. Yes, it was true; he was an American, a soldier of America. The Dane was a tenderfoot; he didn't know that Hugo's old friends were Yankee soldiers. In a dream of ancient days, walking through a vision of rattling harness, the charge of lean-faced young men in tilted forage caps, the evening choruses and the fantastic boyish cursing at dawn, Hugo rambled to the theatre, and was ushered to the section reserved for the G.A.R., whose silvery polls glimmered in the half-light—his friends!

He had missed the first reel of the film. The second was just beginning. He was excited. Hitherto he had seen only two motion-pictures, both cheap melodramas. This was his first feature film.

It was the highly successful photo-play *Columbia Awaken!* in which three army aeroplanes and a regiment of real soldiers were used. To Hugo Bromenshenkel it was overwhelming. He was startled to see before him, moving, real, the khaki-uniformed soldiers of America today. He was proud; these were his younger comrades.

On the screen a squad ran forward, scattering, and leaped into a trench. Above them burst a shell. They ducked, grinned, rammed clips of cartridges into their rifles, and began firing at a mass of trees.

Hugo leaned forward, his mouth open. His stringy horn-hard fingers clawed at the seat-arm. "Get 'em! Get 'em!" he was muttering. It seemed to him that he himself was there in the trench, fighting to hold it. They *had* to hold it, and keep back the enemies hidden in those woods! His hands twitched and closed on an imaginary rifle-stock. He pulled breathlessly at a trigger. He groaned as the lieutenant commanding the squad slumped down, dead. He kept urging, "Get 'em! Get 'em! Hold the outpost!"

Now, foreign soldiers were sneaking out from the woods; were charging, in a dodging, bobbing, irresistible mass. They had to be kept back! To stop them Hugo was ready to die with the plucky, pitiful little bunch in the trench. He hated those rushing devils who were coming, coming —

With a gasp that could be heard three seats away Hugo recognized the nationality of the attacking force.

They were Germans. He was witnessing, he was actually sharing, the struggle between his own Brideland and his own Fatherland.

A very old, very tired, utterly heartsick lover of men, whose love was proven folly, crumpled in his seat, and no longer looked at the screen. He wanted to cover his eyes with his hands, but round about him were more people than the whole population of Curlew, and it was quite human of him that even in his agony he should not have dared to make so public a demonstration, or protest, or leave the hall. . . . Not yet. But black spirits circled over him.

The film ended. The lights came on. The Honorable Mr. Vickery, the silver-tongued siren of the state senate, arose.

Perhaps Hugo didn't want to comprehend; at any rate he was slow in comprehending the fact that the orator, after a vague tribute to German-Americans in general, and a very definite tribute to all German-Americans who were voters in his district, was proceeding toward a declaration that Germany's object in her submarine policy was to force America into the world-war.

Something, not of his conscious self, made the shy old man, Hugo Bromenshenkel, lift himself from his seat, a wrinkled, unheroic figure, and quaver, "That's a lie! Germany, she is surrounded. She try to fight her way out with submarines."

He stopped, appalled. The eyes of the crowd were a bed of coals about him. His comrades were gaping at him. He was condemned.

The orator was going smoothly on: "Far be it from me to contradict our friend who wears the sacred blue coat of the G.A.R., but—"

Hugo was weary of that oily voice, of the staring eyes. He picked up his black slouch hat and shabby ulster and tramped up the aisle. Then he was outside, in silence and cold air, and he was aghast to find that it was he, he himself, this self that was always with him, who was the fellow that had made a disturbance in a public hall. Curlew and Joralemon do not heckle speakers, except for covert foot-scrapings by tough, gum-chewing young men. All the way home to Curlew, in the smoking-car, Hugo fancied that his fellow-passengers were watching him. He was alternately astonished—each time with a new sharp surprise— by what he had done, and galvanized with desire to make others see Germany as the high-breasted crusader, armed with the iron-hilted sword of righteousness. . . . Hugo knew less about Germany's modern economic and military system than did even the Honorable Mr. Vickery. In Germany there doubtless are silver-tongued jingoes and amateur defenders of honor, small, snug bureaucrats and journalists who shout: "Every red-blooded German—!" Hugo Bromenshenkel didn't know about that. He knew only that in a quiet valley, filled with bird sounds, was the grave of his father; and that somewhere in a putrid space between trenches was the body of his nephew Ludwig, the baby. Blood and tears and sweat of his own boyhood and of his own kin had fertilized Germany. With his blood and tears and sweat he loved Germany; and he believed—you can see from this just how simple he was—he believed that Germany was conceivably as honest and human in her warring as the North and the South had been in the Civil War.

Of one thing Hugo dared not think, while he hid behind the red-plush back of a seat in the smoker: he could never go down to the G.A.R., now, never see the boys again.

During the last two miles of the journey he prepared cheerful lies with which to meet his wife.

She was waiting for him at the station, with the democrat wagon and the old, warm buffalo-robe. After one look at him, she ran up and kissed his cheek, lingeringly, and put her arms about him. She asked no questions. As they entered the house he said, "There was a fellow — he spoke against Germany — " Nothing else was said regarding that evening, though for days she grieved that her boy had been robbed of the holiday to which he had gone forth so eagerly. About international policies she thought not at all; her patriotism consisted in keeping the wristlets on Hugo's thin wrists and the gaiety in his eyes.

Very much was said regarding that evening, however, in the two general stores and the saloon at Curlew; and the Dane blurted out to Hugo, the next time he came into town: "Well, you made a fine fool of yourself, they tell me."

Then came news from Germany that Franz, the chemist, the scholar, the creator, had been killed.

Hugo's eldest son, Grant, who lived in Chicago and owned a car, had heard a well-spiced version of Hugo's crime from some Joralemonite, and he wrote to his father with the harshness which the second generation often has for the first generation and Old Country ways: "You make me ashamed of you. What good did you think you were going to do?" Hugo did not answer, but he kept Grant's letter and read it often, and looked ashamed.

He was in Curlew on March seventeenth. The sight of the decorations in Monohan's store brought back all his indignation over the attacks on Germany in the motion-picture and in the speech of Mr. Vickery. He astounded the crowd in the store by shouting:

"St. Patrick's Day! Green and allerlei foolishness. Irish-American! Hyphenated! It's only the Germans that mustn't be hyphenated!"

A week and a half later he was in Curlew again. People stared at him, curious. That doubtless got on his nerves. Otherwise he would never have disturbed the Norwegian-American parade, for he liked the Scandinavians; had been neighborly to them for two-score years. They were dedicating a new Lutheran church. Lines of lanky, tall, ash-blond men and little withered women formed in the muddy chaos of the village street, and marched singing toward the new white-steepled shack that stood in a grove of birches, virgin and rustic as the birches. Hugo listened to their chanting. Beside him was the Danish saloon-keeper.

"Not for a poor wicked boozing devil like me," said the Dane, waving his hand toward the procession. He, too, was beginning to feel a pathos in the growing bitterness of this man who had, even in stormy arguments, always kept a pleading affection for everybody. He tried to think of something diverting to say, while Hugo was complaining: "Norwegian-Americans! Hyphenated! They pray in Norwegian, even! Only the Germans that mustn't love their own flesh and blood, and Germany fighting for her life, and blood, and Germany fighting for her life, and Franz dead—*Gott!*"

Suddenly Hugo bellowed: "Damn you all! Damn you! I hate you!"

The church procession heard, and their singing faltered. The town policeman ran up, caught Hugo's arm, led him off to the absurd lock-up behind the post-office. The Dane tagged behind them, begging: "He didn't mean it. Aw, he didn't say much of anything, Jim."

But the policeman left Hugo in the lock-up. Hugo stood in the middle of the room, his corded and rheumy chin up, and sang all that he could remember of *"Ein feste Burg ist unser Gott."*

In the justice's court he was fined ten dollars. He said nothing. Always he looked at something sacred and awful that stood behind the justice.

III
· · · · ·

The ice was breaking in Curlew Lake, the mold smelled fresh with spring, ducks were calling of adventure, and the farm turned expectantly to its master. But Hugo followed the drill slowly. He said nothing to anyone. He was convinced that he had become a criminal, a traitor, in some manner which he couldn't quite grasp though he went over and over it behind the drill. This seeding might be his last, he felt. His speech and his step were sluggish.

He was roused by an honor. In a letter in thin-looped German script he was invited to the pro-German city of St. Hilary, to attend a German Red Cross rally which was to be addressed by the famous German-American editor and propagandist, Peter Schiller-Lechtner of Chicago. And Hugo was to sit on the platform!

"We have heard," wrote the committee, "of the persecution which you have undergone for the Cause, and we desire to pay you at least this small belated honor."

Hugo read the letter to his wife.

"Well, I must go," he sighed.

He did not want to go. He had got into confused trouble every time he had gone anywhere, lately, and he wanted to spend every moment of what might be his last springtime with her, his *Liebling,* and with the fields that needed him. He was afraid to go from the joyous shine of the spring sun on softly weathered barns, out into the blackness where people laughed at him and put him in jail and reviled his dead nephews as men who had been trying to drag America into the war. Someone—he didn't understand these things any more—had ordered him to come and do something for the Fatherland, and he would obey, of course. But he stared regretfully about the kitchen, at the broad old stove with the glow through its lower draft, at the padded rocking-chairs, the glass bowl filled with balls of darning cotton. Everywhere, in everything, was the spirit of his wife. The wrinkles of his crepe-paper skin were spread out to smoothness in his first smile for days.

"Why, you could go with me!" he cried.

"Yes, I will go."

They packed their pasteboard imitation-alligator-skin tele-scope. It was time to dress. Hugo reached for the garments which he had long associated with festal days—the blue coat and gold-corded hat of the G.A.R. He hesitated. Defiantly, glancing craftily at her while she pretended not to notice, he dragged on the coat and pulled the gold-corded hat low on his head.

"I will!" he quavered. "I got a right to."

"Yes, Hugo," she soothed.

He rested his forehead against her sturdy shoulder, and from her presence drew strength to join the enemies of his land, and hers. For he saw the rally at St. Hilary as actual rebellion against America.

At St. Hilary the Bromenshenkels were met by half a dozen young Germans, not long from the Old Country, and they were ceremoniously driven to the house of an ardent writer of pro-German letters to the state press. In a dining-room hung with German mottoes and pictures of Zeppelins, the young zealots laughed and argued and exploded in German songs. They courted Hugo. Because they were not exactly sure what it was he had "done for the Cause" at Joralemon and Curlew, they told him he was a hero, a lone outpost of the Empire, and aside from the large quantities of sauerkraut and leberwurst and hasenpfeffer which were pressed on him, they all kept handing him buttered compliments, which embarrassed him. Yet he reveled in the surging Germanism of everything about him. Not for years had he been in so Teutonic an atmosphere, or talked so volubly. . . . If you were a Princeton man, say, or Yale, and after scores of years in Petrograd you met some Princeton undergraduates, singing the old songs, would you not forget Russia for a little hour? . . . Hugo ranted and stammered in his glorification of Germany. The young men encouraged him, and he worked up to a high-pitched excitement that was not far from real madness.

He sprang up. Solemnly, in a cracked, trembling voice, he toasted the martyred Franz and Ludwig, and he loved the young men as they cheered and drank the toast—and understood.

Arm in arm with a perfervid young German schoolmaster, his wife stumping behind him, Hugo marched with the others to Turn Hall. After a dark passage through a rear door and among stacks of scenery his party came suddenly out on a platform, and were facing at least one thousand people, in sharply marked curving rows, all of them staring at him, all in a haze of lights and German flags and portraits of Von Hindenburg and the Kaiser. As Hugo's glance crept up to the great arched rafters, where hung an enormous imperial eagle, ringed with electric lights; he began to realize that this rising applause was for his own group—for him!

He sank down in the nearest chair, almost hidden in the wings, and appealingly grasped his wife's hand, to pull her down beside him, regardless of the polite efforts of his hosts to conduct him to a chair near the center of the platform. Hugo shrank into himself; he dared not peep out at the audience till the arrival of the speaker of the evening diverted the applause from his own group.

The audience was roaring, "Lechtner! Unser Peter!"

Hugo expected a bearded Teutonic warrior. He found a manikin, delightedly bobbing to the audience—Unser Peter. For the famous Peter Schiller Lechtner, editor of three new pro-German publications and friend of active German consuls, looked like a cross between a naive child and a malicious monkey who would chatter his own praise from any bush that would lift him above the marveling bunnies of the wood. Hugo, being rustic and ignorant, had never learned that Unser Peter was the New Bismarck. All he saw was a little, pimply young man, much like the sleazy youths who hang about the depot lunch-room at Joralemon. Hugo shook his head, puzzled.

The chairman announced that they were all about to derive

high inspiration from that editor who had so valiantly defended Germany against the paid propagandists of France and perfidious Albion, that prophet of Teutonic supremacy, Herr Peter Schiller Lechtner.

Unser Peter darted up, raised his hands, demanded, *"'Die Wacht am Rein!' Zusammen!"*

With the others sang Hugo, stirred to tears.

Unser Peter Schiller Lechtner let a moment of silence creep through the hall, then leaped into shrill eloquence. He was, it seemed, violently in favor of the Germans using their combined vote as a weapon in this year's presidential election. Why? Did they ask him why? Because American munitions had made millionaires of the Americans and corpses of the Germans.

Hugo Bromenshenkel wasn't used to hearing his Brideland mentioned in quite such a tone of hatred. But he uneasily assured himself, "Yes, I don't like those munition-exports. *Gott!* Maybe my sister's boys were killed by American shells!"

Unser Peter was darting across the stage. With a hysterical jerk he pulled down an American flag that was twined with the German colors. He waved it frenziedly, bawling, "This Yankee rag! Do you know what it means? Red for blood! White for false neutrality! Blue for—"

Hugo Bromenshenkel half rose from his chair. He no longer saw the audience, the committee on the platform. He saw only the claws of Unser Peter clutching the flag he had worshiped for fifty years. He stooped, and picked up his G.A.R. hat. He carefully brushed the hat with his sleeve. He carefully put it on. He walked to the center of the platform. He snatched the American flag from the hands of Unser Peter.

Unser Peter stopped in mid-sentence. He clenched his fist, drew back his arm. Old Hugo faced him, quietly smoothing the folds of the flag, arranging it over his arm.

"Shame! The old mann iss all right!" a Germanic voice shouted from the audience.

Unser Peter's arm began to relax.

Hugo turned to look for his wife. She was just back of him, waiting, patient.

"Come, *Liebling,* we will go home," he said.

Still smoothing the torn flag, Hugo stalked down the steps from the platform, up the center aisle of the hall. His wife trotted beside him. They both ignored the crowd that hemmed them in. On either side of the aisle Germans began to rise, to clap, then to cheer. While Unser Peter shouted unheard on the platform, a vast-shouldered, red-faced German in a box led the audience in a thunderous singing of "America."

At the door of the hall Hugo stopped. He folded up the flag. He began to laugh, and in his laughter was no madness, now. He said judiciously: " Unser Peter would make a fine scarecrow for the beggie-field, if he wasn't so easy scared!"

The old lovers chuckled comfortably, and arm in arm they started happily for the station.

"It looks like rain. We'll have a good crop this year, after all," said Hugo.

THE TAMARACK LOVER

PLUMED WITH SPRUCE AND TAMARACK, or smirched by forest fires, these pine-tracts of northern Minnesota sweep toward the Mesaba Iron Range. This village of Larch is merely a sandy trail lined by three aimless blocks of tar-paper shacks and log-cabins. The one large structure is a flat-faced barracks which stands alone in a block prickly with pine stumps. It is the Bjorken Hotel; boarding-house and saloon in one.

The dining-room, a litter of oilcloth-covered tables about a sheet-iron stove, opens on the barroom, where the guests are cheerily hopeful of bloodshed just now. They are men of the woods: lumberjacks, mill-hands, railroad-construction laborers; Norwegian and Canuck, Finn and German. Hank Killeen, the section boss, calls Joe Kmoska something which expresses a doubt regarding the domestic purity of Joe's ancestors. Joe produces a razor. Hank handily throws a bottle of gin. The guests pack in a circle. . . .

From the dining-room rolls a deep voice, and a women hurtles into the bar—a tall, powerful, white-hot woman bawling: "You cut that out! I want you boys to under-by-jolly-well-stand I don't allow no scrapping here. G'wan out in the yard." Coaxingly: "Now, boys, be nice, or I won't darn your socks no more!" To the onlookers, laughing: "Honest, ain't them two the brace of cowards! Afraid to fight with their mitts! Afraid to! Dassant start a man-size fight without they got a knife to protect themselves!"

"Aw, I ain't afraid of no Mick boss," says Kmoska, while Hank Killeen dutifully goes on record, "I ain't afraid of any Roosian wop."

"Then go and lick the stuffin's out of each other—unless you're liars," suggested the woman, as though she were begging refractory children to run along and play. Her woolly lambs troop out.

Hearst's Magazine, February 1918

44

She strides back into the dining-room, and shakes her head at the book she has been reading: a curious book for this swart hole: *The Household Compendium of Famous Prose and Poetry, by Mrs. Hemans, Young, Beattie, Gray, and Other Immortal Bards, also 200 Valuable Recipes, Games and Recitations for the Refined Hearth and Home.* The title is lettered in three kinds of hairy type, and ornamented with rather a nice thing in the way of a gilt bird that is something like a robin and something like a sofa-pillow.

"Thank heaven for the quiet," says the woman. "I wish I could get myself to read some more of this poetry stuff. Oh, I guess I'm lonely to-night." In her voice is the ancient longing of disappointed women, but she ends her monologue briskly: "In fact, lonely as a loon, Uly, old girl. You're a grand little whiner!"

Her W's threatened to become V's, but she is not a humorous character with a jolly dialect, as she stands with folded arms, a figure strong, white, solitary as a single marble column amid a ruin. Technically she is not a beauty. Grand-opera *habitués* would say she is a heavy, a warrior, who ought to sing *Brunhilde* and wear a twenty-pound helmet, but be prevented at all costs from cuddling upon davenports. And she does seem a warrior at rest, a Saxon princess, high-cinctured, glorious of thigh, quiet-browed, wheat-colored of hair, mighty to wield the two-handed sword beside her lord, yet quick to comfort in the long days of peace.

Such is the widow Ulrica Bjorken at thirty-four.

A Norwegian-American, born in the pine-lands of Wisconsin, she was early married to Lars Bjorken, a fine big man with an appetite for ankles and alcohol, and none at all for paying debts. Ulrica was lucky enough to lose her husband in a log jam. She is a well-to-do woman now, owner of the hotel, the bar, the Larch general store, and certain rooms over the store where poker is played. She has acquired a section of cut-over land, eight miles west from Larch, and she speculates in iron-mining tracts in the Vermilion Range, which will be valuable when the M.&D.R.R puts through a new branch line.

To her boarders and customers and real-estate associates she talks like a man, tolerating no chuckings beneath the chin. She can swing a sack of wheat into a lumber-wagon, drink whisky neat, and bluff with a bob-tailed flush as well as her men, and because she can compete with them she cannot love them. There is nothing in them to surprise her slow, secret ideals into wonder. Now, by the rusty stove, she is dreaming of the world of silken women and clever men.

She drops her arms, looks alert. The crowd is returning to the barroom, bibulously applauding Hank Killeen. Simultaneously the outside door of the hotel, beyond the dining-room, opens — not to the expected grocery drummer, but to a stranger.

The stranger was a thin, youngish man, dark and moody of face, delicate of hand, and dressed in dour black. Behind him was old Henry R. Tuttle, owner of the local lath-mill, a loud and disapproving man.

"Mrs. Bjorken," said Henry R., "I want to make you 'quainted with the Reverend Felix Sweetwater, the new pastor of our church. Just hit town. The Missus is house-cleaning, and we can't entertain Brother Sweetwater, so he'll stay with you for a little while. Give him your best rate, Mrs. Bjorken, your best rate."

Ulrica was meditating, "The old tightwad," while with a shapely hand she greeted the shy young man. "I'm afraid this ain't much of a place for a Reverend," she said, "but I'll give you our best room, and put all clean sheets on the bed!"

The Reverend Felix Sweetwater smiled with difficulty, shifting from one foot to the other, and peering at the barroom, while the crowd peered back and muttered, "Great snakes! Get onto Henry R. and the preacher!"

Henry R. volubly departed. The crowd surged in from the bar, and Hank Killeen sneered: "Welcome to our city, Your Reverence. Come have a drink. It ain't often us guys — we're tough, we are, we bite through nails, we're so tough, we killed the last school-teacher that was here—not often we get a chance to meet a regular fire-and-brimstone Protestant preacher. Come have a drink, I said."

The gang ringed the Reverend Felix; chins bristling with black stubble were thrust at him, and a huge Swede slapped him on the skinny shoulder-blades. Ulrica Bjorken battered her way into the circle. She shook her fist in Hank's face, and shrieked: "You boys get out of here if you can't be polite to the first Reverend that's ever had the kindness to lodge with you filthy Squareheads! I won't have no noise or cussing in my dining-room, understand? And not one single word of bad language around the Reverend, savvy?"

The Reverend Felix recovered from his temporary paralysis, and spoke in a voice of surprising virility for one of his sallow slightness: "Let me talk to them. . . . Listen here, boys. If I'm going to live here, I want you to understand me. You know I'm a preacher, and I can't booze with you. You know how it is to have a hard-driving boss? Well, I have all the church-going people for my boss—I haven't just one person keeping time on me, but the whole lot of them. And if I have to please them, and please you big husky fellows, what can I do? Pretty hard to work in two crews at once."

"That's right, Father," said Hank. "Sure, I know. These respectable guys are fierce to work for. I know. Come on, boys. The preacher is all right. Come on."

As they shuffled away, Ulrica proclaimed: "You did fine, Reverend. That's the idea; don't be scared of them."

The Reverend Felix confessed: "But I was scared of them—scared to death! But I don't mind their roughness. I envy them. Could you find me a little something to eat, if it isn't too much trouble?"

"Lord love me, I'm clean forgetting! You just sit right down, and I'll dig you out something in two shakes. Like your eggs done on one side, or over?"

The Reverend Felix blanched before the array that she brought: beans and eggs and rewarmed hash and canned apricots and salt pork and coffee with condensed milk and doughnuts and pie and cake—and toothpicks.

He could not know that Ulrica, the mistress, did not ordinarily wait upon guests. He paid no attention to her, as she sat by the stove, heavily staring at him.

She who could pump a taciturn Finn or a "jollying" Duluth drummer, did not know how to approach the reverend and melancholy Felix. She was puzzled. Therefore she was delighted! It had been so long since she had been puzzled by any of these men, with their obvious ways of asking for credit or kisses. She moved away from him, but from the kitchen door she kept watch. He brought out a book from his pocket, propped it against the nickeled cruet-stand. She came in to fill his water glass—in other words, to peep at the book. It was poetry!

To her, musical-comedy lyrics and the epics of Milton and the hymns of Isaac Watts were all poetry—something to admire, but not exactly to read. She was excited. The Reverend Felix's muteness became magic to her.

She wanted to know—oh, everything that these fellows wrote in books. The Reverends who had formerly occupied the Larch pulpit had been cramped, anxious men, addicted to wives and a surf of children, and reading nothing but sermons and grocery bills. But this man—maybe he was one of those poet fellows himself! She galloped back with the water, sat down at the table with him, and babbled:

"Say, Reverend, it sure is nice to see a fellow reading books and literature here. These boys, they're nice boys when they aren't too drunk, but read——! Now me, I always was crazy about reading—not that I ever was much educated, you know how it is, but I just do love books. If I do say it myself, I have the finest library in Larch township. And a piano! Say, don't you just love books?"

"Yes. But I can't afford very many," he sighed.

"I bet you've read everything. You've got such a' educated way of saying things. Look! Me gassing here, and your coffee all gone!" She pounced on his coffee-cup, and fairly charged on the kitchen.

"Huh! Him a regular preacher!" she confided to the soot-crusted coffee-pot. "Why, he ain't asked me once, even yet, if I'm saved. He's no preacher! Can't tell me!"

She hurried back to ask him about "improving books to read."

"Say, I guess you aren't married, like most of these preachers, are you?" she interrupted the Rev. Felix's discourse on Tennyson.

"No, I am not," he beatified her by saying.

After all, he wasn't more than a year younger than herself, she decided. And she had heard of people like him marrying country people. Oh, that was nonsense. . . . But hadn't it been elegant, the way he talked, and the way he put his napkin on his knee, like a drummer, instead of tucking it under his chin!

She went up to her own room. Her face was not heavy now, but lighted with dreams.

It was a room of symbols, thick with the shadows of wistful aspirations. There were symbols in hard, practical things — a stubby cast-iron safe, a pompous little cannon-ball stove and a big wood-box, a cheap wash-stand marked with white rings from the soap-dish. But beside the safe was a bookcase, and shoved behind the bed, as though it had once stood farther out in the room but had gradually been forgotten, was a piano — the only piano in Larch.

She undressed slowly, standing before the locked bookcase, repeating aloud the names of books, mispronouncing many of them, shaking her head, awed, a little unhappy. There were a hundred books, perhaps; a grotesque collection: Howells and Marie Corelli, Balzac and Mrs. E. D. E. N. Southworth, *The Practical Horse-Breeder,* Vol. XVII, and *By-by Tales for Tiny Tots.*

She wrapped a blankety dressing-gown about her coarse night-gown. From a standing wardrobe she took out three evening gowns of satin, blue and white and cerise, heavily spangled.

"But maybe the preacher would think they were immodest," she mourned. "I guess maybe I won't ever get to wear them."

She took from a drawer a scrapbook, and in a tidy-hung rocker by the stove she turned the pages. It was filled with a miscellany of pictures clipped from magazines.

She pored over a picture of two men in a *Georgian* library.

"If I was married to a poet fellow, I wouldn't bother him if he was talking to his tony friends, and I would fry him a nice slice of sugar-cured ham. I guess even a poet likes his vittles."

She reached the last page of the scrapbook. She was fixed upon a picture which clever persons, who know about cubism and orange pekoe and sabotage, would have smiled at as highly sentimental. It was a pitilessly clear photograph of a baby in a ribbon-tied basket.

"Oh, baby," she whispered, faintly, timidly. She was in a trance.

There was a sound from the yard, as of some one singing two or three ballads at once, with imperfect knowledge of harmony.

Ulrica dropped the scrapbook. She listened. She paddled to the window, threw it up. She shouted: "You, Joe Kmoska, you drunken Finnski foreigner, you go to bed — waking everybody up — or I'll come down there and pound your block off, savvy?"

Then she went to bed and for seven hours she slept with perfect soundness and a slight suggestion of a feminine snore.

Ulrica's head hired-girl was a sufferer from corns, but she was a great church-goer. She told Ulrica, along in May, that the thirty people who made up the exclusive congregation were not satisfied with the Reverend Felix Sweetwater. The hired-girl didn't think much of the Reverend Felix as a preacher, though she admitted that he was nice and quiet to wait on at table. She complained that he merely talked. He didn't make his voice go up high and trembly, and then come down in a boom that waked you up.

She sat behind Henry R. Tuttle at prayer-meeting, and heard Henry R. say that the Reverend Felix seemed to think he was so pesky modern that he had outgrown the blood of the Lamb and sanctification by grace; and that four hundred dollars salary, paid pretty promptly, was a lot too much for a fellow that thought he was too good for the old-time Bible salvation.

Henry R. admitted that Brother Sweetwater was a good caller, but he criticized him for remaining at Mrs. Bjorken's, when he could just as well keep his board-money in the flock, seeing as Mrs. Clabber now had room to take him in; and while some said Mrs. Clabber wasn't a big provider, she ran a good Christian home.

Early in June, fairest month in the pines, when the burnt-over stretches were flecked with rag-baby and Indian tobacco and sorrel, the ecclesiastical hired-girl reported that the attendance of Felix's church had fallen to twelve or fifteen at a meeting. The hotel was almost empty, now, with the woodsmen in the cities or out on Red River Valley farms, but one Saturday evening Ulrica secretly assembled nine of her permanent boarders in the dining-room, after Felix had gone up-stairs.

"Now boys," she said, "I got something I want you to do. But first, all have a drink."

"It must be a terror of a job, if the boss passes out free booze," grunted Hank Killeen.

"You shut your trap," said Ulrica, comfortably. "Just for that you don't get a drink. Pass him by, boys," she commanded, as she started a quart of Bourbon circulating.

Joe Kmoska pretended that he wasn't letting Hank have a drink, and Hank pretended that he wasn't getting one, and Ulrica pretended that she was taken in, and they were in immense good-humor when she exploded her request.

"I want you all to go to church tomorrow."

"Huh!" said Hank. "I go to mass at Hennepin City every month."

"I mean Reverend Sweetwater's church here."

"Me sit near Henry R. Tuttle?" protested Mr. Tuttle's straw-boss.

"Why don't you send us off to Sunday-school with a penny in our mitts?" bellowed the next man.

Ulrica pounded on the table. "Now that's enough from you. I'm tired of your wicked, profane ways, you hell-pups, and either you go to church, or you don't get anything but prunes and hash for a week."

"But what do we get out of it?" demanded Henry R.'s loyal straw-boss.

"You get your morals and manners fixed up, you gumbo hog. I'll furnish two bits each for you to put in the pot, if I catch any of you holding it out on me when Henry R. passes that little cloth hat on the long stick I'll eat you."

"Well, all right; anything for quiet," growled Hank. "Guess I could stand a Protestant church once."

"Now, understand, you aren't going because I bully you into it. You all want a little religion. And you want baths. You're goin' to get the baths right now. I've chased the hired-girls out of the kitchen, and there's soap and towels, and a wash-tub standing in the middle of the floor, and plenty hot water in the wash-boiler. Now, in there and strip and scrub, Hank, and hustle up, so the others can have their turn."

She marshaled her nine lambs to church next morning. When Cross-Saw Jones and the Swede carpenter tried to play a private game of poker with a vest-pocket pack on an outspread hymn-book, she kicked them, looking heavily serene the while.

But she was not serene.

Her flock was bored by Felix's sermon, a rather hesitating optimism about internationalism.

Hank Killeen was covertly angry about something; he kept staring at her sternly, his lips moving.

The Reverend Felix Sweetwater seemed confused by their presence. He gaped at their solid red row of faces; seemed to be searching for words to reach them.

Finally, the crusty, dry-baked soul of the church, Mr. Henry R. Tuttle, kept turning around disapprovingly. Ulrica had no sunny Sicilian passion for Henry R., but he represented the small, solid Respectable Society of Larch, and his stare made her uncomfortable. When the service was over and she was whispering to her publicans and sinners, "Now go out quietly, you devils!" Henry R. teetered back to her, and said loudly: "It's a great pleasure to see you in the house of God, Mrs. Bjorken. Too bad you can't come oftener." But he seemed to mean that this was the house of Henry R. Tuttle, and that it was too bad she had ever come.

Ulrica could find nothing to say. Nor could she say anything when Felix, shaking hands at the door, murmured: "Thank you for bringing the boys, Mrs. Bjorken. I'm so sorry I couldn't interest them."

Hank Killeen glanced at her bitterly. She worried over that glance as she plowed home. She did not even care that the dry sand was dimming her red-heeled mail-order slippers. She went to her room and sat with her head in her hands. She looked tired but savage—a she-panther, wearied by the trail.

Her door opened. Hank stood there, leering.

"You get out of here!"

Hank carefully closed the door and laughed. "How about a little kiss, old sweetheart?"

"I'll throw you out of here——"

"Now we had enough of that bluffing stuff last night. You're a beefy wench, all right, but you want to get right over this idea that you're the female Hackenschmidt. You're nothing but a she-woman, and you been taking on a lot too much for a woman." He glared. His thin, long face was formidable. He had not even taken off his hat. "You been leading on a bunch of us, especially me. Well, I've come to collect, see? You know I love you, but you don't know something, see? I'm through with your stalling. Now let's have a little kiss, girlie."

She sprang up. Making no noise except for a hoarse sighing in her throat, she struggled against him. But he was weathered by handling oak ties and steel rails. He bent her face back and kissed her, boisterously.

"I'll kill you!" she said.

"Tut! You didn't used to be so particular. I remember when you was a young widdy, you kissed me when I came back from Superior. And the Lord only knows how many others!"

"Well, I'm different now."

"Huh, I know that all right! You admit it, do you! And do you know why? You—a big strapping two-fisted woman like you— you're in love with this yapping four-flush of a preacher."

"Look here, Hank; we've been pretty good pals. I want you to listen to me. Take your hands off me and listen."

Never before had she looked at him just as a woman, with feminine beseeching. He slowly removed his hands.

"Hank, do you remember when your wife died, how you wanted to kill yourself? How it ached? That's how I feel now. Hank, dear, honest, I haven't told anybody but you about it. Haven't even told myself! Remember how you felt when your kid first went to Hen City and got into the round-house there and made good as a fireman? How you starved yourself to buy him a locomotive manual? That's how I feel about this boy. Hank, he ain't nothing but a boy, this preacher, and he ain't making good, and my breast fairly aches when I think of him trying to please that rock-faced old coffin-robber, Henry R."

"Yes. I see. Say. . . . Uly. . . . Say, honest, I don't think bad of the little man. He's got nerve. He sticks on in a fierce job, him with a real man's soul under his ribs trying to get along with that gossip-hound, Mrs. Clabber."

He stood kicking a rocker, while to herself she was gasping, "Why, it's true! I do love him—just like I was a fool girl. I ain't a husky free-trader now, no more. Good-by Ulrica Bjorken."

She found Hank looking at her, grinning. She blushed.

"Think you got it all settled, now you've run out Hank, don't you!" he jeered. "Just got to yell to the little preacher, and he'll come a-running! But what're you going to do about the skirt that writes to him every week?"

"Don't know what you mean."

"No, of course you don't look over the mail!"

"No, I don't—except my own."

"Oh no, sure not! 'Course you never noticed the letters, that some she-female writes him! There's one down in the dining-room now, in the batch of mail the cookee just brought in from the office. 'Course you won't go down and give it the once-over!"

"No, I won't. And you get out of here. You ain't got no right in a lady's bedroom, anyway."

"All right, old kiddo. . . . Honest, Uly, I'm sorry for you."

She bared her teeth at his back. She stood still. She tiptoed into the hall, and listened till the door of his room closed.

"I always did despise these hens that look at folks' mail," she told herself.

In a panic she tumbled down-stairs, rushed into the dining-room, picked from the tiny pile of mail a letter addressed to the Rev. Felix Sweetwater. It was on the stationery of a real-estate firm of Wabicott, Minn., but it was inscribed in a feminine writing, a script delicate and schooled.

"Oh, it's just some business letter," Ulrica declared, as she laid it down.

But as the Revered Felix came into dinner, Ulrica saw between herself and him the lines of a woman's handwriting, a bar filmy as cobweb and strong as rock, an obstacle that evaded her bold strength and demanded a new strategy.

Ulrica Bjorken, before love had turned her from a brisk boss of men into a passionate woman, had beheld the Reverend Felix Sweetwater as that Culture which every Middle Westerner desires after his kind, whether he is a Finn like Joe Kmoska, or the Senator from Omaha. But now she saw Felix as a man.

She talked more freely with him, and put into her smiles for him all her cheery warmth. In shy, unpoetic compliments Felix showed his respect for Ulrica. He praised her housekeeping, her mania for cleanliness.

August came in; the pine alleys were baking by noon, windless and itching with heat by night; and the mosquitoes and no-see-ums penetrated the cheesecloth screens at every window and over every bed. There were few guests, and even the obstreperous Hank kept to himself.

One evening there was no one at supper but Ulrica and Felix. She flashed on him all her long-constrained womanliness. She laughed, with excitement in her voice. She made the pine table a soft and alluring place, with the touch of her hand on his as she filled his coffee-cup. His tired energy seemed to awaken, and he stammered of his ambitions. He wanted, he said, to be the head of a mission in a city — Fargo or Minneapolis — and to conduct a free-employment bureau.

"Tell me, where do you come from?" she half whispered to him. "I wonder so much about you. I think probably you must be from Milwaukee or New York, one of those learned fellows like my dad used to see in Upsala; he was there one time — it's the biggest college in the world. Tell me, won't you?"

She leaned forward. Her arms were moist, and her gingham sleeves were unevenly rolled; yet those arms were round and of an even pink, fine-textured as linen, as they stretched toward him in the late sunlight that splashed across the glazed white oil-cloth.

"No, I am not learned, not a bit," he said. "You always flatter me by thinking I'm a real preacher, but as a matter of fact I'm just a searcher. I was a Kandiyohi County boy. My father was a farmer. I went to St. Paul and learned stenography and got into the railroad offices. And I didn't make good. I wasn't satisfied with being a clerk, and I wanted to be a preacher, but I hadn't the education, though I read lots of library books, and I was awful interested in Christian Endeavor and Men's League. Then, when I was twenty-seven, I took what little money I'd saved and went through Plato College. I thought it was a pretty fine college, but afterward, when I had two years in theological school, and met fellows from Oberlin and the University of Chicago and Wisconsin, I saw that Plato was just a rural school. And I don't know my profession yet. This is my first charge, except for pulpit-filling in vacations. I do love to read, but I'm ignorant, Mrs. Bjorken, and I guess I'm sort of a liar to talk about books to you in such a high-and-mighty way."

"Huh! That's funny — you telling me you're ignorant!"

"You're a hundred times better educated than I am. I'm a failure, and you know your job — oh, splendid!" He grasped her hand, held it tight, cried: "I've never been able to thank you for the way you've taken care of me. And while of course I can't approve of your owning a saloon, I do know you've lived, while I've crept on, oh, so blindly——"

There were voices in the barroom. He snatched back his hand, looked self-conscious.

Ulrica did not understand the academic distinctions between Plato College and the University of Chicago, but she did understand that at last he was willing to take away the class bars between them. She whispered to him: "Come sit on the side-porch, and read me some of this poetry. All my life I've wanted to hear some one read poetry!"

He read Longfellow and Tennyson to her, on the side-porch, sheltered from the street by a clump of spruce. She had little idea what these violently modern poets were talking about, but she would have enjoyed his version of them had they been written in Alexandrine Greek regarding the Logos. When he laid down the book she begged: "Is there maybe some poetry you like to have? I wish I could buy it for you. Sure! I send to Duluth."

"Buy it for me? Oh, no, no, no. I couldn't — I shouldn't even let you do all that you do now. I take so much from you. It's wicked."

"I don't guess I worry if I spend two-three dollars."

"It isn't that. I haven't any right to take anything from you. It isn't as though you were some motherly old woman. Why, Ulrica, you're a young woman, and a handsome woman, and I'm young, too, and I have been a man once, I seem to remember!"

"You think I'm handsome?"

"I like your looks altogether too much." He looked at her close, breathed quickly. "Yes, and the feeling of your hands. Too much. Not because I'm a preacher, but because I'm engaged."

"Oh! That's what all those letters are! Some woman! I knew it! Every week a letter!"

"Yes, and I write to her every day."

"A letter every day? What about? Me, I couldn't write a letter every day, not even if I was engaged to the King of France. . . . But I write pretty good, too, so anybody could read it."

"Of course you do, but—Ulrica, she's a wonderful girl, Annabel. Annabel Potts."

"That's a fine Yankee name!" Ulrica sighed. "I wish I had a name like that. . . . Where does she live? Is her folks alive?"

She was not entirely free from guile. She had been making a guilty study of these weekly letters post-marked "Wabicott, Minnesota," on the business envelopes of "J. F. Potts, Real Estate and Insurance."

Felix told his shepherd's tale of the fair Annabel, who sat upon porches and talked about Vogner and played pianos and was slender and quick-footed and curly haired, and taught a class of little ones in Sunday-school. Ulrica encouraged him because she wished to know just what she had to fight. For fight she would, now that the Reverend Felix saw her, not as a Larch landlady, but as a human being.

Despite his effusions, he held her hand at parting. Alone, she mourned: "Why did I let him go? Maybe he might have kissed me. I don't think this girl, this Horrible Spots, got warm hands like me, even if she does play her piano. Oh, I want him, *him!* Why did I let him go?"

Like many rudimentary creatures, she knew precisely and shamelessly what she wanted. She was, perhaps, no more resolute than the Annabel Pottses in demanding the love of her Man, but she was more honest in knowing that she did demand it.

Once he had come out of his pastoral retirement, Ulrica would not let the Reverend Felix retreat. She persuaded him to go hunting with Joe Kmoska and herself; he shot as a farm boy should, quick but careful of aim, and brought home nine mallards.

He refused her offer to contribute a hundred dollars yearly to the church, so long as she should be a Woman of the World, and own a saloon and gambling rooms. She closed up the gambling rooms, but the saloon she would not close. She had thought of it often, she said, but a saloon-keeper at Hennepin City was ready to open a tough dive if she closed. Though she would have given body and blood and life to Felix, she would not give up her conviction. In the November days, the bar crowded with gangs of lumberjacks returning to the woods, Ulrica was busy with them and with new, excited speculations in Vermilion Range options. There was secret information that the M.&D.R.R would push a new Vermilion branch through in the spring and she gambled on borrowed money. She had to go to the range often, and when she was home the guests, who filled every room and a dozen cots in the halls, were between her and Felix. With her every investment she thought of him; she might become a very wealthy woman; might be able to give him a sea-facing house, Eastern leisure, a chance to open a dozen missions.

The woman behind the business man, the woman who could darn socks and long for a hand in hers, was lonely for him.

One evening, at supper, Felix received a sick-call to a farm six miles west of Larch.

He smiled at her. "I guess I'll walk out. Isn't very far."

"No, be a fine walk," she said, knowing he could not afford livery hire.

As she said it, her bosom heaved, she started, and said calmly, loud enough for all the dish-clattering table to hear, "Say, Reverend, I'm going out to my claim to-night—got to see how my new shack looks—sent out the carpenters to build it. It's near where you go. You ride out with me, and I'll drop you off, and you can walk back."

"Be glad to."

She telephoned the livery stable to send the grays, the best team in Larch—oh, yes, Larch has a liveryman, though he is also the garage man, undertaker, veterinary, and very handy at odd jobs of carpentry and fiddle-playing.

"You want to drive?" she asked, as they stood outside the house, the horses stamping in the clear and echoing cold.

"Yes!" Later he added: "First time I've driven for months—in fact, since I filled the pulpit at Kildee. Oh, it's thoughtless of me to talk about enjoying the ride, with poor, sick Mrs. Heffner waiting for me."

"You take care of yourself, and don't worry about her. I know these women, drat 'em! She just wants a man to hold her hand.... Maybe I like to have my own hand held!"

"There, then, that ought to satisfy you," he cried, as with his red-flannel mitten he patted her thick glove. He laughed with more flirtatious gallantry than she had ever heard from him before. He hummed "Seeing Nelly Home." He chattered of his boyhood, of driving a bobsled to a dance.

She listened fondly. But she caught only half of what he said.

"You know where the Heffner house is, don't you?" he asked.

"Sure, but it's a cold night. I think maybe you better drive on to my shack with me, and then I come back with you and wait for you at Heffner's."

"Oh, thanks, but I guess I better not."

The wind congealed their jaw muscles, froze their moist breath in a mist of ice about their fur collars. The cold did not, she noted, keep him from driving well over the chunks of frozen sand.

. . .

He marveled, presently, "Why, it's only six miles out to Heffner's, they said. Haven't we gone that?"

"Just a little way now." There was panting exultation in her voice.

After perhaps half a mile she cried: "Goodness! Say, Reverend, it was Joe Heffner's you wanted to go to, wasn't it?"

"Why no! Albert Heffner's."

"Then I've gone and let you go a mile and a half beyond. Oh, that's a shame! Albert lives back by the popple grove. What made me think: here we are at my place. I tell you. You just wait a minute, and I hurry and look at my house and then we drive back. Turn in here."

They came in the darkness to the mass of a low house, the new unpainted pine clapboards vague in the hard starlight.

"Jut wait while I get the lantern and look around," she said. She went into the house.

From inside she cried, "Oh, Reverend! Come! Quick."

"What is it?" He leaped from the buggy, hastened to the door. "Some one in there?"

"Oh, no," she said naïvely. "But would you fight him for me if there was?"

"Why, I guess so, if I had to, though I'm not much of a hand at fighting."

"For me would you fight?"

"Ulrica, you've been the one person that's enabled me to stick on in Larch. Of course I'd fight for you."

Her laugh was glorious, but it ended, in a humorous diminuendo, with: "All right, then, maybe you'll light a fire for me! I'm so cold."

The new shack was furnished only with a sheet-iron stove, a tumbled cot, a bare cupboard, two kitchen chairs — things sent out with the carpenters.

He hastened as he heaped paper and pine cones in the stove. She seemed constrained, warming her hands by the ephemeral blaze. She did not glance at him till he said: "Have you looked it over? We must be getting back."

Her whole spirit seemed to flame, like the pine cones. "No! We're not going till we have a talk."

"Why, what about?"

"Us! Here we stay——"

"Why, my dear woman, are you trying to kidnap my valuable self?"

"Yes! I am! If things were like they were in the Big Woods ten—fifteen years ago, I would kidnap you for all winter, carry you off to a claim and keep you there."

"B-but——" The bewildered boy dropped from him and he laughed. "Ulrica, this is positively funny. Come. We'll talk as we drive back."

"Why are you afraid to be alone with me here where it's quiet? You are afraid! Tell me you aren't, and I'll let you go."

She put both her hands on his shoulders. They were of about the same height. Her cornflower-blue eyes were frank in their demand. Her huge coonskin coat was open and hung from her shoulders in long straight lines, her head was back; and in the lantern light she was impressive as a great prima donna.

He looked at her, trembled. "Ulrica, don't put me in this rotten, priggish, Galahad position, as though I were a scary girl, and you were the man, urging me. I can't stand that."

"It's because you are a finer man, more understanding and brighter and all than these big-footed husks, that I love you. Maybe you don't understand how it is; but I was brought up like a boy doing chores and getting licked, and if I wanted anything I didn't have any mother to go and whine to for it; I just had to grab it. And my husband—if I wanted anything, I had to grab it. And now I'm in love—why, I'm going to grab love! If I sat back and waited I would be a poor widow, keeping roomers, and I would die a lonely old woman. That's why I bring you here—to talk straight. It ain't respectable, I guess, but, oh, they never gave me

time to be respectable. Always it was hustle—and grab. This respectable world—oh, hang the respectable folks; they expect us
women to be oxen for work and little whisper-doves for love. I
work—and I love! . . . But I'm tired, tired of begging you. If you
would come to me and ask for my love—then I would be willing
to be a dove."

Suddenly the pride went out of her; her erect figure seemed to give
way, her magnificent head, with one ashen coronet braid visible
under the dark, soft fur cap, dropped on his shoulder, and her
boasting slumped to a weary sigh.

He put his arm about her, he smoothed her cheek, for an in-
stant he held her tight. Then he fled to the rumpled cot, and sat
there, the forlorn dignity of his little learning gone.

"Ulrica," he mourned, "I know you're beautiful. When I see
your cheeks so close to my lips—I've been blind; I never knew a
woman's skin could be so frightfully alive and warm. Why, I've
simply got to fight myself to make myself consider the obligations
I have. But—I've never much known what I wanted to do in life,
but I have got respect for you even if I haven't very much for myself, dear, and I want——"

She had come to sit beside him, woe-begone, like a big unhappy girl. Now she laughed, a rolling laughter wholesome as the
wind among Norway pines. "You talk so fon-ny!" she shouted.
"Just like a big preacher! And I know you are just a little boy,
same as Ulrica is nothing but a hungry girl. So fon-ny! 'Consider
obligations!' My man, he is a fine educated fellow, I t'ink!"

"Yes, yes, but Ulrica——"

She laid her fingers over his lips, she locked her fingers with
his. As they looked at each other they were not Ulrica of the woods
and the Reverend Felix Sweetwater, but man and woman.

"You do care," she murmured. "Maybe you don't know it. I
think that. But you do care! You were glad to have my head on
your shoulder!"

"If Annabel were———"

"You know something? I never did like that girl! I think she is too selfish to come up to Larch and share your salary with you!" said Ulrica, in a most genial conversational tone.

He was silent. He shrugged. He smiled at her, sadly. He went to replenish the stove, but he came back to her, and this time it was he who took her hand and held it. The room was small, warm and still. The stove crackled. Pine shavings, still heaped in a corner, smelled with a resinous fragrance. They two were close together, in that drowsy and betraying warmth, that lantern-blurred dusk. Her throat was the one white startling thing that shone out of the dimness; he bent forward and touched it with his quick fingers. She was swaying toward him.

The stove-fire roared suddenly as it devoured a pitch-pine chunk. Through the front-draft a barred light swept the room for a second.

Felix sprang up. He jerked from his inside pocket a leather case. He flipped it open and held it toward her. She could just make out, inside, the photograph of a girl.

"Annabel," he said.

"What does she matter?" wailed Ulrica, all woman now.

"She's between us. I love you. But I shouldn't. Oh, I don't know, I can't think. We must go."

"No, no!" she sobbed, holding out her hands to him, as the whipped child that does not understand holds out its arms to the angry mother. "No, no! Kiss me. That's all I want. So many years I have worked, so hard. See, my fingers are calloused—see, here and here. So ugly! I could not keep them soft for you. But I have kept my heart for you. When many ask for it, many, many. Once, kiss me once."

He held between them the picture of Annabel, as though it were a crucifix.

"Ulrica, I do love—I think I love—I did love Annabel. She is so bright and young and jolly. When I was trying to tell her what I wanted to do, she would look at me—do you see how big her eyes are?—her eyes would open and open, and she would say: 'Oh, yes, you will do splendid things.' You are wiser. You know I'm nothing but a yearner who hasn't even found his work yet. But I loved her for—oh, for coddling me, I suppose."

Ulrica snapped: "Oh, that Annabel! She wins! Me, I got nothing but a pair of black deuces. And she, she got big black eyes and girly hair and one admiring look, and I guess that counts for three queens, and she win the pot. And you, God help you, you win the Potts. Sure, me, I can make jokes. What do I care! Come."

She buttoned her coat. She stalked out. As they climbed into the buggy, he implored, "Ulrica!"

No answer.

"Ulrica!"

"Say, you better hurry. Mrs. Heffner is still waiting to hold your hand. These women—Ulrica and the whole lot. Don't get ahead. Man-crazy. Keeps 'em back."

"Ulrica, will you forgive me? You must remember I've taken a good many years becoming a book, and it's hard trying to be a to-hades-with-everything man. I suppose I seem ridiculous to both you and Annabel. I know I am to myself."

"Oh, no! I understand. I'll wait. This can't be all. All my life I wait to want a man—it isn't the kiss, it's wanting to be kissed. I won't believe I won't ever have your lips near mine again. You won't go away from me? You won't go to Mrs. Clabber's to board?" In a prosy and highly indignant tone: "Honest, Felix, she give her boarders prunes for breakfast every day in the year! I swear she do! And who would darn your socks?"

"No, I won't go," he said, as he lashed the horses.

Whether or not someone had seen them go to Ulrica's shack, there spread through Larch next day a small-town scandal to the effect that though the Reverend Mr. Sweetwater was engaged to a girl somewhere, he and Mrs. Bjorken were "carrying on." A voluble Montenegrin brought tidings of the scandal to Ulrica. . . . They say that to this day the Montenegrin avoids the vicinity of the Bjorken Hotel.

Two evenings later, the trustees of the church called upon Felix in his room. Ulrica crept to listen, through the thin partition. Henry R. Tuttle, who was a square man according to his rep-curtained lights, grated out that, though he knew Brother Sweetwater was a milk-and-water preacher, he would never believe that Henry R. Tuttle's own pastor could care for a big, strapping, rum-selling, Norske clodhopper.

"She is the best woman I know, and I'll trouble you to speak respectfully of her," Felix was heard to answer.

"Well, never mind that. The point is: We've thought it over, and we've arranged for you to go board with Mrs. Clabber."

"No thank you."

"Mean to say you want to stay in this house of licker and wrath?"

"If Larch considers this place good enough for its workmen, then it's good enough for the workmen's pastor."

"Look here, young man, I'm older than you, and if you can't show a little respect——"

"I know. You'll ask for my resignation. Well, you won't get it, unless the whole church, assembled in business session, demands it. Now bring up any accusations you may have, and I'll answer them. But understand, first of all, that I'm proud to have a clean, strong, fighting woman like Mrs. Bjorken for my friend."

Ulrica, listening, had made up her mind. She would get rid of Annabel. And then—Ulrica could have laughed full-throated— she would be able to close up her Vermilion land deals, and lavish the money on her man, Felix. It was a critical time in the Vermilion deals, but here was something more critical.

To the Wabicott Hotel came a woman, tall, youngish, Norse-haired, in painfully correct mourning-veil and gown. Timidly she asked for a room and meekly trailed up-stairs after the night-clerk.

"That all, ma'am?" he said, with a tone that hinted he might be insolent to lone ladies if he were not tipped.

"Yes, I think so. Please, mister, is there a real-estate man in town—his name is Mr. Potts?"

The "Please, mister," betrayed to the epochally wise night-clerk that she was merely an expensively dressed country woman.

"Yuh, I guess so."

"Don't you know?" she wondered, opening wide her patient blue eyes.

"Aw, a clerk can't know everything. Say, the folks usually slips me two bits for lugging their grips up-stairs; all the swell city folks do."

"I guess you're from the city, maybe?"

"Sure. Born and raised there."

Somehow the good-looking country-woman had circled between him and the door. She now leaned against the jamb, and began to laugh boisterously.

"I guess I know the kind of city you come from. You come from Axelbrod Prairie. You poor kitchen cat, I own a bigger hotel than what this is, and I wouldn't have a steak-stealing, money-sneaking clerk like you working for me. Now you listen. I ain't got but a little time. I'll give you five dollars if you give me the information I want about this dead town, savvy?"

"Say, you're all right, kid! You took me in! Say, what's your graft?"

"Never mind that. *Sit down!*"

He sat. He told her the life history of Mr. J. F. Potts, Real Estate, and Insurance; also of Annabel the fair, and how she was a cute kid, and loved a jeweler, oh yes, and they say she had been interested in a preacher named Sweetwater, quiet fella, who had preached in First Church, one vacation time, but nobody knew what had become of this fella, and anyway Annabel was going with the jeweler, who was a swell guy that wore fancy vests, and nobody could understand why they didn't get hitched; maybe the jeweler was holding off, because Maizie Denver, the banker's daughter, liked the jeweler pretty good herself. And thanks for the five bucks.

At eight-seventeen next morning Ulrica saw that Beau Brummell among jewelers, made an offer which caused him to deem her mad, talked earnestly, showed her bankbook, slapped the repair bench, asked questions, went with the jeweler to lunch at the Wabicott House, and at two P.M. made him promise to give up his reasonably good chance of marrying the banker's daughter, and elope with Annabel Potts who was, he said, really engaged to this Sweetwater, but would be tickled to death to throw over a choosey preacher for a good fellow who could play auction and dance the fox-trot.

In consideration, the jeweler was to receive three thousand dollars in bills upon the day of his wedding, money to be deposited with a Minneapolis Trust Company, which would notify him of the deposit.

At three o'clock Ulrica caught the train for Minneapolis. When she got out of it, she staggered with the strain of deals in land and matrimony, and she took a taxicab for the first time in her life. The trust company, with which she was to make a deposit, was closed. She went to a hotel. From one of the telephone booths in the lobby she called up her lawyer, at Hennepin City, to learn how the Vermilion option deals were going.

"I've been telegraphing all over the State, trying to get hold of you!" wailed the lawyer. "It's fallen through! Railroad isn't going to run in a branch, maybe not for years. They decided they have enough iron on the Mesaba and the developed part of the Vermilion. Options are worthless. Got to find the money to make our notes good."

Ulrica was found, huddled in the booth. She refused to go to a hospital. They got her to bed in the hotel. All evening she lay in bed, a white figure, apparently smaller than the woman of Larch. She stared at the tiled bathroom, the florid wall-paper. Over and over she mumbled: "Now I can't get any fixings like these for him. He will be poor, still."

Next morning she deposited with the trust company three thousand dollars to be paid, under certain conditions, to a jeweler at Wabicott. That left her only three hundred dollars.

She spent two days in hunting down various officials of the M.&D.R.R at the head offices at St. Paul; made one trip to the Vermilion range, and a number of long-distance calls to her lawyer and various money-lenders; at last she saw the one exalted railway official whom she had been trying to reach. During this time she had talked quickly, demandingly, but she staggered when she stood still; and when she was relaxed, on trains, her eyes were like water-soaked ashes. At the end, standing in the street, she said aloud: "Well, I'm wiped out. Pay the notes if I sell the whole caboodle. I'll have my farm left. For him — nothing."

She arrived in Larch twelve days after she had left Wabicott. She had telephoned again, and a hotel man from New Antonia was awaiting her at her hotel. Without stopping to greet any of her acquaintances she showed to this man the hotel, the bar, her general store, and her several ledgers. He made an offer; it was accepted; he departed.

She stood in the middle of the dining-room and looked about strangely. It wasn't her dining-room any more. She had promised to give immediate possession.

She didn't even try to see Felix. What was the use? She couldn't carry out any of those plans which she had fashioned from fire and mist and love. She had even taken his Annabel away. She had harmed him, not blessed him.

She telephoned again to her lawyer, informing him that she would meet all the notes. She summoned her bartender, her hired-girls, and the chief-clerk in the store, and informed them of the change in ownership. She was going out to her claim next day.

. . .

Next morning she packed a duffle-bag with extra stockings and shoes, food for two days, matches and head-ax and a pack of cards for solitaire. The rest of her personal possessions, and groceries for two months, would be brought out by bobsled. While she was packing, she first had word of Felix, from the religious hired-girl, who informed her that the congregation had asked for Felix's resignation and had received it. Felix had not left Larch, but he was keeping to his room, said the girl, and he seemed "kind of funny, the way he looks at you." Ulrica heard the news without comment, merely with tightened lips.

She was going to tramp out to her farm. Though the day was January at its bitterest, the distance was only eight miles, and she wasn't going to waste any money on a livery team. Her time, she told herself scornfully, was worth nothing till spring, when she could go to work on the land. She slipped out through the back door. She said good-by only to the two hired-girls.

The snow was almost three feet deep on the level, but the sun was out, tumultuously brilliant on that unstained crust, and the sky was hard and smooth and unfriendly, like a plate of blue enamel. She was a showy figure as she tramped the road—a tall, quick-swinging woman, in a Canadian winter suit and fur cap, with short skirt and high laced boots, a pack on her back, a staff in her fur-gloved hands. Her cheeks were flushed. But her eyes had the steadiness of death. And when she had gone a mile her stalwart swing became a plodding. She was very tired.

She could not think; she could only lament: "I will be alone . . . I won't see Hank or Joe or Sarah, or the train coming in, or the movies at Hen City . . . I won't even hear about Felix. I won't know when he marries some baby-faced Annabel, and she bears him a man-child. . . . Always alone there, till I am wrinkled like an old Chippewa squaw!"

She was exhausted when she passed a wire fence and knew she was on her own land.

It was a cloudy, freezing, unfeeling dusk now, and this land, where she was to live forever and alone, was penetratingly desolate. It was unwelcoming; it was not home. And her shack would be cold with many weeks of unoccupation.

She started. She had come over the frozen bog through the tamaracks into sight of her shack. The window was a lighted square. Some one was in there! The whole night seemed full of sneaking, sinister figures. "Oh, don't be a nervous baby!" she snarled at herself, and clumped up to the window.

Inside, on the cot, covered to the chin with the stained red quilt, was Felix Sweetwater. He was asleep. His face was pale, clean beat.

She tiptoed through the door of the shack. She did not heed the warmth from a dying fire in the stove. She crept to the side of the cot, her face great with the genius of tenderness. She knelt there, crooning, while her snow-caked boots turned wet and streams of melting water ran along her legs and made a puddle about the hem of her skirt. She did not move till he stirred. Then she lifted her head to look at him, laughing, content. He opened his eyes, slung his arm about her neck, kissed her, full-lipped. He sprang from the cot. He saw the muddy wetness of her skirt. He cried: "Already taking care of me, and me asleep! That's enough of your caring for me. My turn! Off with that skirt. It's frightfully wet. Pop under the quilt while I fix the fire." She obeyed, content. Now it was he who came to kneel by her, he who wooed. His voice had changed from doubt and botherment to a bold confidence. "I was fired from the church," he said. "It wasn't on your account, though; I guess it was because I was such a poor preacher. I don't hardly know whether I am a preacher at all any more. Annabel's gone, too. I had a letter from her; she said I was a nice little saint, but she had married a fellow in Wabicott, a watchmaker or something." He did not sound forlorn. "Sorry?" she said.

"How could I be, if you still love me? Ulrica, why didn't you let me know you were broke? I waited and waited for you to come back from the Twin Cities, and stayed by myself, and I never learned till this morning that you had sold out and started for here. I hustled after you—I don't know how I passed you on the way here. Frightfully scared when I got here and found you hadn't arrived. Sorry I had to bust the padlock to get in."

"Why did you come?"

"Maybe I can do something for you, now that you're broke. Got almost a hundred dollars saved! And I can work for you. I'm a good farmer! Oh, Ulrica, can you love a wabbling, questing———"

"Say, have I got to stay in bed still?" she demanded. "I'm warm now. I don't think I catch pneumonia! I can't kiss you if I am all smothered up with quilts and Lord knows what-all dirty stuff those carpenters left! And if I can't kiss you this time I am going to smash something, let me tell you!"

He solved the problem and commanded: "Now you snuggle down till I get some supper for you. Packed some food out. You darling!"

She sighed. "I think it's pretty good to have someone boss me and make love to me for a change."

When she was rested and warm, when she had drawn on her skirt and made a fête of eating his rather dubious flapjacks and bacon and coffee, they sat side by side, obscured figures in the lantern light, their hands warm and quiet together. He said briskly: "Well, to-morrow I'll tramp to Kildee and get a marriage license and a preacher—a real preacher! That is, if you still like me?"

"Like you? Why, I ain't even going to let you go to Kildee alone! Some Annabel might see you and grab you and marry you, before fat old Ulrica could waddle up. But don't say you ain't a real preacher—you, the finest preacher ever came north of Aitkin County! Say! I bet you marry me to reform me! Well, I fool you. I sell my saloon, but I buy me a pipe and smoke him every day, or else you won't think I'm the hell-roaring Ulrica that needs reforming, and you go off to a mission in the city———"

"Nope. I'm not going to a mission. I'm going to stay right here, and preach with a plow, and make my pastoral calls on the stumps on this farm with a stick of dynamite under my arm. Shall I?"

"Sure!"

But, as he went to stoke the fire, she murmured to herself: "No, I won't let him monkey with no dynamite. He can plow, if he wants to, but me, I do all the stump-blowing, by jiminy crickets!"

GOPHER PRAIRIE

A WOMAN BY CANDLELIGHT

I
. . . . .

THE HEART OF WOMAN was hidden from Wilbur Cole; to him
that secret beauty was as unfamiliar as great music. He was not
hard, but he was young, and blind with first success. This January
day he had finished his first trip as traveling salesman—as grip-
man for the St. Sebastian Wholesale Grocery Company.

He was a conqueror, and St. Sebastian was a city worthy to
greet a conqueror's triumph. Snobs from the East, from Chicago
and Eau Claire, say that St. Sebastian is a scattering of dumpy
buildings; but in the silo country we consider it oppressively
grand.

It has twelve thousand inhabitants and a round-house and a
state normal school.

To Wilbur Cole, reared in a farm shanty concealed only by a
willow windbreak from the devouring prairie, and trained in a
crossroads general store, St. Sebastian was a metropolis crammed
with fascinating people—people who had six-cylinder cars and
knew about dress suits and auction bridge.

As soon as he had reported to the office he began to wait for
half past seven, when he would be able to go and call on Myrtle
Hillbridge, who wore a wrist watch and was the daughter of the
head of the Hillbridge Farm Machinery Agency. He went to his
room and tried to read the accumulation of St. Sebastian papers;
but he fidgeted and spent an hour manicuring his nails, occasionally rushing to the window on the totally unreasonable chance
that Myrtle might be passing. He pictured her, in the jumper and
linen skirt she usually wore, as a combination of out-door whole-
someness and city smartness. He saw clearly the triangle of cheek

Saturday Evening Post, July 28, 1917
Collected in *I'm a Stranger Here Myself and Other Stories* (1962)

beneath each of her eyes. He would sit near her — this same evening! — just a few hours, now! Perhaps he would dare to touch her hand. Then she would become silent, and he would move nearer to her.

Though her house was luxurious, what did he care for the cabinet of cut glass, the lace table cover, or the expensive framed color photographs from Yellowstone Park, which proved that the Hillbridges had traveled? No; he would adore Myrtle if she were a squarehead on a cleared farm.

He could not sit through supper at his boarding house; to the grief of the landlady, he couldn't get down any of the lemon meringue pie. He wanted to be out and alone, thinking of the goddess. He may have been a bulky figure for a lorn lover, in the coonskin overcoat, sealskin cap, red flannel wristlets and knee overshoes of the region; but his chin was high and his breath made passionate puffs of steam as he tramped past the Hillbridge house, which he managed to do six several times. At first he went by on the theory that he was hastening to some important engagement a great distance off, and didn't even see the house. Then he half stopped, as though he were startled by the revelation of architectural charms in the front porch, which had turned columns and diamond-shaped shingles of red and green and yellow.

He was trying to keep himself from arriving before half past seven; but at twenty minutes past he could stand this exile no longer, and he rang the bell. . . . She herself was coming down the hall! He could see her shadow against the ground glass of the door. During the seven seconds while she put an inquiring hand up to her back hair and fumbled with the knob, he was boiling with anticipation. She was going to be more beautiful than he had pictured! She was going to look at him with tremulous shyness. Maybe she would be wearing the lovely yellow dress with that lace stuff at the neck.

He was frightened. He wanted to bolt. He wouldn't dare to look at her — much less touch her magnetic hand.

Then Miss Myrtle Hillbridge had opened the door and was saying:

"Oh, hello! Oh, it's Mr. Cole! Oh, I thought you were out of town! Oh, you must have got back!"

"Yes, I got back." He beamed fatuously.

"Oh! Oh, isn't it cold! Oh, do come in, so I can shut the door. Oh, you missed it, going away; we had the peachiest party at Hildy's! Oh, I wish I'd known somebody was coming tonight; I would have dressed up. Isn't this flannelette blouse dreadful! Oh, let me take your hat. Isn't it cold! Let's sit in the sitting room; it's so much warmer there. Papa and mamma have gone over to aunty's to play cribbage. Oh, did you have a good trip? Oh, let me tell you the latest—you mustn't tell a soul; it isn't supposed to be out—Bessie is engaged to Ben! Who would ever have thought it! Don't you think Bessie is a perfect fright in that pink charmeuse? Oh, listen; I've got a trade last for you."

"Well, I—uh—can I give you a compliment of my own for the trade last? I thought about you lots while I was on the trip. Say, by the way, I had a slick trip. I tell you, it's pretty darn' important—a fellow's first trip out on the road for a house. Of course I know the retail grocery business O.K., but I didn't know how it would be selling to dealers, but it went fine, and I landed a new customer for the house———"

"That's nice; it isn't a trade last at all unless it's something you heard somebody else say, all right, Mister Smarty; I won't give you my trade last at all. Oh, I must tell you about the funny thing that happened at Hildy's party: You know how her house is, with that dinky little conservatory—it isn't really a thing in the world but a bay window, even if Hildy does call it a conservatory—you know, on the dining room—"

As Wilbur had hoped, they were sitting side by side. He told himself that she was an "awful cute kid—not many girls can jolly a fellow along like this." Also, the Hillbridge house was of an even more gorgeous fancifulness than he had remembered, in its tapestry and velours rockers with carved arms, and the storm of light from the bracket lamps and from the electrolier of crimson, pearl and orange mosaic glass. But in the midst of these observations, so comforting to one recently returned from a round of smoking cars and uncarpeted hotels, Wilbur made two startling discoveries: He wasn't afraid of trying to hold Myrtle's hand, and he didn't want to hold her hand, anyway!

While she was confiding to him — but he mustn't tell a single soul! — that she could have snitched Ben from Bessie, Wilbur smiled politely, and nodded his head at regular intervals, and didn't hear a word she said.

He was wondering how he had lost all that exquisite fear of her. He wasn't in the least awed. To prove it he seized her hand.

She blushed and squeaked, though she let him keep the hand. But he did not wish to keep it. He was decidedly embarrassed by the possession of it. He did not know what to do with it. A plump hand — not a tingling electrode, but just an ordinary smallish hand, such as almost everybody had — seemed a foolish thing to be holding. Her knuckles were puffy and her fingers were fat, he noted.

She babbled "My, but you are the fresh thing!" and he tried to live up to this new rôle as a perfect devil with the ladies by stroking her hand. A point in the setting of her small turquoise ring jabbed his finger. He carefully laid the hand down on the couch. She left it there for a moment, then took it back, drooping her head toward him and sighing in a pleased manner: "Oh, aren't you the bad one!"

He felt like different kinds of a fool and made an excuse to flee. She followed him to the door, and he combined an impression that he was highly honored with a desire to dodge.

His boarding-house room seemed as bare to him as the hotels. In it he began to remember how warm and filled with curtains and newish furniture was the Hillbridge mansion, and again he saw Myrtle as something costly and beautiful.

Two days later, as he took the northbound train during the first gray blast of a coming blizzard, he was certain that he was longing for Myrtle.

II
. . . . .

Wilbur should have reached Gopher Prairie in seven hours, with a stop at Joralemon; but for twenty-four hours the train struggled in the blizzard. Between gusts it made a mile, two miles, gasped a little, balked, and stopped. Wilbur covered himself with his coonskin coat and a strip of coco matting from the aisle in the cold car and watched the outside world turn to roaring steam. Through the night he slept raggedly, and smoked till his throat was parched, and talked to the seven passengers and the trainmen till they reached religion and politics and became personal.

The train was finally stalled three miles from Gopher Prairie. It would not move till the rotary plow dug its way through from Ferguston. The storm passed; the world was a level plain of snow, which covered the track from embankment to embankment, all achingly brilliant with sun from a blue porcelain sky. Farmers began to fight through with bobsleds. With his bags, Wilbur was bundled into the hay-covered bottom of a sled, and thus did he crawl into the town of Gopher Prairie.

The rows of two-story brick stores running off into straggling frame houses, which made up Gopher Prairie, were covered with snow like a counter of goods with a linen cover smoothly drawn across them. Lovely was the molding of the snow; it swooped in long curves from eaves to sidewalk; it was eight feet deep beside windbreak fences; it made of the squat buildings a series of Chinese pagodas. But none of this too-familiar beauty was interesting to Wilbur Cole. It meant only that he would be imprisoned here till the trains were running again. To north, south and east the service was shut off. Telephone and telegraph wires were down. There would be no mail, not one message from the world beyond the waste of snow, for two or three days. And Wilbur knew no one in Gopher Prairie. On his previous trip he had met two men in the grocery dealing with his house; but they had not warmed to him yet.

He stumbled along the paths that were being gouged through the drifts and spent an hour in the store. The clerks were affable, but they were too busy telling of their heroism in reaching the store to listen to his account of being stalled; and they did not invite him to supper. At last there was nothing to keep him from toiling to the hotel, mountain-climbing over drifts on the way.

He hoped to find a bunch of jolly fellow salesmen; but the only other guests at the hotel were a cranky old jewelry salesman who regarded himself as in some way an artist, as a superior person entitled to glance at you over his eyeglasses, together with a silent man who seemed to Wilbur to have no purpose whatever in existing except to monopolize the warmest hot-air register in the office.

A floor which has been scrubbed for so many years that the knots stand up out of the soft pine boards can be more desolately bare than a dirty floor scattered with different interesting things; and the hotel office was nothing but a waste of scrubbed floor, dotted by a desk of grained wood, a brown writing table decked with advertisements of the bus line, and a row of wooden chairs. Even less adorned was Wilbur's bedroom, its bureau listed to starboard, its one chair, and the bed with the dirty red comforter—which was so much like the other dirty red comforters in all the other hotel rooms on his route that it might have been a pursuing haunt.

He walked up and down the office, made halting efforts to get acquainted with the two morose salesmen and the sleepy night clerk, and crept out into the cold, to go to the movies. It was like ice water, that cold; he was gasping and struggling with it the moment he plunged into it. He made his way a block down to the movie theater only by darting in at stores to get another supply of warmth.

Over the theater was the sign "Closed tonight, acct. storm."

He struggled back to his room and made an occupation of getting ready to read. He did not undress—he took off his coonskin coat, and shivered, and hastily put the coat on again. He moved his chair two inches to the right, then an inch to the left, and sat with his feet on the bed. For two hours he solemnly read a two-days-old copy of the *Minneapolis News.* He turned the pages very carefully, exactly creasing the paper each time. He rattled it rather unnecessarily—the sound was cheerful in this room, surrounded by the bulky silence of the snowbound village.

Now and then he looked up and said, aloud: "Let's see: Tomorrow the train might get through—I'll get to— No, I don't suppose there'll be a train—wish I could see Myrtle and sit and jolly with her! Oh, this is a sweet life! Let's see: Larsen took two cases of apricots this time. . . ." He was comforted by his own voice. But he hadn't much to say. His brain felt dead as a bone, dead as the silence packed in about him.

He read every obituary and want ad in the paper. He considered the desirability of jobs as textile chemist, curtain hanger, Italian-Greek salesman, actuary, oxyacetylene welding expert, designer of little gents' garments, and bright boy. He learned the diverting news that "peas, Scotch, choice, 100 lbs., were 13.50 @ 13.75"; that the "Fifth Race, for three-year-olds, selling, one mile and seventy yards," would be run by an amazing company consisting of Garbage, Springtide Reverie, Oh You Kid, Tippytoes and Pink Suspenders; that " John Swan, Mary Ammond Swan, and their heirs-at-law, devisees, and next of kin, and other persons, if any there be, and their names are unknown to the plaintiff," were warmly invited to a guessing party; that "deb 5s, ctfs of dep, stpd"; that "1 do cvt 4s ser B55 55 55"; and that "J.B. Terrell as exrx &c of S. L. Barnes dec'd pltf."

In the midst of this last thriller he hurled the newspaper across the room and, as it fell in a shower of detached sheets, he cried:

"I want you so, my dear Myrtle——"

They are heroes, these salesmen and agents, who sit so quietly in trains and small hotels.

For all of another day the train service was interrupted, and Wilbur trudged through drifts, unnoticed, while about him were the shouting of men shoveling walks or driving horse plows down the street, and the laughter of children skiing. He managed to spend two hours in the grocery store, helping the clerks arrange a display of canned goods. As he returned to his hotel in the early darkness, he could see happy families in lighted homes, and the prospect of this second evening of loneliness was not boredom — it was fear.

He got to the hotel at five. He skipped when he heard the voices of Fred Oberg and two companions in the office!

Fred Oberg was one of the best-known traveling men in the state. He was a practical joker, a teller of stories, a maker of love, and an inspired player of poker. His two companions were noisy of tie and laughter. They had got through from Curlew by bobsled, and they were going to make a night of it. Would Wilbur join them in a little game, with a few bottles, in Fred's room? Wilbur thankfully would. He sat down with these older, more poised men, and laughed with them. He sounded a little hysterical.

Now it is a rule of the road that young traveling men must be broken in, and there are certain tricks that may lawfully be played upon them, to the joy and righteous approval of all beholders. . . . Fred Oberg slipped out of the hotel. He went to the drug store, next door, where there was a telephone. Fred Oberg could make his voice soft and feminine. . . .

While the other salesmen were encouraging Wilbur to tell them all about how successful his first trip had been, the telephone in the hotel office rang. It was a call for Mr. Wilbur Cole, said the night clerk, coughing and hiding his mouth with his hand.

Wilbur rushed to the telephone and heard a voice as of a large pleasant woman with a cold:

"Hel-lo-uh? Oh! Oh, is this Mr. Cole? Oh, Mr. Cole, this is

Miss Weeks, the milliner. I just heard that you were in town. I am a cousin of Mr. Gasthof, of your firm. I'm so sorry to hear of your having to stay at that horrid hotel. Won't you come over and have a homy supper tonight? I'd just love to have you! I live over my shop, one block down Main Street, toward the depot."

Wilbur did a two-step down the office to the other salesmen, who grunted: "What's the excitement, little one?"

"I'm invited out for supper!"

"The deuce you are! Gwan! Don't believe you."

"You bet I am! Oh, you fellows can stick to the roast pork and apple sauce. Watch little Wilbur wade into the fried chicken!"

"Who's the fall guy?"

"Never you mind who it is."

"Gwan—tell a fellow."

"It's Miss Weeks, the milliner. She's a cousin of a friend of mine."

"The little Weeks? Oh, you lucky dog! Why, she's the swellest skirt in town."

"Is she—honest?"

"Is she? Why, don't you know her? Why, say, she's pretty as a magazine cover—nice and round and plump, and not a day over twenty, and lively— Say, I bet you have some evening! Now ain't that luck for you! Some men are just nachly born lucky."

Wilbur's cheerfulness was in no wise lessened by the envy headlined in the faces of the two salesmen; and when Fred Oberg returned, and was informed of Wilbur's good fortune, Fred sighed that he wished he could make a hit with the ladies like that. Wilbur tried to look modest; but he cocked his hat over one eye and lit a cigar.

"Say, we got to help the boy dress up for the occasion." Fred tenderly proposed; and the three of them dragged Wilbur upstairs.

They insisted that he ought to wear a red necktie; and Fred produced from his grip a tie like a fireman's shirt. Solicitously Fred said:

"We got to brush your hair right, kid. Stand there in front of the bureau. I got a slick new patent hairbrush that shines 'em up like a St. Paul barber."

The three of them seemed to have a good deal of difficulty in getting just the right light on Wilbur's hair, and during an altercation as to whether he ought to stand on the right or left of the incandescent they almost rended him.

"Ouch! Say, quit! Quit, I say! You're almost tearing my arm off," wailed Wilbur.

The salesmen dropped his arms. In tones of deepest grief Fred Oberg protested:

"Gosh, that's what you get when you do your best to help a brother knight of the grip make a hit with a squab! All right, sir. Sorry we bothered you."

"Aw, thunder, Fred; I didn't mean to be ungrateful."

"Well, stand there then."

He stood there, while Fred brushed his hair with an instrument of torture which dug its claws into his scalp. Wilbur tried to look patient, though he winced at every stroke. One of the salesmen had a fit of coughing that sounded somehow like laughing, and Wilbur became suspicious.

"That's enough, Fred. You don't need to take my scalp off."

"Well, maybe I was digging in a little more than I had to; but I had to get even with you for swiping the swellest little chicken in town. But you're wise to all these rough-house stunts, all right, Wilbur. You're going to make a great hit on the road."

"Well, I hope I'm not entirely a darn fool," said Wilbur, much pleased.

One of them polished his shoes with a dirty handkerchief. Another offered him a drink from a pint flask of rye; but he politely refused. The three kept up their sighs of envy: A home supper with a peach! Oh, but Wilbur was the society favoryte! And would Wilbur be so good as to join them in the poker game when he got back?

They accompanied him to the street door, bidding him hurry and not keep the fair one waiting.

Wilbur found Miss Weeks' Millinery Emporium in the Colby Block, a row of two-story brick stores adorned with a galvanized iron cornice. It occupied half of a shop, the other half of which belonged to a jeweler and optician. Beside the shop was a stairway, an incredibly broad and dark stairway, smelling of yellow soap. He stumbled up it, and stopped under a small incandescent, which showed the K.P. Hall on one side and an attorney's office on the other. Miss Weeks' rooms must be at the back. Through the darkness he felt along the wall, stumbled over a door mat, and knocked at a door.

"Yes?"—in a weary voice.

"Is this Miss Weeks' residence?" said Wilbur elegantly.

"Yes."

The door opened. He saw a woman three or four years older than himself, a tired-eyed, restrained, businesslike woman in a spinsterish blue-and-white wash dress. Gentle she seemed, but not round nor jolly.

"Miss Weeks?"

"Yes."

"This is Mr. Cole."

"Yes?"

"Wilbur Cole."

"Why—who were you looking for?"

"Didn't you telephone me at the hotel?"

"I'm afraid there is some mistake."

Then was Wilbur aware that down the hall was a rustle and a masculine giggle, as of two or three men. He was filled with fury that he had been tricked; that they had even followed, to watch him make a fool of himself. But he had to relieve Miss Weeks. She was holding the door tight, beginning to close it, looking anxious.

He spoke softly, so that his tormentors should not hear:

"I know what it is now. I'm new on the road—salesman—and

some of the boys at the hotel were kidding me, and pretended it was you telephoning to invite me to supper. I don't care about myself—I can get back at them; but, honest, Miss Weeks, I'm terribly sorry it was you I had to bother. I guess maybe it must be kind of scary, living here alone; but don't be scared. I'll beat it now. It was a good joke on me—heh? You see, I been stuck in town, with the storm tying up the trains, and I was so proud of being invited to a home feed that prob'ly I boasted a little; so I guess I deserved all I got."

"You poor boy—you are only a boy—it was horrible of them!"

"Oh, I'm not a boy. I'm twenty-eight."

Her weariness smoothed out in a darting smile as she mocked:

"Oh, so old; so very old! I'm older than that myself."

"Say, sometime on some other trip, may I drop into the store and have a chat, and make up for those other fellows? But I know they didn't mean to get you in Dutch. They were just kidding— they're a wild bunch—but they don't mean any harm; and a fellow sure is ready for any kind of a jamboree to break the monotony when he's on the road."

"Yes." Her face lighted again, as though she had an inspiration. "Well, good night."

"Wouldn't you like to really stay and have supper?"

"Do you mean it?"

"Yes. . . . I think I do."

As he followed her in, she banged the door shut with a sudden nervous energy and sighed:

"There! Let's shut out the loneliness. I know how it is at your hotels. I get that way myself, living alone; and I've never dared to invite a man to supper, because people gossip so here. But we'll forget all that tonight, and I'll see what I can scratch up for supper. I was going to have scrambled eggs and tea; but we'll have to have something grander than that—for company."

While she searched the cupboard he sat on the edge of a chair and clung to his cap. No man feels entirely abandoned to a situation so long as he keeps hold of that symbol of his royalty, his headgear. Wilbur would have felt more independent had it been a derby; but still, a sealskin cap was a solid masculine thing.

He was puzzled by her and by her living room. He told himself that she was like a school-teacher. The room seemed bare. There was no carpet; only a large rag rug. The table was of reddish wood, with something like a double set of legs. It seemed to be the dining table as well as library table. There wasn't a real sideboard, with the beveled glass and brass handles, and rows of cut glass, which spelled elegance in St. Sebastian, but only another reddish-wood thing, very plain, with small glass knobs, and covered with a plain blue cloth, set with two brass jars.

The only chairs were black wooden things — not even rockers. He "liked them, sort of," he announced to himself; "they were kind of pretty, but awful plain and old-fashioned."

Most curious of all was the fact that the room was lighted only by candles.

Even on the farm they had had lamps, and every nice house in St. Sebastian had so many electric clusters that you could read fine print in the farthest corner. Yet somehow it was "restful, the way the candlelight shone on the reddish wood, even if it was tabby."

"How do you like my candles and mahogany?" Miss Weeks interrupted his inspection.

"Oh, is that mahogany, that red wood? I've heard of that."

"Yes; my grandfather brought that table from Vermont to Minnesota. It's a gate-legged table."

"Oh, is it? I've read about them."

"Do you disapprove of my candles much? All my women friends here in Gopher tell me that candles are used only in the log cabins, way up North; but then an old maid needs a dim light to look attractive in."

"Oh, they're just envious. Don't get silver candlesticks like those in any log cabin, let me tell you! I like candlelight. It's — oh, it's——"

"Yes; it really is. Do you think you could stand some shirred eggs with canned mushrooms and some nice little sausages for supper?"

"That would be corking!" he breathed. He was telling himself "I bet she's educated."

While she prepared supper he was uneasy. He did not feel that he had a right to be here, and he pictured Fred Oberg and his confederates waiting for him in the hall, possibly knocking at the door or sending a foolish message to him. He did not gain confidence till he sat opposite to her at supper.

She still seemed to him of the forbiddingly bluestockinged sort who "expected a fellow to be interested in suffrage and all that high-brow stuff." But his heart, which was so hungry for beauty without knowing that it was hungry, was pleased by her fine nose, her intelligent eyes, her quick and fragile fingers. He had a perplexed feeling that the supper table, with its four candles and thin china, was more impressive than even a Sunday dinner table of St. Sebastian. He tried to tell her his feelings:

"I've never been brought up to real pretty things much. I was raised on a farm; and then I got busy *mit* groceries at Jack Rabbit Forks; and then—oh, you know—a boarding-house at St. Sebastian and out on the road. I guess I'm pretty ignorant about this decoration stuff, and so on and so forth, never being in the furniture line or anything."

"Ignorant? Heavens, so am I!" Her eyes glowed. He had a sense of impersonal friendship such as he had never known with women.

She mused, while he was pleased by the turn of her wrist as she dropped lumps of sugar in his tea.

"Yes, I'm afraid I'm a bluffer about silver and candles. I talk so glibly about grandfather's table—it was his; but, just the same, dear old granddad died in the poorhouse, and I never was able to get his mahogany back till a few years ago. A farm? Heavens, child, I lived on a farm for eighteen years. And taught district school, and made the fires every morning, and sometimes scrubbed the floor. But I always wanted to handle pretty things; and so, when mother died and I didn't have to be a schoolma'am any more, I went to Winona and learned millinery, so I could play with pieces of velvet and ribbon and jet ornaments—and oh, things from Paris and Vienna, and all sorts of far, far-off places—long red feathers that make me think of the tropics—palms and parrots———"

"Yes, I know; I've always wanted to travel too."

They laughed at each other—friends now, these children of the new settlements.

Because they did belong to the new settlements they could not keep up the strain of rhapsodizing. It didn't seem to Wilbur quite decent to talk about beauty. As though the label on a tomato can had any use except to make it sell! They gossiped about the blizzard, the governor, and the prospect for a good crop. Wilbur was permitted to smoke after supper, and he was in a state of fullness and friendly comfort, though not in any artistic fervor. But when she brought out a genuine Rue de la Paix hat ornament, set with brilliants, and laughed at herself because she could not bear to sell it, he began to confess that he had felt emotions in the presence of wild roses.

She read aloud a poem from a magazine—a slight verse with none of the boom and red-bloodedness of the verses he had approvingly read in newspapers. It concerned an English watering place and a seller of periwinkles. There was a line which Miss Weeks repeated:

"The 'winkie woman's coming in the twilight by the sea."

Wilbur knew but little regarding periwinkles and the vending of periwinkles, and he had never thought of the sea except as a means of importing olive oil; but always he was enthralled by dusk, and wondered whether he wasn't a little "soft." Now he perceived that there might be others like himself.

He took leave in such a high mood of goodness and happiness

as he had not known since Sunday afternoons on the farm. He thanked her for taking him in, and they shook hands at the door.

He crept into the hotel, avoiding Fred Oberg and his associated jesters. He could not endure the questions and rib-pokings with which they would soil his memory of the evening. Next morning the trains were running again, and he slipped away from town, the memory in his heart like something delicate and of pearl.

III
· · · · ·

Through springtime and summer Wilbur covered his territory, not by train, but by a little runabout motor, such as traveling men were beginning to use everywhere. These were the good days of youth and first success, travel and discovery, dawns of starting and dusks of whistling arrival, great skies, and the vast and breathing land.

He issued early from frame hotels to rush to the garage and be chummy with the repair man, and wise about mixtures, and that heat pipe which was working loose. He started in the cool hour of dew and meadow larks.

He drove from the larger towns to German or Norwegian settlements, each with a large brick church, a large saloon, a small smithy, with the smith in wooden shoes, and a hum of flies about the hitching posts in the street.

His laugh became more confident; his cheeks resumed the tan of farm days; his eyes, pale amid the brick red of his flesh, were calm with visions. He followed fenceless roads that were close in amid the grain, while overhead rolled the bellying clouds. He was alone most of the day, but he was not friendless now. The grocers had come to accept him; they liked his eagerness and truthfulness.

At one end of the route, which he covered once every two weeks, he had Myrtle Hillbridge for stimulant, and he was on first-name terms with her; he strolled with her beneath the lindens and box elders, and laughed a good deal, and pretended he was going to try to kiss her.

Midway on the route he had an inspiration in a Gopher Prairie milliner named Miss Weeks.

He could not again have supper in her rooms. The little town, with its poverty of melodrama, was hungry for scandal, and she clung to her immaculate reputation. She scorned herself for her timidity, she said; but there it was. He called on her at the millinery shop and touched with his horny, blunt forefinger the bits of colored fabric she loved. They planned that some day, when he was the owner of a chain of five hundred grocery stores, they would buy a yacht and sail off to Hong-Kong and the isles of the sea, and bring back carved ivory and dusky opals, and the feathers of cockatoos.

Most of this fancy was hers; it was she who, from her yearning study of magazines, had garnered the names that studded their game: Taj Mahal and Singapore and Colombo, Kioto and the Hôtel du Chemin de Fer of Buitenzorg. His contribution was an insistence that the yacht should have stores of city food and enormous boxes of candy; and mahogany and candles, for which decorations he had come out strongly.

On a moonlit evening in August he begged Miss Weeks to walk out beyond the town to see the moon on the prairie.

He was excited; he was proud of her, as a treasure he had found. But he talked casually, trying to be very cultured. They passed a house on a hill. He knew it was a noble edifice, because it was like the Hillbridge mansion in St. Sebastian.

"That's an elegant place—don't you think so?" he said in selected accents of politeness and intellectuality.

"No; I'm afraid I think it's pretty ugly. It's— Oh, I wish I knew something about architecture! I don't know why I don't like it, except that it looks to me like a fat woman with lots of paste diamonds, and too dressy, and a stenciled garden hat on top of that. It's so lumpy, and it's got scrollamajigs all over the porch; and that round tower is just silly—don't you think?"

"Yes. I guess—yes; that's so," he sighed.

He told himself that, after all, this monstrosity was not like the chaste Hillbridge mansion. But he knew it was.

"Our towns aren't beautiful—not yet. Maybe they will be when they stop trying to be showy."

"Yes. I guess—yes; that's so. . . . Though, golly, the towns looked pretty good to me when I came off the farm. Oh, I'm an ignorant brat! I don't know how you can stand me."

"My dear, you're not! You're good and sweet and honest. It's myself who am ignorant. Look at me—old enough to be your grandmother; the perfect catty old maid, daring to criticize these towns that the pioneers built out of sweat and blood. And what am I? Just a small-town milliner, with half a shop—tinkering and making a few silly hats."

"You're not! You're not! You're—oh, so cultured and everything— And you're young; you aren't hardly a bit older than me by the family Bible; and your—oh—your imagination is so young; and— Oh, I don't know how to say it, but you know what I mean."

He put his arm about her shoulder, on a corner shadowed by a bank of lilac bushes. There was a hush, rhythmic with a distant chorus of frogs. The angel of quiet affection bent lulling wings about them. She patted his arm as they walked on.

The town broke off abruptly. One moment they were hedged in by one-story cottages; the next, with the town forgotten, they faced the splendor of the open prairie, brown and honest and elemental by day, but charmed now to an uplifted radiance. It was not a flat, dull plain, but dipping and winsome. Nothing save the stormy ocean could be so broad, so far-stretching to that pale shimmer of horizon.

They were on a slight rise, and they looked across ten miles of meadow and corn patch and fifty-acre wheat fields. The moon was still low and touched the veils of mist that rose from hollows. Beyond these apparitions the eye lifted till the spirit was swimming and dizzy with the sweep of the shining land. The groves of willows, the alder bushes marking a curving creek, and the eye of a slew were sparkling points on the plate of silver. The yellow light of a distant farmhouse stirred the poignant thought of home.

Unspeaking, with one strong emotion linking them, unconsciously hand in hand and their arms swinging together, they moved forward into that world of light. Their eyes were solemn. They passed from the road into a meadow. The long grasses whispered to their slow tread.

He ignored the heavy dew, which soaked his shoes, till he realized that he was not caring for her, and urged:

"Sakes alive! You'll catch your death o' cold. Let's sit on this gate."

He had spoken so softly that the charm was not shattered; and, swathed in glory, they perched on the three-barred wooden gate of a barbed-wire fence, which had been enchanged into a spider web. She sat on a lower bar and leaned her head against his knee. The faint pressure made him tender, conscious that she belonged to that wistful beauty.

He instinctively stroked her cheek. Slowly the full ecstasy of the holy hour welled in him till he could no longer be mute. He identified her with it, and demanded her.

"I've never felt—oh, so happy before! I don't want to ever lose you, dear. Can't we be married? I ain't—I am not worthy——"

She straightened up; stood by the fence.

"Boy, you don't love me! It's just moonlight and walking with a woman. You don't know what you want yet. I've always had such big visions of love that— No, no, no! You wouldn't propose to me if it were a hot afternoon, a muggy, wilty afternoon, and we were walking down Main Street."

"But you do like me; and when we're both lonely——"

"Probably no one will ever love me as I want. Oh, why should they? What am I but a little hat trimmer, with a love for tea and cats!"

"You aren't; you are the one person I could love—if you could only understand how much I mean it!" And as he said it he knew he didn't quite mean it; he knew he was merely living up to the magic moment, and he listened to his own high-pitched voice going on in poetic periods unnatural to him: "Your soul shines like the prairie there; and when I look into your eyes I see all the fairy stories my mother used to read to me——"

"But, my dear boy, you don't want a lady reciter. You want a nice home and somebody to send out the laundry for you. That's all right! I understand. I often want a home myself. But I'm a funny old silly. Frightfully sentimental. So I distrust sentimentality. Wait. Think it over tomorrow. Oh——"

Suddenly she was crying, in sobs accumulated through years of loneliness. She crouched on the lower bar of the gate and hid her eyes against his knee. Her hat fell off and her hair was a little disordered. Yet this touch of prosaicalness did not shock him. It brought her near to him; made her not a moon wraith, but a person like himself. He patted her shoulder till she sat up and laughed a little; and they strolled toward the town.

The overwrought self that had sung of love was gone. But he felt toward her a sincere and eager affection.

Twenty-four hours later, back in St. Sebastian, he was calling on Myrtle Hillbridge. They put a humorous monologue record on the phonograph and laughed loudly over it and ate fudge; and he was perfectly sincere about that too.

IV
. . . . .

He was to spend two weeks in St. Sebastian, helping take stock. It was his longest stay there since he had met Miss Myrtle Hillbridge at a church social. On his first call he criticized the Hillbridge house to himself for having a foolish little tower and a battlement. He was uneasy in the glare of electric light falling upon bright green velours upholstery in Myrtle's parlor, and he decided that Myrtle's smooth cheeks were stupid in that hot shine. He thought of the gentle vividness of Miss Weeks' ever-changing face. But he reasoned with himself:

"Thunder, they can't everybody have the same kind of a house! . . . Rats, they can't everybody be the same kind of a person! . . . Miss Weeks is the finest woman I know; but Myrtle is a mighty jolly girl. . . . Gosh, that's a funny record! I wonder if Myrtle has any of this jazz music."

He was invited to an Advertisement Party at Myrtle's, and by reason of much reading of magazines upon trains he won the guessing contest. He danced the fox trot with damages to the slippers of not more than one or two girls, and told a good story about the Chippewas at Cass Lake.

When the young married couples were departing, and the girls were being persuaded to let various young men take them home, Myrtle whispered:

"Don't go yet, Wilbur. Wouldn't you like to stay and help me eat up the rest of the cake and lemonade?"

She looked confidential; and he felt confidential and superior to the rest of the party as he whispered:

"Yes."

They sat in chairs drawn up to the polished expanse of the dining table and nibbled crumbs of coconut filling, and laughed at the rest of the guests. The least he could do was to hold her hand. This duty he performed to the perfect satisfaction of all immediately concerned. She hung her head; and, while she shyly traced the design on his cuff button with her finger, she murmured:

"Why am I so bad? Why do I let you hold my hand?"

He didn't know the answer, and he felt guilty that she was so moved by his caress. How could he, as a regular man, stop now when she was so innocently happy? He seized her hand more boldly; and, because the tension of the moment demanded that he should say something complimentary at once, he sighed:

"Pretty little hand!"

She glanced at him sharply and snatched away her hand.

"I don't believe you care a bit about holding my hand; and I'm not going to let you, either! You're nothing but just a lady-killer, going round playing make love."

"I am not, either!" he insisted, and tried to capture the hand again.

She would not let him, and informed him that she should never have yielded to his petition to be allowed to stay and finish up the cake if she had not supposed he would behave himself. He was crushed by her coldness and convinced that to hold the hand of Miss Myrtle Hillbridge was a very close approximation to heaven.

She sent him home; but relented at the door and let him kiss her good night, which he did with rapturous thrills, and went out exultant. When he got home, and began to smoke a cigar of triumph, he wondered whether Myrtle was entirely unwilling to be kissed. He informed himself that she was maneuvering, but that he was an ungrateful dog to think anything of the sort; that Myrtle would like to drag a promising young man to the altar, but also that she was just a kindly girl whom said ungrateful dog had sore offended; that she was more human than Miss Weeks, but that Miss Weeks' little finger was worth more than Myrtle's whole body. He repeated this highly consistent analysis over and over, and went to bed in a whirl of perplexity, out of which emerged only one fact — that he liked to kiss Miss Myrtle Hillbridge.

It was past one, three hours after the canonical bedtime in St. Sebastian, when he went to bed. He was sleepy next day, and all his opinions regarding women could have been summed up in "Drat them; they disturb a man's work!" But Myrtle called him up and invited him to drop in after supper. After having kissed the poor, trusting girl — why had he ever been such a scoundrel! — he couldn't be cold to her; and he thanked her ardently, though his warmest desire was to get to bed directly after supper.

He hoped that she wouldn't be too affectionate or talkative that evening. She wasn't. They sat on the front steps, upon flattened doughnuts of willow, leaning against the porch pillars; and they talked drowsily of Ben and Bessie, and of how admittedly superior Myrtle was to Bessie. He found himself kissing her good night at the gate, and he went home feeling bound to her.

Never, he meditated, could he tell her that he hadn't really meant those kisses. Why, it would break her heart! He had to go on now. . . .

How come he had kissed her again? He certainly hadn't meant to. He didn't understand. Well, anyway, it wouldn't be so bad to marry Myrtle. She was a splendid girl and a normal-school graduate. . . . But he plaintively wished he had met Miss Weeks earlier. He wondered, with excitement, why he couldn't correspond with Miss Weeks. Never thought of that before! . . . No; too late! . . . Besides all that—oh, that moonlight stuff was too highbrow for a jay like himself! Oh, well———

V
. . . . .

He was invited to supper at the Hillbridges. It was a party meal, with olives and candied orange peel. Mr. Hillbridge treated Wilbur as one accepted by the established set in St. Sebastian. He asked him questions about the grocery business outlook, and boomed: "Have some more of the lamb, Wilbur, my boy. And don't you two young people go holding hands under the table there!" Mrs. Hillbridge smiled, and said "Now, Chan!" to her husband; and, to Wilbur, "Don't mind him, Mr. Cole; he's a terrible joker."

Myrtle was moody, but she gave Wilbur secret smiles. And Mr. Hillbridge gave him a two-for-a-quarter cigar.

The Hillbridges were temporarily without a maid—most families in St. Sebastian are permanently temporarily without a maid. After supper Myrtle commanded her parents: "You two go off to the movies, and Wilbur and I will wash the dishes—won't we, Wilbur?"

Yes—Wilbur would, indeed; there was no sport he admired so much as the washing of party supper dishes. Mrs. Hillbridge protested for a suitable period, then winked at her husband and jerked her head backward at him; and they departed, leaving Wilbur in a comfortable fancy that this was his house and Myrtle his jolly little wife.

They laughed as they washed the dishes. He dropped some cold water down her neck, and she chased him about the kitchen, snapping the dish towel at him till he begged for mercy. They did not talk of solemn beauty or the misty plains; neither of silver nor of candlelight; but lustily sang together a pleasing melody:

> *Oh, myyyyyy E-GYP-shun queen,*
> *You're the best I ever-rever-rever seen;*
> *And your winks put the jinx on the sphinx,*
> *so I thinks,*
> *My dreamun Ejup que-en!*

"Isn't that a dandy song?" glowed Myrtle. "Oh, I'd die if I could just write one song like that! They say this man made a hundred thousand out of "Poor Butterfly"; but I don't know— maybe it would be more fun to write movie scenarios. Oh, just think of being a scenario writer and going out to Los Angeles and meeting Douglas Fairbanks! Isn't he a peach! I wonder if he is married. I was reading—why, just yesterday—it was an advertisement in the paper, where you can learn to write scenarios in six lessons; and you get from a hundred to a thousand dollars apiece for them. Think of that! Maybe I wouldn't buy an automobile that would put it all over Doctor Julian's! But still, think of writing a song like that—My dreammun Ejup que-en!"

"Yes; that's so," Wilbur agreed.

It had been a good supper. He certainly did like corn fritters.

He contrasted this big kitchen, its enamel refrigerator, its cabinet, its new range, with the closet which Miss Weeks called a kitchen and in which she cooked one thing at a time on a kerosene burner.

It was good to be on kitchen terms of intimacy after months in the bedrooms and offices of hotels. It was good to have Myrtle acknowledge that he was on such terms and to say, when they had gone out to the front porch: "Oh, do run in and get me a glass of ice water, Wilbur. You know where the ice box is."

He swaggered through the hall, the dining room, the kitchen, as though all this were his. He was no longer a farm boy on sufferance in the great mansion of the great city.

He cheerfully let the tap run cold, chopped ice, filled the glass, made the ice tinkle, switched off the kitchen light, started toward the hall—and stopped.

Someone, a block away, was playing a violin. The kitchen window was open; and as he looked from the darkened room he was conscious of a honeysuckle bush rustling in the yard, of slumberous trees and the quiet night, while the music wound a thread of faint, fine emotion about him. And instantly he was identifying that mood with Miss Weeks; and he knew that he was doing it, and wanted to run away from the admirable young woman awaiting him on the front porch.

"It isn't Myrtle's fault—she's a lot better than I am. I'm a hound; but, Lord, I don't want to settle down yet! I don't want to look fat after supper, like Pa Hillbridge. I guess probably she is eight, maybe ten, years older than Myrtle; but still, she's so much younger; and she always will be. I want to play yet, like a kid—like her."

"Her" meant Miss Weeks to him. "Her" would always mean Miss Weeks to him, he knew.

Myrtle was waiting. He trailed out to the porch. She was cuddled on the porch swing. She patted a cushion and said amiably:

"Sit here and be comfy."

Then, because he was afraid he would kiss her, he did kiss her, and felt himself to be a traitor and a fiend and a scared rabbit, all at once. Again he wanted to run. Also, he wished to kiss her. Suddenly he was standing beside the porch swing and listening to his own stammering:

"Oh, I mustn't kiss you—I mustn't—you're so good and bully; and—I guess I better go."

"I didn't—I didn't mind. I like you!" she whispered.

If she would only be angry—only tell him to go! He couldn't be churlish to her. But never again would he be so weak as to kiss her! She was a stranger to him; and always would be, though they were married with bell, book and candle. But he could say nothing. He was afraid of the serene power of commonplaceness in her. He could only stand in a cold numbness, wondering why he couldn't find anything to say.

"Wilbur, what is the matter?"

He did not answer; could not answer.

"Wilbur!"

Nothing.

She sat on the edge of the swing and stared at him. She drew an angry breath. He turned his head away. Then:

"Well, Mr. Wilbur Cole, if you think I am so crazy about you that I am going to stand for your being silent and queer and cranky, as if you had done me a favor by—by kissing me—and now you guess maybe you want to run along home, then I guess you have another guess coming, Mr. Wilbur Cole. You can go; and you can't go one bit too soon for me!" Her voice was round and resolute, young and hard.

He moved toward the gate.

"Wilbur!" It was a sound of relenting.

He turned back, and heard a queer vulgar little old man in him piping: "Darn it! I thought she was going to let me go now."

"Wilbur, don't you think you ought to apologize before you go? What is it, dear? Come, tell me the matter."

Terrified, he cried:

"I can't—not tonight. Oh, I'm so sorry, honey! You're sweet; and—I'll call you up tomorrow."

He bolted; and not for a mile did he slacken his half run.

He sat on a pile of ties overlooking a cindery railroad yard for three hours or more; and he was no longer young. He was suffering, and he was not enjoying the spectacle of himself. Youth makes a dramatic picture of itself as heroic in suffering. Past youth blames itself and wants either to heal or to cause the suffering of others.

The moon came up in its last quarter—riding like a wrecked galleon in a lost sea of grasses. It seemed to bind him to Miss Weeks, up there, sixty miles away. The night breeze was ever cooler and more fresh. He muttered:

"Gee! I'm free! It isn't too late now, no more. Myrtle, poor kid! Hope she gets a new beau in couple of weeks. . . . Bet she does, too. . . . Why don't I go? I'll do just that."

He walked sedately to the garage. He awoke an irate night attendant. He cheerfully filled the tank of his little car, and even took care to fill a grease cup. At three o'clock he started due north, toward Gopher Prairie.

He no longer blamed himself or justified himself. He merely growled:

"Bet there's lots of fellows get married when they don't specially want to—just drift along, and see they're expected to buy a ring; lots more than will ever admit it. Tell you, me, if I ever get married it's going to be—oh, like one of these here pilgrimages. Kind of religious. I've crawled up from a farmhouse attic to this little ole car, and I ain't going to stop with just being a solid citizen. No, sir! Read books. Not just selling talk, but music. Mahogany. Tropics. . . . Candlelight . . . All that stuff. . . . Motor sure does run a lot better at night!"

The road was free of traffic and there was exhilaration in slashing through villages barren with sleep; in chasing an imbecile of a jack rabbit that hadn't sense enough to get out of the road, but kept ahead for half a mile, humping itself ludicrously in the circle of gliding light.

The darkness trembled; the fields awoke in choruses of insects; the tremendous prairie sunrise boomed across the land; the early goldenrod was cheerful beside a red barn; a meadow lark fluttered up to a fence wire and caroled—and Wilbur came riding into Gopher Prairie.

He ran up the stairs in the Colby Block, past the K.P. Hall; pounded at her door. Miss Weeks opened it—yet somehow it was not Miss Weeks.

Love had performed its old miracle of alchemy—this ordinary human face had been changed; somehow; to him it had become beautiful and imperishably young. She exclaimed:

"Why, what are you doing here? I thought you had to stay in St. Sebastian for two weeks."

"Huh? Just a moment—gee, out of breath! Do you know how pretty you are? Especially when you smile? Just ran up here to tell you I want to try that stunt of walking up Main Street on a hot afternoon; and twice in every block I want to tell you about you and me and all kinds of things— Dear, will you listen? Will you?"

She searched his eyes; then stretched out her hands. There was a skylight in the hall. Morning sunshine fell upon the lovers.

A ROSE FOR LITTLE EVA

THE ORCHESTRA, which consisted of Miss Gussie Jorgenson, the popular and talented daughter of the station-agent, interpreted "Old Black Joe" at the piano. The strains which she had been discoursing died in caramel sweetness upon the air. In that exciting pause before the play began, the elite of Gopher Prairie—even Pup Mason, the leader in hardware and social circles—leaned pantingly forward. The curtain rose majestically, with certain hitches, one complete drop, and an audible reference to eternal punishment made by Nels Peterson, the janitor, manager, and stage-hand of the G.A.R. Hall.

Most realistic was the old-time plantation scene which entranced the eye. A large, handsome, and recklessly expensive Kentucky mansion, fully twenty feet long, together with its slave quarters, was portrayed on the back-drop, in front of which were grouped a Southern gentleman with a secret sorrow, a slave-trader with a chew, and a horde of four darkies, who burst out in that chief occupation of colored persons, namely, caroling about the joys of cotton-picking.

The soloist was a pretty quadroon boy with glossy ringlets, who insisted upon the ethnological value of spooning, in June, with a coon, pretty soon, oh, Mister Moon. With a debonair bow which hinted that he was not a colored lad at all, but a lady actress of great charm and ability, the quadroon flung into a clog in which, he, she, or it was joined by the entire staff of negroes, to such a degree of mirth and noisiness that the repining heart longed for those days when all plantations must have been exactly like cabarets without the cover-charge.

To the magic fancy of the Muse are all delicate miracles possible, and without breaking the illusion of bygone years, the soloist

McClure's Magazine, February 1918

was able to add a dramatic novelty to her more accurate ante-bellum ballads. Her lyric was set to the tune of that National Anthem of all New York restaurants, "Dixie":

"Yessah, darkies, we all has happy times on Mas'r Shelby's place here in old Kaintuck, so I'll sing you one more song for my old Kentucky home:

> *The United States has 'most gone dry,*
> *At banquets they drink toasts in pie,*
> *In chewing gum, in beef stew, and maple walnut sundae.*
> *The Kaiser has an awful pain*
> *When he sees Uncle Sam in an aeroplane,*
> *In destroyers, in dreadnoughts, and other dreadful weapons.*

"Where's good old Uncle Tom, my lads? Ah, there comes the brave fellow, whom Mas'r Shelby trusts e'en as he would a brother, and ne'er would sell. Shake a foot, me lads. Greet Uncle Tom with an old-time hoe-down."

It may have been the spectacular entrance of Thomas, or it may have been a realization by the audience that the author of this timely interpolation was none other than the soloist herself, which prompted the applause that now shook the rafters, or at least the lathes of the G.A.R. Hall. The demonstration was as much enjoyed by the audience as by the bowing talent, since it gave the three rows of young men at the back a chance to pound their feet, and to kick one another's caps along the line.

But every sunny cloud has a German silver lining, and just when the general good-will and festivity was at its highest, the slave-trader seized his whip, drove the unfortunate darkies from the stage, and in coarse tones began to bargain with Mr. Shelby for the immediate delivery on contract of the following goods, to wit: Harry, quadroon, son of Eliza, and Uncle Tom, laborer.

Concealed from everyone save the audience and the orchestra, Eliza listened to the bargaining. Horror stole o'er her face. She clasped Harry, the former soloist, to her bosom, and prepared to flee. The curtain did the same thing, with equal success.

When the curtain crawled up again, the stage-hand had removed the entire plantation, and brought out of the crates a grim and dismal swamp, consisting not only of a back-drop, somewhat holey and faded, but also a rubber-plant in a pot, and a whole practicable tree.

It was to be the most thrilling scene in *Uncle Tom's Cabin*, as presented by the Cushman Bland International Theatrical & Uncle Tom's Cabin Company, with a Stupendous Aggregation of Talent and Actors, Carrying a Trainload of Scenery, the Sunny South Darky Chorus in Plantation Melodies and Hoe-Downs, with New Modern Feature, Hawaiian Music and Dancing by Famous Native Artists Imported from New York and Honolulu for this Company, and World-defying Pack of Huge, Man-eating Bloodhounds. Specialties between Each Act. Price Only 25 and 35 cents. Children below Five Free. SEE the Darktown Prize Cakewalk Contest, the Death of Little Eva, the Horrible Persecution of Uncle Tom, the Hair-raising Pursuit of Eliza. Remember Not a Moving Picture but a Real Show, Free Concert Every Noon location annc'd on hand bills, SEE Cushman Bland as Uncle Tom, Dulcie Damores as Little Eva, Mimosa Booth in Side-splitting Pranks and Fun of Topsy, H. Rutherford Savoy as Simon Legree, Three Nights Only in Your City, Tonight, Tonight, Tonight.

The most memorable three events of our history are the battle of Gettysburg, the first home-run of Mr. Baker, and Eliza's crossing of the ice, which was the beginning of the prohibition movement. It is true that the Cushman Bland Company, the last *Uncle Tom's Cabin* agency remaining in the territory, had by competition with the movies been compelled to make up a highly revised version of the play, to pepper it with vaudeville acts, and to use Jazz music instead of the two Lawyer Markses who used to attract the drama-lovers of the good old days of twenty years ago. But it was not legal nor ethical to have any *Uncle Tom's Cabin* performance whatsoever, unless Eliza should be pursued by bloodhounds. Cushman Bland, that survivor of those days of Booth and high art that never existed, had improvised upon the Eliza motif till the scene had, without losing any of the fine strong flavor of the soil, become as modern as an electric milker.

Mr. Bland was often heard to say, however, that he had no patience with the old-fashioned companies who had Eliza cross the ice. Wooden blocks of ice were not convincing art. . . . Besides, the price of Eliza Ice Blocks in the mail-order catalogue had gone up.

We now understand the philosophy behind the powerful scene that was about to be fearlessly enacted.

The stage was slightly darkened. The audience shuddered, or was supposed to shudder, at the swamp. Silence and gloom. Not one actor was in sight, not even a maid dusting a gilt chair and soliloquizing, "Well, Master will catch it if he comes home drunk again. He is a rich insurance agent, and he has a son who is a great practical joker, but this time he has gone too far! Ah, the doorbell! There he is now!"

No, the stage was deserted. Then, off-stage, a wail. The audience bent forward, with breaths not only baited but hooked and reeled in. Out staggered Eliza and Harry. Eliza was not carrying Harry because the bonny boy was about twelve pounds heavier than his mother, and two inches larger around the ankle; but they both stumbled, while Eliza sobbed:

"I can guh nuh futhuh, muh poh boee, muh own Harry darlun, but ere I let thu crool slave-traduh catch youh, I will dash yuh and muh poh self to death. You remember that I have now walked all night, with you slumberun in muh arms, them dee lil hands clasped tight about muh neck, panic-stricken but nevuh ceasun in muh flight, but now I can guh nuh futhuh, though we are nearly to thu Ohio Rivuh whenee we can cross into Ohio, where the kind Quakuhs will take care of us. But we must sleep for a momunt. Lay yuh head on mothuh's breast, and do not repine."

While Harry did not see his, or her, way clear to comply with this request, the fugitives reclined side by side. Suddenly Eliza lifted her head in horror. . . . From afar came the baying of bloodhounds.

It was not so afar but that the audience could hear it perfectly. Indeed, it is probable that had you been in on the secrets of dramaturgy, you would have known that Alfred, who composed the Cushman Bland Company's pack of huge, man-eating hounds, was baying to the lure of a pork chop held in front of his quivering nose just three feet from the stage.

Although Eliza did not realize that Alfred was so near, that famous maternal instinct warned her that all was not well for Harry. She pulled Harry's hundred and thirty-seven pounds, and together they fled forth into the night. They may have missed their way, or the stage may have been moved on a little; anyhow, twice more they were beheld dashing across the scene. The second time the entire pack of hounds was hurtling in pursuit, with his ears fluttering, his brow wrinkled, his mouth dripping, his dewlap swinging, his deep roar making the footlights tremble. The third time Eliza was just a neck ahead of the pack, but for her heroic nature, there was time. She climbed the practicable tree!

Alfred the bloodhound obliging gave her time to kick the bottom peg in more firmly, to climb up peg by peg, to perch in the branches, to give a hand to her son and, when they were settled, to whisper *sotto voce* to Harry, "Ouch, ma, look out! You're sittin' on me hand!" But once the victims were out of his reach the pack circled about the tree, uttering again and again that melancholy yammering that is known to be so blood-chilling to fugitive slaves when they are hidden in dark and snake-filled swamps and clinging to property trees that were none too secure when they were new, and have now been used steadily for seven years.

The sunset spread its lavish colors upon the scene—at least they were pretty lavish when you consider that they were produced by a broken kerosene spotlight. The darkness grew thick. The pack of hounds modestly withdrew, as it became bedtime for the ladies. The fugitives slumbered in the tree, discussing behind their hands that night's supper at the Star Hotel. Black seemed their plight. But rescue was at hand! Across the swamp toiled a band of two Quakers, carrying lanterns and saying "thee." Fair virtue in distress had foiled the diabolical schemes of the slave-trader and Alfred the hound.

The curtain fell as though reluctant to hide this triumph of innocence, or else as though Nels Peterson, the theatre staff, had slipped out for just one more beer too many times. Skinny Swankhof, who had sat in the front row and talked with Miss Gussie Jorgenson, the orchestra, during all of the first act, muttered:

"Gosh, it's a punk show, Gussie! I drather see a movie any time. But say, that bloodhound is some dog! Fierce-looking brute. I was almost scared when he howled like that. He's the best actor in the bunch. Say, Gussie, are you going to the I.O.O.F. dance tomorrow night?"

Behind the scenes Nels Peterson was bringing out the set which had been the kitchen in *Is Your Girlie Safe?* the week before. With the addition of four dining-room chairs and an imitation hand-painted picture, all hired from the Boston Furniture & Undertaking Bazaar for ten passes, the set made a delightful New Orleans mansion in which Uncle Tom would soon be giving good advice to St. Clare, recently the slave-trader, and to Little Eva, recently Harry, while Topsy, recently the unfortunate Eliza, diverted them all with her merry tricks and her discussions of the economics of expropriation.

Alfred, the bloodhound, ate his pork chop and rested till he should again be needed, to assist in the villainies of Simon Legree. His square forehead was thoughtful with the dignity of the true artist, and even in the slow tongue with which he had licked his porky lips, there was a hint of the tradition of Henry Irving.

The chief members of the Cushman Bland Company gathered in Little Eva's hotel room after the show. In that white-browed professional with the languid hands you would scarce have recognized him who had uplifted the audience with his double visualizations of Uncle Tom and Phineas the Quaker. Nor would you in the plump white-corduroy-suited lady with the large hat and the white near-kid shoes have discerned her who was called Dulcie Damores by the wide world, but among her intimates was known to be Mrs. Cushman Bland, the gifted interpreteuse of the rôles of Little Eva, Harry, and Cassy. Hardly a day older did she seem than her daughter, Mlle. Mimosa Booth, otherwise known as Liz Bland, who has been our Eliza and our Topsy; and even younger did Dulcie appear than her son Hank, alias H. Rutherford Savoy, who has been so well suited to the parts of the slave-trader of St. Clare, and of Simon Legree—a fellow of infinite wit and whip-snapping.

With the Blands was the most instinctive artist of them all—Alfred the bloodhound. His interpretation of the character of the venomous canine cataclysm of the swamps was sheer creation. Upon the stage his red eyes glared, his horribly hanging mouth slavered, his bay rolled out in the ecstasy of genius. Yet in private life Alfred was a gentleman and a scholar, with affable manners and the morals of a Sunday school. Despite the terribleness of his sagging countenance, he really was humble when he begged for a pork chop: he sat mildly upon his hind legs, and with paws drooping, waited till he was given the word before snapping. He always slept at the foot of Eliza's bed, and if he was forbidden, he would stand in a corner and mew pitifully. His one vice was his guilty love of chops.

But Alfred was too sensitive. He was as cowardly as he was kindly. He was afraid of sparrows, street cars, landlords, and ants. Now he had retreated into an imaginary cave beneath the bed, and in his sleep he whimpered as he dreamed of playing with butterflies and kittens.

The four minor actors who played the Quakers, abolitionists, plantation singers, Hawaiian dancers, overseers, and swampnoises—low souls with no devotion to art or to anything else save making money—had gone to bed, but the Blands sat up for after-theatre supper in the room of Cushman and Little Eva. Cushman Bland called it their "itinerant green-room," and submitted that nowhere else, in this crass age, was there to be found the stately manners and noble converse of a past generation. They were engaged in that noble converse right now. Removing the top of a milk-bottle with a hairpin, Little Eva, otherwise Mother Bland, piped:

"Say, Cushie, we didn't do such bad business tonight. I'm glad we got three days here. With that construction gang that's going to be in town tomorrow night, we ought to pull another swell crowd."

The great Cushman sighed:

"Ah, but to strut for dullards, to play the antic mime before these ambulatory fellows of the lesser sort———"

"And if we don't get a full house, we're going to quit: get me, Cushie?"

"You're dead right, ma," Eliza commented, pouring the cocoa out of a cold-cream jar. "I ain't no rube, but if business goes the way it has been, it's us for the farm, all right. Hank will do a grand little dance behind the plow. Ouch, quit, you quit, Hank! Don't you dast to put no cocoa down my neck, hear me?" Eliza got the slave-trader in a hammer-lock and held him till he squealed, and Alfred, beneath the bed, booed in sympathy.

Ignoring them Cushman Bland despaired, "Pity 'tis 'tis true. The Uncle Tom game is going on the fritz. The low morale of the motion pictures has put to naught the passion and splendor of the spoken word, and the art even of the greatest Uncle Tom in the profession. But I never will be easy about that blamed farm. We never will get the mortgage paid up, without touching our poor little ready cash. You know I never will get to like your scheme of buying it, Dulcie. Think of the hand that once clasped that of the elder Southern picking potato bugs."

"Well, cheer up, old man, the farm won't be so bad. And I'll see the mortgage gets cleared off, all rightee," said Little Eva briskly.

Her liveliness dissipated the fear of going to work which had hung over the entire Bland family since the day when it had become evident that the Uncle Tom furor was past, and she had made them invest in a farm to which to retire. That same busy cheerfulness always charmed audiences. She was almost as much an attraction as Alfred the bloodhound, the following noon, when she appeared in the free street concert, in her hussar uniform, with the banner inscribed, "Dulcie Damores, Champion Lady Cornetist of the Middle West."

Movies, flat, gray, silent movies, with your blackly shiny "stills" before the Eureka or the Bijou or the Novelty, where are your street concerts? where your blares that announce the arrival of an aggregation of priests of the high dramatic arts? where your stars who can double in brass? Children of the movie age, soon will you know no more, even under canvas, that troupe of soldierly musicians, ladies and gents, who stood reverently in the shade of the temple of the Muses while the champion cornet of Dulcie Damores made "The Bonny Banks of Loch Lomond" and "Nelly Was a Lady" as pleasantly lugubrious as a funeral. Round them gathered farmers in lumber wagons, shirt-sleeved clerks, and every child who dared approach the vicinity of the dreadful, slave-hunting, death-fanged demon of devastation, Alfred the Bloodhound.

A large gang of laborers who were being shipped north on railroad construction work were in town overnight. They gathered with the music-inspired street crowd, and to them especially did Cushman Bland address his daily, "Ladies and gemun, it is my priviluge to 'nounce that tonight, in your palatial Grand Army Hall, will again be presented that epochal enactment of the celebrated en-tuh-tainment, *Uncle Tom's Cabin*, which so delighted your beautiful community lahst evenun."

Apparently the gang of laborers were moved by this chance to pluck the tail-feathers of Art as she flitted past. They occupied most of the first rows of the theatre that evening. The rest of the house was well filled. Cushman Bland stood discoursing musically upon the size and intelligence of the gathering, with his round and rolling eye fixed to the hole in the curtain, till Little Eva came and propelled him to their dressing-room.

The rows of hulking roustabouts were noisy and tough. They shouted to one another, and pounded the backs of seats with the heels of their laced boots. But they were simple and trusting souls, and when the first scene was magically recreated, and Harry sang about the Southland, the Northland, the Middlewestland, and the Northwesteastofspokaneland, they applauded heavily, and scarcely misbehaved at all, except possibly for throwing a couple of boiled onions on the stage, tripping up the usher, and singing not very nice words to the choruses. It is true that the street-corner boys of the town were encouraged to a certain noisiness and a peculiarly irritating whistling through the teeth by the example of these older strangers, but Harry said cheerily to Eliza, "They won't raise much roughhouse; and wait till I pull the Death of Little Eva. That always gets 'em. They'll can the rough stuff. Watch your ma make 'em weep, Liz. But what's the matter with Alfred? He looks nervous."

Alfred *was* nervous.

Not only was the dog of death agitated by the stamping in the front of the house, but also, with that affable nature that ever strove to please, he was trying to be friendly with a kitten. Alfred loved kittens. Their playful ways and fluffy gentleness were akin to his own delicacy. But this kitten was not gentle, no, nor play-ful. It was a bad, suspicious cynical, picaresque alley kit, which had strayed in through the stage door. Its experience with previous dogs had been unfortunate. It demanded free and equal suf-frage for cats, and the conscription of dogs. It was ready at any time to take the stump for these doctrines, and indeed when Al-fred companionably sidled up to it, the kit did take the stump upon Little Eva's wardrobe trunk, and publicly denounced Alfred as a "Mrrowr." It offensively arched its back and swelled its tail, while Alfred looked up at it and panted. He gamboled before it;

he pretended to pat a little mud pie with his huge paws; but the kitten merely sneered down at his invitation to come and play, and observed, unjustly, "Phrowrrr meameon hpsst."

It was time for the swamp scene, and for Alfred's first cue. Already Eliza and Harry had staggered into the midst of the morass, and pillowed their heads upon the moccasin snakes for a moment's rest.

The alley kit came down from the trunk and crouched behind that copy of the Chicago directory which was one of the most valuable stock props of the G.A.R. Hall, serving as it did as a library, a stage telephone book, a Bible for stage ministers to carry under their arms throughout all scenes in which they appeared, and as a block to keep dressing-room doors open. In the fly, behind the directory, Alfred discovered his little friend, and with bounding heart and a wide-open countenance, he began to lick its fur. His was a hearty and rather rough lick. It plastered down the fur, and reduced the kitten to the naked appearance of a wet rat.

Uncle Tom appeared with the pork chop which was Alfred's cue for the off stage bay before bounding upon the scene. Alfred bayed, oh, tremendously. The kitten, released from the licking, raised its poisonous paw and swiped Alfred across the nose. The baying slackened and turned into a foolish squeak. The kitten sailed straight up into the air, widespread, and landed upon Alfred's back, clawing and squalling. The man-eating monster of the marshes, with his tail sheathed, his cat covered back humping, his legs entirely folding under him in his bounding flight, and his voice uplifted in a quavering whinny, bolted upon the stage, upset Eliza, and exited R.C., with speed.

The audience saw only a thunderbolt of inextricable dog and cat, a streak of yammering brown and red, and the exquisite humor of Eliza's sitting down hard and rubbing her knees. The crowd rose — not as one man, but as a lot of men, delighted and noisy — and the words that it said were words of lumber camp and frontier saloon.

To her son Harry, Eliza groaned, "Come on: quick, ma! We'll climb the tree."

They ran for it. As Eliza reached the second peg of the tree, Alfred came roaring through again, muffler cut out, throttle wide open, and steering gear shot away. He collided head on with the property tree, the old and feeble tree, which wavered, and collapsed. The kitten went flying off into the air, and it was already running before it touched the floor. It vanished; Alfred vanished, leaving a trail of "ki-yi, ki-yi, ki-yiiiii;" and Eliza sat bewildered amid the shell shattered forest ruins.

The roustabouts in the front rows had all the encouragement they needed to wreck the show. While Gussie Jorgenson fled from the piano, they climbed upon the stage, followed by the younger and tougher townites. They drove Eliza and Harry from the stage, they stamped on the property tree, they invaded the flies, broke up wardrobe trunks, and slashed the plantation drop, and before the town policeman could be retrieved from the back room of Knudsen's Harness Shop where he was playing pitch, they had howlingly escaped through the stage entrance. The policeman did arrest William Lloyd Garrison Mizzle, the mildest youth in town, who was hiding beneath a seat, but this gallant punitive expedition did not satisfy the Cushman Bland Company. Upon the stage which, with its flats torn out, gaped back to the plaster walls like an empty barn, they stood weeping.

"We might as well end our tour right here and now—our scenery is gone—them devils even busted all our banjos!" wailed Eliza.

"Yes, and Alfred is gone. I can't find the poo' fellow nowhere. He may never come back. . . . Fall'n and conquered and ab-so-lute-ly vamoosed," lamented Cushman Bland. His hands trembled.

Harry of the imbecile youthful expression hastily turned into Little Eva, the brisk and cheerful mother of the clan. "Never mind, chickens. Looks like this was the hand of fate pointing for us to beat it to the farm right now. We'll be country gents. We'll rig up a stage in our barn, and only play when we want to. I wish we had—a little more—money, but— Well, we got each other, folkses, and there ain't many families can say that." She pulled off her black velvet tam-o'shanter, threw it up, and yelped. "Us for the cunnin' cows! No more havin' to do a fool clog for hick audiences. We'll be the hicks; we'll go to every show that comes to Ojibway Falls, and kid the performers."

Her husband could, in an emergency, stop presenting his perpetual role of The Great Cushman Bland. Now he thundered in the index, "You're a good kid, Dulcie darling. Children, wipe off the tears, and let's see if we can't be as plucky as your ma."

Mimosa Booth and H. Rutherford Savoy kissed Little Eva back of each ear, and engaged in a tussle which, feeble though it was, gave them a devil-may-care manner. They were beginning to pick up their scattered wardrobes, Mimosa shrieking that Cushman Bland's Richard III sword would make a peach of a hoe for string beans, when through the deserted auditorium strode the human exclamation point.

It was a tall, thin, intellectual young woman, with chained eyeglasses—presumably chained to keep them at their dangerous task of riding the mountainous bridge of the lady's Nearly Roman nose.

"I have just heard of this outrage, and I have come to the rescue," stated this ghost of Hamlet's maiden aunt. "I am Miss Dill."

"Pleased meecher, Miss——" conceded Little Eva. Eliza had taken one look, and gone back to packing, declaiming, "—and then I'm going out to look for Alfred. Poor doggie, wandering around, and nasty little boys stoning him, and I just couldn't sleep a wink without him lying on the foot of my bed——"

"I am afraid that you did not catch my name. I am Mabel Rockland Dill."

"Oh, yes. Miss Rock Randal. What can I do for you, honey?" Little Eva soothed.

"De-oo? Do for me? My dear woman, I don't see how you can

do anything for me! I'm afraid you don't know who I am, after all. I am, perhaps, of some little significance in this community. I am president of the Jolly Knitters, and the Two Orphans Dramatic Association, and recording secretary of the Blackhaw University Alumni Association of Radisson County, but I am not what we show-people call a provincial. I am a graduate of the Halsted Street Dramatic School of Chicago, and as such, I say it with all modesty, something of an authority on stage-craft, in fact, my professor—and while his own practical experience is not large, he is a Master of Elocutionary Public Reading from a special course in Vassar to which he was the only man admitted!—and he himself told me that I was qualified to take a leading part in any Ibsen company, but of course you understand I do not financially need to follow my career professionally, in fact, I would not care to commercialize my art, but rather confine myself to being an influence here for more elevated drama, and I have come to tell you that it would be much better for all of you to go back to the factory, or wherever you came from, instead of perpetuating this silly old-fashioned melodrama, and if you want my opinion——"

Little Eva's arms were akimbo, and so was her voice: "And if you want my opinion, Miss Panhandle, you amachoors make me so sick——"

"Thank you, I don't know that I really do care for your opinion! I have——"

"Well, you're going to get it."

"—come to tell you that immediately upon hearing of the discourtesy of the audience, which should have charity even for an *Uncle Tom's Cabin* company, I decided that I would get up a benefit for you, for tomorrow evening, and raise at least enough for you to get home."

"A benefit?" Little Eva's hands were pressed together. Her pugnacious eyes became visionary. "I've always wanted to have a benefit! I always read about the New York benefits in the *Clipper* and— But could you pull it off, Miss? Would the town——"

"The town better! It is I who alone am responsible for the planting by the city council of no less than seven maples in the park! Very well. —I must hurry out, now, and get the talent for the occasion, and start the *Cyclone* office printing the bills. You may, if you wish, give the Death of Little Eva scene, as it only requires a plain interior."

Mabel Rockland Dill folded her name about her and departed, while Cushman Bland chanted, "A courtly and gracious woman, despite a certain imperiousness of manner, my dear. I must rebuke you for having taken her ignorant—by gum, they were ignorant, all right!—taking her amateur remarks in ill part. Behind her brusque dictatori—dictatorish—dictatoriality of *une belle chatelaine*, 'twas a true and womanly heart. . . . Gosh, a reg'lar benefit!"

"Well, I still maintain she's a fried-mush-faced cat," murmured the mother, in her most angelic Little Eva tones, "but still— Cushie, when we came from Douglas County and made our first hit in *East Lynn*, and was reckonized even by the most jealous in the profession, we didn't think, did we, that some day we would have a benefit!"

Fifty cents, instead of thirty-five, was charged at the benefit, but every seat was taken, and a crowd standing. The full high-school orchestra played all of its seven pieces, including the wedding march and the funeral march and the waltz composed by the local barber, to the immense satisfaction of everybody except the ex-orchestra, Gussie Jorgenson, and of Adolph Tretska, the trombone player, who had lost his gum down the mouth of his instrument just before the first selection.

The benefit was regularly opened by Squire Stevens, the popular sewing-machine agent and justice of the peace, and convention-addresser of the town, who had introduced seven congressmen to audiences. He now gracefully referred to these seven several stalwarts, along with the eagle, the broad acres of the Midland Empire and in the gold of wheat not of mines is our treasure, the prospective cow-pea crop, George Washington, the three Muses whose names he remembered, Mike who said that funny thing to Pat, Harriet Beecher Stowe, Sarah Bernhardt, the Kaiser, and, as an afterthought, Cushman Bland and Dulcie Damores. His address and frock coat were received with delight by all, especially by the Blands, glowing behind the hastily repaired scenes, and patting Alfred, who had sneaked back, matted with cockleburs and disillusioned regarding kittens and innocence.

The Squire might have kept up his judicious remarks so long that there wouldn't have been any other feature at the benefit, but when he absently reached out his hand for the pitcher and glass of water, and didn't find any, he became confused, and with a quotation from Dan'l Webster, he retreated.

The Main Street Quartette pleased in selections from *Pinafore, The Wizard of Oz,* and the *Collegians' Own Pocket Songster.* Miss Gussie Jorgenson, after looking sniffily down at her rival orchestra, played the Intermezzo from *Cavalleria.* John J. Tampole, the well-known bookkeeper of the Gopher Prairie Flour Mills, gave recitations from Kipling, and for many a long day the ravished ears of the audience will ring to his awed:

"You're a betta—man—than—I ahm, Goonguh Deen!"

It being a Roman Nose holiday, Miss Dill did not permit the Blands to appear at their own benefit, except in the Death of Little Eva, which went off despite the fact that just as Eva was succumbing she saw one of the rioters of the previous night, and snapped to Uncle Tom, "Lemme up, and I'll catch him and snatch him bald-headed." But Uncle Tom was the stronger, and by holding her down while he was murmuring to St. Clare, "Mas'r, Ah hopes you take wahnin' from this—see, the sweet and forgivin' spirit is flown," he compelled her to die peacefully.

Then burst the feature of the evening.

Miss Mabel Rockland Dill had been unable to bestow her histrionic gifts upon Gopher Prairie oftener than twice a year, and then in plays which were contaminated by the rest of the cast. Now she appeared before the curtain, in a Russian blouse from Minneapolis and Russian boots from her father's hunting kit, and announced that alone, single-handed, she would face the celebrated, that is, foreign, one-act play, *The Blood Drips*, by Serge Klopotsky.

She was, it seemed, a gentleman murderer, who repented, feared, briefly outlined anarchism, and suicided, in the manly straightforward way of all heroes of the New Drama. Compelling was that speech of hers delivered with Swedish movements in front of a somewhat Americanized ikon:

"Drip. . . . Drip. . . . . Drip." A high lob, a fierce rally. "Dead — dead!" A net ball, but a superb serve with the second ball, leaping straight up in a splendid exhibition of MacLaughlin's American service. "Corpse. . . . Gray. . . . But I'm a better man than you. I dared the last fine splendor of a murder." Quick backward run, and back-hand return almost equal to Pell's. Score, thirt-love, "And now — I shall be consistent — I shall end the unsocial line of the Trofimovitches by my own hand!!" Vantage out. Game!

They called her to the curtain twice, and twice more she took a chance and came out anyway. On her last call she led out Squire Stevens, the Quartette, Gussie Jorgenson, and even those strangers whom the town couldn't be expected to applaud as they did their fellow-citizens, namely, members of a certain Cushman Bland Company.

In her appreciation of Miss Dill's generosity in giving them a benefit, Little Eva hadn't minded her stealing the show. Twenty-four hours before, with their scenery ruined and Alfred not yet returned, all had been tragic, but now the world was neighborly again, and as she bowed to the people, she loved them. Amid rustling and craning, a small boy came down the aisle bearing a basket of roses. He was so scared that he could not lift them over the footlights. He looked appealing at Little Eva, and she darted out, took the flowers from him, and stood with them clasped in her arms. They were the first floral tribute of her career. In the hush she stammered, "Thank you! oh — that's all I can say!" and began to cry while the audience cheered.

The stage career of the Cushman Blands was over, in roses and glory.

The four Blands were in Cushman's dressing-room when Mabel Rockland Dill, changed back into her baggy Norfolk suit, loomed among them. Little Eva received her with a lavish smile, but Mabel did not seem cheerful. She poked out a roll of bills, and as Little Eva reached for it, Mabel gave her a look which said, "These intellectual eyes of mine can behold thee nowhere, low one." She turned her shoulder on Eva and handed the bills to Cushman Bland, remarking:

"There are the receipts, two hundred and fifty dollars — far more than you deserve, but let that pass. And now, my friends, let me advise you that, if you are so dull that in this age of Klopotsky, you still stick to inane melodrama, then you'd better give up even trying to understand the Spirit of the Stage Beautiful, and go and earn your living honestly! Now —" pointing to Eva's triumphal bouquet — "if you will give me my roses, I will go."

"Your roses? Whatcha mean 'your roses'?" Little Eva rounded the promontory of Mabel's shoulder and confronted her.

"I simply mean that they were intended for me!"

"Now where do you get that——"

"My dear Miss Damores, or whatever you call yourself, do you suppose that Gopher Prairie is interested in you? No, in me — me who got up this benefit, who have compelled every barber in town to put up a placard forbidding cursing in his shop, who have made the city council plant——"

"Yes, I know; seven maples. You'll spoil them maples if you go on digging 'em up and replanting 'em. Now you look here, my dear Miss Squill, or whatever you call yourself. I want to know what makes you think them roses were for you? Didn't the boy bring them straight to me?"

"I know it because — I—— Didn't you see that the urchin was frightened and confused? I knew beforehand that a, well, a certain person was going to send them to——"

"Say, I got you now. You sent them roses to yourself! You're right. They're yours. Take 'em and beat it!" Little Eva smothered her with the basket.

"'Beat it'?" shouted Mabel. "This to me, but for whom you beggar players would have had to walk home——"

"Oh! Oh, we would, would we? You look here!" Little Eva snapped.

She dragged the struggling Mabel to a suitcase, yanked from it a pile of little books, and slapped them one by one upon a table, crying, "See those savings-bank books? Ten of 'em! And three thousand in each of 'em! See the balance in that book? See it? And in that one? And would you like to see the deed to our, uh, country villa, to which we are about to retire? No? Pleasure to show it! You know what? You got up our benefit so you could show off! Now you take your roses and go!"

As Mabel rushed terrified away, Little Eva wept into her rouge pot. "And I won't have any benefit bouquet after all!" She was blind with unhappiness. Cushman Bland and the children slipped away.

Cushman dropped his stateliness. He humped across the way to a candy and news store, and bought a pink basket, and a plain card upon which he wrote something. Not like a high soul but like a frightened and eager husband he trotted down the street, his elegance of black broadcloth trousers flapping about his Cassian legs. . . . He had noticed that there was a rose garden beside a house a block away, not too near a street light.

Ten minutes later another small boy knocked at the door of Eva's dressing-room, and to the still weeping lady presented a pink basket of roses bearing a card, "To Mlle. Damores, with the admiration of a Committee of Citizens of Gopher Prairie for the greatness of her art."

When Cushman Bland came in again, she was hugging the roses, and exulting, "Oh, Cushie darlin', look at this! I have got a real floral tribute, after all! . . . Oh hon, I thought I wasn't goin' to get one, this very last, last night of our career."

Cushman bent grandiosely over her hand, declaiming, "Sweets to the sweet—and ne'er was tribute half so well bestowed." Liz and Hank galloped in to join the family tableau, and chant, "Ma, that's simply elegant." Round them was the triumph of farewell.

But Alfred the bloodhound had sneaked out. He stood on the apron of the stage, looking at the empty seats. The Blands might be content with roses, but they were not conscientious and inspired artists like Alfred. For the last time he saw the altar of his genius. Stilled was the clapping; the painted palaces were crumbled now and dust; and the pomp of ceremony dwindled to a senile emptiness of flea-hunting and the long sleep. Down the furry nose of the old actor rolled one doggish tear.

MAIN STREET'S BEEN PAVED!

WHEN *The Nation* asked me to visit Gopher Prairie, Minnesota, and ask the real he-Americans what they thought of the presidential campaign, I was reluctant. Of all the men whom I met in Gopher Prairie years ago, during that college vacation when I gathered my slight knowledge of the village, Dr. Will Kennicott was the one whom I best knew, and for him I held, and hold, a Little Brother awe. He is merely a country practitioner, not vastly better than the average, yet he is one of these assured, deep-chested, easy men who are always to be found when you want them, and who are rather amused by persons like myself that go sniffing about, wondering what it all means.

I telegraphed the doctor asking whether he would be home, for sometimes in summer he loads his wife and the three boys in his car and goes north for a couple of weeks' fishing. He answered — by letter; he never wastes money by telegraphing. Yes. He was in Gopher Prairie till the middle of August; would be glad to talk with me; knew Carrie (his wife) would enjoy a visit with me also, as she liked to get the latest gossip about books, psychoanalysis, grand opera, glands, etc., and other interests of the intellectual bunch in N.Y.

I arrived in Gopher Prairie on No. 3, the Spokane Flier. Many people will be interested to know that No. 3 is now leaving Minneapolis at 12:04, that the St. Dominick stop has been cut out, and that Mike Lembcke, the veteran trainman so long and favorably known to every drummer traveling out of Mpls., has been transferred to the F line, his daughter having married a man in Tudor.

I was interested to see the changes in Gopher Prairie in the past ten years. Main Street now has three complete blocks paved in ce-

The Nation, September 10, 1924
Collected in *The Man from Main Street* (1953)

ment. The Commercial and Progress Club had erected a neat little building with a room to be used either for pleasure and recreation or for banquets; it has card tables, a pool table, a top-notch radio; and here on important occasions, like the visit of the Congressman or the entertainment of the Twin City Shriners' Brass Band, the ladies of the Baptist Church put up a regular city feed for the men folks. The lawns are prettier than they used to be; a number of the old mansions — some of them dating back to 1885 — have been rejuvenated and beautified by a coating of stucco over the clapboards; and Dave Dyer has a really remarkable California bungalow, with casement windows, a kind of Swiss chalet effect about the eaves, and one of the tallest radio aerial masts I have seen west of Detroit.

But quite as striking was the change in Dr. Kennicott's office.

The consulting-room has been lined with some patent material which looks almost exactly like white tiling — the only trouble with it, he told me, is that lint and so on sticks to it. The waiting-room is very fetching and comfortable, with tapestry-cushioned reed chairs and a long narrow Art Table on which lie *Vogue,* the *Literary Digest, Photo Play,* and *Broadcasting Tidings.*

When I entered, the doctor was busy in the consulting-room, and waiting for him was a woman of perhaps forty, a smallish woman with horn-rimmed spectacles which made her little face seem childish, though it was a childishness dubious and tired and almost timid. She must once, I noted, have been slender and pretty, but she was growing dumpy and static, and about her was an air of having lost her bloom.

I did not at first, though I had often talked to her, recognize her as Carol, Dr. Kennicott's good wife.

She remembered me, however, by my inescapable ruddiness and angularity; and she said that the doctor and she did hope I'd drop in for a little visit after supper — she was sorry they couldn't invite me to supper, but the new hired girl was not coming along as well as they had hoped, as she was a Pole and couldn't speak a word of English. But I must be sure to come. There would be a really fine concert from WKZ that evening—of course so much of the broadcast stuff was silly, but this would be a real old-time fiddler playing barn-dance music—all the familiar airs, and you could hear his foot stamping time just as plain as though he were right there in the room—the neighbors came in to enjoy it, every Thursday evening. Oh! And could I tell her— There'd been such an argument at the Thanatopsis Club the other day as to what was the *dernier cri* in literature just now. What did I think? Was it Marcel Proust or James Joyce or *So Big* by Edna Ferber?

She couldn't wait any longer for the doctor. Would I mind telling him to be sure to bring home the thermos bottle, as they would need it for the Kiwanis picnic?

She whispered away. I thought she hesitated at the door. Then the big, trim doctor came out of the consulting-room, patting the shoulder of a frightened old woman, and chuckling, "So! So! Don't you let 'em scare you. We'll take care of it all right!"

From his voice any one would have drawn confidence; have taken a sense of security against the world—though perhaps a sense of feebleness and childishness and absurdity in comparison with the man himself; altogether the feeling of the Younger Brother.

I fumbled at my mission.

"Doctor, a New York magazine—you may not have heard of it, but I remember that Mrs. Kennicott used to read it till she switched over from it to the *Christian Science Monitor*—*The Nation,* it's called; they asked me to go around and find out how the presidential campaign is starting, and I thought you'd be one of the ——"

"Look here, Lewis, I've got a kind of a hunch I know exactly what you want me to do. You like me personally—you'd probably take a chance on my doctoring you. But you feel that outside of my business I'm a complete dumbbell. You hope I'm going to pull a lot of bonehead cracks about books and writings and politics, so you can go off and print 'em. All right. I don't mind. But before you lash me to the mast and show me up as a terrible reactionary—that's what you parlor socialists call it, ain't it?—before you kid me into saying the things you've already made up your mind you're going to make me say, just come out and make a few calls with me, will you?"

As I followed him downstairs I had more than usual of the irritated meekness such men always cast over me.

He pointed to a handsome motor with an inclosed body.

"You see, Lewis, I'm doing all the Babbitt things you love to have me do. That's my new Buick coop, and strange to say I'd rather own it—paid for in advance!—than a lot of cubist masterpieces with lop-jawed women. I know I oughtn't to get that way. I know that if I'd just arrange my life to suit you and the rest of the highbrows, why, I'd make all my calls on foot, carrying a case of bootlegged wood alcohol under one arm and a few choice books about communism under the other. But when it drops much below zero, I've got a curious backwoods preference for driving in a good warm boat."

I became a bit sharp. "Hang it, doctor, I'm not a fool. Personally, I drive a Cadillac!"

This happened to be a lie. The only mechanical contrivance I own is not a Cadillac but a Royal typewriter. Yet I was confused by his snatching away my chance to be superior by being superior to me, and for the second I really did believe I could beat him at motor-owning as I can beat him at theories of aesthetics.

He grinned. "Yeh, you probably do. That's why you haven't got any excuse at all. I can understand a down-and-outer becoming a crank and wanting to have Bob La Follette or this William Z. Foster—or, God! even Debs!—for President. But you limousine socialists, a fellow like you that's written for the real he-magazines and might maybe be right up in the class of Nina Wilcox Putnam or even Harry Leon Wilson, if you did less gassing and drinking and more work and real hard thinking—how you can go on believing that people are properly impressed by your pose of pretending to love all the lousy bums — well, that's beyond me. Well, as I said: Before we go into politics and Coolidge, I want to show you a couple of things to point out what I mean."

He called to Dave Dyer, in the drug-store. Dave is really an amiable fellow; he used to keep me supplied with beer; and we would sit up, talking science or telling dirty stories or playing stud poker, till a couple of hours after everybody else in town had gone to bed — till almost midnight.

Dave came out and shouted: "Glad to see you again, Lewis."

"Mighty nice to see you, Dave."

"I hear you been up in Canada."

"Yuh, I was up there f'r little trip."

"Have nice trip?"

"You bet. Fine."

"Bet you had a fine trip. How's fishing up there?"

"Oh, fine, Dave. I caught an eleven-and-a-half pound pickerel — jack-fish they call 'em up there — well, I didn't exactly catch it personally, but my brother Claude did — he's the surgeon in St. Cloud."

"Eleven naf pounds, eh? Well, that's a pretty good-sized fish. Heard you been abroad."

"Yes."

"Well. . . . How'd the crops strike you in Canada?"

"Fine. Well, not so good in some parts."

"How long you planning stay around here?"

"Oh, just a couple days."

"Well, glad to seen you. Drop in and see me while you're here."

I was conscious, through this agreeable duologue, that Dr. Kennicott was grinning again. Dave Dyer's amiability had lubricated my former doubtfulness and I was able to say almost as one on a plane of normality with him: "Oh, what are you sniggering at?"

"Oh, nothing, nothing — posolutely Mr. Leopold, absotively Mr. Loeb. (Say, that's a pretty cute one, eh? I got it off the radio last night.) I just mean it always tickles me to see the way you loosen up and forget you're a highbrow when you run into a regular guy like Dave. You're like Carrie. As long as she thinks about it, she's a fierce Forward Looker and Deep Thinker and Viewer with Alarm. But let the hired girl leave the iron on a tablecloth and burn it, and Carrie forgets all about being a Cultured Soul and bawls hell out of her. Sure. You write about Debs, but I'd like to see you acting natural with him like you do with Dave!"

"But really, I'm very fond of Gene."

"Yeh. Sure. 'Gene' you call him—that's the distress signal of your lodge—all you hoboes and authors and highbrows have to say 'Gene.' Well, I notice when you talk to Dave, you talk American, but when you get uplifty on us, you talk like you toted a monocle. Well, climb in."

I considered the sure skill, the easy sliding of the steering-wheel, with which he backed his car from the curb, slipped it forward, swung it about the new automatic electric traffic signal at the corner of Main and Iowa, and accelerated to thirty-five.

"I guess you've noticed the paving on Main Street now," he said. "People that read your junk prob'ly think we're still wading through the mud, but on properly laid cement the mud ain't so noticeable that it bothers you any! But I want to show you a couple of other things that otherwise you'd never see. If I didn't drag you out, your earnest investigation would consist of sitting around with Carrie and Guy Pollock, and agreeing with them that we hicks are awful slow in finally making Gopher Prairie as old as Boston. . . . Say, do you play golf?"

"No, I haven't——"

"Yeh. Thought so. No Fearless Author or Swell Bird would condescend to lam a pill. Golf is a game played only by folks like poor old Doc Kennicott of G.P., and the Prince of Wales and Ring Lardner and prob'ly this H. G. Wells you're always writing about. Well, cast your eye over that, will you."

We had stopped, here on the edge of Gopher Prairie—this

prairie village lost in immensities of wheat and naïvetés, this place of Swede farmers and Seventh Day Adventists and sleeve-garters—beside a golf course with an attractive clubhouse, and half a dozen girls wearing smart skirts and those Patrick sweaters which are so much more charming, more gay, than anything on Bond Street or Rue de la Paix.

And in a pasture beside the golf course rested an aeroplane.

I could say only: "Yes. I see. But why the aeroplane?"

"Oh, it just belongs to a couple more Main Streeters from some place in Texas that are taking a little tourist trip round all the golf courses in the country—terrible pair, Lewis; one of 'em is a Methodist preacher that believes hard work is better for a man than whiskey—never would dare to stand up in a bacteriological argument with this give-'em-the-razz scientist friend of yours, De Kruif; and the other is a cowardly lowbrow that got his Phi Beta Kappa at Yale and is now guilty of being vice-president of a rail-road. And one other curious little thing: I went into Mac's bar-bershop to get my shoes shined this morning, and Mac says to me: 'Afraid you got to let 'em go dusty, Doc—the bootblack is out playing golf.' Now, of course, we're a bad, mean, capitalistic bunch that 're going to vote for that orful Wall Street hireling, Coolidge. In fact, we're reg'lar sadists. So naturally we don't mind playing golf with the bird that blacks our shoes, and we don't mind the hired girl calling us by our first names, while you earnest souls——"

He had forced me to it. "Oh, go to hell!"

He chuckled. "Oh, we'll save you yet. You'll be campaigning for Cal Coolidge."

"Like hell I will!"

"Look, Lewis. May I, as a rube, with nothing but an A.B. from the U of Minn (and pretty doggone good marks in all subjects, too, let me tell you!) inform you that you pulled 'hell' twice in successive sentences, and that the first person singular future indicative of the verb 'to be' is 'shall' and not 'will'? Pardon my hint-ing this to a stylist like you. . . . Look, I'm not really trying to razz you; I'm really trying the best method of defense, which I believe is attack. Of course you don't think so. If the Japs were invading America, you'd want to have a swell line of soap boxes built along the California coast, and have this bird Villard, and this John Haynes Holmes, and this Upton Sinclair—and prob'ly Lenin and Trotzky and Mother Eddy and some Abrams practitioners and Harry Thaw—all get up on 'em and tell the dear artistic Japs how you love 'em, and then of course they'd just be too *ashamed* to come in and rape our women. But, personally, I'd believe in going out with one grand sweet wallop to meet 'em."

"Doctor, you have two advantages. Like all conservatives, all stout fellows, you can always answer opponents by representing them as having obviously absurd notions which they do not possess, then with tremendous vigor showing that these non-existent traits are obviously absurd, and ignoring any explanation. But we cranks try to find out what is the reality of things—a much less stout and amusing job. And then, while we admit enormous ignorances, you never try to diagnose anything you can't physic or cut out. You like to do an appendectomy, but an inquiry into the nature of 'success'———"

"I've noticed one funny thing in all your writings and stuff, Lewis. Whenever you have to refer to a major operation, you always make it an appendectomy. Have you a particular fondness for 'em, or don't you know the names of any others? I'd be glad to buy you a medical dictionary. All right. I'll quit. Now I want to show you a few other changes in G.P."

He drove back into town; he pointed out the new schoolbuilding, with its clear windows, perfect ventilation, and warm-hued tapestry brick.

"That," he said, "is largely Vida Wutherspoon's doing. Remember her and you and Carrie used to argue about education? You were all for having Jacques Loebs and Erasmuses and Mark Hopkinses teaching, and she concentrated on clean drinking-pails. Well, she pounded at us till we built this. . . . Meantime, what've *you* done for education?"

I ignored it, and asked what sort of teachers in this admirably ventilated building were explaining Homer and biochemistry and the glory of God to the youth of Gopher Prairie.

"The teachers? Oh, I guess they're a bunch of dubs like the rest of us; plain ordinary folks. I guess they don't know much about Homer and biochemistry. . . . By the way, in which school are *you* giving your superior notions about Homer and biochemistry, and meanwhile correcting themes, and trying to help the girls that get so inspired by the sort of junk you and Mencken write that they blow home at three G.M., lit to the guards? You hint—of course you haven't met any of 'em but you know it all beforehand—you aren't satisfied with our teaching; we've got a bunch of dumbbells. . . . Willing to come here and teach Latin, math, and history, so they'll be done right? I'm on the school board. I'll get you the job. Want to?"

At my answer he sniggered and drove on. He showed me the agreeable new station—depot, I think he called it—with its flower-bordered park; the old-fashioned English garden put in by a retired German farmer; and the new State fish-hatchery. He demanded: "Well, how about it? Main Street seem to be existing almost as well as the average back alley of some burg in Italy?"

"Certainly. You have them completely beaten—materially!"

"I see. Well, now we've got one other exhibit that we, anyway, don't think is just 'material'—how birds like you love that word! We've got a baseball team that's licked every town of our size in the State, and we got it by hiring a professional pitcher and coach for five months, and going down into our jeans, without any 'material' return, and paying him three hundred dollars a *week!*"

"How much do you pay your teachers a *month?*" was all I had to say, but it provided voluble, inconclusive debate which lasted the twenty-odd miles to a hamlet called New Prague.

Dr. Kennicott stopped at a peasant-like cottage in the Polish settlement of New Prague, and as he knocked I beheld him change from a Booster to the Doctor. What he did in that house I do not know. I do not understand these big suave men who go in to terrified women and perform mysteries and come out — calm, solid, like stockbrokers. During his fifteen minutes within there was the shriek of a woman, the homicidal voice of a man speaking some Slavic tongue — and as he started off he said to me only: "Well, I think I've got her to listen to reason."

"Good Lord, what reason? What do you mean? What happened in there? Who was the man? Her husband or another?"

I have never seen quite so coldly arrogant a cock of the eyebrow as Kennicott gave me.

"Lewis, I don't mind explaining my financial affairs to you, or my lack of knowledge of endocrinology, or my funny notion that an honest-to-God Vermont school-teacher like Cal Coolidge may understand America better than the average pants-maker who hasn't been over from Lithuania but six months. If you insist on it, of course I shouldn't mind a bit discussing my sexual relations to Carrie. *But* I do not ever betray my patients' confidence!"

It was splendid.

Of course it didn't happen to be true. He had often told me his secrets, with the patients' names. But aside from this flaw it was a noble attitude, and I listened becomingly as he boomed on:

"So! Let that pass. Now, why I brought you out here was: Look at this cross-roads burg. Mud and shacks and one big Ford garage and one big Catholic church. The limit. But look at those two Janes coming."

He lifted his square, competent hand from the steering-wheel and pointed at two girls who were passing a hovel bearing the sign "Gas, Cigarettes, Pop and EATS"; and those girls wore well-cut skirts, silk stockings, such shoes as can be bought nowhere in Europe, quiet blouses, bobbed hair, charming straw hats, and easily cynical expressions terrifying to an awkward man.

"Well," demanded Kennicott. "How about it? Hicks, I suppose!"

"They would look at home in Newport. Only——"

He exploded. "Sure. 'Only.' You birds always have to pull an 'only' or an 'except' when we poor dubs make you come look at facts! Now, do stop trying to be a wise-cracker for about ten seconds and listen to a plain, hard-working, damn successful Regular Guy! Those girls—patients of mine—they're not only dressed as well as any of your Newports or Parises or anywhere else, but they're also darn' straight, decent, hard-working kids—one of 'em slings hash in that God-awful hick eating joint we just passed. And to hear 'em talk—Oh, maybe they giggle too much, but they're up on all the movies and radio and books and everything. And both their dads are Bohemians; old mossbacks; tough old birds with whiskers, that can't sling no more English than a mushrat. And yet in one generation, here's their kids—real queens. That's what we're producing here, while you birds are panning us—talking—talking——"

For the first time I demanded a right to answer. I agreed, I said, that these seemed to be very attractive, probably very clever little girls, and that it was noteworthy that in one generation they should have arisen, in all their radio-wise superiority, from the bewildered peasants one sees huddling at Ellis Island. *Only,* was it Doc Kennicott and Dave Dyer and the rest of Main Street who were producing them? Dr. Kennicott might teach them the preferability of listening to the radio instead of humming Czech folk-songs, but hadn't they themselves had something to do with developing their own pretty ankles, buying their own pretty silk stockings, and learning their own gay manners?

And, I desired to be informed, why was it that to Dr. Kennicott the sleek gaiety of socialistic Slavic girls in New York was vicious, a proof that they were inferior, a proof that no one save Vermont conservatives should be allowed to go through Ellis Island, while the sleek gaiety of movie-meditating Slavic girls on Main

Street was a proof of their superiority? Was it because the one part had Dr. Kennicott for physician and the other did not?

There was debate again. I perceived that I had not begun to get my interview; that I was likely to be fired by Mr. Villard. I calmed the doctor by agreeing that his ideas were as consistent as they were practical; and at last I had him explaining Coolidgeism, while he drove back to Gopher Prairie at thirty-five on straight stretches, twenty on curves.

"Well, I hope you're beginning to get things a little straighter now, Lewis. I wanted you to see some of the actual down-to-brass-tacks things we've *accomplished*—the paving on Main Street, the golf course, the silk stockings, the radios—before I explained why everybody around here except maybe a few sorehead farmers who'll vote for La Follette, and the incurable hereditary Democrats who'll stick by Davis, is going to vote for Coolidge. We're people that are doing things—we're working or warring—and in the midst of work or war you don't want a bunch of conversation; you want results.

"Now, first you expect me—prob'bly you've already got it written; darn' shame you'll have to change it—you expect me to pan hell out of Bob La Follette. You expect me to say he's a nut and a crook and a boob and a pro-German. Well, gosh, maybe I would've up till a couple of years after the war. But as a matter of fact, I'm willing—I'm glad to admit he's probably a darn' decent fellow, and knows quite a lot. Maybe it's even been a good thing, some ways, to have a sorehead like him in the Senate, to razz some of the saner element who otherwise might have been so conservative that they wouldn't have accomplished anything. I imagine prob'bly La Follette is a good, honest, intelligent man, a fighter, and a fellow that *does* things. But that's just the trouble. We mustn't be doing too many things, not just now. There's a ticklish situation in the world, with international politics all mixed up and everything, and what we need is men that, even if maybe they haven't got quite so much imagination and knowledge, know how to keep cool and not rock the boat.

"Just suppose a couple of years ago, when Banting was working out insulin for diabetes but his claims weren't confirmed yet, suppose you and all the rest of you Earnest Thinkers, including La Follette, had come to me hollering that I was wrong to go on doing the honest best I could just dieting my diabetes patients. You tell me about Banting—but equally you tell me about some other scientist named, say, Boggs, who had something new for diabetes. What'd I have done? Why, I'd of gone right on being a stingy old conservative and dieting my cases!

"Now, when it proves Banting is right and Boggs is wrong, I follow Banting and kick out Boggs, but I don't do either till I *know.* Boggs might have been a wiz, that took his degree of X.Y.Z. at Jena, but he was premature—he was wrong—he wanted to do too much. Well, La Follette is Boggs, a beaner but plumb wrong, and I and some twenty-thirty million other Americans, we're Coolidge, sitting back and watching, handing it to Banting and such when they prove they've got the goods, but never going off half-cocked.

"The trouble with La Follette isn't that he'd lay down on his job or not understand about railroads and the tariff but that he'd be experimenting all the time. He'd be monkeying around trying to fix things and change things all the time. And prob'ly there's lots of things that do need fixings. But just *now,* in these critical times, we need a driver that won't try to adjust the carburetor while he's making a steep hill.

"So. Not that I mean we're worried—as long as we have a cool head like Cal's at the wheel, with his Cabinet for four-wheel brakes. We ain't been half so worried as you Calamity Howlers. You say that unless La Follette is elected, gosh, the dome of the Capitol will slide off into the Potomac, and Germany will jump on France, and prob'ly my aerial mast will get blown down. Well, far's I can see, most of the folks around here are getting their three squares a day, and the only thing that seems to keep agriculture from progressing is the fact that the farmers can get three bucks a quart for white mule, so they're doing more distilling than manuring.

"Oh, yes, we've had bank failures and there's an increase of tenant-farming. But d' ever occur to you that maybe it's a good thing to close up a lot of these little one-horse banks, so we can combine on bigger and better ones? And about this tenant business; is that any worse than when every farmer owned his own land but had such a big mortgage plastered on it that he didn't really own it at all?

"No, sir, you got to look into these things scientifically. . . . Say, is that left front fender squeaking or do I imagine it? There, don't you hear it now? I do. I'll have Mat fix it. Gosh, how I hate a squeak in a car!

"Now I imagine this sheet *The Nation* tries to let on that the whole country is rising against the terrible rule of Coolidge. And I saw a copy of this *American Mercury* — Guy Pollock lent it to me — where some bird said Coolidge was nothing but a tricky little politician with nothing above the eyebrows. . . . By the way, notice that Ford and Edison and Firestone are going to call on him? Of course those lads, that 're merely the most successful men of affairs and ideas in the country, they're plumb likely to call on a four-flushing accident! Oh, sure!

"Well, now look here. First place, did you ever see a four-flusher that went on holding people's confidence? I never did — Oh, except maybe this chiropractor that blew into town three years ago and darned if he isn't still getting away with it! In the second place, suppose Cal were just a tricky little politician, without a he-idea in his bean. Well, what do you need for the office of President?

"For medicine, and for writing, too, I imagine, some ways, you need *brains*. You're working single-handed, no one to pass the buck to, and you got to show results. But a preacher now, all he's got to do is to make a hit with his sermons, and a lawyer simply has to convince the poor cheeses on the jury that his learned opponent is a lying slob. In the same way, for President you need a fellow that can pull the wool over everybody's eyes, whether it's in the primaries back home in Hickville or whether it's dealing with Japan or Russia. If Cal can get by without having any goods whatever, then he's the boy we want, to keep the labor unions in order and kid along the European nations!

"Then, next place. . . . Oh, all this talk is just wasted energy. You know and I know that Coolidge is going to be elected. Be better if they called the election off and saved a lot of money, and damn the Constitution! Why, nobody is interested, not one doggone bit.

"As you ride around the country, do you hear anybody talking politics? You hear 'em talking about Leopold and Loeb, about Kid McCoy, about the round-the-world fliers, about Tommy Gibbons's battle in England, about their flivvers and their radios. But politics—nix! And why? Because they know Coolidge is already elected! Even the unregenerate old Democrats, that would love to have Brother Charlie run the country on the same darned-fool, unscientific, they-say basis on which William Jennings has the nerve to criticize evolution!

"I haven't met one single responsible well-to-do person who's for La Follette. Who've we got boosting him, then? Well, I can tell you—I can tell you mighty darn' quick! A lot of crank farmers that because they don't want to work and keep their silos filled want to make up for it by some one who, they hope, will raise the price of wheat enough so they can get by without tending to business! The fellows that 've always followed any crazy movement— that ran after the Populists and the Nonpartisan League! And a lot of workmen in the cities that think if some crank comes into office they'll all become federal employees and able to quit working!

"But aside from these hoboes . . . Well, I guess I've asked a hundred people who they were going to vote for, some around G.P. and some on the smoker down to St. Paul, and ninety out of the hundred say: 'Why, gosh, I haven't thought much about it. Haven't had time to make up my mind. I dunno. Besides, anyway, I guess Cal is going to win.'

"Now, about these so-called 'exposures' of the Attorney General and so on. Well, I've always suspected there was a lot more to it than you saw on the surface—lot of fellows trying to make political capital out of it—and the fact that Wheeler is running with La Follette proves my contention, and I for one don't propose to let him get away with it, let me tell you that right now!

"Nope. Unless we have an awful' bad crop failure, and the crops never looked better than they do this year, we've got you licked. Cal is elected. It's all over but the shouting."

I called on Kennicott and his wife after six o'clock supper, but I could not get the talk back to the campaign. Carol hesitated that, yes, she did admire La Follette, and Davis must be a man of fine manners if he could be ambassador to the Court of St. James's, but just this year, with so many bank failures and all, it wasn't safe to experiment, and she thought she would vote for Coolidge; then some other time we could try changes. And now—brightening— had I seen *The Miracle* and *St. Joan?* Were they really as lovely and artistic as people said?

It was time to tune in on the barn-dance music from WKZ, and we listened to "Turkey in the Straw"; we sat rocking, rocking, the doctor and I smoking cigars, Carol inexplicably sighing.

At ten I felt that they would rather more than endure my going, and I ambled up a Main Street whose glare of cement pavement, under a White Way of resplendent electric lights, was empty save for bored but ejaculatory young men supporting themselves by the awning-cords in front of Billy's Lunch Room and the Ford Garage. I climbed to the office of Guy Pollock, that lone, fastidious attorney with whom Carol and I used once, in the supposition that we were "talking about literature," to exchange book titles.

He was at home, in his unchanged shabby den, reading Van Loon's *Story of the Bible.*

He was glad to see me. With Kennicott I had felt like an intruder; to Carol I seemed to give a certain uneasiness; but Guy was warm.

After amenities, after questions about the death of this man, the success of that, I murmured, "Well, there've been a lot of changes in the town—the pavement and all."

"Yes, a lot. And there's more coming. We're to have a new water system. And hourly buses to the Twin Cities—fast as the trains, and cheaper. And a new stone Methodist church. Only——"

"'Ware that word!"

"I know it. Only—only I don't like the town as well as I used to. There's more talk, about automobiles and the radio, but there's less conversation, less people who are interested in scandals, politics, abstractions, gallantries, smut, or anything else save their new A batteries. Since Dr. Westlake died, and this fellow Miles Bjornstam went away, and Vida Sherwin's become absorbed in her son's progress in the Boy Scouts, and even Carol Kennicott— Oh, well, the doctor has convinced her that to be denunciatory or even very enthusiastic isn't quite respectable—I don't seem to be awakened by the talk of any one here.

"And in the old days there were the pioneers. They thought anybody who didn't attend an evangelical church every Sunday ought to be lynched, but they were full of juice and jests. They're gone, almost all of them. They've been replaced by people with bath-tubs and coupés and porch-furniture and speed-boats and lake-cottages, who are determined that their possessions of these pretty things shall not be threatened by radicals, and that their comments on them shall not be interrupted by mere speculation on the soul of man.

"Not, understand me, that I should prefer the sort of little people you must find in Greenwich Village, who do nothing but chatter. I like people who pay their debts, who work, and love their wives. I wouldn't want to see here a bunch of superior souls sitting on the floor and dropping cigarette butts in empty hootch glasses. Only——"

He scratched his chin. "Oh, I don't know. But it depresses me so, the perpetual bright talk about gas-mileage and mah jong here. They sing of four-wheel brakes as the Persian poets sang of rose leaves; their religion is road-paving and their patriotism the relation of weather to Sunday motoring; and they discuss balloon tires with a quiet fervor such as the fifteenth century gave to the Immaculate Conception. I feel like creeping off to a cottage in the Massachusetts hills and taking up my Greek again. Oh, let's talk of simpler things!"

"Then tell me your opinion of the presidential campaign. I suppose you'll vote for Coolidge. I remember you always liked books that the public libraries barred out as immoral, but you wanted to hang the I.W.W. and you thought La Follette was a doubtful fellow."

"Did I? Well, this time I'm going to vote for La Follette. I think most of the people who resent, when they go calling, having good talk interrupted by having to listen to morons saying 'Well, good evening, folks!' amid the demoniac static from the loud-speaker — most of them *must* vote for La Follette, and if we don't elect him this year, some time we shall. I have faith that the very passion in the worship of the Great God Motor must bring its own reaction."

"Kennicott feels he has us beaten forever."

"If he has, if the only voice ever to be heard at the altar is Coolidge on the phonograph and the radio, then our grandsons will have to emigrate to Siberia. But I don't believe it. Even the Kennicotts progress — I hope. His ancestors ridiculed Harvey, then Koch, and Pasteur, but he accepts them; and his grandsons will laugh at Coolidge as Kennicott now laughs at the whiskers of Rutherford B. Hayes.

"But meanwhile I feel a little lonely, in the evenings. Now, that the movies have, under the nation-wide purification by fundamentalism and the rigid Vermont ideals of the President, changed almost entirely from the lively absurdities of cowpuncher films to unfaithful wives and ginny flappers in bathing suits, I can't even attend them. I'm going—and, Lord, how I'll be roasted by the respectable lawyers!—I'm going out to campaign for La Follette!

"We must all do it. We've been bullied too long by the Doc Kennicotts and by the beautiful big balloon tires that roll over the new pavement on Main Street—and over our souls!"

MAIN STREET GOES TO WAR

A RADIO SCRIPT BY SINCLAIR LEWIS

TWENTY-ONE YEARS AGO came Sinclair Lewis' novel, *Main Street.* Here appear some of the same characters — particularly Carol Kennicott, her husband — Dr. Will Kennicott — Vida Sherwin Wutherspoon, Maude Dyer, and Nat Hicks. But they are all twenty years older; the Kennicotts have a daughter, Betty, who is now twenty-one; new people have come to the Kennicotts' village of Gopher Prairie; and certain recent events have changed their whole prairie world.

CHARACTERS

(In order of speaking.
*Those marked * appeared in the novel* Main Street.*)*

THE NEW YORKER, a middle-aged business man, suave but not affected.

THE MAN FROM MAIN STREET, also a middle-aged business man, slightly countrified but not too much so.

*DR. WILL KENNICOTT, of Gopher Prairie, Minnesota. Now 67. A solid, competent professional man, but his voice suggests hunting and fishing as much as it does the consulting-room.

*CAROL KENNICOTT, his wife. Now 55. Rather charming voice, suggesting much reading. She is just a little timid, but she warms to the security of friendship.

MRS. SCHLOSS, the Altbauers' grand-daughter. 28. Hard but efficient. No German accent.

BARNEY ALTBAUER, farmer of 65, with a German accent — not too marked.

MARTA, his wife — heard only in her sick moaning.

BETTY KENNICOTT, daughter of Will and Carol; 21, brisk, com-

Written 1942; never before published

petent, possessed of much humor, much excitement about life.
INGA, the Kennicotts' maid. Slight Swedish accent — very slight,
for she was born in America.

*NAT HICKS, the Gopher Prairie tailor. Nearly seventy. Voice may
be a little harsh. He was born in Ohio, has spent most of his life in
Minnesota.

*MRS. MAUDE DYER, wife of Dave, the druggist. Slightly over
50. Voice a little insinuating and coquettish.

*MRS. VIDA SHERWIN WUTHERSPOON. 65. She is a bit senti-
mental, but not a fool about it. Was for years a school-teacher.

OTTO GROSS, butcher, and mayor of Gopher Prairie. He is about
45. He has a German accent — that must be distinct — but it must
never be comic. It is warm and sympathetic. He is universally
known in Gopher Prairie as a "grand guy."

KNUTE OLESON, dirt-farmer and state legislator. 50. He was
born in Norway, and still has a considerable accent, but he is lu-
cid and impressive.

GERTRUDE OLMSTED, of Yankee stock, trained nurse, 32,
competent.

> (SCENE: The living-room of an apartment fifteen stories up
> above Fifth Avenue, New York City. You hear the sound of
> crowds and of a military parade — shuffling feet, marching feet,
> cheers, automobile horns, a band just below, and other bands
> farther away.
>
> (Against this constant background of sound, which is not
> too loud, we hear two voices.)

THE MAN FROM MAIN STREET: Yes, it certainly gives me a
kick to look down there on Fifth Avenue, with a parade on.

THE NEW YORKER: And tonight, at the mass-meeting, you'll
see an audience of twenty-five thousand people.

THE MAN: Hm! That's just ten times the population of my little
burg — Gopher Prairie, Minnesota.

THE NEW YORKER: And you'll hear a whole bunch of celebrities speaking — generals and bishops and senators and journalists. Yes, I do think we do things right, here in New York. Now tell me: Out in a Middlewestern village like yours — are you really doing anything to help win the war? Just how much attention are you paying to Democracy and Freedom?

THE MAN: Oh, nothing to make headlines, I'm afraid. No bishops and no generals! And I don't know as we *say* much about Freedom and Democracy. We just kind of plug along and do our best. Now you take a fellow like Dr. Will Kennicott, of Gopher Prairie — just a plain, every-day Main Street fellow——

> *(The sounds of New York and of the parade fade, and we hear an irritable TELEPHONE BELL, ringing again and again; then DR. WILL KENNICOTT's voice answering it. His sleep has been interrupted at 3 A.M. He is at first sleepy and grouchy, then interested, competent, and not unkindly. But in everything, he is authoritative.)*

WILL: Hel-LO! . . . Yuh, this is the doctor. . . . Bernhard Altbauer? . . . Yes, I'm taking Dr. Gould's families — he's in the army. What seems to be the trouble, Barney? . . . Well, why didn't you call me last evening? Here it is three o'clock in the morning — and raining! . . . I see. Now how do I get out there? . . . Yuh, the red barn with the two silos. Then right or left? . . . How'll I get through, if the creek is flooded? . . . All right. Have the rowboat ready for me. I'll start right away.

> *(Sound of hanging up receiver. Sound of his dressing.)*

WILL: Doggone that doggone belt. Where is it? . . . Oh.

Carol *(drowsily)*: You going out, Will?

WILL *(but good-naturedly)*: No, I'm just dressing for exercise!

CAROL: Three o'clock? That's a shame! How far do you have to go?

WILL: Seven miles north, beyond Nelson's Grove.

CAROL: And you have to do that operation on old Emil when you get back! Why, you won't get three hours sleep!

WILL: Yuh, I don't love it any too much. Not so young as I used to be, Carol. And I'm kind of spoiled for night practice since I took Hugh into partnership. Used to enjoy lying here snoozing while that poor kid did the night driving. But I don't grudge his going into the army, mind you! I'm glad he's in the service, and I'll try and do his work and Dr. Gould's and my own too. Makes up for not being able to take a crack at the Heinies and the Japs personally. *(Chuckles.)* Huh! I'd hate to tell you what I think about sometimes when I lance a boil! And maybe Mr. Shicklegruber would hate to know. Well—see you at breakfast, dear.

CAROL: Oh, do take care of yourself.

WILL: I been failing to take care of myself for sixty-seven years now, and it's too late now to learn. Yes, and I have my key! Go back to sleep.

> *(Sound of garage door being rolled open, of car being started and in motion. Sound of it stopping, then of* WILL *running up a couple of steps and knocking, several times, impatiently, at the door of a small cottage.)*

MRS. SCHLOSS *(calling from inside the cottage; her voice muffled but alarmed, aggressive)*: Who's that? What do you want?

WILL: Dr. Kennicott.

MRS. SCHLOSS *(more amiable, but still astonished)*: Oh. What is it, Doctor?

> *(Sound of door being unlatched, unlocked, and opened. From here on,* MRS. S*'s voice is not muffled.)*

WILL: Your grand-dad, Barney Altbauer—he just phoned me your gramma is pretty sick—way he describes it, might be typhoid. She'll need a nurse, and all our nurses in town are in the service or awful overworked. Understand you had some practical nurse training in Minneapolis.

MRS. SCHLOSS: That's right. *(Then astonished.)* But do you mean to say Grampa told you to bring a nurse? He's never heard of nurses. He's never heard of the Battle of Waterloo!

WILL: That's part of a country doctor's duties — to bring a nurse before the customers have a chance to say they won't want one! Can you come?

MRS. SCHLOSS: I suppose so. I'll get dressed.

WILL: You better — unless you want me to pick you up and carry you off in that negligee. But hustle — hustle!

MRS. SCHLOSS: Okay, I won't take ten minutes.

WILL: Okay, you won't take five minutes!

MRS. SCHLOSS *(but admiringly)*: You're such a bully. You ought to be in the war.

WILL: I am! Right now. Four minutes and fifty seconds!

> *(Sound of motor horn, then of a meadow lark, possibly transition MUSIC before it.)*

WILL: We've waked up a meadow lark. I'll bet he hates us.

MRS. SCHLOSS: You wouldn't think that, would you, doctor? I'm sure he just LOVES to be waked up at three-thirty A.M. — like me! There we are — that's it — now turn right. . . . Now down the dirt road. . . . Oh! *(In alarm.)* The bridge has been washed out. The whole gully's flooded.

> *(Sound of car stopping, or rushing water.)*

WILL *(shouting)*: Barney! Hey! Barney! It's the doctor. *(Lower, to MRS. SCHLOSS.)* There he is — lantern bobbing. *(Pause, during which rushing water is heard.)* Gosh, what a current!

BARNEY ALTBAUER *(He is an oldish man, with a German accent — but more tragic than comic. He is shouting to them from thirty feet away.)*: Doctor! Doctor! I can't get the boat out of the barn. Too heavy. Nobody here to help me. You got to drive back around Skagmo — six mile — bad road.

WILL *(shouting)*: Haven't got the time! I'm going through!

(*To* MRS. SCHLOSS.) All right, girl. Hold on to the door. (*Sound of motor roaring, in first speed.*) Here we go.

> (*Motor roaring louder, water wildly splashing against the hood, wheels squealing on gravel,* MRS. SCHLOSS's *prolonged "Ohhhhh!"* BARNEY's *"You can't do it," and a farm dog barking. Then* WILL's *voice, in triumph.*)

You can't stop the home medical corps! . . . Morning, Barney. Let's take a look at the patient.

> (*Sound of entering the farmhouse, three people clumping upstairs,* BARNEY *"It's you, Sadie" to his grand-daughter. Then sound of his old wife, moaning.*)

Hm. . . . No, don't look like typhoid. Let's see. . . . Hm. Belly hard. Looks to me like acute appendicitis. I'm going to examine her a little better, but meanwhile—Mrs. Schloss, I want you to sterilize the instruments.

MRS. SCHLOSS: You haven't got any along, have you? You thought it was typhoid. Or anesthetic.

WILL: A country doctor that knows his business *always* goes prepared—for anything from pulling teeth to playing polo. Now skip downstairs and start a fire and get the kettle boiling and see if you can dig out a clean sheet, and scrub the kitchen table. I'll have to bring it up here for an operating table. . . . Barney, you collect all the lanterns you can get your hands on, and hang 'em up in this room.

BARNEY: Doctor! We can't afford an operation! I can't pay for it!

WILL: Who said anything about paying? . . . Go on, Mrs. Schloss. Get busy. Lots of hot water. (*Sound of her leaving the room, descending the stairs, while* WILL *continues.*)

I'll tell you what you can do, though, Barney. You can buy a couple of ten-dollar Victory bonds. Can you manage *that*?

BARNEY: Oh, yah, sure.

WILL: And—would you *like* to?

BARNEY: Oh, yah, sure! You know, Doctor, I was born in the old country. People around here, all the Scandinavians, they think

I'm nothing but an old Dutchman! Doctor—Doctor—I ain't a German now no more. I'm an American! Forty years I live here, clearing these fields, yanking out the stumps with an ox-team, building this house—building America!

It's *my* America! I just wanted somebody should tell me what to do. You want I should buy bonds? I buy 'em! And if I get a good crop this fall, I pay you, every cent, every cent, Doctor!

WILL: Don't worry about that, Barney. . . . Well, I want to examine your woman a little better. You go down and help—— *(Sudden acute moan from the old woman.* WILL *speaks cheerfully— the doctor, confident and giving confidence.)* Coming to, Mrs. Altbauer? Feel pretty bad, eh? Well, we'll just fix that pain up in a jiffy—in a jiffy—you bet!

(MUSIC.)
(SCENE: The Kennicott dining-room, breakfast time.)

BETTY KENNICOTT *(21 and charming and very active)*: Inga!

INGA *(The maid, calling from the kitchen. She is fairly young, herself. She has a slight Swedish accent.)* Yeh, Miss Betty—Miss Kennicott?

BETTY: What's for breakfast?

INGA: French toast and honey.

BETTY: Goody!

INGA: And fresh raspberries.

BETTY: Out of this world!

INGA: And priority coffee.

BETTY: What's that?

INGA: One cup and one lump and like it!

BETTY: No! This is a democracy! You have to do it, but you don't have to like it. *(Sound of her running into the hall, then calling up to her mother.)* Moth-er!

CAROL *(from upstairs)*: Yes, dear?

BETTY: Breakfast.

CAROL: I'll be right down.

BETTY: With priority sugar.

CAROL: What's that?

BETTY: I get your sugar — and you like it. *(Sound of hall door opening.)* Oh, Daddy, Daddy, where have you been? Traipsing around all night!

WILL: Oh, I just operated on a woman, and saved her life. But what's important — I've sold my first Victory bond!

CAROL *(just coming downstairs)*: Good morning, darling. But let's not hear any more about bonds till I've had my morning coffee. I've got to sell bonds all this evening. Will! Do I seem to remember your walking out on me, about three o'clock this morning?

WILL: I believe there was something of the sort.

CAROL: And not a wink of sleep since. Poor darling!

WILL: I'm beginning to like it. Being in this war is making me young and husky again. That's practical psychiatry — keep so darn busy you got no time to worry over yourself. And at that, I'll bet that Hugh, in the medical corps, gets less sleep than I do.

BETTY *(calling from the dining-room)*: Hey, are you two lovers coming in to breakfast, or aren't you? My generation has more trouble teaching you discipline.

CAROL *(almost whispering)*: Will! Don't ever let her know, but I think she's right. These children *are* teaching us!

(MUSIC.)
(SCENE: At breakfast.)

WILL: More French toast?

BETTY: I'm stuffed! Do you think we'll get breakfasts like this if the war goes on two more years?

WILL: Would you mind much?

BETTY: Not so much. It's funny what a kick I get out of doing without things — like that new suit. I sort of feel as if we're stronger and clearer than we were a few months ago.

CAROL: I love the feeling that we can have a will and a purpose, and not just appetites.

WILL: Yuh? Well all I can say is, there's a lot of superior women in this house, but Hugh and me—I'll bet he grouses all the time, in the army, and I know I do. And you, young woman——

BETTY: Yes, *mon petit pappa.*

WILL: If you take the car out and take Wes Stowbody to a barn dance and waste a lot of rubber just one more time, I'll murder you, my fine young idealist.

BETTY: Okay, Colonel. Besides! Wes has joined the State Guard. He's drilling almost every evening—learning all he can before he goes into the service. Gee, between me in business college all day and him marching all evening, a pair of romantic young lovers like us are lucky if we can have a malted milk together. Oh, Dad! Do you know what I'd like to do?

WILL: Don't tell me. I didn't get enough sleep.

BETTY: Couldn't I quit studying shorthand—after all, my dear, think of my going back to school after graduating from the University! Couldn't I go somewhere and learn parachute jumping?

CAROL: That's ridiculous!

WILL (*thoughtfully*): No, it's not ridiculous. Way things are going, with the Japs sneaking up on us, God knows who might have to be parachute jumping. . . . But I want you to complete your shorthand *first,* Betty. We know that'll be useful, war or peace. A little discipline, my pet.

BETTY: Okay. Maybe some day I can take letters from my parachute commander while we're floating through the summer skies together.

WILL: And speaking of discipline, I want you to get here on time for dinner, this noon. You ought to know by this time that dinner in *this* house is twelve o'clock sharp—not ten minutes past twelve!

BETTY: Yes, darling, I ought to know, by now! But I won't be here, this noon.

CAROL: Why not?

BETTY: Bunch of new recruits from Sauk Centre and Alec and Fergus changing trains, this noon. The Service Club is giving 'em a feed, and some of us girls are to dance with 'em. Well, I got to hustle. Bye, everybody! *(Sound of street door slamming.)*

CAROL: Oh, these young people today—they make fun of themselves, but they're so eager I could cry.

WILL: It's a funny new world we got, old lady. Think of an America that's quit wasting everything! I'm glad we lived to see it. We got to take some bitter medicine, but boy, what a prognosis!

(MUSIC.)

CAROL: Oh, Inga!

INGA: Yah?

CAROL: Have you started saving the kitchen fat?

INGA: And how!

(MUSIC.)
(CAROL is in HICKS' tailor shop.)

CAROL: Oh, Mr. Hicks, the doctor thinks maybe you could clean and turn this gray suit of his, and make it last another year.

NAT HICKS *(a little rough and rustic, but amiable)*: I guess I could, at that. I'm just as bad as all the other merchants in town—doing ourselves out of a lot of business—like Joe Tilton at the garage—chasing people right away from his own filling station and telling 'em to walk and save rubber. I don't know what's got into us!

CAROL: I do.

NAT: What?

CAROL: The religion of humanity.

NAT: Oh—*that!*

(MUSIC.)
(SCENE: Red Cross sewing room.)

MAUDE DYER *(flippant, though not young)*: ——and believe it or not, girls, I saw that red-headed school-teacher with a Minneapolis travelling man every night last spring——

VIDA WUTHERSPOON *(She is sentimental, on the uplift side, but she is decidedly not a fool.)*: Maude!

MAUDE: What is it, Vida?

VIDA: Listen, ladies! I know you'll think I'm sentimental, but here we are sewing on layettes for the refugees and knitting scarves for the soldiers, and I don't think we ought to sew or knit hatred into 'em!

MAUDE: I don't get the idea.

CAROL: I do.

VIDA: I'm sure you do, Carol. These gifts are going to strangers, and we've all worked so hard, every day, and I think they ought to have woven into them all our pride in our community, our country. Don't you honestly think so, Maude?

MAUDE: I think a nice little scandal never hurt anybody, but I'll shut up if you girls want me to. *(Sighs loudly.)* Oh dear. I'm getting so good that it hurts.

(MUSIC.)
(SCENE: At the Kennicotts'. Will is entering, shouting:)

WILL: Carol!

CAROL *(upstairs)*: Yes, Will?

WILL: Two minutes to twelve! Dinner ready? Guess what I got!

CAROL: Not a letter from Hugh?

WILL: That's it.

CAROL: Oh! Let's see! *(Pause. Sound of paper crackling.)* This is terrible!

WILL: What's trouble?

CAROL: He's enjoying himself! He's experimenting with these sulfa drugs, and he says he likes it!

WILL: Aren't you glad?

CAROL: I suppose I am. It just doesn't seem right, though—his being happy away from us.

WILL: Pass me the muffins. . . . Young people today seem different. We're scared of seeing our old world change, but they like it. Golly, think of us living right in history—like we were Cromwell and Queen Elizabeth!

CAROL: Will!

WILL: Yuh?

CAROL: About Hugh——

WILL: Come on!

CAROL: I'm going out with Joe Tilton, the garageman, this afternoon and stir up the farmers that haven't brought in their rubber scrap yet. And—well, I told Joe we'd turned in all our old rubber, but I find——

WILL: Come out with it!

CAROL: Well, I've found a few more things, and one of 'em is that little toy rubber dog that Hugh used to love when he was a baby—the little gray rubber dog that squeaks. Do you think I ought to— Oh, I know I'm silly!

WILL (*gravely, affectionately*): Honey, I don't suppose one toy dog would make more 'n a couple dozen truck tires. But you're one of these perfectionists. If you start anything, you want to go the whole way. So you'll never be happy unless you sit down and have a good cry and then turn in that rubber pup.

CAROL: I will not! . . . All right, I will!

(*MUSIC.*)
(*SCENE: The Gopher Prairie Armory, that evening; a Victory Bond meeting. Sound of many voices, feet scuffling. The village band plays—badly but not grotesquely—a few bars of patriotic music. Then speech by* OTTO GROSS, *the mayor.*)

He has a slight German accent, but it is sympathetic, not comic.)

OTTO GROSS: Fellow-citizens of Gopher Prairie! When you done me the honor of electing me your mayor, there was a lot of voters that said, "Otto Gross? Why, he ain't nothing but a dumb platt-deutsch butcher." You know what? I agreed with 'em. I never went to school beyond the sixth grade, and I been cutting up your meat since I was fourteen. But I figured, with my faults the only way I could get by was to tell you the plain truth, every time.

And I want to tell you tonight that I'm ashamed of you, all of you! You haven't bought your quota of Victory Bonds, not two-thirds — a great, big town like this, twenty — five — hundred — people!! — and us laying down on the job, while a little burg like Benedict's Grove, only three-hundred-and-twenty-seven folks, and them nothing but poor Heinies, and they doubled their quota! Now I want you should wake up———

(His voice has faded out on this last, broken sentence, and comes up on:)

And so I have the honor of presenting to you our state senator, that great tax expert and plain dirt-farmer, the Honorable Knute Oleson!

(Applause.)

KNUTE OLESON *(He has a slight Norwegian accent, rather pleasant.)*: Fellow Americans, my old uncle, back in Norway, would be proud of me tonight if he knew I was being allowed to address you, to lead you in this drive to provide wings for the flight to victory. So permit me tonight, my fellow citizens———

(KNUTE's voice fades on this last sentence, then OTTO's voice breaks in.)

OTTO: ———and now I come to our real fighting military leader, a hometown girl that sure has made good—Second-Lieutenant Gertrude Olmsted, of the A.N.C.!

(Applause; shouts of "Good girl" and "Hey, Gertie" and "Go to it, lieutenant," then a couple of bars from the band.)

GERTRUDE OLMSTED *(a competent, pleasant voice, not too sweet)*: Fellow townsmen, I've just come back from a visit in my grandfather's old home town, in the State of Maine—it took him three months to get here and took me only nine hours, by aeroplane, to get back. Seventy-five years separate that old town from us, but as I talked to my relatives, what do you think I found them doing? Putting on a Bond drive, like us here, and that old town just as wild as——

(Her voice fades out on "old town just as," etc. and OTTO's *voice cuts in:)*

OTTO: And now the captain of ushers, Mrs. Doctor Kennicott, and the fine crew of home town girls will bring you pledge blanks and I want to sign the first one myself. Come on!

(His voice is drowned out by vigorous music, supposedly by the Gopher Prairie band. The scene changes to the Kennicott home. WILL *and* CAROL *are going to bed.)*

WILL: Great meeting, all right. *(Yawns.)* Gosh, I'm sleepy.

CAROL: We're over our quota. I don't know whether it was just mass hypnotism, but I loved it.

WILL: So did I. Say, where's my Palm Beach pants? I think it's going to be hot as the dickens tomorrow. *(Sudden suspicion.)* Saaaay—look—here!

CAROL *(guiltily)*: Something wrong, dear?

WILL: I should say there is! Where's my hot water bottle? It's always on that second closet shelf. Right—there—on—that—shelf! Has been for years!

CAROL *(stoutly)*: Well, you *know* I was collecting rubber!

WILL: You mean to tell me that you turned in my good new hot water bottle?

CAROL: It was not new! You've had it for years! It was all patched up with adhesive tape!

WILL (*rueful*): It was just a little patched!

CAROL: You let Hugh's poor little rubber dog be sacrificed, and your horrible old collapsed hot water——

WILL: You win! All right! You win!

CAROL: Next winter, I'll get a brick and make you a lovely calico cover for it, and we can heat it in the oven, like our parents did. Oh! You don't suppose there'll be any restrictions on bricks, do you?

WILL: I think you're safe. Good night. (*Yawn. Pause.*) Just the same—it was a darn good hot water bottle!

CAROL (*yawn*): And it was a darn good little rubber dog. Good night, my dear. (*TELEPHONE rings, insistently.*) Will! Not again!

WILL: Cheer up. This is war. (*On the telephone.*) Yes? . . . Yes, this is the doctor. . . . All right. Come in tomorrow morning. (*Hangs up.*) Grand! Maybe I'll get some sleep. Good night, soldier.

(*MUSIC.*)

ZENITH

BE BRISK WITH BABBITT

I
A Booster for Coolidge
. . . . .

THOUGH I HAD BEEN SENT to Zenith to interview Mr. George F. Babbitt in the matter of the presidential campaign, I did not see him for two days after my arrival. I felt that as a background to the story I ought to consider the city, study its changes in the three years since I had viewed it.

I was not altogether ingenuous in my purpose. The fact is that a Tory in New York had accused me of encountering in various American cities only the highbrows, and, after denying it with the indignation which the truth of the statement naturally aroused, I privately repented and vowed that I would go into the plain, simple, normal, wholesome, and otherwise painful aspects of some Hundred Per Cent American Community.

So for two days of six hundred hours each I trudged the unending streets of Zenith. I saw that there were numbers of delicatessens, laundries, trolley cars, radio supply shops, billboards, people, and new fall felt hats, but otherwise I have no revolutionary discoveries to report.

Now, among the more select and intellectual circles of Zenith I am somewhat known because of three lectures on the "The Influence of the Atharva Veda and Duns Scotus on the Manner of Edith Wharton," which I delivered at Symphony Hall in 1920. Or it may have been my impersonation of a clergyman at the Press Club Get-together Dinner. Anyway, I know most of the newspapermen, and toward evening of my second lonely day I came into the Hotel Thornleigh to find Eddie Morrissey of the *Advocate-Times* waiting for me.

The Nation, October 15, 22, 29, 1924

"Hello, why didncha let me know you were in town say is this the right dope Ernest Boyd pulled about Scott Moncrieff's translation of Proust what you in town for say the city editor says I gotta interview you got any preferences or shall I just write it how about a little poker this evening say do you think I could get a job in New York or London there'll be just five or six of us playing," observed Eddie.

During the evening I admitted to him, with secrecy, that I contemplated interviewing Mr. Babbitt.

Next morning, at eight, a peculiarly gloomy portion of the dawn, I was aroused by the telephone.

"This is George Babbitt speaking. Heard you wanted to see me. Just drop in at the office at any time," said a brisk but manly voice.

"Well——"

"I hate being interviewed. What I feel is that if a man can't conduct his business without a lot of this personal publicity and social items, he'd better quit. But it's always a pleasure to meet you boys from out of town, and if there's anything I can tell——"

"I think I'd better come in this afternoon."

"All right. Any time. Whenever it's convenient."

I seemed safe till noon. But at nineteen minutes past nine there was a knock, a lot of knocks, and sulkily I opened the door on a beaming, ruddy, well-padded, round-faced gentleman with large rimless spectacles—Mr. George F. Babbitt.

"Well, well, well, well," said Mr. Babbitt. "Going by the hotel and thought I'd save you the trouble of looking me up. Now, look here, I don't want you to get the idea I like being interviewed, or that I think my political ideas are of significance——"

"Come in. Mind sitting— Oh, just throw that shirt and stuff on the floor."

"—or, to be perfectly frank, even of interest to the body politic as a whole. In fact, I feel that as a plain business man who has no share in politics except to build up his party and play the role of good citizen so far as it may be in his power I have no right to even try to influence others. But— Eddie Morrissey 'phoned me that you'd like to know my opinion on Cal and La Follette and Davis, so I said if I can help him out in any way——

"Now, here's how I figure it out. Trying to put aside all prejudices, I've finally decided that any vote except one cast for Coolidge is a vote thrown away. You see, all things considered, it's like this: I feel there's been a lot of misjudgment of Cal. I know he isn't as showy as Harding and Bill Bryan and Dawes and a lot of obviously brainy men like that, but my feeling is that he's a fellow who takes his time to make up his mind and to weigh all sides of the question. He's not a fellow that goes off half-cocked, or that yields to every passing wave of the ill-balanced popular winds of fashion. And then another thing:

"I've had an opportunity of getting a viewpoint on America and its relations to the world such as mighty few folks are lucky enough to have. Fact, I've been to Europe!"

"Really?"

"Yump. Seen the whole thing from Puncture to Blowout, as the fellow says. Do you remember Paul Riesling—great friend of mine—skinny fellow with black hair? (Lord, you'd love Paul! Honestly, he's the real goods, and you ought to hear him fiddle— I've been told, on good authority, that if he took it up professionally instead of sticking to the roofing business, he'd put Kreisler and all these birds right out of the running. One of these dreamers, but right on the job just the same.)

"Well. Paul 'd had a lot of trouble, one kind and another, and he was sort of going to pieces. I had a hunch—the poor kid has always wanted to go to Europe—I says to him, 'If the wife will give me the time off, I'm going to lug you over to Gay Paree and get your mind off your worries.' Well, sir, you certainly got to hand it to Myra. All she said was: 'Go the limit as long as you don't bring home one of these Paris cuties with you!' and so off we went.

"Well, sir, of course I'd always known that Europe wasn't efficient like the U. S., but I'd never appreciated what that *meant.* The very first thing we hit on the steamer was an Englishman, and I said to him: 'Well, what's your impression of the States?'

" 'Magnificent country,' he says.

" 'Glad you liked it,' I says.

" 'Splendid machinery,' he says.

" 'Well,' I says, 'I'm glad you liked it.'

" 'There's only one thing,' he says. 'There isn't any hospitality.'

"Well, of course that knocked me for a row of radio sets, because anybody that knows anything about the U. S. knows that while we may have our faults, we're the most hospitable people on earth. Look at the good time we gave the Prince of Wales, polo and everything—prob'ly you noticed how grateful he was in this letter he gave out when he was leaving. So I thought probably this English fellow was trying to jolly me, and I says, 'Yes, It's a shame. We don't hardly ever give our guests anything more than the madame's pearl necklace and the baby's bottle.'

"You know how these blinkin' Britishers look at you sometimes—as if they thought it was somebody else they'd been talking to and suddenly discovered it was only you? Well, that's how he looked, and then he says:

" 'No, seriously. I'd bloomin' well heard———'

"I can't do the English accent the way he did it. You know how funny they talk—the way they keep dragging in Fancy and Quite and all those trick words. But I mean: He said:

" 'I'd always blinkin' well heard—and not just from you bloomin' Americans alone—that you're so all-fired hospitable. What I found was that in America my host didn't hesitate one jolly bit to lug me out to a gathering where we weren't even expected, and I'd be taken in as one of the family. A bunch of birds would slap me on me back and call me by me jolly old first name, don'cha know, and I'd feel awfully welcome and all that sort of thing.' (You know how they talk, but I can't exactly get it, even though I was in England, and one of my best friends is Sir Gerald Doak, this famous steel man, regular bang-up member of the aristocracy, they say he knows Lord Leverhulme intimately. But I'll just give you an idea of the way he put it.)

"'But, then,' he says, 'after I'd met all these folks so darn' chummy-like,' he says, 'I never would come to know them one jolly bit better, and if I ever handed them out any ideas or opinions or anything that was different from their own, they'd throw me out.

"'Now, in England,' he says, 'you don't slap a fellow on the back—if you ever do that sort of thing—till you're gol-blimey well sure you know him, and after that he's one of your own folks. In America you have railroad-station hospitality—everybody welcome to come in and then invited to keep right on moving, but in Great Britain we have fireside hospitality, the kind that lasts.'

"I'm telling you all this because it's such a good sample of the way Europeans don't get America. Talking about it on the steamer coming home, a lot of folks were wondering why it was, but I explained it—you see a fellow gets onto a lot of human slants and psychology in the real estate business. I explained to 'em that the reason Europeans don't understand us is because they're all *jealous* of us, and so they simply won't let themselves be adaptable and consider new viewpoints and take the trouble to get a real genuine insight into other nations, the way Americans do.

"Well. We had a pretty good time, at that. O course London is awful' slow, after New York and Chicago—hardly a skyscraper in the whole burg, and no cabarets or elevateds or anything—people so darn' conservative and old-fashioned that they can't see the need of getting down to business and hustling if they're going to take their part in modern competition. But I had a fine time with Sir Gerald Doak. Unfortunately Lady Doak was away, so he couldn't invite us to Nottingham, but he took us to lunch at his club, and he slipped us a lot of real inside information—how this Ramsay MacDonald was in the pay of the Soviets.

"And we found one awfully nice place—the Cheshire Cheese—that's where this Dr. Johnson, you know, the famous author that wrote a lot of books, where he used to hang out, and say, they've got a dandy book there that all the visitors write in—some of the cutest things you ever saw, poetry and sketches and everything, and almost all of 'em by Americans—I was mighty proud of my country after I saw that book. I remember there was one piece written by a gentleman from Omaha that ran something like this:

Here's to the good old Cheshire Cheese,
That tries hard every Yank to please;
And when I drink old ale in prime condition,
I don't know as I think so much of prohibition.

"Well, I saw the whole works—Westminster Abbey and Buckingham Palace and the Tower and everything, and made a study of business conditions—looked over several department stores and so on—not one-two-three beside the American stores.

"I could see Paul was still feeling touchy, and I let him go off by himself. At the Cheshire Cheese I ran into a dandy couple—Mr. and Mrs. Smith of San Francisco, I wonder if you ever met him, he's in the insurance business—and we three chased around together, and evenings we'd look for some regular American movie and kind of take it easy and get back at ourselves for working so hard at sight-seeing all day.

"And we did the English country, too. Paul had some crazy idea about wanting to moon around some out-of-town cathedral all day (some big Episcopalian cathedral, I think it was), so I let him beat it off by himself, and I and the Smiths and another dandy couple, Mr. and Mrs. Apstein of Milwaukee, he's in the machinery business, and their three kids, we all hired an automobile, and say, we made two hundred and thirty-seven miles in one day, including a stop for lunch.

"Then we went over to Paris, and Paul, he wanted to see some museums, I guess it was, so I hooked up with a peach of a fellow from Rochester, N. Y., that I met at the New York Bar—Evans, his name was—and him and Mrs. Evans and I, we certainly did that old town up brown—the Moulin Rouge and the Rat Mort and Zelli's (that's that dancing place—fellow runs it is an American, even if he has got a Dago name, and they have a swell American orchestra).

"And then on to Rome—met Dr. and Mrs. Simmons of Fargo on the train going down there, and we three bummed around together—not much to see there, if you want to know the truth—and then Florence (wasn't it?)—that's where I ran onto Reverend and Mrs. Jackson—no, in Madrid it was I met the Jacksons and—Oh, a slew of other places. Amsterdam and Switzerland and all over.

"Well, as you can see, I got a pretty thorough notion of Europe. And now here's where I come to the point.

"Europe is picturesque and quaint and historical and all that, but it's a gone goose; it hasn't got any pep. Why, I've seen streets right in Rome, which the guide book calls the Eternal City, that they wouldn't stand for in Punkin Center—dirty, narrow, stinking alleys worse 'n any runway behind a garage!

"Now, of course a lot of fellows will tell you and talk about there not being any bathtubs in Europe. That shows they aren't observant. Makes me tired to hear a fellow just quoting conventional opinions and not using his eyes and being original. Paul and I didn't have a bit of trouble getting rooms with baths, at the Cecil in London or the Continental in Paris or anywhere. *But——*

"People over there don't know how to be friendly. When we landed in London, the bell-boy that took our grips up to the room was a bright-looking little tad, so I gave him a quarter—a shilling they call it—and I says to him, 'Say, buddy, are they pulling off any good movies in town this evening?' Well, sir, I bet I had to repeat it half a dozen times before I could make him understand.

"You see over there in England, they don't have regular public schools like ours, way I understand it, and there's a lot of hick dialects back in what they call the counties, so a lot of the common people don't hardly understand the Queen's English at all. And even when this boy did understand, and I kidded him a little about being so slow on the come-back, he didn't kid me back like a nice bright American bell-hop would. No democracy and friendliness. Same with the cops, when you'd try to stop and pass the time of day with 'em — looked at you like you were a Heathen Chinee.

"Now, another thing. They can talk about London being the big noise, but do you realize that the price per front foot of some of the best business properties in London is actually less than it is for corresponding locations right here in Zenith? That's a thing that ain't generally understood, and somebody ought to write it up and bring it to the attention of the general public more strongly.

"Then the taxicabs. Why, say, some of those old taxis in London couldn't make a two per cent grade on second! And the cocktails in London — why, right in the Cecil itself, which as you know is the bon-ton classy hotel of the whole country, where all the dukes and everybody stays, the clerk himself told me so — they didn't mix as good a cocktail as I can.

"And you hear so much about the food, but you couldn't get as good coffee at the Cecil as we have right at home, and when I asked How's chances on their digging up some corn on cob, the head waiter simply passed out.

"I'm glad to see this Scott Fitzgerald shows up French cooking, too, here in a recent *Saturday Evening Post.* He shows where all the wise birds in France duck these fancy sauces and everything and stick to American crackers and American cheese. Glad he explained that to people.

"And say, darned if every dining car in France didn't have toothpicks right on the table. Why, you take the greenest American boob you could find, and if you caught him swinging a toothpick publicly, he'd just about die of shame. And this is the country that thinks it has so much more class than the U. S. A.!

"So there you are. We've got it all over Europe. They simply want to make all they can out of us. And so—a thing that so many Americans can't understand, without they've had the privilege of studying Europe first-hand—our game is to keep clear of Europe, and it's my firm conviction, first, last, and all the time, that the man who can best keep us clear of European entanglements is that most American and even Yankee of all our greater statesmen— Calvin Coolidge!

"Now, of course there are those that insist La Follette is basically and fundamentally American. I heard a man in this town—Seneca Doane his name is, crank lawyer, I used to like him, fact he was a classmate of mine, and I agree with him that labor has its rights just as much as capital, providing it doesn't get funny and pull a lot of obstructive strikes and otherwise interfere with the conduct of necessary and constructive business—but I mean, I heard this Doane give a smart-aleck talk about how in Wisconsin La Follette duplicated the simplicity and democracy of the old days, and Doane said he was agin the Supreme Court because the Supreme Court itself was agin the Constitution, and how *he* was the One Hundred Per Cent American and not Daugherty. *All* that junk.

"Now, what are the facts? La Follette is a man that's always talk-ing about public ownership, and from that to communism and chaos there's only one step. And a boy from here that was in Wash-ington representing the *Advocate* for several months tells me that he was on the inside and got all the dope, and seems La Follette has entertained Germans and Russians right in his own home. He lets on to be opposed to the League of Nations and foreign entangle-ments, but didn't he deliberately go over to Moscow and get right in with that murderous Soviet crowd, here not long ago?

"In other words, he's the sort of fellow that if he once got to be President and was given a free rein, he'd be negotiating with Ger-many and Russia and France and God knows what all nations, and getting us mixed up with that bunch of has-beens and hoboes and highfalutin' four-flushers over there instead of sticking to business and growing corn and selling real estate.

"Maybe Davis ain't as bad. The papers all say he's a Southern Gentleman, and of course the Southerners are great folks for the home virtues, but still, he's been ambassador to England, and when you think of the way the papers say the Prince of Wales was staying up till all hours dancing every night when he was here, you can readily see that isn't the kind of training you want for a man that's going to keep us free of foreign entanglements, and enable business to have that feeling of security and progress which will enable it to make such extensions as are necessary if we are ever to fulfill our manifest destiny of controlling the industrial affairs of the world and you can't shake a hoof all night and be down at the office at nine. And without that, how is business going to have sufficiently rapid turnovers to assure to every working man that high standard of comfort——

"There was a cartoon in the *Saturday Evening Post* that showed where, unlike Europe, every American laborer owns a nice automobile and a dandy little detached cottage, and you don't find *that* in Europe, do you!

"So that's why I'm going to vote for Coolidge, and I hope I've made my line of reasoning clear to you.

"You see, I've done pretty well in the real-estate game, all things considered. And I want to be permitted to go right on doing well, you can bet your life on that! And if La Follette thinks I'm going to hand my business over to a lot of European paupers or to the Government—well, he guessed wrong, that's all!"

II

Are Americans Timorous Tabbies?

· · · · ·

I was so encouraged by the comparative ease of persuading Mr. George F. Babbitt to confide his opinions that I went, in the afternoon, to call on his friend, Mr. Paul Riesling, whom I knew as a rather fine, very sensitive little man, really (despite Babbitt's commendation) an excellent amateur violinist.

I found him in the office of his small factory for the manufacture of prepared-paper roofing. When I hinted that his friend Babbitt had sent me, he became reluctantly cordial.

"Vote?" said Mr. Riesling, "I'm going to vote for La Follette.

"So you saw Georgie Babbitt. Good man. He has all the reasoning of a child of eight. He's the real majority-rule Democrat— he repeats whatever he hears the majority of his friends in the Zenith Athletic Club and the Boosters' Club saying. And at the same time he's one of the kindest, most loyal, most trustworthy friends a man could have, and if you intend to make fun of him in your interview——"

"Not at all. I'm going to quote him without comment."

"Hm. With most of us, the unkindest thing an interviewer could do would be to quote us exactly, without comment. But anyway:

"Know why I'm going to vote for La Follette? Because I've had a lot of personal and business complications lately, and they've shaken me out of myself—made me think.

"We've all gone ahead, generation after generation, being cautious, being afraid, insisting that if the wrong people were married, or if an industry was underpaying its employees, or if a man that ought to be writing music stuck at his job of selling roofing, why, we ought not to take any chance on changing these conditions. Then opposed to us were a little group of left-wingers who wailed that if anything did exist at all, that was a sufficient reason for changing it right away. But in between there were people like La Follette, who weren't afraid of change but who did advocate a man's paying his debts and doing his work and being loyal to his friends.

"I don't know. I may be wrong. But it seems to me La Follette is almost the first presidential candidate since Lincoln (the first with a chance to win—that's why I leave out Debs) who has had *greatness,* who has combined a desire to let human life be free and happy with a hard, solid, practical, food-raising competence.

"Another thing. I've had the opportunity of getting a detached view of America. In fact, I've recently been in Europe."

"You went with Babbitt, didn't you?"

"Yes, but we were apart a good deal. As I said, Georgie (don't repeat this to him—it would hurt his feeling)—Georgie is the kindest fellow in the world, but he does have the habit when he's traveling of keeping himself from seeing anything by digging in with all the fellow members of the Boosters' Club that he runs into along the way. I remember him and some osteopath from Fargo standing in the middle of the Coliseum discussing wardrobe trunks!

"So I got the habit of sneaking away from him as much as I could and— Oh, I don't know that I learned much. I'm afraid I never once did my duty as a tourist and saw the places to which you go, as Georgie always puts it, 'so you could say you'd been there.' I just wandered—talked to policemen, to bar-maids in pubs, to vergers in cathedrals, to a man I ran into at the British museum— apparently he was a retired British general—and to a Hyde Park communist orator, who walked along Edgeware Road with me and bought me a drink of milk! They were so friendly! They were so simple, so eager to find out what Americans really were like. . . . I used to pretend to them that I was a professional violinist.

"And it was just the same in Paris and Florence and Rome, with the people who spoke English—waiters and concierges and a few taxi-drivers. And everywhere, in all those queer old streets, where you felt that people would rather have ease and laughter than facilities for parking flivvers, there was such peace.

"You may not see how this touches La Follette. It's like this. It seems to me that he combines, and Wheeler combines, American adventurousness and initiative with the scorn of empty hustle and noisy professional good-fellowship which the Europeans have. Oh, for once we have running for the Presidency not an ambitious, trimming, boot-licking politician but a real man who wants us to go on clearing the fields as we've always done, but not to become peddlers. *Gallant*—that's the word I always think of in connection with both him and Senator Wheeler. . . . I wonder if we're actually going to turn them down for a Vermont undertaker and a husky college pipe-smoker who's never grown up?

"I have a queer notion that in this election the American people is showing itself up. We're going to announce whether we're a nation of Coolidges, of La Follettes, or of Brother Charlies. We're going to say that we're content to be known as tight, cautious, timorous tabbies; or as loose and confused and purposeless followers of a party which has no policy and which in a generation has had no great man except Woodrow Wilson perhaps; or as mature and fearless people who are no longer colonial shop-keepers."

III
"I've Done Very Well, Thank You!"
. . . . .

It was with hesitation that I sought my third Zenith interview—with Mr. Charles L. McKelvey, president of the Dodsworth-McKelvey Construction Company, which built the Zenith Union Station and the State capitol. McKelvey is a big, suave, immaculate, quick-thinking man; a baron of the new feudalism; a man to whom, I fancy, Babbitt is a counter-jumper and Paul Riesling a sentimental fool. McKelvey would be a far more suitable symbol for use on the dollar than any antiquated goddess of liberty.

I was admitted, not too glowingly, to his enormous house on Royal Ridge.

"I suppose you're going to vote for Mr. Coolidge," I said, with the meekness suitable to a journalist in the presence of a potentate who can borrow a million dollars between noon and three.

McKelvey glanced at me with that friendly, knowing, devastating eye which has enabled him to control legislators without buying them—much. He tapped his teeth with his thumb nail, he made a gesture with his cigar, and spoke abruptly:

"Nope. For La Follette."

"Eh?"

"I don't suppose you regard that as much of a boost for La Follette though! I have no doubt you believe that anybody whom I and my bunch of cradle-snatchers vote for must be a crook. Well— Confound it, I don't enjoy supporting the man! But I've had a conversion.

"I'm what you people call a Big Business Man. I've done very well, thank you! And naturally I've always stood in politics for the candidates who would let me carry out my plans and not butt in. I've always admired men like General Dawes—a great executive, a man with a big vision in business and yet with complete practicalness, and, I imagine, the best fellow and the best friend in the world—a real he-man. I've certainly always been against La Follette—he struck me as a chap who didn't understand the hard fact that one honest-to-God executive was worth more than a thousand of the dub workmen whom you can replace just around the corner in half an hour.

"Then, I've always been against La Follette's asinine doctrine that monopolies have to be broken up. Yes, and I'd have been against it if I'd been a workman instead of a boss.

"It seems fairly evident to me that the days of small, competitive industries are dead as Moses. Deader! If the country wants to grab off the big companies and run 'em, all right—if they can!— but to go back to a one-man barbershop kind of amateur business is simply childish. Why, we haven't even begun to consolidate! Before you and I pass out, we'll see international corporations that will make Ford and Standard Oil and Sir Basil Zaharoff's combinations look like lemonade stands at a county fair.

"And absolutely right. The old-time way was for any farmer who got tired of plowing to move in town and start a grocery store, and then out of sheer ignorance and laziness to sell dirty let-

tuce and rotten eggs till he failed and was replaced by some other
boob. Today we have organizations in which an egg-seller is cho-
sen because he does it well or he gets moved on to something he
can do well. You talk about 'public service'! Why, good Lord, the
United Cigar Stores give the people a kind of service nobody ever
dreamed of!

"So I was against La Follette both because of sound self-inter-
est and from a knowledge of economics. (Oh, they'll tell you in
this town that I'm a hard-boiled grafting contractor. Well, I spe-
cialized in economics in the State University, and I bet that right
today I read more economics and sociology than the whole bunch
you'll find hanging around this arty, socialistic book-shop of Lloyd
Mallam's put together!)

"Well, then I got the contract to put up the new block of dor-
mitories at the U. The president had a good idea—he wanted the
architect and me to talk with a bunch of students and get their notion of what they wanted in dorms. So I met a lot of the present
brood of undergrads, and I didn't talk to them like an alumnus of
the vintage of 400 B.C., either, but like a shop-mate. And politics
crept in—this was here just the other day, beginning of the fall
term.

"Well, I had a shock. I found that all the good, solid, foot-
ball-playing birds were for Coolidge, but all in the same words
—and when I asked 'em what they wanted in the way of dormi-
tories, they answered like Mongolian idiots making a sound in-
dicating they needed food. But the others—lot of 'em were girls,
and a lot of those Jews, keen little devils, awfully honest and decent and hard-working, and Lord how they liked bawling me
out!—they knew what dorms ought to be, *and* they all seemed
to look at the La Follette campaign as if it were some kind of a
damned crusade.

"Then I had to go on to New York, and while I was there I got
dragged to a highbrow evening at the house of a parlor socialist,
and the speaker of the evening was a pro-Soviet Communist—the

whole works — left-wing as a rattlesnake. And he converted me to La Follette. By attacking him!

"It may raise cain with me, but still, it's been sort of a relief — sort of the old-fashioned rejoicing in salvation that my aunt used to talk about when I was a kid and used to visit her in a small town up-State — to be standing for a candidate who you think is necessary for the country, instead of always feeling you have to be a good loyal slave to the party and backing the lad who promises you to see your grafting doesn't get you into jail!

"This Communist explained to us that there were two philosophies of reform politics — the belief that everything was so bad that the only hope was a complete revolution, and the other a belief that perfection comes slowly. He was of the first faith — oh, something violent! It seems that La Follette, like Ramsay MacDonald, was merely trying to bolster up our wicked democracy and palliate the evil, and so keep the day of judgment from arriving quicker, and those of us that wanted to hustle up the blood and revolution should either vote for William Z. Foster (who, he admitted, would get fully seven votes outside of such members of the *Liberator* staff as took the trouble of voting) or else we ought to come out plumb for Coolidge.

"He was strong for Coolidge. Why, he was stronger for him than the Ku Klux Klan and the Rotary Club and the Bankers' Association put together. If we just elected Coolidge and a few successors like him, said my Communist friend, things would finally get so bad that we'd have the whole nation rising, and all American Institutions would be dumped into the garbage can, where they belonged, and the blessed Russian Institutions would be installed in the United States instead.

"In fact, he said, La Follette was as much of a boob, old-time, non-Marxian American as Jefferson.

"Well, when I heard this fellow (and a good fellow he was, too — bully to go hunting with, I imagine) I got so stirred up I almost forgot about the profits of the Dodsworth-McKelvey Construction Company. I felt I was an old-time American myself. I was ashamed — a little — of all the graft I'd pulled at various times. I felt that La Follette, like William Allen White, represented my own people and that I, who'd been croaking about Immigration and the Furriners, had been so closely associated with Hunkies and Wops — in the interesting position of their employer — that I'd forgotten to be an American.

"I started my own private movement for the Americanization of American Big Businessmen right then and there. And I got to thinking about La Follette on monopoly again. I realized — I'm still agin him on that; but I realized that Coolidge and Davis hadn't *any* positions; they didn't mean anything whatever; whereas La Follette, right or wrong, did have things for which he stood. And that if he was wrong sometimes, he was only part of a movement.

"So, intellectually, I was pretty near converted to La Follette. But not quite. I still couldn't visualize myself voting for a knocker, and I had a hunch that my Board of Directors wouldn't care much for my new religion.

"Well, I walked down Fifth Avenue and passed a rich-man's club — the kind that I'd eventually belong to myself, if I moved to New York and got a little flabbier, and there was a whale of a big Coolidge and Dawes sign across the face of the building. I got to thinking. How few rich men sitting around clubs are for Davis, and how darn much fewer of 'em for La Follette! Struck me as kind of a give-away of my class. And the sign — 'absolute devotion to our country,' along with the names of Coolidge and Dawes — somehow it made me sore, the smug way in which they assumed that only their herd of sacred white cows could be devoted to America. So I did some more fretting, but I still couldn't see myself lined up with what I'd always called a bunch of cranks.

"I came back on the Twentieth Century Limited and happened to get talking to a man who hinted that he was the Klosmic Klamor or something like that of the Ku Klux Klan. And he ordered me both to join the Klan and to vote for Kloolidge — say, I must hand that slogan over to my orthodox Republican friends; ought to win a million votes:

KLEEP KLAREFUL WITH KLOOLIDGE.

"Well— It happens that an ancestor of mine, some darned old Scotchman that turned Catholic just out of pure cussedness had to flee to the Quakers in Nantucket to keep from being imprisoned by the holy Puritans in Massachusetts. Myself, I'm about as much of a Catholic as Rabbi Wise, but when this earnest soul on the train told me that if I didn't vote for Coolidge the Catholics would be appointing a cardinal (preferably a Negro one who lived kosher) as President of the United States, in 1928, why, it got my goat, and I told him I came from a line of Americans, ten generations or so, who'd taken chances on liberal thought, and I wasn't too badly scared that America would be ruined by the adventurers, and I guessed I'd vote for La Follette.

"But—it's been hell having to clean up my business and run it without bribery, as I've had to do since I came out for La Follette!"

IV
What Mr. Schnaufknabel Thinks
· · · · ·

The man whom I interviewed after Mr. Babbitt, Mr. Riesling, and Mr. McKelvey is unknown to glory. I had once known him as a garage mechanic, but he is now a foreman in the Zenith Steel and Machinery Company. His name is Schnaufknabel, August Schnaufknabel.

"Me?" said Mr. Schnaufknabel, when approached by Our Representative, "I'm going to vote for Coolidge, you can bet your sweet life on that!"

"But don't you think La Follette is much more pro-labor than Coolidge, and you take such an interest in labor unionism——"

"Used to, you mean. I've cut that out. That stuff was all right when I was on the jump changing tires or running my fool head off looking for monkey-wrenches for you fellows, but now I've got a job with some responsibility and a future to it, and I've got no time to waste looking out for the interests of a lot of lazy bums that are too inefficient to get on by themselves. I used to fall for this solidarity junk, but that was when I was a kid, and now — Why, say, here in couple more years I'll be able to strike out with a garage of my own, and I'll have men working for me, and suppose I want them pulling a lot of union talk on me?"

"So you've gone back———"

"Oh, I know what you're going to say. Nobody so strong for labor loyalty as a lot of you New York arm-chair liberals that never did a stroke of work in your lives and that couldn't wedge into even the Sandwichmen's Union. No, sir; I've got myself and my family to look out for, and Coolidge represents the kind of conservative enterprise that a man who's making a success of things ought to stand for. Then another thing," concluded Mr. August Schnaufknabel. "La Follette is sympathetic toward the Germans, and that's one thing that makes me hostyle. I'd have been in the war, if I hadn't had a family to support, and I hate any man who's so dumb he doesn't realize what devils all these Germans are."

V

Coolidge Is "Almighty Careful"
. . . . .

I found Mr. Vergil Gunch, past-president of the Boosters' Club and Exalted Ruler of the Benevolent and Protective Order of Elks, in a snug corner of the Zenith Athletic Club, on a cozy settle of green-stained oak with a jolly colored-glass window let into the high back. He greeted me with breezy affability:

"I'll tell you how I feel. I feel that Cal is a fellow that takes his time before he makes a judgment and weighs all sides of a question. He never goes off half-cocked. He may not be as showy as Davis or Lodge or Volstead, but he's almighty careful, and that's what we need in times like these."

VI

"If I Could Make People Realize——"
. . . . .

Seneca Doane is a lawyer who has at once the worst reputation and the best reputation in Zenith. He is called a "dangerous radical," yet the wealthy cannot get along without him in criminal and divorce cases. It was he who got Sam Dodsworth's daughter her divorce from the bogus Vicomte de Montigny without having to pay that delightful almost-nobleman a cent of blackmail, and he who, within the year, was without fee defending the impoverished labor union which Sam Dodsworth had been fighting. He is a veteran single-taxer; a friend in old times to Golden Rule Jones, Tom Johnson, Horace Traubel, and Prince Kropotkin.

When I had seen him three years before, he had looked tired. A sense of the futility in all politics had enervated him; he was thinking of roaming round the world; of losing himself in Java or Italy.

I had trouble in finding him. He was not at his office, not at home. He would be, they informed me, at La Follette headquarters. But there I had to wait half an hour to see him, so many were the callers, so many the telephone messages. I found a new Doane.

He had the placidity which comes less from loafing than from exhilarating work. His eyes were gay, his voice gusty.

"We're going to do it!" he cried. "If we don't elect La Follette this time, we'll elect a Progressive candidate four years from now. I'm not talking propaganda; I mean it! And I think there's an incredibly good chance of electing La Follette right now. You see, a lot of cautious business men and careful workmen, who don't talk about it for fear people won't think they belong to the Conservative Church, are going to sneak out and vote for La Follette. It'll be as much of a surprise result as the last general election in Great Britain, when people woke up to Lloyd George and Stanley Baldwin. There's a magnetic heroism in La Follette, and it's only because we're all so sheep-like that more of us don't come out and shout for him.

"I'm enjoying this campaign—Lord, how I'm enjoying it! It's the first political fight since Tom Johnson's that has seemed to me not merely a throwing of lots between two puppets. I worked for the Committee of Forty-Eight, of course, and I admired the members, but that never seemed to me an authentic, spontaneous movement coming from the people—it was an artificial enthusiasm with too much intellection and too little blood and sweat. I wish I had a thousand tongues, so I could tell the whole country what the La Follette campaign means—the breaking up of the dry, hard rind that's encased our hearts all these years! If I could make people realize——"

VII

"See How I Mean?"
. . . . .

On the train east, I talked to the news-butcher. He wasn't one of the breed of blatting youngsters but a seasoned, professionally good-natured man of forty-five.

"Of course you're working for La Follette," I said.

"Well—" He scratched his chin. "I dunno. I haven't thought much about it yet. I'll tell you. I figure I got a lot of responsibility here on my job, and I tend to my business and let the fellows that understand politics tend to them."

"And that's how people may let Coolidge slip in," I reflected.

"Well, now look here. Don't know as that would be so bad, at that. I'll tell you. Maybe you never thought about this, but the way I've figured it out is:

"Coolidge is a man that maybe he isn't as showy as a lot of fellows that a man like me that's in the magazine business keeps reading about—birds like Ford and Sam Gompers and Nicholas Murray Butler and John Roach Straton and Frank Crane and Billy Sunday. *But* he's mighty careful; he looks at all sides of a question and takes his time before he makes a decision. Maybe that's something you never thought of. Oh, I don't believe in going off half-cocked. If I've been able to get along as good as I have by industry and knowing which kind of detective-story magazines different kinds of traveling men will buy—and believe me I ain't done so badly; we got a flivver at home and a new radio set and the Cross-Word Puzzle Book—why, I guess there's nothing wrong with prosperity and the way the two old parties have run things. I don't see any reason for getting all het up over La Follette. Trouble with a lot of you fellows is you don't think things over; see how I mean?"

Then to the brakeman I hinted:

"Working for La Follette?"

"You bet! He's the only candidate except Bill Foster that knows people like me are anything but machines done up in uniforms," said the brakeman.

So I came back from Zenith.

VERNON, JORALEMON, AND OTHER TOWNS

THINGS

I
. . . . .

THIS IS NOT THE STORY OF Theodora Duke and Stacy Lindstrom, but of a traveling bag with silver fittings, a collection of
cloisonné, a pile of ratty school-books, and a fireless cooker that
did not cook.

Long before these things were acquired, when Theo was a girl
and her father, Lyman Duke, was a so-so dealer in cut-over lands,
there was a feeling of adventure in the family. They lived in a
small brown house which predicated children and rabbits in the
back yard, and a father invariably home for supper. But Mr. Duke
was always catching trains to look at pine tracts in northern Minnesota. Often his wife went along and, in the wilds, way and beyond Grand Marais and the steely shore of Lake Superior, she
heard wolves howl and was unafraid. The Dukes laughed much
those years, and were eager to see mountains and new kinds of
shade trees.

Theo found her own freedom in exploring jungles of five-foot
mullein weeds with Stacy Lindstrom. That pale, stolid little Norwegian she chose from her playmates because he was always ready
to try new games.

The city of Vernon was newer then — in 1900. There were no
country clubs, no fixed sets. The pioneers from Maine and York
State who had appropriated lumber and flour were richer than the
newly come Buckeyes and Hoosiers and Scandinavians, but they
were friendly. As they drove their smart trotters the leading citizens shouted "Hello, Heinie," or "Evenin', Knute," without a feeling of condescension. In preferring Stacy Lindstrom to Eddie
Barnes, who had a hundred-dollar bicycle and had spent a year in

Saturday Evening Post, February 22, 1919
Collected in *Selected Short Stories of Sinclair Lewis*

a private school, Theo did not consider herself virtuously democratic. Neither did Stacy!

The brown-haired, bright-legged, dark-cheeked, glowing girl
was a gorgeous colt, while he was a fuzzy lamb. Theo's father had
an office, Stacy's father a job in a planing mill. Yet Stacy was the
leader. He read books, and he could do things with his hands. He
invented Privateers, which is a much better game than Pirates. For
his gallant company of one privateers he rigged a forsaken dump
cart, in the shaggy woods on the Mississippi bluffs, with sackcloth
sails, barrel-hoop cutlasses, and a plank for victims to walk. Upon
the request of the victims, who were Theo, he added to the plank
a convenient handrail.

But anyone could play Ship—even Eddie Barnes. From a territorial pioneer Stacy learned of the Red River carts which, with
the earthquaking squawk of ungreased wheels and the glare of
scarlet sashes on the buckskin-shirted drivers, used to come plodding all the redskin-haunted way from the outposts of the Free
Trappers, bearing marten and silver fox for the throats of
princesses. Stacy changed the privateers' brigantine into a Red
River cart. Sometimes it was seven or ten carts, and a barricade.
Behind it Stacy and Theo kept off hordes of Dakotas.

After voyaging with Stacy, Theo merely ya-ah'd at Eddie
Barnes when he wanted her to go skating. Eddie considered a figure eight, performed on the ice of a safe creek, the final accom-
plishment of imaginative sport, while Stacy could from imme-
morial caverns call the Wizard Merlin as servitor to a little playing
girl. Besides, he could jump on ski! And mend a bike! Eddie had
to take even a dirty sprocket to the repair shop.

The city, and Theo, had grown less simple-hearted when she
went to Central High School. Twenty-five hundred boys and girls
gathered in those tall gloomy rooms, which smelled of water pails
and chalk and worn floors. There was a glee club, a school paper, a
debating society and dress-up parties. The school was brisk and
sensible, but it was too large for the intimacy of the grade buildings. Eddie Barnes was conspicuous now, with his energy in man-

aging the athletic association, his beautifully combed hair and his real gold watch. Stacy Lindstrom was lost in the mass.

It was Eddie who saw Theo home from parties. He was a man of the world. He went to Chicago as calmly as you or I would go out to the St. Croix River to spear pickerel.

Stacy rarely went to parties. Theo invited him to her own, and the girls were polite to him. Actually he danced rather better than Eddie. But he couldn't talk about Chicago. He couldn't talk at all. Nor did he sing or go out for sports. His father was dead. He worked Saturdays and three nights a week in an upholstery shop—a dingy, lint-blurred loft, where two old Swedes kept up as a permanent institution a debate on the Lutheran Church versus the Swedish Adventist.

"Why don't you get a good live job?" Eddie patronizingly asked Stacy at recess, and Theo echoed the question; but neither of them had any suggestions about specific good live jobs.

Stacy stood from first to fifth in every class. But what, Eddie demanded, was the use of studying unless you were going to be a school-teacher? Which he certainly was not! He was going to college. He was eloquent and frequent on this topic. It wasn't the darned old books, but the association with the fellows, that educated you, he pointed out. Friendships. Fraternities. Helped a fellow like the dickens, both in society and business, when he got out of college.

"Yes, I suppose so," sighed Theo.

Eddie said that Stacy was a longitudinal, latitudinous, isothermic, geologic, catawampaboid Scandahoofian. Everybody admired the way Eddie could make up long words. Theo's older sister, Janet, who had cold, level eyes, said that Theo was a fool to let a shabby, drabby nobody like that Stacy Lindstrom carry her books home from school. Theo defended Stacy whenever he was mentioned. There is nothing which so cools young affection as having to defend people.

After high school Eddie went East to college, Stacy was a clerk in the tax commissioner's department of the railroad—and the

Dukes became rich, and immediately ceased to be adventurous.

Iron had been found under Mr. Duke's holdings in northern Minnesota. He refused to sell. He leased the land to the iron-mining company, and every time a scoop brought up a mass of brown earth in the open pit the company ran very fast and dropped twenty-five cents in Mr. Duke's pocket. He felt heavy with silver and importance; he bought the P. J. Broom mansion and became the abject servant of possessions.

The Broom mansion had four drawing rooms, a heraldic limestone fireplace and a tower and a half. The half tower was merely an octagonal shingle structure with a bulbous Moorish top; but the full tower, which was of stone on a base of brick, had cathedral windows, a weather vane, and a metal roof down which dripped decorative blobs like copper tears. While the mansion was being redecorated the Duke senior took the grand tour from Miami to Port Said, and brought home a carload of treasures. There was a ready-made collection of cloisonné, which an English baron had spent five years in gathering in Japan and five hours in losing at Monte Carlo. There was a London traveling bag, real seal, too crammed with silver fittings to admit much of anything else, and too heavy for anyone save a piano mover to lift. There were rugs, and books, and hand-painted pictures, and a glass window from Nuremberg, and ushabti figures from Egypt, and a pierced brass lamp in the shape of a mosque.

All these symbols of respectability the Dukes installed in the renovated Broom mansion, and settled down to watch them.

Lyman Duke was a kindly man, and shrewd, but the pride of ownership was a germ, and he was a sick man. Who, he meditated, had such a lamp? Could even the Honorable Gerard Randall point to such glowing rods of book backs?

Mrs. Duke organized personally conducted excursions to view the Axminster rug in the library. Janet forgot that she had ever stood brushing her hair before a pine bureau. Now she sat before a dressing table displaying candlesticks, an eyelash pencil, and a powder-puff box of gold lace over old rose. Janet moved graciously, and invited little sister Theo to be cordially unpleasant to their grubby friends of grammar-school days.

The accumulation of things to make other people envious is nothing beside their accumulation because it's the thing to do. Janet discovered that life would be unendurable without an evening cloak. At least three evening cloaks were known to exist within a block of the Broom mansion. True, nobody wore them. There aren't any balls or plays except in winter, and during a Vernon winter you don't wear a satin cloak — you wear a fur coat and a muffler and a sweater and arctics, and you brush the frozen breath from your collar, and dig out of your wraps like a rabbit emerging from a brush pile. But if everybody had them Janet wasn't going to be marked for life as one ignorant of the niceties. She used the word "niceties" frequently and without quailing.

She got an evening cloak. Also a pair of fifteen-dollar pumps, which she discarded for patent leathers as soon as she found that everybody wore those — everybody being a girl in the next block, whose house wasn't anywhere near as nice as "ours."

II
. . . . .

Theo was only half glad of their grandeur. Oh, undoubtedly she was excited about the house at first, and mentioned it to other girls rather often, and rang for maids she didn't need. But she had a little pain in the conscience. She felt that she hadn't kept up defending Stacy Lindstrom very pluckily.

She was never allowed to forget Stacy's first call at the mansion. The family were settled in the house. They were anxious for witnesses of their nobility. The bell rang at eight one Saturday evening when they were finishing dinner. It was hard to be finishing dinner at eight. They had been used to starting at six-thirty-one and ending the last lap, neck and neck, at six-fifty-two. But by starting at seven, and having a salad, and letting Father smoke his cigar at the table, they had stretched out the ceremony to a reasonably decent length.

At the sound of the buzz in the butler's pantry Janet squeaked: "Oh, maybe it's the Garlands! Or even the Randalls!" She ran into the hall.

"Janet! Jan-et! The maid will open the door!" Mrs. Duke wailed.

"I know, but I want to see who it is!"

Janet returned snapping: "Good heavens, it's only that Stacy Lindstrom! Coming at this early hour! And he's bought a new suit, just to go calling. It looks like sheet iron."

Theo pretended she had not heard. She fled to the distant library. She was in a panic. She was ashamed of herself, but she didn't trust Stacy to make enough impression. So it was Mr. Duke who had the first chance at the audience:

"Ah, Stacy, glad to see you, my boy. The girls are round some place. Theo!"

"Lyman! Don't shout so! I'll send a maid to find her," remonstrated Mrs. Duke.

"Oh, she'll come a-running. Trust these girls to know when a boy's round!" boomed Mr. Duke.

Janet had joined Theo in the library. She veritably hissed as she protested: "Boys-s-s-s! We come running for a commonplace railway clerk!"

Theo made her handkerchief into a damp, tight little ball in her lap, smoothed it out, and very carefully began to tear off its border.

Afar Mr. Duke was shouting: "Come see my new collection while we're waiting."

"I hate you!" Theo snarled at Janet, and ran into the last of the series of drawing rooms. From its darkness she could see her father and Stacy. She felt that she was protecting this, her brother, from danger; from the greatest of dangers—being awkward in the presence of the stranger, Janet. She was aware of Janet slithering in beside her.

"Now what do you think of that, eh?" Mr. Duke was demanding. He had unlocked a walnut cabinet, taken out an enameled plate.

Stacy was radiant. "Oh, yes. I know what that stuff is. I've read about it. It's cloysoan." He had pronounced it to rime with moan.

"Well, not precisely! Cloysonnay, most folks would call it. Culwasonnay, if you want to be real highbrow. But cloysoan, that's pretty good! Mamma! Janet! The lad says this is cloysoan! Ha, ha! Well, never mind, my boy. Better folks than you and I have made that kind of a mistake."

Janet was tittering. The poisonous stream of it trickled through all the rooms. Stacy must have heard. He looked about uneasily.

Suddenly Theo saw him as a lout, in his new suit that hung like wood. He was twisting a button and trying to smile back at Mr. Duke.

The cloisonné plate was given to Stacy to admire. What he saw was a flare of many-colored enamels in tiny compartments. In the center a dragon writhed its tongue in a field of stars, and on the rim were buds on clouds of snow, a flying bird, and amusing symbols among willow leaves.

But Mr. Duke was lecturing on what he ought to have seen:

"This is a *sara,* and a very fine specimen. Authorities differ, but it belonged either to the *Shi sinwo* or the *Monzeki*—princely monks, in the monastery of *Nin-na-ji.* Note the extreme thinness of the cloisons, and the pastes are very evenly vitrified. The colors are remarkable. You'll notice there's slate blue, sage green, chrome yellow, and—uh—well, there's several other colors. You see the ground shows the *kara kusa.* That bird there is a *ho-ho* in flight above the branches of the *kiri* tree."

Stacy had a healthy suspicion that a few months before Mr. Duke had known no more about Oriental art than Stacy Lindstrom. But he had no Japanese words for repartee, and he could only rest his weight on the other foot and croak "Well, well!"

Mr. Duke was beatifically going on: "Now this *chatsubo,* you'll notice, is not cloisonné at all, but champlevé. Very important point in studying *shippo* ware. Note the unusually fine *kiku* crest on this *chawan*."

"I see. Uh—I see," said Stacy.

"Just a goat, that's all he is, just a giddy goat," Janet whispered to Theo in the dark room beyond, and pranced away.

It was five minutes before Theo got up courage to rescue Stacy. When she edged into the room he was sitting in a large leather chair and fidgeting. He was fidgeting in twenty different but equally irritating ways. He kept recrossing his legs, and every time he crossed them the stiff trousers bagged out in more hideous folds. Between times he tapped his feet. His fingers drummed on the chair. He looked up at the ceiling, licking his lips, and hastily looked down, with an artificial smile in acknowledgment of Mr. Duke's reminiscences of travel.

Theo swooped on Stacy with hands clapping in welcome, with a flutter of white muslin skirts about young ankles.

"Isn't the house comfy? When we get a pig we can keep him under that piano! Come on, I'll show you all the hidey holes," she crowed.

She skipped off, dragging him by the hand—but she realized that she was doing altogether too much dragging. Stacy, who had always been too intent on their games to be self-conscious, was self-conscious enough now. What could she say to him?

She besought: "I hope you'll come often. We'll have lots of fun out of——"

"Oh, you won't know me any more, with a swell place like this," he mumbled.

As women do she tried to bandage this raw, bruised moment. She snapped on the lights in the third drawing room, and called his attention to the late Mr. P. J. Broom's coat of arms carved on the hulking stone fireplace. "I got the decorator to puzzle it out for me, and as far as he could make out, if Pat Broom was right he was descended from an English duke, a German general and a Serbian undertaker. He didn't miss a trick except——"

"Well, it's a pretty fine fireplace," Stacy interrupted. He looked away, his eyes roving but dull, and dully he added: "Too fine for me, I guess."

Not once could she get him to share her joy in the house. He seemed proud of the virtue of being poor. Like a boast sounded his repeated "Too darned fine for me — don't belong in with all these doo-dads." She worked hard. She showed him not only the company rooms but the delightful secret passage of the clothes chute which led from an upstairs bedroom to the laundry; the closet drawers which moved on rollers and could be drawn out by the little finger; the built-in clock with both Trinity and Westminster chimes; the mysterious spaces of the basement, with the gas drier for wet wash, and the wine cellar which — as it so far contained only a case of beer and seven bottles of ginger ale — was chiefly interesting to the sense of make-believe.

Obediently he looked where she pointed; politely he repeated that everything was "pretty fine"; and not once was he her comrade. The spirit of divine trust was dead, horribly mangled and dead, she panted, while she caroled in the best nice-young-woman tone she could summon: "See, Stace. Isn't this cun-ning?"

It is fabled that sometimes the most malignant ghosts are souls that in life have been the most kindly and beloved. Dead though this ancient friendship seemed, it had yet one phase of horror to manifest. After having implied that he was a plain honest fellow and glad of it, Stacy descended to actual boasting. They sat uneasily in the smallest of the drawing rooms, their eyes fencing. Theo warned herself that he was merely embarrassed. She wanted to be sorry for him. But she was tired — tired of defending him to others, tired of fighting to hold his affection.

"I certainly am eating the work in the tax commissioner's office. I'm studying accounting systems and banking methods evenings, and you want to watch your Uncle Stacy. I'll make some of these rich fellows sit up! I know the cashier at the Lumber National pretty well now, and he as much as said I could have a job there, at better money, any time I wanted to."

He did not say what he wished to put into the railroad and the bank—only what he wished to get out of them. He had no plans, apparently, to build up great institutions for Vernon, but he did have plans to build up a large salary for Stacy Lindstrom.

And one by one, as flustered youth does, he dragged in the names of all the important men he had met. The conversation had to be bent distressingly, to get them all in.

He took half an hour in trying to make an impressive exit.

"I hate him! He expects me to be snobbish! He made it so hard for me to apologize for being rich. He— Oh, I hate him!" Theo sobbed by her bed.

III
· · · · ·

Not for a week did she want to see the boy again; and not for a month did he call. By that time she was used to doing without him. Before long she was used to doing without most people. She was left lonely. Janet had gone East to a college that wasn't a college at all, but a manicurist's buffer of a school, all chamois, celluloid, and pink powder—a school all roses and purring and saddle horses and pleasant reading of little manuals about art. Theo had admired her older sister. She had been eager when Janet had let her wash gloves and run ribbons. She missed the joy of service. She missed too the conveniences of the old brown house—the straw-smelling dog house in the back yard, with the filthy, agreeable, gentlemanly old setter who had resided there; and the tree up which a young woman with secret sorrows could shin resentfully.

Not only Janet and Eddie Barnes but most of Theo's friends had escaped domestic bliss and gone off to school. Theo wanted to follow them, but Mrs. Duke objected: "I wouldn't like to have both my little daughters desert me at once." At the age halfway between child and independent woman Theo was alone. She missed playing; she missed the achievements of housework.

In the old days, on the hired girl's night out, Theo had not minded splashing in rainbow-bubbled suds and polishing the water glasses to shininess. But now there was no hired girl's night out, and no hired girls. There were maids instead, three of them, with a man who took care of the furnace and garden and put on storm windows. The eldest of the maids was the housekeeper-cook, and she was a straight-mouthed, carp-eyed person named Lizzie. Lizzie had been in the Best Houses. She saw to it that neither the other servants nor the Dukes grew slack. She would have fainted at the sight of Sunday supper in the kitchen or of Theo washing dishes.

Mr. Duke pretended to be glad that they had a furnace man; that he no longer had to put on overalls and black leather gloves to tend the furnace and sift the ashes. That had been his before-supper game at the shabby brown house. As a real-estate man, he had been mediocre. As a furnace man, he had been a surgeon, an artist. He had operated on the furnace delicately, giving lectures on his technic to a clinic of admiring young. You mustn't, he had exhorted, shake for one second after the slivers of hot coal tumble through the grate. You must turn off the draft at exactly the moment when the rose-and-saffron flames quiver above the sullen mound of coal.

His wife now maintained that he had been dreadfully bored and put upon by chores. He didn't contradict. He was proud that he no longer had to perch on a ladder holding a storm window or mightily whirling the screw driver as the screws sunk unerringly home. But with nothing to do but look at the furnace man, and gaze at his collections of jugs and bugs and rugs, he became slow of step and foggy of eye, and sometimes, about nothing in particular, he sighed.

Whenever they had guests for dinner he solemnly showed the cloisonné and solemnly the guests said, "Oh," and "Really?" and "Is it?" They didn't want to see the cloisonné, and Mr. Duke didn't want to show it, and of his half-dozen words of Japanese he was exceedingly weary. But if one is a celebrated collector one must keep on collecting and showing the collections.

These dinners and private exhibits were part of a social system in which the Dukes were entangled. It wasn't an easy-fitting system. It was too new. If we ever have professional gentlemen in this country we may learn to do nothing and do it beautifully. But so far we want to do things. Vernon society went out for businesslike activities. There was much motoring, golf and the discussion of golf, and country-club dances at which the men's costumes ran from full evening dress through dinner coats to gray suits with tan shoes.

Most of the men enjoyed these activities honestly. They danced and motored and golfed because they liked to; because it rested them after the day in the office. But there was a small exclusive set in Vernon that had to spend all its time in getting recognized as a small exclusive set. It was social solitaire. By living in a district composed of a particular three blocks on the Boulevard of the Lakes Mr. Duke had been pushed into that exclusive set—Mrs. Duke giving a hand in the pushing.

Sometimes he rebelled. He wanted to be back at work. He had engaged a dismayingly competent manager for his real-estate office, and even by the most ingenious efforts to find something wrong with the books or the correspondence he couldn't keep occupied at the office for more than two hours a day. He longed to discharge the manager, but Mrs. Duke would not have it. She enjoyed the ownership of a leisure-class husband.

For rich women the social system in Vernon does provide more games than for men. The poor we have always with us, and the purpose of the Lord in providing the poor is to enable us of the better classes to amuse ourselves by investigating them and uplifting them and at dinners telling how charitable we are. The poor don't like it much. They have no gratitude. They would rather be uplifters themselves. But if they are taken firmly in hand they can be kept reasonably dependent and interesting for years.

The remnants of the energy that had once taken Mrs. Duke

into the woods beyond the end of steel now drove her into poor-baiting. She was a committeewoman five deep. She had pigeon-holes of mysteriously important correspondence, and she hustled about in the limousine. When her husband wanted to go back and do real work she was oratorical:

"That's the trouble with the American man. He really likes his sordid office. No, dearie, you just enjoy your leisure for a while yet. As soon as we finish the campaign for censoring music you and I will run away and take a good trip—San Francisco and Honolulu."

But whenever she actually was almost ready to go even he saw objections. How ridiculous to desert their adorable house, the beds soft as whipped cream, the mushrooms and wild rice that only Lizzie could cook, for the discomforts of trains and hotels! And was it safe to leave the priceless collections? There had been a burglar scare—there always has just been a burglar scare in all cities. The Dukes didn't explain how their presence would keep burglars away, but they gallantly gave up their lives to guarding the cloisonné while they talked about getting a caretaker, and never tried to get him.

Thus at last was Lyman Duke become a prison guard shackled to the things he owned, and the longest journey of the man who had once desired new peaks and softer air was a slow walk down to the Commercial Club for lunch.

IV
. . . . .

When Janet and Eddie Barnes and the rest of Theo's friends came back from college; when the sons went into their fathers' whole-sale offices and clubs, and the daughters joined their mothers' lecture courses and societies, and there was an inheriting Younger Set and many family plans for marriages—then Theo ceased to be lonely, and remembered how to play. She had gone to desultory dances during their absence, but only with people too old or too young. Now she had a group of her own. She danced with a hot passion for music and movement; her questioning about life disappeared in laughter as she rose to the rushing of people and the flashing of gowns.

Stacy Lindstrom was out of existence in this colored world. Stacy was now chief clerk in the railroad tax commissioner's office, and spoken of as future assistant cashier in the Lumber National Bank. But he was quite insignificant. He was thin—not slim. He was silent—not reserved. His clothes were plain—not cleverly inconspicuous. He wore eyeglasses with a gold chain attached to a hoop over one ear; and he totally failed to insist that he was bored by the vaudeville which everybody attended and everybody sneered at. Oh, he was ordinary, through and through.

Thus with boarding-school wisdom Janet dissected the unfortunate social problem known as Stacy Lindstrom. Theo didn't protest much. It was not possible for youth to keep on for five years very ardently defending anybody who changed as little as Stacy. And Theo was busy.

Not only to dances did Janet lead her, but into the delights of being artistic. Janet had been gapingly impressed by the Broom mansion when the family had acquired it, but now, after vacation visits to Eastern friends, she saw that the large brown velvet chairs were stuffy, and the table with the inlaid chessboard of mother-of-pearl a horror. What Janet saw she also expressed.

In one of the manuals the girls had been tenderly encouraged to glance through at Janet's college it was courageously stated that simplicity was the keynote in decoration. At breakfast, dinner, and even at suppers personally abstracted from the ice box at two A.M., Janet clamored that their ratty old palace ought to be refurnished. Her parents paid no attention. That was just as well.

Otherwise Janet would have lost the chance to get into her portable pulpit and admonish: "When I have a house it will be absolutely simple. Just a few exquisite vases, and not one chair that doesn't melt into the environment. Things—things—things—

they are so dreadful! I shan't have a thing I can't use. Use is the test of beauty."

Theo knew that the admirable Janet expressed something which she had been feeling like a dull, unplaced pain. She became a member of an informal art association consisting of herself, Janet, Eddie Barnes, and Harry McPherson, Janet's chief suitor. It is true that the art association gave most of its attention to sitting together in corners at dances and giggling at other people's clothes, but Janet did lead them to an exhibit at the Vernon Art Institute, and afterward they had tea and felt intellectual and peculiar and proud.

Eddie Barnes was showing new depths. He had attended a great seaboard university whose principal distinction, besides its athletics, was its skill in instructing select young gentlemen to discuss any topic in the world without having any knowledge of it whatever. During Janet's pogrom against the Dukes' mosque-shaped brass lamp Eddie was heard to say a number of terribly good things about the social value of knowing wall sconces.

When Janet and Harry McPherson were married Eddie was best man, Theo bridesmaid.

Janet had furnished her new house. When Theo had accompanied Janet on the first shopping flight she had wanted to know just what sort of chairs would perform the miracle of melting into the environment. She wondered whether they could be found in department stores or only in magic shops. But Janet led her to a place only too familiar—the Crafts League, where Mrs. Duke always bought candle shades and small almond dishes.

Janet instantly purchased a hand-tooled leather box for playing cards, and a desk set which included a locked diary in a morocco cover and an ingenious case containing scissors, magnifying glass, pencil sharpener, paper cutter, steel ink eraser, silver penknife. This tool kit was a delightful toy, and it cost thirty-seven dollars. The clerk explained that it was especially marked down from forty-five dollars, though he did not explain why it should be especially marked down.

Theo wailed: "But those aren't necessary! That last thingumajig has four different kinds of knives, where you only need one. It's at least as useless as Papa's cloisonné."

"I know, but it's so amusing. And it's entirely different from Papa's old stuff. It's the newest thing out!" Janet explained.

Before she had bought a single environment-melting chair Janet added to her simple and useful furnishings a collection of glass fruit for table centerpiece, a set of Venetian glass bottles, a traveling clock with a case of gold and platinum and works of tin. For her sensible desk she acquired a complicated engine consisting of a tiny marble pedestal, on which was an onyx ball, on which was a cerise and turquoise china parrot, from whose back, for no very clear anatomical reason, issued a candlestick. But not a stick for candles. It was wired for electricity.

As she accepted each treasure Janet rippled that it was so amusing. The clerk added "So quaint," as though it rimed with amusing. While Theo listened uncomfortably they two sang a chorus of disparagement of Mid-Victorian bric-a-brac and praise of modern clever bits.

When Janet got time for the miraculous chairs——

She had decided to furnish her dining room in friendly, graceful Sheraton, but the clerk spoke confidentially of French lacquer, and Theo watched Janet pledge her troth to a frail red-lacquered dining-room set of brazen angles. The clerk also spoke of distinguished entrance halls, and wished upon Janet an enormous Spanish chair of stamped leather upholstery and dropsical gilded legs, with a mirror that cost a hundred and twenty dollars, and a chest in which Janet didn't intend to keep anything.

Theo went home feeling that she was carrying on her shoulders a burden of gilded oak; that she would never again run free.

When Janet's house was done it looked like a sale in a seaside gift shop. Even her telephone was covered with a brocade and china doll. Theo saw Janet spending her days vaguely endeavoring to telephone to living life through brocade dolls.

After Janet's marriage Theo realized that she was tired of going to parties with the same group; of hearing the same Eddie tell the same stories about the cousin of the Vanderbilts who had almost invited him to go yachting. She was tired of Vernon's one rich middle-aged bachelor; of the bouncing girl twins who always rough-housed at dances. She was peculiarly weary of the same salads and ices which all Vernon hostesses always got from the same caterer. There was one kind of cake with rosettes of nuts which Theo met four times in two weeks—and expected to meet till the caterer passed beyond. She could tell beforehand how any given festivity would turn out. She knew at just what moment after a luncheon the conversation about babies would turn into uneasy yawns, and the hostess would, inevitably, propose bridge. Theo desired to assassinate the entire court of face cards.

Stacy Lindstrom had about once a year indicated a shy desire to have her meet his own set. He told her that they went skiing in winter and picnicking in summer; he hinted how simply and frankly they talked at dinners. Theo went gladly with him to several parties of young married people and a few unmarried sisters and cousins. For three times she enjoyed the change in personnel. As she saw the bright new flats, with the glassed-in porches, the wicker furniture, the colored prints and the davenports; as she heard the people chaff one another; as she accompanied them to a public skating rink and sang to the blaring band—she felt that she had come out of the stupidity of stilted social sets and returned to the naturalness of the old brown house.

But after three parties she knew all the jokes of the husbands about their wives, and with unnecessary thoroughness she knew the opinions of each person upon movies, Chicago, prohibition, the i.w.w., Mrs. Sam Jenkins' chronic party gown, and Stacy's new job in the Lumber National. She tried to enliven the parties. She worked harder than any of her hostesses. She proposed charades, music. She failed. She gave them one gorgeous dance, and disappeared from their group forever.

She did go with Stacy on a tramp through the snow, and enjoyed it—till he began to hint that he, too, might have a great house and many drawing rooms some day. He had very little to say about what he hoped to do for the Lumber National Bank in return.

Then did Theo feel utterly deserted. She blamed herself. Was something wrong with her that she alone found these amusements so agonizingly unamusing? And feeling thus why didn't she do something about it? She went on helping her mother in the gigantic task of asking Lizzie what orders Lizzie wanted them to give her. She went on planning that some day she would read large books and know all about world problems, and she went on forgetting to buy the books. She was twenty-six, and there was no man to marry except the chattering Eddie Barnes. Certainly she could not think romantically about that Stacy Lindstrom whose ambition seemed to be to get enough money to become an imitation chattering Eddie Barnes.

Then America entered the war.

V
. . . . .

Eddie Barnes went to the first officers' training camp, and presently was a highly decorative first lieutenant in a hundred-dollar uniform. Stacy Lindstrom made his savings over to his mother, and enlisted. While Eddie was still stationed at a cantonment as instructor Stacy was writing Theo ten-word messages from France. He had become a sergeant, and French agriculture was interesting, he wrote.

Stacy's farewell had been undistinguished. He called—a slight, commonplace figure in a badly fitting private's uniform. He sat on the piano stool and mouthed: "Well, I have a furlough. Then we get shipped across. Well—don't forget me, Theo."

At the door Stacy kissed her hand so sharply that his teeth bruised her skin, and ran down the steps, silent.

But Eddie, who came up from the cantonment at least once a month, at least that often gave a long, brave farewell to Theo. Handsome, slim, erect, he invariably paced the smallest drawing room, stopped, trembled, and said in a military tone, tenor but resolute: "Well, old honey, this may be the last time I see you. I may get overseas service any time now. Theo dear, do you know how much I care? I shall take a picture of you in my heart, and it may be the last thing I ever think of. I'm no hero, but I know I shall do my duty. And, Theo, if I don't come back———"

The first two times Theo flared into weeping at this point, and Eddie's arm was about her, and she kissed him. But the third, fourth and fifth times he said good-by forever she chuckled, "Cheer up, old boy." It was hard for her to feel tragic about Eddie's being in the service, because she was in the service herself.

At last there was work that needed her. She had started with three afternoons a week at Red Cross; chatty afternoons, with her mother beside her, and familiar neighbors stopping in the middle of surgical dressings to gurgle: "Oh, did you hear about how angry George Bangs was when Nellie bought a case of toilet soap at a dollar a cake? Think of it. A dollar! When you can get a very nice imported soap at twenty-five cents."

Theo felt that there was too much lint on the conversation and too little on their hands. She found herself one with a dozen girls who had been wrens and wanted to be eagles. Two of them learned motor repairing and got across to France. Theo wanted to go, but her mother refused. After a dignified protest from Mrs. Duke, Theo became telephone girl at Red Cross headquarters, till she had learned shorthand and typing, and was able to serve the head of the state Red Cross as secretary. She envied the motor-corps women in their uniforms, but she exulted in power—in being able to give quick, accurate information to the distressed women who came fluttering to headquarters.

Mrs. Duke felt that typing was low. Theo was protected by her father.

"Good thing for the girl to have business training," he kept insisting, till the commanding officer of the house impatiently consented.

It was the American Library Association collection which turned Theo from a dim uneasiness about the tyranny of possessions to active war. She bounced into the largest drawing room one dinner time, ten minutes late, crying: "Let's go over all our books tonight and weed out a dandy bunch for the soldiers!"

Mrs. Duke ruled: "Really, my dear, if you would only try to be on time for your meals! It's hard enough on Lizzie and myself to keep the house running———"

"Come, come, come! Get your hat off and comb your hair and get ready for dinner. I'm almost starved!" grumbled Mr. Duke.

Theo repeated the demand as soon as she was seated. The soldiers, she began, needed———

"We occasionally read the newspapers ourselves! Of course we shall be very glad to give what books we can spare. But there doesn't seem to be any necessity of going at things in this—this—hit-or-a-miss! Besides, I have some letters to write this evening," stated Mrs. Duke.

"Well, I'm going over them anyway!"

"I wish to see any books before you send them away!"

With Theo visualizing herself carrying off a carload of books, the Dukes ambled to the library after finishing dinner—and finishing coffee, a cigar and chocolate peppermints, and a discussion of the proper chintz for the shabby chairs in the guest room. Theo realized as she looked at the lofty, benign, and carefully locked bookcases that she hadn't touched one of the books for a year; that for six months she hadn't seen anyone enter the room for any purpose other than sweeping.

After fifteen minutes spent in studying every illustration in a three-volume history Mrs. Duke announced: "Here's something I think we might give away, Lym. Nobody has ever read it. A good many of the pages are uncut."

Mr. Duke protested: "Give that away? No, sir! I been meaning to get at that for a long time. Why, that's a valuable history. Tells all about modern Europe. Man ought to read it to get an idea of the sources of the war."

"But you never will read it, Papa," begged Theo.

"Now, Theo," her mother remonstrated in the D.A.R. manner, "if your father wishes to keep it that's all there is to be said, and we will make no more words about it." She returned the three volumes to the shelf.

"I'll turn it over to you just as soon as I've read it," her father obliged. Theo reflected that if any soldiers in the current conflict were to see the history they would have to prolong the war till 1950.

But she tried to look grateful while her father went on: "Tell you what I was thinking, though, Mother. Here's these two shelves of novels—none of 'em by standard authors—all just moonshine or blood and thunder. Let's clear out the whole bunch."

"But those books are just the thing for a rainy day—nice light reading. And for guests. But now this—this old book on saddlery. When we had horses you used to look at it, but now, with motors and all——"

"I know, but I still like to browse in it now and then."

"Very well."

Theo fled. She remembered piles of shabby books in the attic. While the Dukes were discovering that after all there wasn't one of the four hundred volumes in the library which they weren't going to read right away Theo heaped the dining-room table with attic waifs. She called her parents. The first thing Mrs. Duke spied was a Tennyson, printed in 1890 in a type doubtless suitable to ants, small sand-colored ants, but illegible to the human eye. Mrs. Duke shrieked: "Oh! You weren't thinking of giving that handsome Tennyson away! Why, it's a very handsome edition. Besides, it's one of the first books your father and I ever had. It was given to us by your Aunt Gracie!"

"But Moth-er dear! You haven't even seen the book for years!"

"Well, I've thought of it often."

"How about all these Christmas books?"

"Now, Theodora, if you wouldn't be so impatient, but kindly give your father and me time to look them over,——"

Two hours and seventeen minutes after dinner, Mr. and Mrs. Duke had almost resignedly agreed to present the following literary treasures to the soldiers of these United States for their edification and entertainment:

One sixth-grade geography. One *Wild Flowers of Northern Wisconsin.* Two duplicate copies of *Little Women.* The *Congressional Record* for part of 1902. One black, depressed, religious volume entitled *The Dragon's Fight With the Woman for 1260 Prophetic Days,* from which the last seven hundred days were missing, leaving the issue of the combat in serious doubt. Four novels, all by women, severally called *Griselda of the Red Hand, Bramleigh of British Columbia, Lady Tip-Tippet,* and *Billikins' Lonely Christmas.*

Theo looked at them. She laughed. Then she was sitting by the table, her head down, sobbing. Her parents glanced at each other in hurt amazement.

"I can't understand the girl. After all the pains we took to try to help her!" sighed Mrs. Duke later, when they were undressing.

"O-o-o-oh," yawned Mr. Duke as he removed his collar from the back button—with the slight, invariable twinge in his rheumatic shoulder blades. "Oh, she's nervous and tired from her work down at that Red Cross place. I'm in favor of her having a little experience, but at the same time there's no need of overdoing. Plenty of other people to help out."

He intended to state this paternal wisdom to Theo at breakfast, but Theo at breakfast was not one to whom to state things paternally. Her normally broad shining lips were sucked in. She merely nodded to her parents, then attended with strictness to her oatmeal and departed—after privily instructing Lizzie to give the smaller pile of books in the dining room to the junk collector.

Three novels from the pile she did take to the public library for the A.L.A. To these she added twenty books, mostly trigonometries, bought with her own pocket money. Consequently she had no lunch save a glass of milk for twenty days. But as the Dukes didn't know that, everybody was happy.

The battle of the books led to other sanguinary skirmishes.

VI
. . . . .

There was the fireless cooker.

It was an early, homemade fireless cooker, constructed in the days when anything in the shape of one box inside another, with any spare scraps of sawdust between, was regarded as a valuable domestic machine. Aside from the fact that it didn't cook, the Dukes' cooker took up room in the kitchen, gathered a film of grease which caught a swamp of dust, and regularly banged Lizzie's shins. For six years the Dukes had talked about having it repaired. They had run through the historical, scientific, and financial aspects of cookers at least once a season.

"I've wondered sometimes if we couldn't just have the furnace man take out the sawdust and put in something else or— Theo, wouldn't you like to run into Whaley & Baumgarten's one of these days, and price all of the new fireless cookers?" beamed Mrs. Duke.

"Too busy."

In a grieved, spacious manner Mrs. Duke reproved: "Well, my dear, I certainly am too busy, what with the party for the new rector and his bride——"

"Call up the store. Tell 'em to send up a good cooker on trial," said Theo.

"But these things have to be done with care and thought——"

Theo was stalking away as she retorted: "Not by me they don't!"

She was sorry for her rudeness afterward, and that evening she was gay and young as she played ballads for her father and did her mother's hair. After that, when she was going to bed, and very tired, and horribly confused in her thinking, she was sorry because she had been sorry because she had been rude.

The furnace went wrong, and its dissipations were discussed by Mr. Duke, Mrs. Duke, Mrs. Harry McPherson *née* Duke, Lizzie, the furnace man, and the plumber, till Theo ran up to her room and bit the pillow to keep from screaming. She begged her father to install a new furnace: "The old one will set the house afire — it's a terrible old animal."

"Nonsense. Take a chance on fire," said he. "House and everything well insured anyway. If the house did burn down there'd be one good thing — wouldn't have to worry any more about getting that twelve tons of coal we're still shy."

When Mr. Duke was summoned to Duluth by the iron-mining company Mrs. Duke sobbingly called Theo home from the midst of tearing work.

Theo arrived in terror. "What is it? What's happened to Papa?"

"Happened? Why, nothing. But he didn't have a chance to take a single thing to Duluth, and he simply won't know what to do without his traveling bag — the one he got in London — all the fittings and everything that he's used to, so he could put his hand on a toothbrush right in the dark———"

"But, Mother dear, I'm sure bathrooms in Duluth have electric lights, so he won't need to put his hand on toothbrushes in the dark. And he can get nice new lovely brushes at almost any drug store and not have to fuss———"

"Fuss? Fuss? It's you who are doing the fussing. He just won't know what to do without his traveling bag."

While she helped her mother and Lizzie drag the ponderous bag down from the attic; while her mother, merely thinking aloud, discussed whether "your father" would want the madras pajamas or the flannelette; while, upon almost tearful maternal request, Theo hunted all through the house for the missing cut-glass soap case, she was holding herself in. She disliked herself for being so unsympathetic. She remembered how touched she had been by exactly the same domestic comedy two years before. But unsympathetic she was, even two days later, when her mother triumphantly showed Mr. Duke's note: "I can't tell you how glad I was to see good old bag showing up here at hotel; felt lost without it."

"Just the same, my absence that afternoon cost the Red Cross at least fifty dollars, and for a lot less than that he could have gone out and bought twice as good a bag—lighter, more convenient. Things! Poor Dad is the servant of that cursed pig-iron bag," she meditated.

She believed that she was being very subtle about her rebellion, but it must have been obvious, for after Mr. Duke's return her mother suddenly attacked her at dinner.

"So far as I can make out from the way you're pouting and sulking and carrying on, you must have some sort of a socialistic idea that possessions are unimportant. Now you ought——"

"Anarchist, do you mean, Mother dear?"

"Kindly do not interrupt me! As I was saying: It's things that have made the world advance from barbarism. Motor cars, clothes you can wash, razors that enable a man to look neat, canned foods, printing presses, steamers, bathrooms—those are what have gotten men beyond living in skins in horrid damp caves."

"Of course. And that's why I object to people fussing so about certain things, and keeping themselves from getting full use of bigger things. If you're always so busy arranging the flowers in the vase in a limousine that you never have time to go riding, then the vase has spoiled the motor for——"

"I don't get your logic at all. I certainly pay very little attention to the flowers in our car. Lizzie arranges them for me!" triumphed Mrs. Duke.

Theo was charging on. She was trying to get her own ideas

straight. "And if a man spends valuable time in tinkering with a worn-out razor when he could buy a new one, then he's keeping himself in the damp cave and the bearskin undies. That isn't thrift. It's waste."

"I fancy that people in caves, in prehistoric times, did not use razors at all, did they, Lyman?" her mother majestically corrected.

"Now you always worry about Papa's bag. It was nice once, and worth caring for, but it's just a bother now. On your principle a factory would stop running for half the year to patch up or lace up the belting, or whatever it is they do, instead of getting new belting and thus— Oh, can't you see? Buy things. Use 'em. But throw them away if they're more bother than good. If a bag keeps you from enjoying traveling—chuck it in the river! If a man makes a tennis court and finds he really doesn't like tennis, let the court get weedy rather than spend glorious free October afternoons in mowing and raking——"

"Well, I suppose you mean rolling it," said her mother domestically. "And I don't know what tennis has to do with the subject. I'm sure I haven't mentioned tennis. And I trust you'll admit that your knowledge of factories and belting is not authoritative. No. The trouble is, this Red Cross work is getting you so you can't think straight. Of course with this war and all, it may be permissible to waste a lot of good time and money making dressings and things for a lot of green nurses to waste, but you girls must learn the great principle of thrift."

"We have! I'm practicing it. It means—oh, so much, now. Thrift is doing without things you don't need, and taking care of things as long as they're useful. It distinctly isn't wasting time and spiritual devotion over things you can't use—just because you happen to be so unfortunate as to own 'em. Like our eternal fussing over that clock in the upper hall that no one ever looks at——"

Not listening, her mother was placidly rolling on: "You seem to think this house needs too much attention. You'd like it, wouldn't you, if we moved to a couple of rooms in the Dakota Lodging House!"

Theo gave it up.

Two days later she forgot it.

Creeping into her snug life, wailing for her help, came a yellow-faced apparition whose eyes were not for seeing but mere gashes to show the suffering within. It was — it had been — one Stacy Lindstrom, a sergeant of the A.E.F.

Stacy had lain with a shattered shoulder in a shell pit for three days. He had had pneumonia. Four distinct times all of him had died, quite definitely died — all but the desire to see Theo.

His little, timid, vehemently respectable mother sent for Theo on the night when he was brought home, and despite Mrs. Duke's panicky protest Theo went to him at eleven in the evening.

"Not going to die for little while. Terribly weak, but all here. Pull through — if you want me to. Not asking you to like me. All I want — want you to want me to live. Made 'em send me home. Was all right on the sea. But weak. Got touch of typhoid in New York. Didn't show up till on the train. But all right and cheerful — Oh! I hurt so. Just hurt, hurt, hurt, every inch of me. Never mind. Well, seen you again. Can die now. Guess I will."

Thus in panting words he muttered, while she knelt by him and could not tell whether she loved him or hated him; whether she shrank from this skinny claw outstretched from the grave or was drawn to him by a longing to nurse his soul back to a desire for life. But this she knew: Even Red Cross efficiency was nothing in the presence of her first contact with raw living life — most rawly living when crawling out from the slime of death.

She overruled Mrs. Lindstrom; got a nurse and Doctor Rollin — Rollin, the interior medicine specialist.

"Boy's all right. Hasn't got strength enough to fight very hard. Better cheer him up," said Doctor Rollin. "Bill? My bill? He's a soldier, isn't he? Don't you suppose I wanted to go into the army

too? Chance to see beautiful cases for once. Yes. Admit it. Like to
have fool salutes too. Got to stay home, nurse lot of dam-fool
women. Charge a soldier? Don't bother me," he grumbled, while
he was folding up his stethoscope, and closing his bag, and trying
to find his hat, which Mrs. Lindstrom had politely concealed.

Every day after her work Theo trudged to the Lindstrom
house—a scrubbed and tidied cottage in whose living room was
a bureau with a lace cover, a gilded shell, and two photographs of
stiff relatives in Norway. She watched Stacy grow back into life.
His hands, which had been yellow and drawn as the talons of a
starved Chinaman, became pink and solid. The big knuckles,
which had been lumpy under the crackly skin, were padded
again.

She had been surprised into hot pity for him. She was saved
equally by his amusement over his own weakness, and by his irri-
tableness. Though he had called for her, during the first week he
seemed to dislike her and all other human beings save his nurse. In
the depths of lead-colored pain nothing mattered to him save his
own comfort. The coolness of his glass of water was more to him
than the war. Even when he became human again, and eager at her
coming, there was nothing very personal in their talk. When he
was able to do more than gasp out a few words she encouraged in
him the ambition to pile up money which she detested.

Uncomfortably she looked at him, thin against a plump pillow, and her voice was artificially cheery as she declared: "You'll
be back in the bank soon. I'm sure they'll raise you. No reason why
you shouldn't be president of it some day."

He had closed his pale eyelids. She thought he was discour-
aged. Noisily she reassured, "Honestly! I'm sure you'll make
money—lots of it."

His eyes were open, blazing. "Money! Yes! Wonderful thing!"
"Ye-es."

"Buys tanks and shells, and food for homeless babies. But for me—I just want a living. There isn't any Stacy Lindstrom any more." He was absorbed in that bigger thing over there, in that Nirvana—a fighting Nirvana! "I've got ambitions, big 'uns, but not to see myself in a morning coat and new gloves on Sunday!"

He said nothing more. A week after, he was sitting up in bed, reading, in a Lindstromy nightgown of white cotton edged with red. She wondered at the book. It was *Colloquial French.*

"You aren't planning to go back?" she asked casually.

"Yes. I've got it straight now." He leaned back, pulled the bed-clothes carefully up about his neck and said quietly, "I'm going back to fight. But not just for the duration of the war. Now I know what I was meant for. I can do things with my hands, and I get along with plain folks. I'm going back on reconstruction work. We're going to rebuild France. I'm studying—French, cottage ar-chitecture, cabbages. I'm a pretty good farmer—'member how I used to work on the farm, vacations?"

She saw that all self-consciousness was gone from him. He was again the Stacy Lindstrom who had been lord of the Red River carts. Her haunted years of nervousness about life disappeared, and suddenly she was again too fond of her boy companion to waste time considering whether she was fond of him. They were making plans, laughing the quick curt laughs of intimates.

A week later Mrs. Lindstrom took her aside.

Mrs. Lindstrom had always, after admitting Theo and nodding without the slightest expression in her anemic face, vanished through the kitchen doorway. Tonight, as Theo was sailing out, Mrs. Lindstrom hastened after her through the living room.

"Miss! Miss Duke! Yoost a minute. Could you speak wit' me?"

"Why, yes."

"Dis—ay—da boy get along pretty gude, eh? He seem werry gude, today. Ay vish you should——" The little woman's face was hard. "Ay don't know how to say it elegant, but if you ever— I know he ain't your fella, but he always got that picture of you, and maybe now he ban pretty brave soldier, maybe you could like him better, but—I know I yoost ban Old Country woman. If you and him marry—I keep away, not bother you. Your folks is rich and—Oh, I gif, I gif him to you—if you vant him."

Mrs. Lindstrom's sulky eyes seemed to expand, grow misty. Her Puritanical chest was terribly heaving. She sobbed: "He always talk about you ever since he ban little fella. Please excuse me I spoke, if you don't vant him, but I vanted you should know, I do anyt'ing for him. And you."

She fled, and Theo could hear the scouring of a pot in the kitchen. Theo fled the other way.

It was that same evening, at dinner, that Mrs. Duke delicately attempted social homicide.

"My dear, aren't you going to see this Lindstrom boy rather oftener than you need to? From what you say he must be convalescing. I hope that your pity for him won't lead you into any foolish notions and sentiment about him."

Theo laughed. "No time to be sentimental about anything these days. I've canned the word——"

"'Canned'! Oh, Theo!"

"—'sentiment' entirely. But if I hadn't, Stace wouldn't be a bad one to write little poems about. He used to be my buddy when——"

"Please—do—not—be—so—vulgar! And Theo, however you may regard Stacy, kindly do stop and think how Mrs. Lindstrom would look in this house!"

The cheerful, gustatory manner died in Theo. She rose. She said with an intense, a religious solemnity: "This house! Damn this house!"

The Lindstroms were not mentioned again. There was no need. Mrs. Duke's eyebrows adequately repeated her opinions when Theo came racing in at night, buoyant with work and walking and fighting over Stacy's plans.

Theo fancied that her father looked at her more sympathetically. She ceased to take Mr. Duke as a matter of course, as one more fixed than the radiators. She realized that he spent these autumn evenings in staring at the fire. When he looked up he smiled, but his eyes were scary. Theo noticed that he had given up making wistful suggestions to Mrs. Duke that he be permitted to go back to real work, or that they get a farm, or go traveling. Once they had a week's excursion to New York, but Mrs. Duke had to hasten back for her committees. She was ever firmer with her husband; more ready with reminders that it was hard to get away from a big house like this; that men oughtn't to be so selfish and just expect Lizzie and her——

Mr. Duke no longer argued. He rarely went to his office. He was becoming a slippered old man.

VII
. . . . .

Eddie Barnes was back in Vernon on the sixth of his positively last, final, ultimate farewells.

Theo yelled in joy when he called. She was positively blowzy with healthy vulgarity. She had won an argument with Stacy about teaching the French to plant corn, and had walked home almost at a trot.

"Fine to see you! Saying an eternal farewell again?" she brutally asked Eddie.

For one of the young samurai Eddie was rather sheepish. He stalked about the largest drawing room. His puttees shone. Eddie really had very nice legs, the modern young woman reflected.

"Gosh, I'm an awful fareweller. Nope, I'm not going to do a single weep. Because this time—I've got my orders. I'll be in France in three weeks. So I just thought—I just thought— maybe—I'd ask you if you could conveniently— Ouch, that tooth still aches; have to get this bridge finished tomorrow sure. Could you marry me?"

"Ungh!" Theo flopped into a chair.

"You've queered all my poetic tactics by your rude merry mirth. So just got to talk naturally."

"Glad you did. Now let me think. Do I want to marry you?"

"We get along bully. Listen—wait till I get back from France, and we'll have some celebration. Oh, boy! I'll stand for the cooties and the mud till the job's done, but when I get back and put the Croix de Guerre into the safe-deposit I'm going to have a drink of champagne four quarts deep! And you and I—we'll have one time! Guess you'll be pretty sick of Red Cross by——"

"No. And I know a man who thinks that when the war is over then the real work begins."

Eddie was grave, steady, more mature than he had ever seemed. "Yes. Stacy Lindstrom. See here, honey, he has big advantages over me. I'm not picturesque. I never had to work for my bread and butter, and I was brought up to try to be amusing, not noble. Nothing more touching than high ideals and poverty. But if I try to be touching, you laugh at me. I'm— I may get killed, and I'll be just as dead in my expensible first lieut's pants as any self-sacrificing private."

"I hadn't thought of that. Of course. You have disadvantages. Comfort isn't dramatic. But still— It's the champagne and the big time. I've——"

"See here, honey, you'd be dreadfully bored by poverty. You do like nice things."

"That's it. Things! That's what I'm afraid of. I'm interested in tractors for France, but not in the exact shade of hock glasses. And beauty— It's the soul of things, but it's got to be inherent, not just painted on. Nice things! Ugh! And— If I married you what would be your plans for me? How would I get through twenty-four hours a day?"

"Why—uh—why, how does anybody get through 'em? You'd have a good time—dances, and playin' round and maybe children, and we'd run down to Palm Beach——"

"Yes. You'd permit me to go on doing what I always did till

the war came. Nope. It isn't good enough. I want to work. You wouldn't let me, even in the house. There'd be maids, nurses. It's not that I want a career. I don't want to be an actress or a congresswoman. Perfectly willing to be assistant to some man. Providing he can really use me in useful work. No. You pre-war boys are going to have a frightful time with us post-war women."

"But you'll get tired———"

"Oh, I know, I know! You and Father and Mother will wear me out. You-all may win. You and this house, this horrible sleek warm house that Mrs.—that she isn't fit to come into! She that gave him———"

Her voice was rising, hysterical. She was bent in the big chair, curiously twisted, as though she had been wounded.

Eddie stroked her hair, then abruptly stalked out.

Theo sat marveling: "Did I really send Eddie away? Poor Eddie. Oh, I'll write him. He's right. Nice to think of brave maiden defiantly marrying poor hero. But they never do. Not in this house."

VIII

. . . . .

The deep courthouse bell awakening Theo to bewildered staring at the speckled darkness—a factory whistle fantastically tooting, then beating against her ears in long, steady waves of sound—the triumphant yelping of a small boy and the quacking of a toy horn—a motor starting next door, a cold motor that bucked and snorted before it began to sing, but at last roared away with the horn blaring—finally the distant "Extra! Extra!"

Her sleepy body protestingly curled tighter in a downy ball in her bed on the upper porch, but her mind was frantically awake as the clamor thickened. "Is it really peace this time? The armistice really signed?" she exulted.

In pleasant reasonable phrases the warm body objected to the cold outside the silk comforter. "Remember how you were fooled on Thursday. Oo-oo! Bed feels so luxurious!" it insisted.

217

She was a practical heroine. She threw off the covers. The indolent body had to awaken, in self-defense. She merely squeaked "Ouch!" as her feet groped for their slippers on the cold floor. She flung downstairs, into rubbers and a fur coat, and she was out on the walk in time to stop a bellowing newsboy.

Yes. It was true. Official report from Washington. War over.

"Hurray!" said the ragged newsboy, proud of being out adventuring by night; and "Hurray!" she answered him. She felt that she was one with awakening crowds all over the country, from the T Wharf to the Embarcadero. She wanted to make great noises.

The news had reached the almost-Western city of Vernon at three. It was only four, but as she stood on the porch a crush of motor cars swept by, headed for downtown. Bumping behind them they dragged lard cans, saucepans, frying pans. One man standing on a running board played Mr. Zip on a cornet. Another dashing for a trolley had on his chest a board with an insistent electric bell. He saw her on the porch and shouted, "Come on, sister! Downtown! All celebrate! Some carnival!"

She waved to him. She wanted to get out the electric and drive down. There would be noise—singing.

Four strange girls ran by and shrieked to her, "Come on and dance!"

Suddenly she was asking herself: "But do they know what it means? It isn't just a carnival. It's sacred." Sharply: "But do I know all it means, either? World-wide. History, here, now!" Leaning against the door, cold but not conscious that she was cold, she found herself praying.

As she marched back upstairs she was startled. She fancied she saw a gray figure fleeing down the upper hall. She stopped. No sound.

"Heavens, I'm so wrought up! All jumpy. Shall I give Papa the paper? Oh, I'm too trembly to talk to anyone."

While the city went noise-mad it was a very solemn white small figure that crawled into bed. The emotion that for four years had been gathering burst into sobbing. She snuggled close, but she did not sleep. Presently: "My Red Cross work will be over soon. What can I do then? Come back to packing Papa's bag?"

She noticed a glow on the windows of the room beside the sleeping porch. "They're lighting up the whole city. Wonder if I oughtn't to go down and see the fun? Wonder if Papa would like to go down? No, Mother wouldn't let him! I want the little old brown shack. Where Stacy could come and play. Mother used to give him cookies then.

"I wish I had the nerve to set the place afire. If I were a big fighting soul I would. But I'm a worm. Am I being bad to think this way? Guess so—committed mental arson, but hadn't the nerve— My God, the house *is* afire!"

She was too frightened to move. She could smell smoke, hear a noise like the folding of stiff wrapping paper. Instantly, apparently without ever having got out of bed, she was running by a bedroom into which flames were licking from the clothes chute that led to the basement. "That dratted old furnace!" She was bursting into her parents' room, hysterically shaking her mother.

"Get up! Get up!"

With a drowsy dignity her mother was saying, "Yes— I know—peace—get paper morning—let me sleep."

"It's fire! Fire! The house is afire!"

Her mother sat up, a thick gray lock bobbing in front of one eye, and said indignantly, "How perfectly preposterous!"

Already Mr. Duke was out of bed, in smoke-prickly darkness, flapping his hands in the air. "Never could find that globe. Ought to have bedside light. Come, Mother, jump up! Theo, have you got on a warm bathrobe?" He was cool. His voice trembled, but only with nervousness.

He charged down the back hall, Theo just behind. Mrs. Duke remained at the head of the front stairs, lamenting, "Don't leave me!"

The flames were darting hissing heads into the hall. As Theo looked they caught a box couch and ran over an old chest of drawers. The heat seemed to slap her face.

"Can't do anything. Get out of this. Wake the servants. You take your mother down," grumbled Mr. Duke.

Theo had her mother into a loose gown, shoes, and a huge fleecy couch cover, and down on the front porch by the time Mr. Duke appeared driving the maids—Lizzie a gorgon in curl papers.

"Huh! Back stairs all afire," he grunted, rubbing his chin. His fingers, rubbing then stopping, showed that for a split second he was thinking, "I need a shave."

"Theo! Run down to the corner. Turn in alarm. I'll try to phone. Then save things," he commanded.

Moved by his coolness to a new passion of love Theo flung her arm, bare as the sleeve of her bathrobe fell from it, about his seamed neck, beseeching: "Don't save anything but the cloisonné. Let 'em burn. Won't have to go in there, risk your life for things. Here—let me phone!"

Unreasoning she slammed the front door, bolted him out. She shouted their address and "Fire—hustle alarm!" at the telephone operator. In the largest drawing room she snatched bit after bit of cloisonné from the cabinet and dumped them into a wastebasket. Now the lower hall, at her back, was boiling with flame-tortured smoke. The noise expanded from crackling to a roar.

The window on the porch was smashed. Her father's arm was reaching up to the catch, unlocking the window. He was crawling in. As the smoke encircled him he puffed like a man blowing out water after a dive.

Theo ran to him. "I didn't want you here! I have the cloisonné——"

As calmly as though he were arguing a point at cards he mumbled, "Yes, yes, yes! Don't bother me. You forgot the two big *saras* in the wall safe."

While the paint on the balusters in the hall bubbled and charred, and the heat was a pang in her lungs, he twirled the knob of the safe behind the big picture and drew out two cloisonné plates. Flames curled round the door jamb of the room like fingers closing on a stick.

"We're shut off!" Theo cried.

"Yep. Better get out. Here. Drop that basket!"

Mr. Duke snatched the cloisonné from her, dropped it, hurled away his two plates, shoved her to the window he had opened, helped her out on the porch. He himself was still in the burning room. She gripped his arm when he tried to dart back. The cloisonné was already hidden from them by puffs of smoke.

Mr. Duke glanced back. He eluded her; pulled his arm free; disappeared in the smoke. He came back with a cheap china vase that for a thing so small was monumentally ugly. As he swung out of the window he said, "Your mother always thought a lot of that vase." Theo saw through eyes stinging with smoke that his hair had been scorched.

Fire engines were importantly unloading at the corner, firemen running up. A neighbor came to herd the Dukes into her house, and into more clothes.

Alone, from the room given to her by the neighbor, Theo watched her home burn. The flames were leering out of all the windows on the ground floor. Her father would never read the three-volume history that was too valuable for soldiers. Now the attic was glaring. Gone the elephant of a London traveling bag. Woolly smoke curled out of the kitchen windows as a fireman smashed them. Gone the fireless cooker that would not cook. She laughed. "It's nicely cooked itself! Oh, I'm beastly. Poor Mother. All her beautiful marked linen——"

But she did not lose a sensation of running ungirdled, of breathing Maytime air.

Her father came in, dressed in the neighbor-host's corduroy hunting coat, a pair of black dress trousers and red slippers. His hair was conscientiously combed, but his fingers still querulously examined the state of his unshaven chin.

She begged: "Daddy dear, it's pretty bad, but don't worry. We have plenty of money. We'll make arrangements——"

He took her arms from about his neck, walked to the window. The broken skeleton of their home was tombed in darkness as the firemen controlled the flames. He looked at Theo in a puzzled way.

He said hesitatingly: "No, I won't worry. I guess it's all right. You see—I set the house afire."

She was silent, but her trembling fingers sought her lips as he went on: "Shoveled hot coals from the furnace into kindling bin in the basement. Huh! Yes. Used to be good furnace tender when I was a real man. Peace bells had woke me up. Wanted to be free. Hate destruction, but—no other way. Your mother wouldn't let me sell the house. I was going mad, sticking there, waiting— waiting for death. Now your mother will be willing to come. Get a farm. Travel. And I been watching you. You couldn't have had Stacy Lindstrom, long as that house bossed us. You almost caught me, in the hall, coming back from the basement. It was kind of hard, with house afire, to lie there in bed, quiet, so's your mother wouldn't ever know—waiting for you to come wake us up. You almost didn't, in time. Would have had to confess. Uh, let's go comfort your mother. She's crying."

Theo had moved away from him. "But it's criminal! We're stealing—robbing the insurance company."

The wrinkles beside his eyes opened with laughter.

"No. Watched out for that. I was careful to be careless, and let all the insurance run out last month. Huh! Maybe I won't catch it from your mother for that, though! Girl! Look! It's dawn!"

THE KIDNAPED MEMORIAL

WAKAMIN is a town with a soul. It used to have a sentimental soul which got thrills out of neighborliness and "The Star-Spangled Banner," but now it wavers between two generations, with none of the strong, silly ambition of either. The pioneering generation has died out, and of the young men, a hundred have gone to that new pioneering in France. Along the way they will behold the world, see the goodness and eagerness of it, and not greatly desire to come back to the straggly ungenerous streets of Wakamin.

Those who are left, lords of the dead soul of Wakamin, go to the movies and play tight little games of bridge and aspire only to own an automobile, because a car is the sign of respectability.

Mr. Gale felt the savorlessness of the town within ten minutes after he had arrived. He had come north to wind up the estate of his cousin, the late proprietor of the Wakamin Creamery. Mr. Gale was from the pine belt of Alabama but he did not resemble the stage Southerner. There was a look of resoluteness and industry about his broad red jaw. He spoke English very much like a man from New York or San Francisco. He did not say "Yessuh," nor "Ah declah"; he had neither a large white hat nor a small white imperial; he was neither a Colonel nor a Judge. He was Mr. Gale, and he practiced law, and he preferred lemonade to mint juleps. But he had fought clear through the War for the Southern Confederacy; and once, on a gray wrinkled morning before a cavalry battle, he had spoken to Jeb Stuart.

While he was settling up the estate, Mr. Gale tried out the conversational qualities of the editor and the justice of the peace, and gave up his attempt to get acquainted with the Wakamites — except for Mrs. Tiffany, at whose house he went to board. Mrs. Captain Tiffany was daughter and widow of Territorial Pioneers.

Pictorial Review, June 1919
Collected in *Selected Short Stories of Sinclair Lewis* (1937)

She herself had teamed-it from St. Paul, with her young husband, after the War. The late Captain Tiffany had been the last commander of the Wakamin G.A.R. Post, and Mrs. Tiffany had for years been president of the Women's Relief Corps. After the barniness of the Wakamin Hotel Mr. Gale was at home in her cottage, which was as precise and nearly as small as the whitewashed conch shell at the gate. He recovered from the forlorn loneliness that had obsessed him during walks on these long, cold, blue twilights of spring. Nightly he sat on the porch with Mrs. Tiffany, and agreed with her about politics, corn-raising, religion, and recipes for hot biscuits.

When he was standing at the gate one evening of April, a small boy sidled across the street, made believe that he was not making-believe soldiers, rubbed one shin with the other foot, looked into the matter of an electric-light bug that was sprawling on its foolish back, violently chased nothing at all, walked backward a few paces, and came up to Mr. Gale with an explosive, "Hello!"

"Evening, sir."

"You staying with Mrs. Tiffany?"

"Yes, for a while."

"Where do you come from?"

"I'm from Alabama."

"Alabama? Why, gee, then you're a Southerner!"

"I reckon I am, old man."

The small boy looked him all over, dug his toe into the leaf-mold at the edge of the curb, whistled, and burst out, "Aw, gee, you aren't either! You don't wear gray, and you haven't got any darky body servant. I seen lots of Confederuts in the movies, and they always wear gray, and most always they got a body servant, and a big sword with a tossel on it. Have you got a sword with a tossel?"

"No, but I've got a suit of butternuts back home."

"Gee, have you? Say, were you ever a raider?"

"No, but I know lots about raiders, and once I had dinner with Colonel Mosby."

"Gee, did you? Say, what's your name? Say, are you a gen'rul?"

"No, I was a high private. My name is Gale. What is your name, if I may ask you, as one man to another?"

"I'm Jimmy Martin. I live across the street. My dad's got a great big phonograph and seventy records. Were you a high private? How high? Gee, tell me about the raiders!"

"But James, why should a loyal Northerner like you desire to know anything about the rebel horde?"

"Well, you see, I'm the leader of the Boy Scouts, and we haven't any Scout Master, at least we did have, but he moved away, and I have to think up games for the Scouts, and gee, we're awfully tired of discovering the North Pole, and being Red Cross in Belgium, and I always have to be the Eskimos when we discover the North Pole, or they won't play, and I thought maybe we could be raiders and capture a Yankee train."

"Well, you come sit on the porch, James. It occurs to me that you are a new audience for my stories. Let us proceed to defend Richmond, and do a quick dash into Illinois, to our common benefit. Is it a bargain?"

It was, and Jimmy listened, and Mrs. Tiffany came out and listened also and the three lovers of the Heroic Age sat glowing at one another till from across the village street, long and thin and drowsy, came the call, "Jim-m-m-ee Mar-r-r-tin!"

Later, Jimmy's mother was surprised to discover her heir leading a Confederate raid, and she was satisfied only when she was assured that the raid was perfectly proper, because it was led by General Grant, and because all the raiders had voluntarily set free their slaves.

It was Jimmy Martin who enticed Mr. Gale to go spearing pickerel, and they two, the big slow-moving man and the boy who took two skips to his one solid pace, plowed through the willow thickets along the creek all one Saturday afternoon.

At the end of the trip, Jimmy cheerfully announced that he would probably get a whale of a licking, because he ought to have been chopping stovewood. Mr. Gale suggested strategic measures; he sneaked after Jimmy, through a stable door to the Martins' woodshed, and cut wood for an hour, while Jimmy scrabbled to pile it.

In the confidences of Jimmy and in Mrs. Tiffany's stories of her Vermont girlhood and pioneer days in Minnesota, Mr. Gale found those green memories of youth which he had hoped to discover, on coming North, in comradely talks with veterans of the Wakamin G.A.R.

But now there was no G.A.R. at all in Wakamin.

During the past year the local post had been wiped out. Of the four veterans remaining on Decoration Day a year before, three had died and one had gone West to live with his son, as is the Mid-Western way. Of the sturdy old men who had marched fifty strong to Woodlawn Cemetery a decade before, not one old man was left to leaven the land.

But they did live on in Mrs. Tiffany's gossip, as she begged Mr. Gale to assure her that there would be a decorating of the graves, though the comrades were gone. This assurance Mr. Gale always gave, though upon sedulous inquiry at the barber shop he discovered that there was very little chance for a celebration of the Day. The town band had broken up when the barber, who was also the band-leader, had bought a car. The school principal had decided that this year it was not worth while to train the girls to wear red-white-and-blue cheesecloth, and sing "Columbia, the Gem of the Ocean" from a decked-over hay wagon.

Mr. Gale endeavored to approve this passing of Decoration Day. He told himself that he was glad to hear that all of his old enemies had gone. But no matter how often he said it, he couldn't make it stick. He felt that he, too, was a derelict, as he listened to Mrs. Tiffany's timid hopes for a celebration. To her, the Day was the climax of the year, the time when all her comrades, living and dead, drew closer together. She had a dazed faith that there would be some sort of ceremony.

She went on retrimming the blue bonnet which she had always worn in the parade, at the head of the W.R.C. Not till the day before the holiday did she learn the truth. That evening she did not come down to supper. She called in a neighbor's daughter to serve Mr. Gale. The young woman giggled, and asked idiotic questions about Society Folks in the South, till Mr. Gale made his iron-gray eyebrows a line of defense. He tramped out the road eastward from town, after supper, growling to himself between periods of vacuous unhappiness:

"Feel's if it's me and the boys I fought with, not them I fought against, they're going to neglect tomorrow. Those Yanks were lively youngsters. Made me do some tall jumping. Hate to think of 'em lying there in the cemetery, lonely and waiting, trusting that we—that the Dam-yanks—will remember them. Look here, J. Gale, Esq., you sentimental old has-been, what do you mean, whimpering about them? You know good and well you never did like Yanks—killed your daddy and brother. But—poor old codgers, waiting out there——"

His walk had brought him to a fenced field. He peered across. It was set with upright and ghostly stones. He had come to the cemetery. He stopped, prickly. He heard creepy murmurs in the dusk. He saw each white stone as the reproachful spirit of an old soldier robbed of his pension of honor. He turned away with a measured calmness that was more panicky than a stumbling retreat.

The morning of the empty Decoration Day was radiant as sunshine upon a beech trunk. But nowhere was the old-time bustle of schoolgirls in bunting, of mothers preparing lunch baskets, of shabby and halting old civilians magically transformed into soldiers. A few families mechanically hung out flags. Mrs. Tiffany did not. When Mr. Gale came down to breakfast he found her caressing an ancient silken flag. She thrust it into a closet, locked the door, hastened out to the kitchen. She was slow in the serving of breakfast, looked dizzy, often pressed her hand against her side. Mr. Gale begged her to let him help. She forbade him sternly. She seemed to have a calm and embittered control of herself.

He hastened out of the house. There was no business to which he could attend on this holiday. He made shameless overtures for the company of Jimmy Martin, who was boisterous over the fact that summer vacation had begun, and his dear, dear teachers gone away. The Martin family was not going to any of the three or four picnics planned for the day, and Jimmy and Mr. Gale considered gravely the possibility of a fishing trip. They sat in canvas chairs on the tiny lawn, and forgot a certain difference in age.

The door of the Tiffany house slammed. They stopped, listened. Nervous footsteps were crossing the porch, coming along the gravel walk. They looked back. Running toward them was Mrs. Tiffany. She wore no hat. Her hair was like a shell-torn flag, thin gray over the yellowed skin of her brow. Her hands dabbled feebly in the air before her glaring eyes. She moaned:

"Oh, Mr. Gale, I can't stand it! Don't they know what they're doing? My boy lies there, my husband, and he's crying for me to come to him and show I remember him. I tell you I can hear him, and his voice sounds like a rainy wind. I told him I'd go to Woodlawn all by myself, I said I'd fill my little basket with flowers, and crabapple blossoms, but he said he wanted the others to come too, he wanted a Decoration Day parade that would honor all the graves. Oh, I heard him———"

Mr. Gale had sprung up. He put his arm about her shoulder. He cried, "There will be a parade, ma'am! We'll remember the boys, every one of them, every grave. You go in the house, honey, and you put on your bonnet, and pack a little sack for you and me to eat after the ceremony, maybe you'll have time to bake a batch of biscuits, but anyway, in an hour or so, maybe hour and a half, you'll hear the parade coming, and you be all ready." Mr. Gale's voice had something of the ponderous integrity of distant cannon. He smoothed her disordered hair. He patted her, like the soft pawing of a fond old dog, and led her to the paint-blistered door of the house.

He went back to his canvas chair, scratching his scalp, shaking his head. Jimmy, who had edged away, returned and sighed, "Gee, I wisht I could do something."

"I bet you would, if you were a little older, James, but—better run away. This old Rebel has got to stir up his sleepy brain and conjure up a Federal parade, with a band and at least twenty flags, out of the sparrows in the street. Good-by."

After five minutes, or it may have been ten, of clawing at his chin, Mr. Gale looked happy. He hastened down the street. He entered the drug store, and from the telephone booth he talked to hotel clerks in three different towns within ten miles of Wakamin.

He hurried to the livery stable which operated the two cars in town that were for hire. One of the cars was out. The second was preparing to leave, as he lumbered up to the door.

"I want that car," he said to the stableman-chauffeur.

"Well, you can't have it." The stableman bent over, to crank up.

"Why not?"

"Because I'm going to take a skirt out for a spin, see?"

"Look here. I'm Mr. Gale who——"

"Aw, I know all about you. Seen you go by. You out-of-town guys think we have to drop everything else just to accommodate you——"

Mr. Gale puffed across the floor like a steam-roller. He said gently, "Son, I've been up all night, and I reckon I've had a lee-tle mite too much liquor. I've taken a fancy to going riding. Son, I've got the peacefulest heart that a grown-up human ever had; I'm like a little playing pussy-cat, I am; but I've got a gun in my back pocket that carries the meanest .44–40 bullet in the South. Maybe you've heard about us Southern fire-eaters, heh? Son, I only want that car for maybe two hours. Understand?"

He bellowed. He was making vast, vague, loosely swinging gestures, his perspiring hands very red. He caught the stableman by the shoulder. The man's Adam's apple worked grotesquely up and down. He whimpered:

"All right. I'll take you."

Mr. Gale pacifically climbed into the car. "Joralemon, son, and fast, son, particular fast," he murmured.

In the speeding car he meditated: "Let's see. Must be forty years since I've toted any kind of a gun—and twenty years since I've called anybody 'son.' Oh, well."

Again, "Let's see. I'll be a Major. No, a Colonel; Colonel Gale of the Tenth New York. Private Gale, I congratulate you. I reckon the best you ever got from a darky was 'Cap'n' or 'boss.' You're rising in the world, my boy. Poor woman! Poor, faithful woman——"

When they reached the town of Joralemon, Mr. Gale leaned out from the car and inquired of a corner loafer, "Where's the Decoration Day parade? The G.A.R.?"

"At the exercises in Greenwood Cemetery."

"Greenwood, son," he blared, and the stableman made haste.

At the entrance to the cemetery Mr. Gale insinuated, "Now wait till I come back, son. I'm getting over that liquor, and I'm ugly, son, powerful ugly."

"All right," growled the stableman. "Say, do I get paid——?"

"Here's five dollars. When I come back with my friends, there'll be another five. I'm going to steal a whole Decoration Day parade."

"How?"

"I'm going to surround them."

"My—Gawd!" whispered the stableman.

The Southerner bristled at the sight of the Northern regimental flag among the trees of the cemetery. But he shrugged his shoulders and waddled into the crowd. The morning's radiance brought out in hot primary colors the red and yellow of flowers in muddy glass vases upon the graves. Light flashed from the mirrory brown surfaces of polished granite headstones, with inscriptions cut in painfully white letters. The air was thick with the scent of dust and maple leaves and packed people. Round a clergyman in canonicals were the eight veterans now left in Joralemon; men to whose scrawny faces a dignity was given by their symbolic garb.

From their eyes was purged all the meanness of daily grinding. The hand of a sparse-bearded Yankee, who wore an English flag pinned beside his G.A.R. button, was resting on the shoulder of a Teutonic-faced man with the emblem of the Signal Corps.

Round the G.A.R. were ringed the Sons of Veterans, the Hose and Truck Company, the Women's Relief Corps, and the Joralemon Band; beyond them a great press of townspeople. The road beside the cemetery was packed with cars and buggies, and the stamp of horses' feet as they restlessly swished at flies gave a rustic rhythm to the pause in the clergyman's voice.

Here in a quiet town, unconscious of the stir of the world beyond, was renewed the passion of their faith in the Union.

Mr. Gale shoved forward into the front row. Everyone glared at the pushing stranger. The voice of the gray, sunken-templed clergyman sharpened with indignation for a second. Mr. Gale tried to look unconcerned. But he felt hot about the spine. The dust got into his throat. The people about him were elbowing and sticky. He was not happy. But he vowed, "By thunder, I'll pull this off if I have to kidnap the whole crowd."

As the clergyman finished his oration, Mr. Gale pushed among the G.A.R. He began loudly, cheerfully, "Gentlemen——"

The clergyman stared down from his box rostrum. "What do you mean, interrupting this ceremony?"

The crowd was squeezing in, like a street mob about a man found murdered. Their voices united in a swelling whisper. Their gaping mouths were ugly. Mr. Gale was rigid with the anger that wipes out all fear of a crowd, and leaves a man facing them as though they were one contemptible opponent.

"Look here," he bawled, "I had proposed to join you in certain memorial plans. It may interest you to know that I am Colonel John Gale, and that I led the Tenth New York through most of the war!"

"Ah," purred the clergyman, "you are Colonel — Gale, is it?"

"I am." The clergyman licked his lips. With fictitious jocularity Mr. Gale said, "I see you do not salute your superior officer. But I reckon a dominie isn't like us old soldiers. Now, boys, listen to me. There's a little woman——"

The clergyman's voice cut in on this lumbering amiability as a knife cuts butter: "My dear sir, I don't quite understand the reason for this farce. I am a 'dominie,' as you are pleased to call it, but also I am an old soldier, the present commander of this post, and it may 'interest you to know' that I fought clear through the war in the Tenth New York! And if my memory is still good, you were not my commanding officer for any considerable period!"

"No!" bellowed Mr. Gale, "I wa'n't! I'm a Southerner. From Alabama. And after today I'm not even sure I'm reconstructed! I'm powerful glad I never was a blue-bellied Yank, when I think of that poor little woman dying of a broken heart up in Wakamin!"

With banal phrases and sentimental touches, with simple words and no further effort to be friendly, he told the story of Mrs. Captain Tiffany, though he did not satisfy the beggar ears of the crowd with her name.

His voice was at times almost hostile. "So," he wound up, "I want you-all to come to Wakamin and decorate the graves there, too. You, my dear sir, I don't care a damaged Continental whether you ever salute me or not. If you boys do come to Wakamin, then I'll know there's still some *men,* as there were in the '60's. But if you eight or nine great big husky young Yanks are afraid of one poor old lone Johnny Reb, then by God, sir, I win another scrimmage for the Confederate States of America!"

Silence. Big and red, Mr. Gale stood among them like a sandstone boulder. His eyes were steady and hard as his clenched fist. But his upper lip was trembling and covered with a triple row of sweat drops.

Slowly, as in the fumbling stupor of a trance, the clergyman drew off his canonicals and handed them to a boy. He was formal and thin and rather dry of aspect in his black frock coat. His voice was that of a tired, polite old gentleman, as he demanded of Mr. Gale, "Have you a car to take us to Wakamin?"

"Room for five."

To a man beside him the clergyman said, "Will you have another car ready for us?" Abruptly his voice snapped: "'Tention. Fall in. Form twos. B' th' right flank. For'ard. March!"

As he spoke he leaped down into the ranks, and the veterans tramped toward the gate of the cemetery, through the parting crowd. Their faces were blurred with weariness and dust and age, but they stared straight ahead, they marched stolidly, as though they had been ordered to occupy a dangerous position and were too fagged to be afraid.

The two rear-line men struck up with fife and drum. The fifer was a corpulent banker, but he tootled with the agility of a boy. The drummer was a wisp of humanity. Though his clay-hued hands kept up with the capering of "When Johnny Comes Marching Home Again," his yellowish eyes were opening in an agonized stare, and his chin trembled.

"Halt!" the clergyman ordered. "Boys, seems to me the commander of this expedition ought to be Colonel Gale. Colonel, will you please take command of the post?"

"W—why, I wouldn't hardly call it regular."

"You old Rebel, I wouldn't call any of this regular!"

"Yes," said Mr. Gale. "'Tention!"

The old drummer, his eyes opening wider and wider, sank forward from the knees, and held himself up only by trembling bent arms. Two men in the crowd caught him. "Go on!" he groaned. His drumsticks clattered on the ground.

Uneasily exchanging glances, the other old men waited. Each face said, "Risky business. Hot day. We might collapse, too."

The clergyman slipped the drum belt over his own head, picked up the sticks. "Play, confound you, Lanse!" he snapped at the pompous banker-fifer, and together they rolled into a rude version of "Marching Through Georgia."

The squad straightened its lines and marched on without even an order from Mr. Gale, who, at the head of the procession, was marveling, "I never did expect to march to that tune!"

The two motor cars shot from Joralemon to Wakamin, with steering wheels wrenching and bucking on the sandy road, and old men clinging to seat-edge and robe-rack. They stopped before the Tiffany cottage.

Mrs. Tiffany sat on the porch, her blue bonnet lashed to her faded hair, with a brown veil, a basket of flowers and a shoe-box of lunch on her knees. As the cars drew up, she rushed out, with flustered greetings. The old men greeted her elaborately. One, who had known Captain Tiffany, became the noisy spokesman. But he had little of which to speak. And the whole affair suddenly became a vacuous absurdity. Now that Mr. Gale had them here, what was he going to do with them?

The quiet of the village street flowed over them. This was no parade; it was merely nine old men and an old woman talking in the dust. There was no music, no crowd of spectators, none of the incitements of display which turn the ordinary daily sort of men into one marching thrill. They were old, and tired, and somewhat hungry, and no one saw them as heroes. A small automobile passed; the occupants scarce looked at them.

The unparading parade looked awkward, tried to keep up brisk talk, and became dull in the attempt.

They were engulfed in the indifferent calm of the day. After the passing of the one automobile, there was no one to be seen. The box-elder trees nodded slowly. Far off a rooster crowed, once. In a vacant lot near by a cud-chewing cow stared at them dumb and bored. Little sounds of insects in the grass underlaid the silence with a creeping sleepiness. The village street, stretching out toward the wheat fields beyond, grew hotter and more hazy to their old eyes. They all stood about the cars, plucking at hinges and door-edges, wondering how they could give up this childish attempt and admit that they were grannies. A sparrow hopped among them unconcernedly.

"Well?" said the clergyman.

"Wel–l——" said Mr. Gale.

Then Jimmy Martin strolled out in front of his house.

He saw them. He stopped short. He made three jubilant skips, and charged on them.

"Are you going to parade?" he shrilled at Mr. Gale.

"Afraid not, Jimmy. Reckon we haven't quite got the makings. The young people don't appear to care. Reckon we'll give up."

"No, no, no!" Jimmy wailed. "The Scouts want to come!"

He dashed into his house, while the collapsed parade stared after him with mild elderly wonder. He came back to the gate. He wore a Boy Scout uniform and a red neckerchief, and he carried a cheap bugle.

He stood at the gate, his eyes a glory, and he blew the one bugle call he knew—the Reveille. Wavering at first, harsh and timorous, the notes crept among the slumberous trees, then swelled, loud, madly imploring, shaking with a boy's worship of the heroes.

Another boy ran out from a gate down the street, looked, came running, stumbling, panting. He was bare headed, in corduroy knickers unbuckled at the knees, but in his face was the same age-less devotion that had made a splendor of the mere boys who marched out in '64 and '65. He saluted Jimmy. Jimmy spoke, and the two of them, curiously dignified, very earnest, marched out before the scatter of old people and stood at attention, their serious faces toward Woodlawn and the undecked graves.

From a box-elder down the street climbed another boy; one popped out of a crabapple orchard; a dozen others from drowsy distances. They scurried like suddenly disturbed ants. They could be heard calling, clattering into houses.

They came out again in Scout uniforms; they raced down the street and fell into line.

They stood with clean backs rigid, eyes forward, waiting to obey orders. As he looked at them, Mr. Gale knew that some day Wakamin would again have a soul.

Jimmy Martin came marching up to Mr. Gale. His voice was plaintive and reedy, but it was electric as he reported: "The Boy Scouts are ready, sir."

"'Tention!" shouted Mr. Gale.

The old men's backs had been straightening, the rheumy redness of disappointment had gone from their eyes. They lined out behind the boys. Even the Wakamin stableman seemed to feel inspiration. He sprang from his car, helped Mrs. Tiffany in, and wheeled the car to join the procession. From nowhere, from everywhere, a crowd had come, and stood on the sidewalk, rustling with faint cheering. Two women hastened to add flowers to those in Mrs. Tiffany's basket. The benumbed town had awakened to energy and eagerness and hope.

To the clergyman Mr. Gale suggested, "Do you suppose that just for once this Yankee fife-and-drum corps could play 'Dixie'?" Instantly the clergyman-drummer and the banker-fifer flashed into "Way Down South in the Land of Cotton." The color-bearer raised the flag.

Mr. Gale roared, "Forward! M——"

There was a high wail from Mrs. Tiffany: "Wait! Land o' goodness! What's Decoration Day without one single sword, and you menfolks never thinking——"

She ran into her house. She came out bearing in her two hands, as though it were an altar vessel, the saber of Captain Tiffany.

"Mr. Gale, will you carry a Northerner's sword?" she asked.

"No, ma'am, I won't!"

She gasped.

He buckled on the sword belt, and cried, "This isn't a Northerner's sword any more, nor a Southerner's, ma'am. It's an American's! Forward! March!"

A MATTER OF BUSINESS

CANDEE'S SLEEPING PORCH faced the east. At sunrise every morning he startled awake and became a poet.

He yawned, pulled up the gray camping blanket which proved that he had gone hunting in Canada, poked both hands behind his neck, settled down with a wriggling motion, and was exceedingly melancholy and happy.

He resolved, seriously and all at once, to study music, to wear a rose down to business, to tell the truth in his advertisements, and to start a campaign for a municipal auditorium. He longed to be out of bed and go change the entire world immediately. But always, as sunrise blurred into russet, he plunged his arms under the blanket, sighed, "Funny what stuff a fellow will think of at six G.M.," yawned horribly, and was asleep. Two hours afterward, when he sat on the edge of the bed, rubbing his jaw in the hope that he could sneak out of shaving this morning, letting his feet ramble around independently in search of his slippers, he was not a poet. He was Mr. Candee of the Novelty Stationery Shop, Vernon.

He sold writing paper, Easter cards, bronze bookends, framed color prints. He was a salesman born. To him it was exhilaration to herd a hesitating customer; it was pride to see his clerks, Miss Cogerty and the new girl, imitate his courtesy, his quickness. He was conscious of beauty. Ten times a week he stopped to gloat over a print in which a hilltop and a flare of daisies expressed the indolence of August. But—and this was equally a part of him—he was delighted by "putting things over." He was as likely to speculate in a broken lot of china dogs as to select a stock of chaste brass knockers. It was he who had popularized Whistler in Vernon, and he who had brought out the "Oh My! Bathing Girls" pictures.

He was a soldier of fortune, was Candee; he fought under any

Harper's Magazine, March 1921
Collected in *If I Were Boss* (1997)

flag which gave him the excuse. He was as much an adventurer as though he sat on a rampart wearing a steel corselet instead of sitting at a golden-oak desk wearing a blue-serge suit.

Every Sunday afternoon the Candees drove out to the golf club. They came home by a new route this Sunday.

"I feel powerful. Let's do some exploring," said Candee.

He turned the car off the Boulevard, down one of the nameless hilly roads which twist along the edge of every city. He came into a straggly country of market gardens, jungles of dead weeds, unpruned crabapple trees, and tall, thin houses which started as artificial-stone mansions and ended as unpainted frame shacks. In front of a tarpaper shanty there was a wild-grape arbor of thick vines draped upon secondhand scantlings and cracked pieces of molding. The yard had probably never been raked, but it displayed petunias in a tub salvaged from a patent washing machine. On a shelf beside the gate was a glass case with a sign:

ToYs for thee chilrun.

Candee stopped the car.

In the case were half a dozen wooden dolls with pegged joints — an old-man doll with pointed hat, jutting black beard, and lumpy, out-thrust hands; a Pierrot with a prim wooden cockade; a princess fantastically tall and lean.

"Huh! Handmade! Arts-and-grafts stuff!" said Candee, righteously.

"That's so," said Mrs. Candee.

He drove on.

"Freak stuff. Abs'lutely grotesque. Not like anything I ever saw!"

"That's so," said Mrs. Candee.

He was silent. He irritably worked the air-choke, and when he found it was loose he said, "Damn!" As for Mrs. Candee, she said nothing at all. She merely looked like a wife.

He turned toward her argumentatively. "Strikes me those dolls were darn ugly. Some old nut of a hermit must have made 'em. They were—they were ugly! Eh?"

"That's so," said Mrs. Candee.

"Don't you think they were ugly?"

"Yes, I think that's so," said Mrs. Candee, as she settled down to meditate upon the new laundress who was coming tomorrow.

Next morning Candee rushed into his shop, omitted the report on his Sunday golf and the progress of his game which he usually gave to Miss Cogerty, and dashed at the shelf of toys. He had never thought about toys as he had about personal Christmas cards or diaries. His only specialty for children was expensive juveniles.

He glowered at the shelf. It was disordered. It was characterless. There were one rabbit of gray Canton flannel, two rabbits of papier-mâché, and nine tubercular rabbits of white fur. There were sixteen dolls which simpered and looked unintelligent. There were one train, one fire engine, and a device for hoisting thimblefuls of sand upon a trestle. Not that you did anything when you had hoisted it.

"Huh!" said Candee.

"Yes, Mr. Candee?" said Miss Cogerty.

"Looks like a side-street notions store. Looks like a racket shop. Looks like a—looks like— Aah!" said Candee.

He stormed his desk like a battalion of marines. He was stern. "Got to take up that bum shipment with the Fressen Paper Company. I'll write 'em a letter that'll take their hides off. I won't type it. Make it stronger if I turn the old pen loose."

He vigorously cleared away a pile of fancy penwipers—stopping only to read the advertisement on an insurance blotter, to draw one or two pictures on an envelope, and to rub the enticing pale-blue back of a box of safety matches with a soft pencil till it looked silvery in a cross-light. He snatched his fountain pen out of his vest pocket. He looked at it unrelentingly. He sharpened the end of a match and scraped a clot of ink off the pen cap. He tried the ink supply by making a line of O's on his thumbnail. He straightened up, looked reprovingly at Miss Cogerty's back, slapped a sheet of paper on the desk—then stopped again and read his mail.

It did not take him more than an hour to begin to write the letter he was writing. In grim jet letters he scrawled:

FRESSEN COMPANY:

GENTLEMEN,—*I want you to thoroughly understand*—

Twenty minutes later he had added nothing to the letter but a curlicue on the tail of the "d" in "understand." He was drawing the picture of a wooden doll with a pointed hat and a flaring black beard. His eyes were abstracted and his lips moved furiously:

"Makes me sick. Not such a whale of a big shop, but it's distinctive. Not all this commonplace junk—souvenirs and bum valentines. And yet our toys— Ordinary! Common! Hate to think what people must have been saying about 'em! But those wooden dolls out there in the country—they were ugly, just like Nelly said, but somehow they kind of stirred up the imagination."

He shook his head, rubbed his temples, looked up wearily. He saw that the morning rush had begun. He went out to the shop slowly, but as he crooned at Mrs. Harry McPherson, "I have some new lightweight English envelopes—crossbar lavender with a stunning purple lining," he was imperturbable. He went out to lunch with Harry Jason and told a really new flivver story. He did not cease his bustling again till four, when the shop was for a moment still. Then he leaned against the counter and brooded:

"Those wooden dolls remind me of— Darn it! I don't know what they do remind me of! Like something— Castles. Gypsies. Oh, rats! Brother Candee, I thought you'd grown up! Hey, Miss Cogerty, what trying do? Don't put those Honey Bunny books there!"

At home he hurried through dinner.

"Shall we play a little auction with the Darbins?" Mrs. Candee yawned.

"No. I— Got to mull over some business plans. Think I'll take a drive by myself, unless you or the girls have to use the machine," ventured Candee.

"No. I think I might catch up on my sleep. Oh, Jimmy, the new laundress drinks just as much coffee as the last one did!"

"Yes?" said Candee, looking fixedly at a candle shade and meditating. "I don't know. Funny, all the wild crazy plans I used to have when I was a kid. Suppose those dolls remind me of that."

He dashed out from dinner, hastily started the car. He drove rapidly past the lakes, through dwindling lines of speculative houses, into a world of hazelnut brush and small boys with furtive dogs. His destination was the tarpaper shack in front of which he had seen the wooden dolls.

He stopped with a squawk of brakes, bustled up the path to the wild-grape arbor. In the dimness beneath it, squatting on his heels beside a bicycle, was a man all ivory and ebony, ghost white and outlandish black. His cheeks and veined forehead were pale, his beard was black and thin and square. Only his hands were ruddy. They were brick-red and thick, yet cunning was in them, and the fingers tapered to square ends. He was a medieval monk in overalls, a Hindu indecently without his turban. As Candee charged upon him he looked up and mourned:

"The chain, she rusty."

Now Candee was the friendliest soul in all the Boosters' Club. Squatting, he sympathized:

"Rusty, eh? Ole chain kind of rusty! Hard luck, I'll say. Ought to use graphite on it. That's it—graphite. 'Member when I was a kid——"

"I use graphite. All rusty before I get him," the ghost lamented. His was a deep voice, humorless and grave.

Candee was impressed. "Hard luck! How about boric acid? No,

that isn't it—chloric acid. No, oxalic acid. That's it—oxalic! That'll take off the rust."

"Os-all-ic," murmured the ghost.

"Well, cheer up, old man. Someday you'll be driving your own boat."

"Oh! Say!"—the ghost was childishly proud—"I got a phonograph!"

"Have you? Slick!" Candee became cautious and inquisitive. He rose and, though he actually had not touched the bicycle, he dusted off his hands. Craftily: "Well, I guess you make pretty good money, at that. I was noticing——

"Reason I turned in, I noticed you had some toys out front. Thought I might get one for the kids. What do you charge?" He was resolving belligerently, "I won't pay more than a dollar per."

"I sharge fifty cent."

Candy felt cheated. He had been ready to battle for his rights and it was disconcerting to waste all his energy. The ghost rose, in sections, and ambled toward the glass case of dolls. He was tall, fantastically tall as his own tall emperors, and his blue-denim jacket was thick with garden soil. Beside him Candee was rosy and stubby and distressingly neat. He was also uneasy. Here was a person to whom he couldn't talk naturally.

"So you make dolls, eh? Didn't know there was a toy maker in Vernon."

"No, I am nod a toy maker. I am a sculptor." The ghost was profoundly sad. "But nod de kine you t'ink. I do not make chudges in plog hats to put on courthouses. I would lige to. I would make fine plog hats. But I am not recognize. I make epitaphs in de monooment works. Huh!" The ghost sounded human now, and full of guile. "I am de only man in dose monooment works dat know what 'R.I.P.' mean in de orizhinal Greek."

He leaned against the gate and chuckled. Candee recovered from his feeling of being trapped in a particularly chilly tomb. He crowed:

"I'll bet you are, at that. But you must have a good time making these dolls."

"You lak dem?"

"You bet! I certainly do. I—" His enthusiasm stumbled. In a slightly astonished tone, in a low voice, he marveled, "And I do, too, by golly!" Then: "You— I guess you enjoy making——"

"No, no! It iss not enjoyment. Dey are my art, de dolls. Dey are how I get even wit' de monooment works. I should wish I could make him for a living, but nobody want him. One year now—always dey stand by de gate, waiting, and nobody buy one. Oh, well, I can't help dat! I know what I do, even if nobody else don't. I try to make him primitive, like what a child would make if he was a fine craftsman like me. Dey are all dream dolls. And me, I make him right. See! Nobody can break him!"

He snatched the Gothic princess from the case and banged her on the fence.

Candee came out of a trance of embarrassed unreality and shouted: "Sure are the real stuff. Now, uh, the—uh— May I ask your name?"

"Emile Jumas my name."

Candee snapped his fingers. "Got it, by golly!"

"*Pardon?*"

"The Papa Jumas dolls! That's their name. Look here! Have you got any more of these in the house?"

"Maybe fifty." Jumas had been roused out of his ghostliness.

"Great! Could you make five or six a day, if you didn't do anything else and maybe had a boy to help you?"

"Oh yez. No. Well, maybe four."

"See here. I could—— I have a little place where I think maybe I could sell a few. Course you understand I don't know for sure. Taking a chance. But I think maybe I could. I'm J. T. Candee. Probably you know my stationery shop. I don't want to boast, but I will say there's no place in town that touches it for class. But I don't mean I could afford to pay you any fortune.

But"—all his caution collapsed—"Jumas, I'm going to put you across!"

The two men shook hands a number of times and made sounds of enthusiasm, sounds like the rubbing of clothes on a washboard. But Jumas was stately in his invitation:

"Will you be so good and step in to have a leetle homemade wine?"

It was one room, his house, with a loft above, but it contained a harp, a double bed, a stove, a hen that was doubtful of strangers, a substantial Mamma Jumas, six children, and forty-two wooden dolls.

"Would you like to give up the monument works and stick to making these?" glowed Candee, as he handled the dolls.

Jumas mooned at him. "Oh, yez."

Ten minutes later, at the gate, Candee sputtered: "By golly! by golly! Certainly am pitching wild tonight. Not safe to be out alone. For first time in my life forgot to mention prices. Crazy as a kid—and I like it!" But he tried to sound managerial as he returned. "What do you think I ought to pay you apiece?"

Craftily Papa Jumas piped: "I t'ink you sell him for more than fifty cent. I t'ink maybe I ought to get fifty."

Then, while the proprietor of the Novelty Stationery Shop wrung spiritual hands and begged him to be careful, Candee the adventurer cried: "Do you know what I'm going to do? I'm going to sell 'em at three dollars, and I'm going to make every swell on the Boulevard buy one, and I'm going to make 'em pay their three bones, and I'm going to make 'em like it! Yes, sir! And you get two dollars apiece!"

It was not till he was on the sleeping porch, with the virile gray blanket patted down about his neck, that Candee groaned: "What have I let myself in for? And are they ugly or not?" He desired to go in, wake his wife, and ask her opinion. He lay and worried, and when he awoke at dawn and discovered that he hadn't really been tragically awake all night, he was rather indignant.

But he was exhilarated at breakfast and let Junior talk all through his oatmeal.

He came into the shop with a roar. "Miss Cogerty! Get the porter and have him take all those toys down to that racket shop on Jerusalem Alley that bought our candlestick remainders. Go down and get what you can for 'em. We're going to have— Miss Cogerty, we're going to display in this shop a line of arts-and-crafts dolls that for artistic execution and delightful quaintness— Say, that's good stuff for an ad. I'll put a ten-inch announcement in the *Courier.* I'll give this town one jolt. You wait!"

Candee did not forever retain his enthusiasm for Papa Jumas dolls. Nor did they revolutionize the nurseries of Vernon. To be exact, some people liked them and some people did not like them. Enough were sold to keep Jumas occupied, and not enough so that at the great annual crisis of the summer motor boat trip to Michigan, Candee could afford a nickel-plated spotlight as well as slip covers. There was a reasonable holiday sale through the autumn following, and always Candee liked to see them on the shelf at the back of the shop—the medieval dolls like cathedral grotesques, the Greek warrior Demetrios, and the modern dolls—the agitated policeman and the aviator whose arms were wings. Candee and Junior played explorer with them on the sleeping porch, and with them populated a castle made of chairs.

But in the spring he discovered Miss Arnold's batik lamp shades.

Miss Arnold was young, Miss Arnold was pretty, and her lamp shades had many "talking points" for a salesman with enthusiasm. They were terra-cotta and crocus and leaf green; they had flowers, fruits, panels, fish, and whirligigs upon them, and a few original decorations which may have been nothing but spots. Candee knew that they were either artistic or insane; he was excited, and in the first week he sold forty of them and forgot the Papa Jumas dolls.

In late April a new road salesman came in from the Mammoth

Doll Corporation. He took Candee out to lunch and was secretive and oozed hints about making a great deal of money. He admitted at last that the Mammoth people were going to put on the market a doll that "had everything else beat four ways from the ace." He produced a Skillyoolly doll. She was a simpering, star-eyed, fluffy, chiffon-clothed lady doll, and, though she was cheaply made, she was not cheaply priced.

"The Skillyoolly drive is going to be the peppiest campaign you ever saw. There's a double market—not only the kids, but all these Janes that like to stick a doll up on the piano, to make the room dressy when Bill comes calling. And it's got the snap, eh?"

"Why don't you—? The department stores can sell more of these than I can," Candee fenced.

"That's just what we don't want to do. There's several of these fluff dolls on the market—not any of them have the zip of our goods, of course. What we want is exclusive shops, that don't handle any other dolls whatever, so we won't have any inside competition, and so we can charge a class price."

"But I'm already handling some dolls——"

"If I can show you where you can triple your doll turnover, I guess we can take care of that, eh? For one thing, we're willing to make the most generous on-sale proposition you ever hit."

The salesman left with Candee samples of the Skillyoolly dolls, and a blank contract. He would be back in his territory next month, he indicated, and he hoped to close the deal. He gave Candee two cigars and crooned:

"Absolutely all we want is to have you handle the Skillyoolly exclusively and give us a chance to show what we can do. 'You tell 'em, pencil, you got the point!'"

Candee took the dolls home to his wife, and now she was not merely wifely and plump and compliant. She squealed.

"I think they're perfectly darling! So huggable—just sweet. I know you could sell thousands of them a year. You must take them. I always thought the Jumas dolls were hideous."

"They aren't so darn hideous. Just kind of different," Candee said, uncomfortably.

Next morning he had decided to take the Skillyoolly agency — and he was as lonely and unhappy about it as a boy who has determined to run away from home.

Papa Jumas came in that day and Candee tried to be jolly and superior.

"Ah there, old monsieur! Say, I may fix up an arrangement to switch your dolls from my place to the Toy and China Bazaar."

Jumas lamented: "De Bazaar iss a cheap place. I do not t'ink they lige my t'ings."

"Well, we'll see, we'll see. Excuse me now. Got to speak to Miss Cogerty about — about morocco cardcases — cardcases."

He consulted Miss Cogerty and the lovely Miss Arnold of the batik lamp shades about the Skillyoolly dolls. Both of them squealed ecstatically. Yet Candee scowled at a Skillyoolly standing on his desk and addressed her:

"Doll, you're a bunch of fluff. You may put it over these sentimental females for a while, but you're no good. You're a rotten fake, and to charge two plunks for you is the darndest nerve I ever heard of. And yet I might make a thousand a year clear out of you. A thousand a year. Buy quite a few cord tires, curse it!"

At five Miss Sorrell bought some correspondence cards.

Candee was afraid of Miss Sorrell. She was the principal of a private school. He never remembered what she wore, but he had an impression that she was clad entirely in well-starched, four-ply line collars. She was not a person to whom you could sell things. She looked at you sarcastically and told you what she wanted. But the girls in her school were fervid customers, and, though he grumbled, "Here's that old grouch," he concentrated upon her across the showcase.

When she had ordered the correspondence cards and fished the copper address plate out of a relentless seal purse, Miss Sorrell blurted: "I want to tell you how very, very much I appreciate the

Papa Jumas dolls. They are the only toys in Vernon that have imagination and solidity."

"Folks don't care much for them, mostly. They think I ought to carry some of these fluffy dolls."

"Parents may not appreciate them, and I suppose they're so original that children take a little time getting used to them. But my nephew loves his Jumas dolls dearly; he takes them to bed with him. We are your debtors for having introduced them."

As she dotted out, Candee was vowing: "I'm not going to have any of those Skillyoolly hussies in my place! I'm— I'll fight for the Jumas dolls! I'll make people like 'em, if it takes a leg. I don't care if I lose a thousand a year on them, or ten thousand, or ten thousand million tillion!"

It was too lofty to last. He reflected that he didn't like Miss Sorrell. She had a nerve to try to patronize him! He hastened to his desk. He made computations for half an hour. Candee was an irregular and temperamental cost accountant. If his general profit was sufficient he rarely tracked down the share produced by items. Now he found that, allowing for rent, overhead, and interest, his profit on Papa Jumas dolls in the last four months had been four dollars. He gasped:

"Probably could make 'em popular if I took time enough. But—four dollars! And losing a thousand a year by not handling Skillyoollys. I can't afford luxuries like that. I'm not in business for my health. I've got a wife and kids to look out for. Still, I'm making enough to keep fat and cheery on, entirely aside from the dolls. Family don't seem to be starving. I guess I can afford one luxury. I— Oh, rats!"

He reached, in fact, a sure, clear, ringing resolution that he would stock Skillyoolly dolls; that he'd be hanged if he'd stock Skillyoolly dolls; and that he would give nine dollars and forty cents if he knew whether he was going to stock them or not.

After the girls had gone out that evening he hinted to his wife: "I don't really believe I want to give up the Jumas dolls. May cost me a little profit for a while, but I kind of feel obligated to the poor old Frenchie, and the really wise birds—you take this Miss Sorrell, for instance—they appreciate——"

"Then you can't handle the Skillyoolly dolls?"

"Don't use that word! Skillyoolly! Ugh! Sounds like an old maid tickling a baby!"

"Now that's all very well, to be so superior and all—and if you mean that I was an old maid when we were married——"

"Why, Nelly, such a thought nev' entered my head!"

"Well, how could I tell? You're so bound and determined to be arbitrary tonight. It's all very well to be charitable and to think about that Jumas—and I never did like him, horrid, skinny old man!—and about your dolls that you're so proud of, but I do think there's some folks a little nearer home that you got to show consideration for, and us going without things we need——"

"Now I guess you've got about as many clothes as anybody ——"

"See here, Jimmy Candee! I'm not complaining about myself. I like pretty clothes, but I never was one to demand things for myself, and you know it!"

"Yes, that's true. You're sensible——"

"Well, I try to be, anyway, and I detest these wives that simply drive their husbands like they were packhorses, but— It's the girls. Not that they're bad off. But you're like all these other men. You think because a girl has a new dancing frock once a year that she's got everything in the world. And here's Mamie crying her eyes out because she hasn't got anything to wear to the Black Bass dance, and that horrible Jason girl will show up in silver brocade or something, and Mamie thinks Win Morgan won't even look at her. Not but what she can get along. I'm not going to let you work and slave for things to put on Mamie's back. But if you're going to waste a lot of money I certainly don't see why it should go to a perfect stranger—a horrid old Frenchman that digs graves, or whatever it is—when we could use it right here at home!"

"Well, of course, looking at it that way——" sighed Candee. "Do you see?"

"Yes, but there's a principle involved. Don't know that I can make it clear to you, but I wouldn't feel as if I was doing my job honestly if I sold a lot of rubbish."

"Rubbish? Rubbish? If there's any rubbish it isn't those darling Skillyoolly dolls, but those wretched, angular Jumas things! But if you've made up your mind to be stubborn— And of course I'm not supposed to know anything about business! I merely scrimp and save and economize and do the marketing!"

She flapped the pages of her magazine and ignored him. All evening she was patient. It is hard to endure patience, and Candee was shaken. He was fond of his wife. Her refusal to support his shaky desire to "do his job honestly" left him forlorn, outside the door of her comfortable affection.

"Oh, I suppose I better be sensible," he said to himself, seventy or eighty times.

He was taking the Skillyoolly contract out of his desk as a cyclone entered the shop, a cyclone in brown velvet, white hair, and the best hat in Vernon—Mrs. Gerard Randall. Candee went rejoicing to the battle. He was a salesman. He was an artist, a scientist, and the harder the problem the better. Mechanically handing out quires of notepaper to customers who took whatever he suggested bored Candee as it would bore an exhibition aviator to drive a tractor. But selling to Mrs. Randall was not a bore. She was the eternal dowager, the dictator of Vernon society, rich and penurious and overwhelming.

He beamed upon her. He treacherously looked mild. He seemed edified by her snort:

"I want a penholder for my desk that won't look like a beastly schoolroom pen."

"Then you want a quill pen in mauve or a sea-foam green."

Mrs. Randall was going to buy a quill pen, or she was going to die — or he was.

"I certainly do not want a quill pen, either mauve or pea-green or sky-blue beige! Quill pens are an abomination, and they wiggle when you're writing, and they're disgustingly common."

"My pens don't wiggle. They have patent grips——"

"Nonsense!"

"Well, shall we look at some other kinds?"

He placidly laid out an atrocious penholder of mother-of-pearl and streaky brass, which had infested the shop for years.

"Horrible! Victorian! Certainly not!"

He displayed a nickel penholder stamped, "Souvenir of Vernon," a brittle, red wooden holder with a cork grip, and a holder of chased silver, very bulgy and writhing.

"They're terrible!" wailed Mrs. Randall.

She sounded defenseless. He flashed before her eyes the best quill in the shop, crisp, firm, tinted a faint rose.

"Well," she said, feebly. She held it, wobbled it, wrote a sentence in the agitated air. "But it wouldn't go with my desk set," she attempted.

He brought out a desk set of seal-brown enamel and in the bowl of shot he thrust the rose quill.

"How did you remember what my desk set was like?"

"Ah! Could one forget?" He did not look meek now; he looked insulting and cheerful.

"Oh, drat the man! I'll take it. But I don't want you to think for one moment that I'd stand being bullied this way if I weren't in a hurry."

He grinned. He resolved, "I'm going to make the ole dragon buy three Jumas dolls — no, six! Mrs. Randall, I know you're in a rush, but I want you to look at something that will interest you."

"I suppose you're going to tell me that 'we're finding this line very popular,' whatever it is. I don't want it."

"Quite the contrary. I want you to see these because they haven't gone well at all."

"Then why should I be interested?"

"Ah, Mrs. Randall, if Mrs. Randall were interested, everybody else would have to be."

"Stop being sarcastic, if you don't mind. That's my own province." She was glaring at him, but she was following him to the back of the shop.

He chirped: "I believe you buy your toys for your grandchildren at the Bazaar. But I want to show you something they'll really like." He was holding up a Gothic princess, turning her lanky magnificence round and round. As Mrs. Randall made an "aah" sound in her throat, he protested. "Wait! You're wrong. They're not ugly; they're a new kind of beauty."

"Beauty! Arty! Tea-roomy!"

"Not at all. Children love 'em. I'm so dead sure of it that I want— Let's see. You have three grandchildren. I want to send each of them two Papa Jumas dolls. I'll guarantee— No. Wait! I'll guarantee the children won't care for them at first. Don't say anything about the dolls, but just leave 'em around the nursery and watch. Inside of two weeks you'll find the children so crazy about 'em they won't go to bed without 'em. I'll send 'em up to your daughter's house and when you get around to it you can decide whether you want to pay me or not."

"Humph! You are very eloquent. But I can't stand here all day. Ask one of your young women to wrap up four or five of these things and put them in my car. And put them on my bill. I can't be bothered with trying to remember to pay you. Good day!"

While he sat basking at his desk he remembered the words of the schoolmistress, Miss Sorrell, "Only toys in Vernon that have imagination and solidity."

"People like that, with brains, they're the kind. I'm not going to be a popcorn-and-lemonade seller. Skillyoolly dolls! Any ten-year-old boy could introduce those to a lot of sentimental females.

Takes a real salesman to talk Jumas dolls. And— If I could only get Nell to understand!"

Alternately triumphant and melancholy, he put on his hat, trying the effect in the little crooked mirror over the water cooler, and went out to the Boosters' Club weekly lunch.

Sometimes the Boosters' lunches were given over speeches; sometimes they were merry and noisy; and when they were noisy Candee was the noisiest. But he was silent today. He sat at the long table beside Darbin, the ice-cream manufacturer, and when Darbin chuckled invitingly, "Well, you old Bolshevik, what's the latest junk you're robbing folks for?" Candee's answer was feeble.

"That's all right, now! 'S good stuff."

He looked down the line of the Boosters—men engaged in electrotyping and roofing, real estate and cigar making; certified accountants and teachers and city officials. He noted Oscar Sunderquist, the young surgeon.

He considered: "I suppose they're all going through the same thing—quick turnover on junk *versus* building up something permanent, and maybe taking a loss; anyway, taking a chance. Huh! Sounds so darn ridiculously easy when you put it that way. Of course a regular fellow would build up the longtime trade and kick out cheap stuff. Only—not so easy to chase away a thousand or ten thousand dollars when it comes right up and tags you. Oh, gee! I dunno! I wish you'd quit fussing like a schoolgirl, Brother Candee. I'm going to cut it out." By way of illustrating which he turned to his friend Darbin. "Frank, I'm worried. I want some advice. Will it bother you if I weep on your shoulder?"

"Go to it! Shoot! Anything I can do——"

He tried to make clear to Darbin how involved was a choice between Papa Jumas and the scent pots of the Skillyoolly. Darbin interrupted:

"Is that all that ails you? Cat's sake! What the deuce difference does it make which kind of dolls you handle? Of course you'll pick the kind that brings in the most money. I certainly wouldn't worry about the old Frenchman. I always did think those Jumas biznai were kind of freakish."

"Then you don't think it matters?"

"Why, certainly not! Jimmy, you're a good business man, some ways. You're a hustler. But you always were erratic. Business isn't any jazz-band dance. You got to look at these things in a practical way. Say, come on; the president's going to make a spiel. Kid him along and get him going."

"Don't feel much like kidding."

"I'll tell you what I think's the matter with you, Jimmy; your liver's on the bum."

"Maybe you're right," croaked Candee. He did not hear the president's announcement of the coming clam bake. He was muttering in an injured way: "Damn it! Damn it! Damn it!"

He was walking back to the shop.

He didn't want to go back; he didn't care whether Miss Cogerty was selling any of the *écrasé* sewing baskets or not. He was repeating Darbin's disgusted: "What difference does it make? Why all the fuss?"

"At most I'd lose a thousand a year. I wouldn't starve. This little decision — nobody cares a hang. I was a fool to speak to Nelly and Darbin. Now they'll be watching me. Well, I'm not going to be an erratic fool. Ten words of approval from a crank like that Sorrell woman is a pretty thin return for years of work. Yes, I'll be sensible."

He spent the later afternoon in furiously rearranging the table of vases and candlesticks. "Exercise, that's what I need, not all this grousing around," he said. But when he went home he had, without ever officially admitting it to himself that he was doing it, thrust a Jumas doll and a Skillyoolly into his pocket, and these, in the absence of his wife, he hid beneath his bed on the sleeping porch. With his wife he had a strenuous and entirely imaginary conversation:

"Why did I bring them home? Because I wanted to. I don't see any need of explaining my motives. I don't intend to argue about this in any way, shape, or form!" He looked at himself in the mirror, with admiration for the firmness, strength of character, iron will, and numerous other virtues revealed in his broad nose and square—also plump—chin. It is true that his wife came in and caught him at it, and that he pretended to be examining his bald spot. It is true that he listened mildly to her reminder that for two weeks now he hadn't rubbed any of the sulphur stuff on his head. But he marched downstairs—behind her—with an imperial tread. He had solved his worry! Somehow, he was going to work it all out.

Just how he was going to work it out he did not state. That detail might be left till after dinner.

He did not again think of the dolls hidden beneath his bed till he had dived under the blanket. Cursing a little, he crawled out and set them on the rail of the sleeping porch.

He awoke suddenly and sharply, at sunup. He heard a voice—surely not his own—snarling: "Nobody is going to help you. If you want to go on looking for a magic way out—go right on looking. You won't find it!"

He stared at the two dolls. The first sunlight was on the Skillyoolly object, and in that intolerant glare he saw that her fluffy dress was sewed on with cheap thread which would break at the first rough handling. Suddenly he was out of bed, pounding the unfortunate Skillyoolly on the rail, smashing her simpering face, wrenching apart her ill-jointed limbs, tearing her gay chiffon. He was dashing into the bedroom, waking his bewildered wife with:

"Nelly! Nelly! Get up! No, it's all right. But it's time for breakfast."

She foggily looked at her wristwatch on the bedside table, and complained, "Why, it isn't but six o'clock!"

"I know it, but we're going to do a stunt. D'you realize we haven't had breakfast just by ourselves and had chance to really talk since last summer? Come on! You fry an egg and I'll start the percolator. Come on!"

"Well," patiently, reaching for her dressing gown.

While Candee, his shrunken bathrobe flapping about his shins, excitedly put the percolator together and attached it to the baseboard plug, leaving out nothing but the coffee, he chattered of the Boosters' Club.

As they sat down he crowed: "Nelly, we're going to throw some gas in the ole car and run down to Chicago and back, next week. How's that?"

"That would be very nice," agreed Mrs. Candee.

"And we're going to start reading aloud again, evenings, instead of all this doggone double solitaire."

"That would be fine."

"Oh, and by the way, I've finally made up my mind. I'm not going to mess up my store with that Skillyoolly stuff. Going to keep on with the Jumas dolls, but push 'em harder."

"Well, if you really think——"

"And, uh— Gee! I certainly feel great this morning. Feel like a million dollars. What say we have another fried egg?"

"I think that might be nice," said Mrs. Candee, who had been married for nineteen years.

"Sure you don't mind about the Skillyoolly dolls?"

"Why, no, not if you know what you want. And that reminds me! How terrible of me to forget! When you ran over to the Jasons' last evening, the Skillyoolly salesman telephoned the house—he'd just come to town. He asked me if you were going to take the agency, and I told him no. Of course I've known all along that you weren't. But hasn't it been interesting, thinking it all out? I'm glad you've been firm."

"Well, when I've gone into a thing thoroughly I like to smash it right through. . . . Now you take Frank Darbin; makes me tired the way he's fussing and stewing, trying to find out whether he wants to buy a house in Rosebank or not. So you—you told the

Skillyoolly salesman no? I just wonder— Gee! I kind of hate to give up the chance of the Skillyoolly market! What do you think?"

"But it's all settled now."

"Then I suppose there's no use fussing— I tell you; I mean a fellow wants to look at a business deal from all sides. See how I mean?"

"That's so," said Mrs. Candee, admiringly. As with a commanding step he went to the kitchen to procure another fried egg she sighed to herself, "Such a dear boy—and yet such a forceful man."

Candee ran in from the kitchen. In one hand was an egg, in the other the small frying pan. "Besides," he shouted, "how do we know the Skillyoollys would necessarily sell so darn well? You got to take everything like that into consideration, and then decide and stick to it. See how I mean?"

"That's so," said Mrs. Candee.

THE HACK DRIVER

I DARE SAY there's no man of large affairs, whether he is bank president or senator or dramatist, who hasn't a sneaking love for some
old rum-hound in a frightful hat, living back in a shanty and making his living by ways you wouldn't care to examine too closely. (It
was the Supreme Court Justice speaking. I do not pretend to guarantee his theories or his story.) He may be a Maine guide, or the old
garageman who used to keep the livery stable, or a perfectly useless
innkeeper who sneaks off to shoot ducks when he ought to be
sweeping the floors, but your pompous big-city man will contrive
to get back and see him every year, and loaf with him, and secretly
prefer him to all the highfalutin' leaders of the city.

There's that much truth, at least, to this Open Spaces stuff you
read in advertisements of wild and woolly Western novels. I don't
know the philosophy of it; perhaps it means that we retain a decent simplicity, no matter how much we are tied to Things, to
houses and motors and expensive wives. Or again it may give away
the whole game of civilization; may mean that the apparently civ-
ilized man is at heart nothing but a hobo who prefers flannel shirts
and bristly cheeks and cussing and dirty tin plates to all the trim,
hygienic, forward-looking life our women-folks make us put on
for them.

When I graduated from law school I suppose I was about as
artificial and idiotic and ambitious as most youngsters. I wanted
to climb, socially and financially. I wanted to be famous and dine
at large houses with men who shuddered at the Common People
who don't dress for dinner. You see, I hadn't learned that the only
thing duller than a polite dinner is the conversation afterward,
when the victims are digesting the dinner and accumulating
enough strength to be able to play bridge. Oh, I was a fine young

The Nation, August 29, 1923
Collected in Selected Short Stories of Sinclair Lewis (1937)

calf! I even planned a rich marriage. Imagine then how I felt when, after taking honors and becoming fifteenth assistant clerk in the magnificent law firm of Hodgins, Hodgins, Berkman and Taupe, I was set not at preparing briefs but at serving summonses! Like a cheap private detective! Like a mangy sheriff's officer! They told me I had to begin that way and, holding my nose, I feebly went to work. I was kicked out of actresses' dressing rooms, and from time to time I was righteously beaten by large and indignant litigants. I came to know, and still more to hate, every dirty and shadowy corner of the city. I thought of fleeing to my home town, where I could at once become a full-fledged attorney-at-law. I rejoiced one day when they sent me out forty miles or so to a town called New Mullion, to serve a summons on one Oliver Lutkins. This Lutkins had worked in the Northern Woods, and he knew the facts about a certain timberland boundary agreement. We needed him as a witness, and he had dodged service.

When I got off the train at New Mullion, my sudden affection for sweet and simple villages was dashed by the look of the place, with its mud-gushing streets and its rows of shops either paintless or daubed with a sour brown. Though it must have numbered eight or nine thousand inhabitants, New Mullion was as littered as a mining camp. There was one agreeable-looking man at the station—the expressman. He was a person of perhaps forty, red-faced, cheerful, thick; he wore his overalls and denim jumper as though they belonged to him, he was quite dirty and very friendly and you knew at once he liked people and slapped them on the back out of pure easy affection.

"I want," I told him, "to find a fellow named Oliver Lutkins."

"Him? I saw him 'round here 'twan't an hour ago. Hard fellow to catch, though—always chasing around on some phony business or other. Probably trying to get up a poker game in the back of Fritz Beinke's harness shop. I'll tell you, boy— Any hurry about locating Lutkins?"

"Yes. I want to catch the afternoon train back." I was as impressively secret as a stage detective.

"I'll tell you. I've got a hack. I'll get out the boneshaker and we can drive around together and find Lutkins. I know most of the places he hangs out."

He was so frankly friendly, he so immediately took me into the circle of his affection, that I glowed with the warmth of it. I knew, of course, that he was drumming up business, but his kindness was real, and if I had to pay hack fare in order to find my man, I was glad that the money would go to this good fellow. I got him down to two dollars an hour; he brought from his cottage, a block away, an object like a black piano-box on wheels.

He didn't hold the door open, certainly he didn't say "Ready, sir." I think he would have died before calling anybody "sir." When he gets to Heaven's gate he'll call St. Peter "Pete," and I imagine the good saint will like it. He remarked, "Well, young fellow, here's the handsome equipage," and his grin—well, it made me feel that I had always been his neighbor. They're so ready to help a stranger, those villagers. He had already made it his own task to find Oliver Lutkins for me.

He said, and almost shyly: "I don't want to butt in on your private business, young fellow, but my guess is that you want to collect some money from Lutkins—he never pays anybody a cent; he still owes me six bits on a poker game I was fool enough to get into. He ain't a bad sort of a Yahoo but he just naturally hates to loosen up on a coin of the realm. So if you're trying to collect any money off him, we better kind of you might say creep up on him and surround him. If you go asking for him—anybody can tell you come from the city, with that trick Fedora of yours—he'll suspect something and take a sneak. If you want me to, I'll go into Fritz Beinke's and ask for him, and you can keep out of sight behind me."

I loved him for it. By myself I might never have found Lutkins. Now, I was an army with reserves. In a burst I told the hack driver that I wanted to serve a summons on Lutkins; that the fellow had viciously refused to testify in a suit where his knowledge of a certain conversation would clear up everything. The driver listened earnestly—and I was still young enough to be grateful at being taken seriously by any man of forty. At the end he pounded my shoulder (very painfully) and chuckled: "Well, we'll spring a little surprise on Brer Lutkins."

"Let's start, driver."

"Most folks around here call me Bill. Or Magnuson. William Magnuson, fancy carting and hauling."

"All right, Bill. Shall we tackle this harness shop—Beinke's?"

"Yes, jus' likely to be there as anywheres. Plays a lot of poker and a great hand at bluffing—damn him!" Bill seemed to admire Mr. Lutkins's ability as a scoundrel; I fancied that if he had been sheriff he would have caught Lutkins with fervor and hanged him with affection.

At the somewhat gloomy harness shop we descended and went in. The room was odorous with the smell of dressed leather. A scanty sort of a man, presumably Mr. Beinke, was selling a horse collar to a farmer.

"Seen Nolly Lutkins around today? Friend of his looking for him," said Bill, with treacherous heartliness.

Beinke looked past him at my shrinking alien self; he hesitated and owned: "Yuh, he was in here a little while ago. Guess he's gone over to the Swede's to get a shave."

"Well, if he comes in, tell him I'm looking for him. Might get up a little game of poker. I've heard tell that Lutkins plays these here immoral games of chance."

"Yuh, I believe he's known to sit in on Authors," Beinke growled.

We sought the barber shop of "the Swede." Bill was again good enough to take the lead, while I lurked at the door. He asked not only the Swede but two customers if they had seen Lutkins. The Swede decidedly had not; he raged: "I ain't seen him, and I don't want to, but if you find him you can just collect the dollar thirty-five he owes me." One of the customers thought he had seen Lutkins "hiking down Main Street, this side of the hotel."

"Well, then," Bill concluded, as we labored up into the hack, "his credit at the Swede's being ausgewent, he's probably getting a scrape at Heinie Gray's. He's too darn lazy to shave himself."

At Gray's barber shop we missed Lutkins by only five minutes. He had just left—presumably for the poolroom. At the poolroom it appeared that he had merely bought a pack of cigarettes and gone on. Thus we pursued him, just behind him but never catching him, for an hour, till it was past one and I was hungry. Village born as I was, and in the city often lonely for good coarse country wit, I was so delighted by Bill's cynical opinions on the barbers and clergymen and doctors and draymen of New Mullion that I scarcely cared whether I found Lutkins or not.

"How about something to eat?" I suggested. "Let's go to a restaurant and I'll buy you a lunch."

"Well, ought to go home to the old woman. And I don't care much for these restaurants—ain't but four of 'em and they're all rotten. Tell you what we'll do. Like nice scenery? There's an elegant view from Wade's Hill. We'll get the old woman to put us up a lunch—she won't charge you but a half dollar, and it'd cost you that for a greasy feed at the café—and we'll go up there and have a Sunday-school picnic."

I knew that my friend Bill was not free from guile; I knew that his hospitality to the Young Fellow from the City was not altogether a matter of brotherly love. I was paying him for his time; in all I paid him for six hours (including the lunch hour) at what was then a terrific price. But he was no more dishonest than I, who charged the whole thing up to the Firm, and it would have been worth paying him myself to have his presence. His country serenity, his natural wisdom, was a refreshing bath to the city-twitching youngster. As we sat on the hilltop, looking across orchards and a creek which slipped among the willows, he talked of New Mullion, gave a whole gallery of portraits. He was cynical yet tender. Nothing had escaped him, yet there was nothing, no matter how ironically he laughed at it, which was beyond his understanding and forgiveness. In ruddy color he painted the rector's wife who when she was most in debt most loudly gave the responses at which he called the "Episcopalopian church." He commented on the boys who came home from college in "ice-cream pants," and on the lawyer who, after years of torrential argument with his wife, would put on either a linen collar or a necktie, but never both. He made them live. In that day I came to know New Mullion better than I did the city, and to love it better.

If Bill was ignorant of universities and of urban ways, yet much had he traveled in the realm of jobs. He had worked on railroad section gangs, in harvest fields and contractors' camps, and from his adventures he had brought back a philosophy of simplicity and laughter. He strengthened me. Nowadays, thinking of Bill, I know what people mean (though I abominate the simpering phrase) when they yearn over "real he-men."

We left that placid place of orchards and resumed the search for Oliver Lutkins. We could not find him. At last Bill cornered a friend of Lutkins and made him admit that "he guessed Oliver'd gone out to his ma's farm, three miles north."

We drove out there, mighty with strategy.

"I know Oliver's ma. She's a terror. She's a cyclone," Bill sighed. "I took a trunk out for her once, and she pretty near took my hide off because I didn't treat it like it was a crate of eggs. She's somewheres about nine feet tall and four feet thick and quick's a cat, and she sure manhandles the Queen's English. I'll bet Oliver has heard that somebody's on his trail and he's sneaked out there to hide behind his ma's skirts. Well, we'll try bawling her out. But you better let me do it, boy. You may be great at Latin and geography, but you ain't educated in cussing."

We drove into a poor farmyard; we were faced by an enormous and cheerful old woman. My guardian stockily stood before her and snarled, "Remember me? I'm Bill Magnuson, the expressman. I want to find your son Oliver. Friend of mine here from the city's got a present for him."

"I don't know anything about Oliver and I don't want to," she bellowed.

"Now you look here. We've stood for just about enough plenty nonsense. This young man is the attorney general's provost, and we got legal right to search any and all premises for the person of one Oliver Lutkins."

Bill made it seem terrific, and the Amazon seemed impressed. She retired into the kitchen and we followed. From the low old range, turned by years of heat into a dark silvery gray, she snatched a sadiron, and she marched on us, clamoring, "You just search all you want to—providin' you don't mind getting burnt to a cinder!" She bellowed, she swelled, she laughed at our nervous retreat.

"Let's get out of this. She'll murder us," Bill groaned and, outside: "Did you see her grin? She was making fun of us. Can you beat that for nerve?"

I agreed that it was lese majesty.

We did, however, make adequate search. The cottage had but one story. Bill went round it, peeking in at all the windows. We explored the barn and the stable; we were reasonably certain that Lutkins was not there. It was nearly time for me to catch the afternoon train, and Bill drove me to the station. On the way to the city I worried very little over my failure to find Lutkins. I was too absorbed in the thought of Bill Magnuson. Really, I considered returning to New Mullion to practice law. If I had found Bill so deeply and richly human might I not come to love the yet uncharted Fritz Beinke and the Swede barber and a hundred other slow-spoken, simple, wise neighbors? I saw a candid and happy life beyond the neat learnings of universities' law firms. I was excited, as one who has found a treasure.

But if I did not think much about Lutkins, the office did. I found them in a state next morning; the suit was ready to come to trial; they had to have Lutkins; I was a disgrace and a fool. That morning my eminent career almost came to an end. The Chief did everything but commit mayhem; he somewhat more than hinted that I would do well at ditch-digging. I was ordered back to New Mullion, and with me they sent an ex-lumber-camp clerk who knew Lutkins. I was rather sorry, because it would prevent my loafing again in the gorgeous indolence of Bill Magnuson.

When the train drew in at New Mullion, Bill was on the station platform, near his dray. What was curious was that the old dragon, Lutkins's mother, was there talking to him, and they were not quarreling but laughing.

From the car steps I pointed them out to the lumber-camp clerk, and in young hero-worship I murmured: "There's a fine fellow, a real man."

"Meet him here yesterday?" asked the clerk.

"I spent the day with him."

"He help you hunt for Oliver Lutkins?"

"Yes, he helped me a lot."

"He must have! He's Lutkins himself!"

But what really hurt was that when I served the summons Lutkins and his mother laughed at me as though I were a bright boy of seven, and with loving solicitude they begged me to go to a neighbor's house and take a cup of coffee.

"I told 'em about you, and they're dying to have a look at you," said Lutkins joyfully. "They're about the only folks in town that missed seeing you yesterday."

ALL WIVES ARE ANGELS

OF ALL THE viciously well-bred female brats that I have know in a long medical practice devoted to keeping the poor out of the hospital and the rich out of jail, the most appalling was that Lydia Turpee who afterward became the very domestic Mrs. Lambert Fenn.

The papers say there are no more family affections these days. Rot! In New York they may use a phone book for family Bible, but out here in Cornucopia we still have four children, and worry about their haircuts and broken hearts as much as our grandfathers did. Even on Agency Hill, where the descendants of our pioneer dollar-trappers live in twenty-room castles that they keep trying to trade for bungalows, we listen to symphonies and Artie Shaw on the radio less than to the nursery and kitchen tips. We are a conservative clan, and that was why we were disturbed by the singularly high-class hellishness that Lydia Turpee displayed even at the age of sixteen.

In the Lavender Walk School for Girls, which is reputed to give the most scholarly instruction in bridge to be found between Lake Forest and San Mateo, Lyddy's classmates used to call her "Turpitude." Maybe the name would better have fitted her father, that old lumber bandit who had taught her that you never get anything unless you grab for it, and that soft words butter no partnerships. She was the school's midnight mosquito.

She organized pajama parades and fried-banana feasts. She kept asking "Why?" in history class, and the refined gentlewoman who taught it, much as Queen Victoria might have, hadn't gone far enough in history to answer any whys that weren't printed out plain in the textbook.

Lyddy even got up a Socialist Club—this was back in 1912,

The Cosmopolitan, February 1943

before it was smart to be Communist—and when the young ladies assembled with well-publicized secrecy, expecting to hear Lyddy advocate the blowing up of President Taft, she appeared wearing a purple military cloak, announced that America ought to become a monarchy with Charley and Bob as royal dukes, and stopped in the middle of her oration to remark that Tess Wallroth's nose was red. Tess howled, and Lyddy Turpee made another trip to the headmistress' office. She had already worn a path there three inches deep in solid-oak flooring.

The headmistress suggested to Lyddy's father that unless she became a day pupil and stayed away from the school except during classes she would have to be expelled. Zeb Turpee was said to have bitten through nails in his early lumbering days, but he was terrified at the threat of his daughter's spending more than three hours a week at home, and he apparently cleared it all up by giving Lavender Walk a new Music Hall.

So Lyddy graduated, after a fashion. I was there, as family doctor and reputed friend, and I saw the headmistress hold out the diploma as though she was afraid Lyddy was going to snap at her hand.

So now Lyddy entered into a wider field of uselessness, and was able to make enemies on a larger scale.

Her father wanted to send her to college, but it just didn't seem as though the better colleges for young ladies needed her. They claimed that she still spelled *was* with too many *z*'s. Of course a bookless barbarian like Jeb Turpee couldn't have his daughter going to any but the most lilylike institutions. Expect her to go to a state university, along with the children of doctors and generals and editors! So she stayed home and took up a life-work of exercising her two private mounts, at the Bridle and Racquet Club. And in all that venerable sanctuary she was the best horsewoman: daring, accurate, graceful. She was inclined to stockiness, but on horseback she looked slender. Poor Lyddy was just born to be a cavalry sergeant, and that was all. I must say that at this time nobody called her "poor Lyddy" except myself and maybe her pastor. People used other words than "poor."

Going out and instantly making enemies was both a talent and an art with her.

It is part of our Agency Hill clannishness that any woman who by birth belongs to our select group of Aristocrats (families of which some are so ancient that they can pretty well guess who their grandfathers must have been and even what their names probably were, back in the Old Country) goes on being accepted and worried about. We felt that we had to keep on including Lyddy in our mild festivities: the horse shows, the deb dances, the reception after the opening of the symphony series. And no one went to them more faithfully than the aggressively bored Lyddy, and at them, nobody built up a more loyal body of enemies.

She was, like too many bright and active women, one of these nonsense-of-coursers. She would say to men, shy, amiable men who hated horsing around, "Nonsense, of *course* you want to leave your office early and come to my bridge tea," and "Nonsense, of *course* you want to address the Junior Assembly Dinner and get your photograph in the paper. Don't try to pull that modesty pose on *me!*"

She was also a Commenter of the highest rating. "My, you think your new sweater is sporting! I think it looks like a sick zebra!" she would offer; and "You weren't really a bit offended by my being rude. You just love it when I kid you. It flatters your vanity!"

The fact is, she had no inhibitions. She didn't have one inhibition big enough to line a mouse's ear.

She blurted out whatever she thought—and she was an awfully quick thinker. And like all such people, she prided herself on what she called her honesty.

And so, by the time she was twenty-four, Lydia seemed to be the one piece of poisoned silk in town that was certain not to get married. Dozens of men had been startled by her hot dark eyes, her bright complexion, her jolly laugh—and maybe by the million or so her father still had left—and she had been willing to be rushed. But within two weeks, if the candidate was almost a teetotaler, she would be certain to jeer publicly that he was a secret souse; or if he was a proud and earnest hoister, she bugled that he always passed out after one glass of beer. And then she would abruptly become a lone spinster again.

Whenever she came to my office to have me look at her tonsils, which she refused to have taken out for the strong reason that I told her she ought to have them out, I would ask her why she tried so hard to alienate everybody she liked; why she took such trouble to make herself miserable. Her answer, once, was to ask me whether I had ever been sued for malpractice, whether I didn't need my own tonsils looked at, and did I have a good doctor of my own?

Just the same, I kept on worrying. I was afraid she might go definitely queer and wind up in one of those private prisons where nurses chirp, "Now, we mustn't be nau-ghty today-ee."

The she started riding with Lambert Fenn.

She must have met him before, but he was ten years older than Lyddy, and no dancing man, though he walked and talked smoothly enough. He was a steady-minded corporation lawyer; he did most of the work and got maybe a tenth of the earnings in the haughty firm of Laverty & Bagg. He was on the edge of the Agency Hill set. His parents had not been rich, but he had gone to Rexford School and to Yale, and been an artillery lieutenant in World War I. And he played golf and said he liked fishing. There was only one doubtful Outsider trait in him: he did paint scenery at our Civic Theater. But Junior Society at Yale had sealed him, and to our liberal and democratic way of thinking he was just as much of a gentleman as if his grandfather had bribed fifty officials and ruined a million acres of virgin forest.

One of our best gossips had told me that she was present at the mounting block at the Bridle Club when Lyddy first showed her interest in Lambert Fenn by briskly insulting him. She looked up at him, trim and easy on his horse, and yelped, "Mr. Fenn, is it true what I hear—that you're the duckiest tennis player in the club?"

He said seriously, as though it had really been a question and not a casual brick, "Yes, I'm quite a good player."

"Oh, you are?"

"But I had to work at it very hard."

"Oh, you did? I know, Mr. Fenn, you're one of these professional men that're so dumb that outside the office you can only keep amused by sports. I bet you play squash."

He said with the utmost civility, "I believe you're dead right. It really is a shame that I don't take more interest in music and so on, but so few people care, or take the trouble to remind you. I do wish I had the chance to go into this with you. You're riding, aren't you? May I tag along? I'll be the best groom I can."

The simp!

I was alarmed when I heard this gossip about Lyddy's latest outrage. I liked Lambert Fenn fairly well. He didn't appreciate a good story, but he was a solid lawyer, and he paid his medical bills within two days. Presently I had a chance to do a little spying on Lyddy and Lam myself. It was during the much-publicized appearance of the farce, *Up in Mabel's Room.* I stood near them in the lobby, both of them so healthy-looking and vigorous in evening dress. They looked well suited, but I heard her snarl with a curious kind of caterwauling tenderness, like a mother lion, "I think this play is very suggestive. I'd like to know what you mean by bringing me to it!"

Gratefully, as though she had told him she adored his hair, he bubbled, "Yes, isn't it strange how we all like suggestive plays? And don't you think this is a brilliant example? So masterfully acted!"

She answered "Grrrrr!" and I waited to see him walk out on her without going in for his hat. He didn't.

A week later Lambert came in to see me at the office. He said in his nice, bright, prim way, "I never felt better, but I would like your advice on a matter of which you'll be a better judge than anybody else."

I was anxious. I knew what the matter was, all right. I was accustomed to being consulted by young men whose complaint was that they had met Lydia. Some of them wanted to know what I thought of suicide, but more of them were sort of figuring on murder. I didn't want to balk my old patient Lyddy of her one chance, but neither did I want to watch Lambert begin to hear voices and chew his thumb.

The astonishment was all mine. I found that Lambert Fenn wasn't a good cynical corporation lawyer at all, but a poet with the regulation professional equipment — wings on his feet and the ability to see a sparrow as a soaring swan. He could sweat out a poem full of gold, roses, sunsets, lambent eyes, ruby lips, and then have the nerve to insist that it was a complete photograph of whatever young lady happened to live across the street.

"I have come to ask you to tell me frankly whether you think I could possibly make Lydia happy," he begged. "Have I any of the qualities that a great-hearted woman like her deserves?"

My first answer was "Uh — uh — uh," which was probably just as reasonable as any other. But I forced myself to get out, "Old man, I know she's a smart girl, but don't you think she's pretty brash for a conservative fellow like you?"

"Brash?"

"I mean 'brash.' She always says the first thing that comes into her head. She never tries to spare anybody's feelings. She seems to think she's a divine agent sent to tell ugly people that their teeth are funny, and poor people that they're contemptible because they can't afford speedboats."

"Oh, no, no! You misunderstand her. I did myself, at first. She has an honesty and a fearlessness that you find only once in a generation — you know, a sort of knightly gallantry. All this aside

271

from her being so beautiful. I've tried to sum it up in — it isn't a very good poem, but you might call it a legal brief in verse and — would you care to hear it?"

I didn't care to very much, but he didn't give me a chance. There he was, in my hitherto aseptic office, putting on his large spectacles and reading aloud some twenty lines that began:

> *Lydia, thou art the huntress moon*
> *That vanquishes each star,*
> *And earthbound dullards shall know soon*
> *Diana's self you are.*
> *That silver fiery purity,*
> *That fierce proud courage that is thee . . .*

I'd had people read me clippings about magic cancer cures, and school report cards, and letters from Aunt Hannah saying I hadn't done 'em one mite of good, but I'd never had to listen to heart throbs. I was certain that fully licensed poets don't ball up the yous and the thous that way, but I was also certain that Lambert Fenn was not reading it to show his rhetorical powers, but as an exact report on his Lyddy.

In some discomfort, I began to question him, and I found that he admired not only her, but pretty much everybody else. He actually liked his own boss, old Laverty, and he thought Lyddy's father oughtn't to be burned alive but merely electrocuted. What could I do? Here was a fellow so imbecile or so superhuman that he believed that politicians and girls in love mean what they say. I let him go with the assurance that he was worthy of his Diana, and I stared wistfully at the office bottle of alcohol.

They were married a month later — in June, of course, with the bishop officiating, of course, and with the family physician in morning clothes, of course. At the end, Lyddy looked at Lambert as though nobody else existed in the world, and she began to cry.

No one had ever seen Lyddy cry before.

. . .

For a year or so we were all restless because there were no bulletins whatever about the Lydia-Lambert encounter. When they appeared abroad, they seemed like any other decent couple, and there wasn't so much as a rumor that he had chased her through the back yard with an icepick. Then we noticed that she was taking part in our community efforts: the Red Cross drive and the orphanage campaign. Slowly, we admitted that she looked happy, that she no longer mauled people's feeling and frequently kept her mouth shut even when there was a chance of getting a laugh by clawing somebody's sore heart.

The miracle had come off. Lambert's faith in her splendor was making her splendid.

But to me it was a little touching, the way she depended on Lam to guide her in a new life that must have been dark and bewildering sometimes, as well as happy and illuminated. At a party, her eyes would grow spiteful, her mouth would open balefully—and then she would turn in panic to Lam, and where she had probably intended to remark, "Mrs. Bjorken, you got the wrong hair dye this time," her husband would purr for her, "How beautifully Mrs. Bjorken's hair shines tonight," and we would all gasp as we heard Lyddy chanting like seven choirboys at Eastertide, "Yes, isn't it beau-ti-ful?"

Sometimes I was sorry for her, having to take her very breath from that smug poet; sometimes I felt a nameless irritation, as though he had cheated us of a grand tragic spectacle on the gallows. I confess that I frequently said to my wife, "It can't last. Lyddy will bust out one of these days, and what a busting that will be!"

But it did last, years and years, and we got used to accepting Lyddy as a human being. By and by she could be pleasant without turning to her husband at all, and most of her set forgot that she had ever been the village pest.

Only once in a while did Lambert have to defend his Diana. When old Mrs. Trojan, our local duchess, said, "I hear your wife acts halfway decent now. I don't believe it," Lam explained, "To me she couldn't do anything wrong, even if I knew legally that she *had* done something wrong, but she *couldn't* do anything wrong."

"I always love to have you lawyers make things clear like that," said Mrs. Trojan.

Lambert and Lydia had two babies, Charles and Donna, and never in the history of Cornucopia had there been more speculation as to how children would turn out. Well, the poor things hadn't a chance; they had to turn out well, for there was that blasted poet and optimist of a father telling them that they were wonderful, that their playmates were wonderful, that little boys simply loved to go to bed at nine and that little girls don't get scared on the jumps because all horses are also wonderful and won't spill their riders, not even on a bet. And so, eventually, the Fenn household became so normal that it engendered less conversation than the love life of the Brussels sprout.

Lam and Lydia played bridge every Thursday evening with Ben and Julia Wetheral, and went to the Bridle Club dance every other Saturday, and each summer they went out to their cottage on Sunset Lake, and so help me, they all worked in the garden and looked as if they liked it. Lyddy's father died, and Lam and she were rich, but they merely moved into the Turpee mansion, without alterations, and every summer they went back to the same lake cottage.

Even as a dear old family friend, I didn't get a chance to enjoy being alarmed about them till the summer of 1929, when Lam went even crazier than the rest of us about everybody in the country becoming a millionaire on that heaven-soaring stock market. He was too poetic about it altogether. I heard him say that this was the turning point in world history, and we would all be eating caviar on gold plates. Apparently nobody would have to work except the sturgeon.

Two days before the crash he was worth three million dollars—

on paper; two days after it he came into my office, said mildly that it was a nice fall day, that he had lost every last cent he had, and would I please give him some sleeping dope to keep him from committing suicide.

It was the third time that day that I had given soporifics to men who had never before known that you can lie awake all night. But Lam looked worse than the others. He was, literally, down to $176.32, he calculated, with all property mortgaged. His eyes were blank, as if there was no longer any faith in them.

I made it my business to drop in at the Turpee-Fenn castle on grand old Paradise Avenue that evening. Lam was low in a chair, his mouth gaping. I don't think he even knew I was there. Lyddy knew it, all right—she made me help her take inventory.

"I'm just seeing which of this handsome junk we can get some money on," she said blithely. "Will you look at that gilt Venus? When I was a kid, I thought it was a work of art, and at three o'clock this afternoon I thought it was a monstrosity, but now it just looks to me like seven dollars at Ike's. I've already signed the lease on the swellest four-room walk-up flat in town. Lam, the lamb, won't even go look at it, but he's going to love it. It has a yellow breakfast nook, and Lam always did have a weakness for canaries. And the kids—I've told them it's an adventure, and all explorers and bohemians live in four-room flats, and if they're very good, I'll let 'em go along with us—the young vipers!

"There's one thing you can do for me, doctor: tell me where I can get a hired girl—not a maid, a hired girl; four dollars a week, live out and do the washing and teach Donna fencing."

Apparently Lam came to, for I know that Lyddy and he themselves, by darkness, in their rakish station wagon, moved most of the furniture they were going to retain for the new flat. Lyddy boasted, and maybe she made herself believe, that it was better fun to have only four rooms and one maid to supervise, and to be allowed now, with no butler to sneer, to make her own bed.

She did not skimp but increased her community work. I saw

her at hospital committees and even, when my wife yanked me there, at the League of Women Voters: a grave, open-eyed, beautiful woman, still quick to speak, but friendly now; too rich a spirit for the barren growth of sneering.

She became more stately and handsome, between 1930 and 1940, and her hair turned entirely gray, and her eyes had a waiting patience in them that sometimes scared me.

Lambert was second partner in his firm by now, and his earnings were good. They did not starve, and before long they moved into a fairly decent house again. And whatever home economies there were, Charles had to go to Rexford School and Donna to Lavender Walk. They had to have sailboats and music lessons and family pride.

"My children are such perfect angels there's nothing too good for them!" said Lambert blissfully, at dinner—and Lyddy winked at me. She was wearing a charming dinner dress five years old.

It was he who healed their sore little modern egos by praising their skiing, their knowledge of Sibelius; but it was Lyddy who was persistent about folding up the napkin, who shooed off the ragtag young beaux for whom Donna occasionally fell—say, once a week—and Lyddy who kept on throwing the verbal harpoons which, through the ages, even the tenderest parents have considered necessary: "If you know so much about it, darling, why do you ask me?" and "Don't monopolize the conversation, sweetheart," and "I'm told that the doctor is simply fascinated by dirty fingernails. Do show him yours, for his collection."

They never seem to do any good, these jabs, but I suppose they must, because a surprising proportion of heedless brats do grow up and become just as nail-cleaned and napkin-folding and dull as the rest of us. Certainly Charles and Donna were ideal children—except once, but that once terrified me.

Most of the boys in Rexford School are high-class fellows worthy of Agency Hill, but a few vicious outlaws do get in, and they are often the fastest drivers, the flashiest dancers in the school. Charles, the grandson of Bandit Turpee, rather admired such mavericks, and one midnight, when I had just gone to bed, I was summoned down to find Lyddy on the stoop, with Charles, aged seventeen, fine and handsome — and dead-drunk.

The first thing she said was, "His father mustn't ever know. He believes so in Charles," and the second was, "And so do I. Look, doctor, couldn't you keep him here all night and when he's in shape in the morning talk to him — give him the works? I've told Lam that he's staying with a friend. Could you, doctor?"

Could I! By that time I was a quarter in love with the woman I had once called "the human carbuncle." I kept Charles there, and I'm afraid I used a little medical magic on him. Anyway, next morning he was a lot sicker — sick and sick and wrenchingly sick — than he would have been normally. Before I got through with him, he understood what he was doing to his father and mother, and he had pretty much ceased to think that it was much of an ambition to become a hobo in a gutter on Harvest Avenue.

The boy's father never knew, and I was sometimes a shade irritated when he went on talking about his "seraphic kids." He hadn't seen how sick the boy seraph could be.

Charles finished Rexford School, not too brilliantly; he went off to college, not too enthusiastically; and on a May evening two and a half years later, when it was a question whether he would be able to finish college before he was drafted, a bland spring evening when my wife and I were at the Fenns' at bridge and Charles was supposed to be in New Haven, fourteen hundred miles away, he slammed into the room where we sat, his hair wild, his eyes wild, his clothing messy, and he observed calmly, "H'are yuh, folks? What's cooking? I have returned to inform you that the curtain has rung down on this farce of my sticking around college. If I see fit, I may enlist. But I think I'd first like a few tonic waters with boon companions of eld, and perhaps a little necking, while I am still a young gentleman of Agency Hill."

It was the old violent Lydia who was screaming, "You're drunk, and not drunk like a gentleman, but like a cheap drugstore sport!"

But Lambert said, as calmly as though we were on a picnic, "Maybe that would be a good idea, son. We all feel sort of strained these days, and you've been very brave to jump out of your rut. If you'd like a drink right now, there's some bourbon on the sideboard."

This time, Lyddy didn't try to hide the boy's wildness from the blind angel-maker.

The day after Charles' return was his twenty-first birthday, and Lambert insisted on giving him a coming-of-age party. But two nights after that I was sent for by the Fenns, and in her new drawing room Lydia remarked, in the manner of Lady Macbeth trying out a new dagger, "Charles has been missing since yesterday noon, when he arose with an interesting hangover. But it's all right now — it's all nice and lovely — we know where he is. He has just sent word that yesterday afternoon he married a little tramp named Winnie Jasper, the daughter of a saloonkeeper in the slums, and they are now happily ensconced, if that's what you call it, in a bijou flat over a pawnbroker's on Harvest Avenue, so it's all right, just lovely——"

Lambert interrupted, not sharply, "We're going down to call on them, and I'd be grateful if you'd come along, doctor, because it may be that Lyddy and I are a bit emotional about it."

Lyddy yelled, "Me? I'm not emotional! I'm just plain mad! And it's about time, too; just — about — time! I've stood plenty all these years, and covered it up. But now I'm going to hammer that young man so that when he gets into the Army he'll think his sergeant major is a choir singer by comparison!"

It was strange and embarrassing to be jerked back twenty-two years, to see the old unchanged Lydia Turpee dominating us, hating and sneering. Neither Lambert nor I said anything but "Oh, now, Lyddy!" as I drove them down to Harvest Avenue.

Charles' honeymoon flat, a flight up over Abe's Loans, was one-

and-a-half rooms, with enough foolish junk in it to fill seven. Cheap new dresses, running to reds and greens, were piled on the three chairs, and on the edge of the unmade bed sat Charles and his Winnie, arms about each other, scared and looking about ten years old.

The girl had black elf locks over a thin, white, lovely face. Not rising, she waved her frail, rather dirty hand and piped, "Is this the old folks, Charley? Welcome, old folks! Have a highball? I can guarantee the hootch. My dad was the best bootlegger in Cornucopia before they sent him up for assault."

Lyddy jumped right in. "This girl isn't just bad, she's a fiend!"

Lambert cried, "Wait!" He held out his hand to Winnie, drew her up, put his arms about her and said cheerfully, "Welcome, my dear! I hope you'll be willing to come home with us and be a new daughter. Or maybe you'd prefer to be independent, when Charles goes into the service. If you would, I know a nice little flat for you. But perhaps you'd be willing to stay with us."

Lydia howled, "She will not! This marriage will be annulled. She's the most impertinent, disgraceful——"

Lambert grew eight feet tall, I swear it, and his face was terrible with flame. "Lyddy! She is very much like you when you were her age. You were the most impertinent, disgraceful, unco-operative young thug that ever lived!"

Lyddy squeaked small, like a mouse. "I thought you thought I was a regular Diana! You said I was an angel!"

"You were—but a warlike angel, as Winnie is. All wives are angels, but they have to be believed in or they fold their wings and die. I've know what you've done for the kids all these years. I wasn't blind. Sometimes great faith and blindness seem alike . . . Charles, I'm glad to find that, like myself, you chose a wife who was above conventions. Would you and your wife like to come home with us for a few days? . . . Winnie, I may not match your dad's liquor, but I can make a good try, angel."

The girl shrieked, "I'm no angel, and I don't want to be!"

"You are now, Winnie, and you might just as well get used to it," Lyddy said bitterly. "No woman can stand out against a man that's so dumb he even *wants* her to be an angel. And maybe some-day——" She turned to Lambert, and suddenly she looked as happy as any woman I've ever seen. "I used to say that you didn't beat me enough. I guess I never understood how much. Come on, Winnie. We'll go home and be a Diana sister team, and like it."

Lambert Fenn was ever so polite. "But you really will like it, darling."

The old Lyddy had one last scream left in her: "I know it! That's what gripes me! Winnie, you don't realize what sweetness you'll be tricked into. A man like that—to know perfectly well when you're bad, but never play fair and lose his temper—what chance have we got? Come on!" And with her arm about the be-wildered Winnie, she moved serenely toward the door, and for the first time Charles looked at his father with the gratitude of a grown man.

NOBODY TO WRITE ABOUT

NOW THIS YOUNG MARRIED WOMAN, Gwynne Winterwax, was a nice sort of girl. She was married to the local Frolic Motor agent, and they had a vacuum cleaner, and a refrigerator with two electric lights in it—one to show the food and one to show the neighbors. Her husband, Bill Winterwax, paid his bills and could laugh when there was anything to laugh about, and they had the brightest yellow bungalow in Walpurgis, which is a very fine town with old maples. Yet Gwynne was unhappy because she had a chronic disease called "I want to write," which causes dizziness and spots before the eyes, and can be cured only by sitting on a hard chair for six hours a day. But Gwynne thought that all authors had high white foreheads and an innocent vegetarian look and sat only on editors.

She had wanted to write ever since her freshman year in high school, when she had won a literary prize for copying out one entire act of *Hamlet* longhand and spelling the Danish gentleman's name as "Hamlett" only twice. She didn't want to write anything in particular—epic poetry or perfume advertisements or love stories about elephants—but she did want to make money, quick, and have her picture in the Literary Club Bulletin.

Whenever she thought her husband was unusually dull, she slipped over next door and sighed to that most patient of old maids, Edna Treakle, "I never have any real reason to complain, and I guess maybe I'm a bad, bad girl, but oh, it's all so futyle—or is it futile or footel? I have to smile when Bill asks me am I happy!"

Probably Gwynne would have got over it, but just about the time when Bill had taken to snarling, "Then why don't you quit talking about it and sit down and write?" she went to Cornucopia, to stay for a week with her cousin, Amanda Jane Deep, the one

The Cosmopolitan, July 1943

that has the coach dog, and Amanda took her to a lecture by the celebrated New York and Westport author, Chichester Mink.

Mr. Mink wasn't much to look at. If he had been, he wouldn't have been an author, but a baseball player or an actor or an information clerk at the Grand Central. He was skinny except in one or two areas, and his hair wasn't so much a covering as just a memory that started something up in your mind that you couldn't quite catch. His nose was long, and his only gesture was to hold up his limp right forefinger and look at it as though he had never noticed it before, and should he grab it or pretend not to have seen it?

But his voice was tremendous. He leaned over the edge of the platform and scooped up the audience and took them to his abstemious bosom and told them that they were all having such a good time together. It did not occur to him to explain to the apprentices like Gwynne the Vorse Law of Authorship—apply the seat of the pants to the seat of the chair—nor to inform them that there is a book out now that tells you how to spell all the words in the language. No, he spent his fifty-nine and seven-tenths minutes of lecturing in recalling what a high time he had had in Paris in 1938 with his friends Vincent Sheehan, George Jessel and the King of Greece.

That, thrilled Gwynne, is the way all authors live, and she returned in a warmer glow than ever to the anxious Bill Winterwax. She privately conveyed to Edna Treakle, "I wonder if anybody in this hick burg can ever understand how I burn with delectable dreams?"

Edna didn't think anybody could.

This time, Gwynne went so far in her artistic enterprise as to buy a lovely notebook with a leather cover and gilt edges and a miniature pink pencil on a silk cord, which would slip into her handbag. She even wrote in it—once:

If I could have known Tschaikowsky that writes these music records and heard him play and seen his understanding brown eyes fixed

*on me — I guess they were brown, there would have been kindled in
me such a flare of inspiration that I would have written books
greater than two hundred thousand copies.*

Thus kindled and inspired by Mr. Mink and her friend
Tschaikowsky, she bravely started to write her first novel about
King Charles the First of England, a fellow who would, she felt,
have appreciated her.

She did a lot of research. She read clear through an article in
the encyclopedia and twice through *The Children's Pictorial History of England*, and one rare inspiring autumn day, she sat down
at the cherry-red steel-topped table in her kitchen and started her
novel:

*It was in the year 1648, and pacing up and down in the shadow
of a mighty battlement ornamented with the coats and arms of a
number of celebrated aristocratic old families, a handsome though
no longer young man and lithe as a leopard of aristocratic bearing,
wearing a fine lace ruffles, was listening to the distant approaching hoofbeats of an approaching steed, and thinking——*

We shall probably never know what King Charles was thinking, because just then the telephone rang to snatch her away for a
game of bridge, which shows how hard it is for a housewife to be
an author. She had to put in four and a quarter hours playing that
afternoon, and lost seventy-eight cents, and by suppertime, she
herself had forgotten what the King thought. Two days later,
when she again remembered that she was an author, she had her
Great Idea. She told Bill to get his own breakfast, and about noon,
she arose and wrote to Mr. Mink, in care of his publishers:

Dear Genius:

*I guess you will be pretty surprised to hear from a perfect
stranger, but I do hope my poor little letter will get past your battery of secretaries.*

I heard you lecture in Cornucopia, and I could not sleep that night, I was so excited. Is it not a shame that so few of your audience appreciated your "fine points" like I did? I wish I knew you better. I feel it would kindle in me such a flare of inspiration that I would begin to turn out masterpieces. I have longed to write ever since I was a little girl, and have a novel about the "gay monarch" almost done, but none here will "understand."

The trouble is, this town is so dull. Nothing ever happens and there is nobody here to write about. What can I do? I would be real pleased to hear from you from time to time, especially about your methods of writing, where do you find all your wonderful plots, and kindly send me an autographed photograph.

Yours sincerely,

Gwynne (Mrs. Wm.) Winterwax

This appeal did get past Mr. Chichester Mink's battery of secretaries, consisting of Mr. Mink and an aged rebuilt typewriter, housed in an ex-chickenhouse behind the charming Connecticut residence that would someday be his if he ever made any payments on it. He sighed a little and cursed a little and sat down to copy out again, with two weary forefingers, his Form AA, 2B:

My dear girl:

I can feel the quiver of talent in your words, but why don't you study the people right on your own block? You may find a world of drama in them, as did Dickens and O. Henry. I regret, have no fotos on hand.

Fraternally yrs

C. Mink

He yelled in to his wife, who was earning their butter and gasoline money by writing gardening articles, "Mag! What say I get a photograph taken? I haven't had a new one in five years now."

His fond helpmate screamed back, "With that nose? No, dear. No pictures."

Bill Winterwax brought the Mink letter home to Gwynne late on a Wednesday afternoon. When she had read it, she went grimly out on the porch, and for two whole minutes she did study her own neighborhood, though it was already tedious with familiarity.

In Walpurgis, the lawns are large, and there were only four houses in that block on Jackpine Avenue. On the south corner was the decrepit Treakle Mansion, rusty red and a little tilted, like an old stagecoach abandoned in a swamp. And what copy, Gwynne demanded, was to be found in the two people living there? Mrs. Treakle was an aged and complaining widow, who talked of nothing but her headaches, and the spinster daughter Edna was a telephone operator, who could remember right off for you the numbers of all the local doctors and bootleggers. The most amusing story about Edna was too ridiculous to write.

For ten years she had been keeping company with that skinny, nervous Nate Jacobus, the dry-goods clerk in the Boston Store. The town giggled when it saw Nate and Edna walking home from Sunday Evening Service at the Plymouth Church and afterward, sitting on the shaky porch of the Mansion, drinking lemonade — lemonade in 1942, when even gin had become old-fashioned!

"There! You see?" Gwynne snarled at the absent Mr. Mink, and turned her literary eye on the north corner house of the block, a flashy new brick Colonial, in which lived George Collister, vice-president of the Suland National Bank, and his overdressed, cocktail-drinking, magazine-cover-pretty wife, Adelle.

Gwynne sniffed, "And those two buzzards, why, nobody but this Upton Sinclair that wrote *Main Street* and is such a savage satirist could do anything with such folks. But you would think that at forty Adelle Collister would take a tumble to herself and quit trying to look like a girl — dancing the rumba and pretending that all her trips down to Cornucopia are to visit the art museum. Do you get me, Mink?"

She passed over the third house in the block without even a look. It was set far back from the street, approached by an unpaved trail among the weeds. It was a one-room shanty in which Old Mr. Bendick untidily bached it, cooking his flapjacks, failing to wash his three dishes and one chipped cup. Nobody knew much about him except that he must be over ninety, and had lived most of his life on a wretched farm in the pine barrens. Certainly the inspired Gwynne Winterwax neither knew him nor wanted to.

As to the fourth house on the block—why, that was Gwynne's own, so there was no story to be tracked down there, unless it should be about herself and her surprising talent. Obviously, there was none in Bill, a man who liked to stick around greasy machinery.

Gwynne returned grimly into the house. Sure! They were all like Mink, these old inside members of the literary ring, plotting to keep their young rivals from succeeding, lolling in paneled libraries, dictating to beautiful young secretaries.

She was silent through supper; she looked indifferent when Bill poked off for a while to his agency. Later, she bitterly tore Mink's letter to pieces, and as she did so she looked scornfully out at the hobbling dullness of Old Mr. Bendick.

For seventy-eight years, since April 14, 1865, Mr. Bendick had lived with the fear that someone would find out his shame.

On that April evening, he was not Old Mr. Bendick but a young cavalryman, brisk and cheerful and brave enough for ordinary use. He had been coming through an alley back of a theater in Washington City when an agitated man limped out of a door, screaming, "I have killed the tyrant!" Who or what a tyrant might be, innocent Dan Bendick had no idea, but he felt that he ought to stop this maniac. He lumbered up, but the fellow waved a pistol at him, and before Dan could make up his mind to grab the

bridle of a waiting horse toward which the crazy man was swaying, the horse and rider were wildly gone.

Next morning, Dan knew that he might have stopped the as-
sassin of Abraham Lincoln.

For two more years of the army, then for seventy years hidden
on a backwoods farm, and these last six years in his village shack,
this ordinary-looking farmer had, day and night, been a boiling of
fears and regret, longing for some heroism that would excuse him.
He had never married; never thought himself a fit man to marry.
Daily, for eight and seventy years, he had argued, "But my stopping Booth wouldn't have saved the President," and daily he had
begged of his implacable self, "Anyway, nobody knows." But he
had never been convinced. He had tried for redemption, had saved
a neighbor from a bull, had led horses out of a burning barn, had
walked through the great February blizzard to bring the doctor
for an unknown hobo. But none of it had been enough.

As Gwynne looked disgustedly out, the trembling old man,
inching up his path, was walking beside an unseen archangel.

"Stupid, sloppy old bach!" raged Gwynne.

Adelle Collister, wife of the banker, had evidently been having another of her flings in Cornucopia, for Gwynne saw her coming
from the late-afternoon train, carrying her pert blue morocco
overnight bag. Her husband met her on the terrace. They were too
far away for Gwynne to hear them.

George said only "Well?" but he said it nervously.

Adelle laughed. "The doctor says not a thing to worry about,
lamb. So let's celebrate! Let's open up the near-champagne
tonight! And look, I'm going to telephone Cousin Ella to come for
a week, after all. We'll have some swell parties for her. And don't
try and tell me you're not half in love with her."

"She's awful easy to look at. And how I love that doc for giving
you good news!"

As a matter of fact, the Cornucopia specialist hadn't been quite so comforting as Adelle pretended. He had said to her, "You really want to know? You can take it? Well, I'm afraid you haven't more than three months to live."

Adelle had fussed with the lapel of her frivolous green wool suit, and said steadily, "How long before my husband will notice anything wrong?"

"I think not for a couple of months."

"Then I'm going to give him the giddiest two months he ever had—and myself too, for that matter. But I'll be careful; I'll stay in bed till noon. I'm glad that it's Ella he likes, next to me. She'll be a good wife. Look, if George snoops in and asks you, tell him I'll live for thirty years. Thanks, doctor. Good-by."

She said nothing more to the doctor, nothing at all. That evening, back in Walpurgis, she told her husband a detailed, copper-riveted convincing lie, and they danced late, to the phonograph.

Gwynne, laying awake, hating the cheerfulness of the dance music, grumbled to herself, "There's a useless pair, really just as uninteresting as an old maid like Edna Treakle."

Edna Treakle and the rabbity Nate Jacobus were sitting on a dry-rotted bench. Their voices could not be heard ten feet away, but in Edna's there was a soft fierceness.

"Why are you trembling so, Nate?"

"I'm scared. Maybe your mother will outlive both of us and we'll never be allowed to get married. When I love you so terrifyingly!"

"But I'm so plain."

"You're the most beautiful woman living! You got such a lot of sweetness and sadness. I hate these expressionless young girls I have to wait on in the store. Hate 'em!"

"Nate, be patient! Mother won't live forever. Put your head on my shoulder."

"I don't dare. I don't hardly dare shake hands with you any more. I'm scared I'll realize how much—— Edna! You got to help me. Sometimes I catch myself planning to murder your mother. Now you're shocked."

"No, I've thought that way. She's so strong and wonderful that she'll boss us as long as she lives. But darling, darling, can't you be sorry for me sometimes, and not just for yourself? Between the two of you, I almost go crazy. I would, too, if I didn't have my fool job—so crazy they'd shut me up. Maybe they will, yet."

"They won't! I'll try to cheer up and be happy and sane, Edna."

"You'll stop thinking about suicide?"

"Yes, yes, sweet, I will. Listen, I got something funny to tell you about a traveling man that come in the store."

He was trembling no longer. He was so concentrated on trying to make her laugh that his voice was louder, and to the wakeful Gwynne it carried the blatant phrases: "'Yes, sir,' I says to him, 'the way I look at it——'"

Gwynne meditated, "Not one person in the whole block, except me, with courage or emotion."

Her husband came upstairs, yawning. "Gwynne, we got to have a talk. With all this gas and rubber rationing, I'm not making a cent. I think we better go off where I can get a munitions job."

"And live in a trailer? Not on your life, my friend! You can just stir yourself, for once, and get some new job here in town. I've just got my novel about King Charles going nicely, and you might try and help me, for once!"

"You really think you can turn out all this writing?"

"Stupid, Chichester Mink wrote to me, 'Everything you do is full of a quiver of talent,' and I'm not going to give it up for any of your alleged patriotic jobs."

"I see." He humped over in the rocker, irritatingly tapping his foot. "Say, I got to thinking, if anything ever happened to me——"

"Nothing will! You haven't even got enough pep to have an accident!"

"Maybe so, but if I did, they're looking for a cook at the Palmer House."

"Well, of all the——"

He did not hear her. He had pointlessly wandered out of the room. She could hear him whistling on the porch.

"One of his idiotic restless fits again. I'm not going to lie awake and wait for him. Not me!" thought Gwynne.

Bill had taken from the lower-hall closet a suitcase hidden there during the evening. He walked to the railroad station. The last train to Cornucopia left at eleven-seven. His friend Jock Wendel was waiting for the train, and said jovially, "Going somewhere or just traveling?"

Bill answered with a curious pleased excitement. "Joke of it is, I dunno. I may get a factory job in Detroit or Dayton, and then again I may ask the generals don't they need me in the Marines. I'd like to see those South Sea islands." He was solemn then. "And I think maybe I will be seeing them! All aboard."

Gwynne half awoke as the train to Cornucopia whistled, and she muttered, "What a dull sound. Every time I hear it, I know that when I wake up tomorrow, I won't find one single thing new or interesting, to live or to write about!"

Acknowledgments

THE MINNESOTA THAT LEWIS WROTE ABOUT is one that still
exists. There are the small towns where the newcomer is treated
with a measure of suspicion and the big cities that have their
boosters. Lewis's hometown of Sauk Centre, however, has been
very welcoming to me, from the first time that I visited, in connection with the celebrations for Lewis's centennial.

I'd like to thank those who nurtured my love of Lewis, including my dissertation director, Dr. Andrew Myers; the members of
the Sinclair Lewis Foundation of Sauk Centre, including Roberta
Olson and Joyce Lyng; and the members of the Sinclair Lewis Society with whom I've corresponded in connection with this project. My gratitude also extends to Sarah McHone-Chase who has
been very helpful in finding the microfilm/microfiche copies of
some of the earlier stories; Christa Sammons and Nancy Kuhl of
Beinecke Library, Yale University, for helping me track down the
earliest of the Lewis stories, "A Theory of Values," and the previ-
ously unpublished "Main Street Goes to War"; and librarians at
both Illinois State University and the New York Public Library.

My gratitude also extends to publisher Gregory M. Britton
who came up with the idea for the collection and his great patience in seeing it to completion and to Ann Regan, who has been
a careful, supportive, and enthusiastic editor.

Finally, I'd like to thank my husband Robert McLaughlin, for
his help in tracking down stories, proofreading, and his endless
love and patience in listening to me talk about my favorite author.

Selected Bibliography

Blakely, Roger K. "Sinclair Lewis and the Baxters: The History of a Friendship." *Minnesota History* 49 (Spring 1985): 166–78.

Bucco, Martin, ed. *Critical Essays on Sinclair Lewis.* Boston: G. K. Hall, 1986.

Dooley, D. J. *The Art of Sinclair Lewis.* Lincoln: University of Nebraska Press, 1967.

Flanagan, John T. "The Minnesota Backgrounds of Sinclair Lewis' Fiction." *Minnesota History* 37 (Spring 1960): 1–13.

Grebstein, Sheldon Norman. *Sinclair Lewis.* New York: Twayne, 1962.

——. "Sinclair Lewis' Minnesota Boyhood." *Minnesota History* 34 (Fall 1954): 85–89.

Hutchisson, James M. *The Rise of Sinclair Lewis, 1920–1930.* University Park: Pennsylvania State University Press, 1996.

Koblas, John. *Sinclair Lewis: Home at Last.* Bloomington, MN: Voyageur Press, 1981.

Lewis, Sinclair. *If I Were Boss: The Early Business Stories of Sinclair Lewis.* Ed. Anthony Di Renzo. Carbondale: Southern Illinois University Press, 1997.

——. *I'm a Stranger Here Myself and Other Stories.* Ed. Mark Schorer. New York: Dell, 1962.

——. *Minnesota Diary 1942–46.* Ed. George Killough. Moscow: University of Idaho Press, 2000.

——. *The Selected Short Stories of Sinclair Lewis.* New York: Doubleday, Doran, 1937. Rpt. Chicago: Ivan R. Dee/Elephant Paperbacks, 1990.

Lingeman, Richard. *Sinclair Lewis: Rebel from Main Street,* New York: Random House, 2002. Rpt. St. Paul: Borealis Books, 2005.

Moodie, Clara Lee R. "The Book That Has Never Been Published." *Sinclair Lewis at 100: Papers Presented at a Centennial Conference.* St. Cloud: St. Cloud State University, 1985. 201–12.

———. "The Short Stories and Sinclair Lewis' Literary Development." *Studies in Short Fiction* 12 (1975): 99–107.

———. "The Shorter Fiction of Sinclair Lewis and the Novel—Anatomy." Dissertation. University of Michigan, 1971.

Schorer, Mark. *Sinclair Lewis: An American Life.* New York: McGraw-Hill, 1961.

Smith, Harrison, ed. *From Main Street to Stockholm: Letters of Sinclair Lewis, 1919–1930.* New York: Harcourt, Brace, 1952.